DRAGONOAK

THE COMPLETE HISTORY OF KASTELIR

Sam Farren

Dragonoak: The Complete History of Kastelir / Sam Farren. -- 1st ed.
ISBN-13: 978-1523285891

For anyone who has delved into a fantasy novel and not seen themselves reflected in the world therein.

CONTENTS

She still went by Sir Ightham, back then. When she came to our village, no one suspected her to be in exile, or that exile was hardly the worst of it.

I was a farmer, raised in a village that had been happily overlooked throughout much of history. We were nestled in a shallow valley with a thicket of trees growing tall on one side, and the only excitement that ever filtered through was the occasional wolf, hoping to make an easy meal of a stray sheep. The surrounding settlements considered ours to be cosy, and my life ought to have been pleasantly mundane.

I shouldn't have had any tales that would give a Knight reason to pause.

Yet in the months leading to Sir Ightham's arrival, I was facing an exile of my own. I already had a story to tell, one that could breathe life into long volumes of texts. I thought I'd long since reached the conclusion of it all; that I was living in my own epilogue.

Despite that, everything started with her arrival. I was twenty-three and all the secrets I'd striven to keep inside had slipped between my fingers and seeped into the dirt, poisoning the village.

But as I said, she still went by Sir Ightham, in those days. We thought it was the start of better things for us all.

PART ONE

The stubborn ground clung to the last of the cold, but clear skies and crisp air marked mid-Mersa and the timely arrival of spring.

Newborn lambs gathered enough courage and coordination to leave their mothers' sides and curiously nudged my knees as I kept watch. They'd inevitably tumble into my lap and bleat, or at least try to. I helped them back onto twitch legs and sent them on their way. Seconds later, they were bouncing through the long grass, convinced they'd never taken an unsteady step in their short lives.

The villagers didn't know I tended to the sheep or toiled in the fields. In their minds, I was confined to the farmhouse and locked in my room, unable to glance at any of the food they'd purchased from my father.

The hills our sheep grazed on were wide and open, but there was nowhere safer for me. I sat atop a tree stump older than I was, able to see everything: the dirt path cutting through the rickety fence at the bottom of the hill, winding around our farmhouse and heading lower into the village itself.

I would've seen anyone approach from a mile away.

I'd imagined a mob coming my way more than once. It was never made of individual villagers or people I recognised, people I'd grown up around. It was a roiling mass, all anger and fear, grasping for simple, bloody solutions. Part of me was convinced I only did it to entertain myself while the sheep slept under the stars I'd charted a hundred times over.

As things were, no one ever wandered further than the farmhouse.

"At least you guys are brave enough to be up here," I murmured to another lamb who'd dared to wobble my way. He stopped on the spot and I offered him a handful of grass from between my bare feet. The lamb ate happily, wagging his stump of a tail as though the whole hillside wasn't covered in more of the same.

Taking what company I could get, I fed the gathering crowd of curious lambs, until something mercifully claimed my attention. Someone was running up the dirt path, completely bypassing the farmhouse. I jumped to my feet and the lambs scattered. For a moment, for one single, blissful moment, I remembered what it was like to be *excited* about something.

4

Until I made out who it was.

My brother. I sat back down but didn't feel the sting of disappointment too keenly. Michael wasn't much of a farmer and never had been. He had a knack for financial matters; he was much better at handling trades and managing our accounts than running through the fields and putting himself to work. It wasn't often he wandered away from the village, much less to the steep hills our sheep roamed.

"Rowan!" he called, waving his hands above his head. His breath puffed out of him and his face was red, but his grin was unmissable. "Hurry it up, would you? Don't make me go any further uphill!"

I jogged down to meet him and he clasped my shoulders with both hands.

"Has something happened?" I asked. The last time I'd seen him that happy, he'd returned from a nearby town, dragging his weight in books behind him.

"Has it ever!" he declared, shaking me. "You'll never guess what, though."

I waited for him to continue but he stared at me, expecting me to guess at something I'd never get right. He shook me again and I shrugged, earning a sigh mixed with a laugh for my ignorance. Luckily for me, Michael had never been good at keeping anything to himself.

"There's a *Knight*. Down in the village, in *our* village. There's a Knight! An actual, breathing, living Knight. In our village!" He brought his hands up and formed fists that near enough trembled with excitement. I tilted my head to the side and he slammed his hands onto my shoulders, trying to drive me into the dirt. "Are you listening? A Knight! In the village! Isn't it amazing?"

I opened my mouth uselessly. Michael was of the opinion that most things he said were amazing, but this time he was selling the story short. A passing merchant drifting into our village would've been amazing; a traveller who'd lost their way and needed a place to stay for the night would've been amazing. We hadn't seen a stranger in our village for five gruelling months. A Knight's arrival was beyond anything most of the Kingdom could ever hope for.

"Are you sure they're a Knight?" I asked. "Why would there be one this far south? Why would they come to *our* village?"

Everyone knew dragons didn't dare to venture too close to the sea,

5

and we were only twenty miles from the coast. On windy days, I could almost taste salt in the air.

"Oh, she's a Knight alright. Not a soldier or a guard or a wandering mercenary. Nothing so mundane as that," Michael said, nodding to himself. He stepped back and clapped his hands together. One of the lambs gave a start and I blinked. "I saw her armour for myself! It's nothing less than dragon-bone, there's no doubting that. It's as white as..."

He tilted his head back but there wasn't a passing cloud in the sky worth comparing it to.

"It's *white*. Not the white of bleached bones. It's something more than that. Well, come on! You've got to see her."

Michael grabbed my wrist. The uphill journey was forgotten and he had more than enough strength left to drag me down the hillside. I went ten, fifteen steps, and reality trailed far behind.

When would I ever get the chance to meet a Knight?

The village would be thrumming with talk of her. Everyone would've rushed from their homes. All three-hundred of the villagers would be gathered in the square, ready to turn their eyes on me and their thoughts against me.

I dug my heels in and skidded to a stop.

"I can't go down to the village," I reminded Michael.

He stared at me like I was being a bore and threw his hands in the air.

"Why not? Did anyone ever *say* you weren't allowed in the village? Have you *tried* going down there?"

Nobody had told me I wasn't welcome. They hadn't given my banishment a voice, though for a time, they'd enjoyed speaking about me when they knew I was within earshot. But their resentment had quickly taken on a new tone: doors slamming, windows latching from the inside. I hadn't dared to venture into the village for four months. Perhaps time had softened them.

"We're just going to *look*," Michael pushed. "You don't need to be there long. It'll be fine, Rowan."

I didn't budge. As scared as the villagers were of me, convinced I had caused last season's crops to fail, I couldn't bring myself to face them, either. Not when there were so many of them. Not when they *knew*. Michael's intentions were good and at heart, he only ever wanted me to join in his enthusiasm for everything beyond village life, but I couldn't take a step forward.

"You don't get it," I said. What I meant was *please don't make me explain*.

Not again.

"Oh, I get it, Rowan. I'm your *brother*. Do you think I don't get it every time I go down into the village? I know how people look at me when they think my attention is elsewhere. I know that people say very different things behind my back than they do to my face at market. So yes, Rowan, I *get it*. I get it more than you do, hiding away in the hills, leaving father and me to deal with the consequences," he said, scowling at a rock on the hillside.

"That's not fair," I mumbled.

I didn't want to argue with him. Not there. Not again.

He sighed.

"No, I suppose it isn't. Not on me and least of all on you." His scowl softened. "Just for a few minutes? You have to try going back eventually, and it's going to be easier on you if it's sooner rather than later. Besides, they're all *terrified* of you. If anyone tries starting trouble, wave your hands in a menacing manner, and they'll run for cover."

He made his case by waving his fingers in the air, and I supposed that I *would* like to see the Knight. It was as good an excuse to go back as I was going to get, and no one had hunted me down in the months I'd been absent. They might want nothing more than to leave me alone. All I had to do was keep my head down and stay out of trouble.

"Alright. If we're quick," I said, sprinting off and jumping the fence. "But only because I'll never believe you if I don't see for myself!"

The hard-packed path had once been riddled with the track marks of carts brought to market from neighbouring towns and villages, but the wind had stolen them. Only footprints remained, and they belonged to my father and brother.

The last time I'd gone into the village, it'd been a month before my birthday and well into winter. The cobbled roads were icy, roofs dusted with a sprinkling of snow, but I expected the village to have changed in more substantial ways than the seasons' whims dictated. It hadn't, of course. The baker's hadn't moved and the butcher's hadn't closed down, yet I took in my surroundings as though standing there for the first time.

7

The mismatched houses were remarkable. Picturesque, almost, as if people couldn't possibly live in them. I wanted to reach out and touch them. I wanted to reach out and touch everything; the street lamps that weren't due to be lit for hours, the worn well, the low benches and the shrine that was older than all else. I wanted to know that I wasn't trapped in the past, or in a dream.

I almost forgot I was there to see a Knight. The tavern alone was incredible.

Whatever hazy quality my return brought with it was soon dispelled. I'd only seen the village gather in force once before and the sight made me tense. They didn't see me. Not at first. They stared at Marmalade Lodge, the only inn our village could boast of, finally occupied after five months. The owners could hardly spare a thought for their past misfortune, now that a Knight was staying there.

Michael's shoulder bumped against mine. He kept close and I pushed myself onto tiptoes, hoping the extra height would let me see through the walls of the inn. Or at least into a window, where a Knight-shaped blur might give my brother and me something to talk about for the next year. I was so caught up in the moment I almost didn't realise someone had seen me.

Not just *someone*. My luck dictated that Thane caught my eye. I sunk flat onto my feet, hoping to sink further still. He didn't say a word and didn't have to. The other villagers looked to him every few seconds, believing he had the power to summon a Knight out into the open.

They followed his gaze, and what should've been familiar faces no longer held the shapes I remembered. They despised me and it darkened their eyes. It made them all the same, somehow.

Thane stepped towards us, breaking from the crowd without daring to come too close. The apothecary's loomed in the background, drawing my gaze over his shoulder. The doors were boarded shut, windows covered. It'd been months but they feared some remnant of me would drift into the air and choke them.

From what my father had told me, the apothecary himself had never returned.

"Northwood," Thane began. He spoke to Michael and Michael alone, voice quiet, controlled. He would've resorted to shouting, had the Knight not been within earshot. "What are you doing, lad? Surely you of all people realise how important this is to us. Run her back to the farmhouse and nothing more'll be said on the matter."

"She only wants to see the Knight. What's wrong with that?"

Michael feigned ignorance and he feigned it well. Thane pinched the bridge of his nose, taking a deep breath.

"Thirty years this village has called me elder, and never have I..." He clenched his jaw. A woman behind him ushered one of the children I'd saved back into their house. "You know what they do to those sorts up in Thule, Michael. We've been plenty lenient thus far, more open-minded than they ever would be, and we've had no reason to be. I thought you'd be smarter than to push your luck."

They were not *open-minded*. They were not *lenient*. Isolation wasn't the villagers' idea of justice, and it certainly wasn't Thane's. Embers of utter resentment had burnt in his eyes when he found out what I was, and I understood what he wanted to do to me; I felt it more than ever in the way he refused to look at me. He'd do worse than they did in Thule, if he only felt a sense of bravery as keenly as he did betrayal.

"Happily, this isn't Thule," Michael pointed out. "We don't have to do *everything* the capital does. We're a hundred miles away! We're practically a different country."

"All the more reason to stay in the Knight's favour. It's for the good of the village, lad. Go on. I'm only being generous because your father's a good man and so are you. I know neither of you asked for this. Get her out of here before she ruins us again."

I stepped forward. Thane stood his ground but the rest of the village flinched. I wondered what would happen if I took another step: would they scatter or surge towards me?

I never found out.

"I still have a name, you know," was all I managed to murmur, feet already moving.

I could always count on myself to run away.

"Rowan!" Michael called. He grabbed my elbow, convinced he would be the one to soften the villagers and pry old prejudices from their fingers, but I walked faster.

"It's alright," I said, staring into the hills. "I know you were telling the truth about the Knight. That's why I came down, remember? So... it's enough. It's enough."

9

It was the most I could ever hope for.

The steep relief didn't stop me. I fled the village faster than Michael and I had charged towards it, feet hitting the dry ground and catching on rocks hidden in the grass. I wanted my legs to ache, for my chest to pull tight, but breathing came easily, despite that. I had grown up in the hills, running, climbing, tumbling. It'd take more than a short sprint to exhaust me, to finally take my mind off what my life had become.

I scrambled over the rickety fence that stopped our sheep from wandering into the village and woods, and saw that I'd been gone for too long. I'd been selfish. I'd wanted something I knew would never be mine again and it was almost too late.

The lambs bleated in confusion, distress, and the sheep circled them, herding the flock to safety when they were just as startled. A wolf had got in. Wolves *always* got in. It was the runt of whatever litter it had belonged to, but that didn't stop its fangs from gleaming as it snarled.

The frustration coursing through me eked away, replaced by a muddled sense of fear and responsibility. My father had left me in charge of sheep; he'd let me remain on the farm, no matter what the villagers had said about me. I had to do something about this, and I couldn't ask the others for help.

I'd left my crook rested against the tree stump. All I had to do was reach it, and then—

What would I do? Hold it over my shoulder, swing, hit the wolf around the head without it sinking its teeth into me first, and not suffer my stomach turning with the sickly crack?

I opted not to move. It did nothing to blind the wolf to me. It tensed, not knowing what to think of me; not knowing if I would put up more or less of a fight than the sheep. I thought my feet would remain rooted to the ground, but the wolf made the decision for me. It lunged at me and I bolted uphill, wet breath on my feet as I dove for my crook.

"Please—look, I don't..." I murmured, rolling onto my back and knocking the wolf away, crook gripped in my trembling hands. "I don't want to hurt you, so..."

But it didn't understand. All it knew was that I had got between it and the sheep, and that it could sink its fangs just as easily into me. The wolf's teeth caught on my arm, tearing skin, though it didn't get the chance to grip on. Panic ruled me. I beat the back of its head with my staff and flailed and kicked, and something in my outburst made the wolf reconsider the situation.

There was easier prey elsewhere.

With a yelp, it skidded back towards the woods. I knelt on the ground, forehead scraping against the dirt, and clutched my bloodied arm. Seething, I told myself it was alright, that it wasn't any worse than the villagers' cutting glares, and my heart began to beat to a steady rhythm as the bite marks smoothed over and my blood had no way of escaping.

"Okay. Okay," I whispered to myself. "It's okay. You're okay."

A few of the sheep edged my way. I sat back up, not wanting to frighten them.

"Easy now. Easy now," I murmured to the trembling sheep, coaxing them back out into the open. Didn't they know they were making it easier for the wolves when they huddled together? "It's alright. The wolf's gone. It can't hurt you."

In the end, the lambs were the bravest of all. They didn't know enough to cling to fear.

I spent my afternoon focused on finding weak spots in the fence. I found a dozen of them, but knew that none were responsible for letting the wolves in. They could scramble over a fence twice as high, whether it was made from wood or stone, but I whittled away my hours fixing the gaps.

I returned to my tree stump and squinted at the village, imagining the colours it must be draped in. Flowers had yet to start blooming in earnest, so the villagers had likely taken out the worn decorations reserved for the Phoenix Festival, still months away. I lingered on the thought that no matter how thrilled the villagers were to have a Knight amongst them, they were forced to dwell on me. They'd be on edge, convinced I'd find a new way to ruin things for them.

It wasn't much of a consolation. I didn't want anyone to fear me any more than I wanted the lambs to grow up fearing wolves.

The sky was smeared a deep, distant orange by the time Michael joined me. He waved at me from the foot of the hill, but I didn't run to meet him.

"Not the year for it, is it?" he said, once he reached me. He spread his arms out in front of me to emphasise what *it* was. "Fifteen hundred years since Kondo-Kana helped chase our ancestors out of the Bloodless Lands! They probably think you're her descendant, here to continue her work."

It was absurd enough for the villagers to believe.

"Anyway, I didn't intend to take so long. I was trying to make them see sense, but they're as thick-headed as ever. After that..."

"You wanted to see the Knight," I said. He nodded, not particularly sorry to have left me alone for so long. "It's alright. I was curious too. What's she like?"

"She's like a *Knight*. She's *exactly* like a Knight! I scarcely know how else to put it. Forget all those stories I wasted my breath on in the past. Even if you were to cobble all the better parts of them together, you'd only get a mere glimpse of the real thing. She's what I've been trying to write about all this time. You feel echoes of how terrified dragons must be around her. Beyond powerful," Michael said. "And dignified, of course. I expect she was of noble blood long before claiming such a ti-tle."

The concept of a Knight was a strange one to me. Michael had shared stories with me from the day I was born, and many of them featured Knights. But they featured merfolk and goblins, too. I saw no reason for Knights to have a firmer place in reality than any of the rest. Had I ever seen a dragon, it might've been a different matter. It was hard to imagine one without the other.

"What's her name?" I asked.

Perhaps that would be enough to help me understand her role in the world.

"Sir Ightham."

Michael practically sang the words.

The names of Knights were probably well known in the bigger cities, but we rarely heard more than a whispering from the capital. Any news that reached us was ever months out of date, ensuring we'd be the last to know when a new monarch came to power.

Still, it was nice to know. Sir Ightham. I thought of the creatures she'd faced to earn such a title. Whatever the truth was regarding dragons, whether or not people exaggerated their size in the same way Michael played up the Knight's virtues, I knew they wouldn't scamper away as wolves did.

"I've got to get back to the hall. There's going to be a feast tonight and I promised I'd help out. To get back on everyone's good side, that sort of thing," he said. To his credit, he made it sound like a momentous chore he reluctantly had to attend to. "You should get some rest, though. Make sure you get something to eat. Someone else'll tend to the sheep."

He was right about one thing. I was *exhausted*, body aching, stomach empty. A hot meal and a long sleep in my own bed weren't going to fix what my life had become, but there was no point in denying myself the basic necessities.

I held out a hand for him to help me to my feet, but Michael started at the sight of it.

"Rowan!" he said, bringing his hand to his forehead. "Don't do that to me. You're sitting there, covered in blood, and you haven't said a word about it! What's wrong? Was it a wolf?"

"I'm not *covered* in blood," I muttered.

I'd wiped most of it off in the grass.

Still, Michael didn't help me up until I offered out my other hand. We walked down the dirt path in glum silence, and he left me on our doorstep, eager to attend the feast. In his defence, five months was a long time, and I didn't want him to be miserable.

"Dad?" I called as I pushed the front door open.

"Out back!"

I shoved my hands in my pockets and headed around to meet my father. He was out by the stables, dragging a pig towards a barn we only ever used for one thing.

I narrowed my gaze suspiciously but said, "There's a Knight in the village, you know. But I'm sure Michael's told you already."

"Your version's a lot easier to digest," he said, smiling at me as he tugged the rope around the pig's neck. "They had her horse brought up to the stables. Beautiful creature. Tan as anything."

Trust my father to focus on a horse over a Knight. Nothing ever shocked or surprised him, and not in a way that left him numb to the world. He was ever upbeat in his own quiet way, content to go along with things, ever as kind as he was busy.

"Wow. Bet Thane wasn't happy about that," I said. Not that they could very well tell a Knight there wasn't anywhere to keep her horse, after the inn's stables had collapsed in last month's storm. "What're you doing with that pig?"

It oinked indignantly at my question.

"The village is putting on a feast, and they want our prized pig," my father said. To his credit, he didn't sound as put out about it as I would've.

"But it could feed us for *months*!" I protested.

The villagers were getting ahead of themselves. They'd drain our resources in one fell swoop, eager to convince Sir Ightham they always lived so lavishly.

"Now, Rowan. Sir Ightham is our guest, and it's up to us to see to it that she has everything she needs," my father told me. It was infuriating how he only ever had kind words for anyone.

There was a feast held in her honour the night after that, too. I supposed there was rather a lot of pig to get through. I watched from the hillside, surrounded by sleeping sheep.

I closed my eyes and strained my ears, pretending I could hear the merriment from within the village hall. Everyone but me had collectively shirked their responsibilities for celebration, as if the Knight's arrival meant we'd never face another famine again and had been granted immunity from the plague slowly creeping along the coast.

The villagers believed fortune hadn't deserted us along with our forgotten gods.

I was always going to be on the outside, alone in the hills. Sir Ightham's arrival was a relief of sorts, but highlighted all I was missing and all I would continue to miss. Another Knight would never grace our village again, but that didn't mean that opportunities for... for *fun*, to laugh and talk to people who weren't my father or brother or sheep wouldn't present themselves again.

I said as much to Michael over breakfast the next morning and he showed more interest in his bread and cheese.

"What are you going to do? Run away? Good luck with that. You don't have the faintest idea how the world works!"

He was right. I'd never left the valley our village was cradled in. The elders had made sure of that a thousand years ago, when I was of use to them.

"I might go." I was more eager to prove him wrong than to leave. "I could find work as... as a healer."

"Back to lying again, is it? That's what caused this whole mess in the first place," Michael chided. "It won't work because you don't *want* it to work. You want the people to know you're here. You want them to know what you are. You want them to know they're cut off from the rest of the world because of you. Say you leave. What happens then? One of the elders will perform a ridiculous cleansing ritual, word will spread, and trade will roll back in. You've cost this village a lot, you know. Don't do the same to some other poor, unsuspecting settlement."

"I didn't *cost* the village anything! I didn't take anything from it. It only... only lost the things I'd got it in the first place," I said. My voice started out loud but faded to an inevitable murmur.

"Yes, well," Michael said, concluding the conversation. He got to his feet, chair legs scraping across the tiled floor of our cramped kitchen. "I have to get back to the village. Thane's planning something special for tonight and needs my help."

He was gone before it occurred to him to wash his dishes.

He didn't mean to be callous. He'd often tell our father that he ought to have been born to a scholar, not a farmer, and my father assured me he knew Michael didn't mean anything cruel by it. He simply had ambitions above his station and could get a little ahead of himself. In his mind, he was probably already Sir Ightham's personal bard.

He'd known what I was years before the villagers found out and had comforted me with secrets of his own, trusting me to hold power over him too.

It didn't compare, but nothing could. I liked knowing that not all of the scholarly expeditions I'd funded were as noble as the village was led to believe, though. As it turned out, Michael was a skilled forger and had made a little money on the side, as well as a name for himself.

A strange thing happened in the days that followed. Michael didn't have much to say about Sir Ightham at all. He didn't refine his initial account of her to include the fact that he'd caught sight of her before anyone else, didn't claim that she'd made eye contact with him. He didn't boast of speaking to her during the feasts, or even of serving her.

I'd expected to hear about nothing but her for years to come, but whenever I asked after Sir Ightham, he'd say, "Well, of course I've seen her today. She's still in the village, isn't she? Ask father, won't you? He sees her as often as I do."

He ushered me out of the kitchen and spent the rest of the day writing letters, commissioned by Thane to boast to the villages and towns that had turned their backs on us.

Why would we ever need a thing from them when the royal family themselves had requested we extend our hospitality to one of their Knights? For that was the truth behind her unannounced arrival, according to the rumours my father returned with. She was heading south across the sea, all the way to the scorching sands of Canth, and needed somewhere to rest and prepare herself for the long journey.

I didn't know they had problems with dragons in Canth. Pirates, yes, but not dragons. I didn't think *anywhere* but Felheim had problems with dragons. Even our neighbours to the west had never suffered the sort of attacks we were plagued by.

All were convinced the King and Queen would never forget our hospitality, and would see us repaid in kind. I knew little of our rulers, or our Princes or Princess, for that matter. I wasn't concerned with them. I couldn't focus on anything but the fact that Sir Ightham would soon be gone, leaving the villagers with no more distractions. There'd be retaliation for the way I'd dared to wander down to the village.

I left the sheep later and later each night, heading back to the farmhouse with rocks in my stomach.

I was convinced they were waiting for me. Thane. The butcher. The former soldiers. Even the children, eager to prove themselves to their scornful parents. It was dark. They could've left the village without me seeing them move along the dirt path. And what if they were holding my father hostage? What if they wouldn't see him safely released until I'd left, or—

I started as I reached for the front door. There *was* someone there.

I gripped the handle and froze. It was faint, but my ears weren't playing tricks on me. Heavy footsteps hit the ground and wood creaked. They weren't inside the house. I could bolt upstairs and hide under my blankets until the sun rose.

But that would be a lot like backing myself into a corner. Something compelled me to edge around the side of the house. It was probably just a pig that had worked its way free of its pen. That was all. I'd be laughing about this over breakfast, because it was just a pig, just a pig—

Clouds drifted across the full moon, and in the darkness, I didn't know *what* I saw I froze in front of a jagged creature, all teeth and sharp angles, and where was my crook now?

Out of reach, by some miracle.

The clouds parted, moonlight making out the shape of Sir Ightham, armour carved to mirror the beasts she was charged with slaying. What she was doing behind my house in the dead of night wasn't immediately as clear. Sir Ightham knew she'd frightened me but didn't apologise.

She didn't say anything.

She opened a bag atop a hay bale and pushed a handful of documents into it.

"Sir...?" I asked, taking a cautious step closer. "Is everything alright?"

"Why wouldn't it be?" she replied dryly.

Her accent was different to mine. Clearer, somehow. Words held more importance when she spoke them. She slung her bag onto her back but there was something folded open across the hay bale. I stole a glance before replying and saw that it was a map, showing all of Felheim with the mountains above and Kastelir to the west.

"Because it's gone midnight and you're sneaking around behind my house," I said.

"Knights don't sneak." She folded the map with her gloved hands and dropped it into one of the bags by her feet, buying me a matter of seconds before we were face to face. I braced myself, but her helm threw shadows across her face. I saw nothing of her expression, but did an impressive job of imagining distain marring her features. She regarded me for a moment and said, quite dismissively, "You're the necromancer, I take it."

It wasn't a question. It wasn't an accusation. She *knew*. Like the rest of the village, she'd decided it was all that mattered. I became uncomfortably aware that Knights were in the habit of carrying swords, and my eyes tore across her unnatural form. Her armoured elbows were carved into spikes and would do as good a job as any blade.

Yet she made no movement other than to ask, "What was your name?"

It almost skidded off my tongue before I had the chance to speak it. "Rowan, Sir."

My mind screamed that she *knew*. She'd said the word *necromancer* as if it was nothing. As if she'd been saying *You're the farmer, I take it.*

17

"What are you doing out at this time?"

She wasn't interested in my answers. She was keeping me distracted while she gathered the last of her belongings.

"I just finished tending to the sheep," I said. I should've known better, but added, "Listen, I won't tell anyone if you're sneaking off. I don't blame you. It must be kind of overwhelming, right? All the attention. You probably haven't had a second to yourself since you got here."

Sir Ightham stared at me. Or I thought she was. I couldn't make out her eyes, but a sliver of moonlight struck the ones carved into her helm and they were narrowed at me.

"Indeed," she allowed, and stepped into the stables.

I followed her. I hadn't been in there for days. My father hadn't needed to say anything for me to know Thane had made him swear I wouldn't go anywhere near the stables while a Knight's horse was residing there.

I didn't know why I went with her. The conversation was hardly flowing, but I'd decided her departure sealed my fate. The villagers would blame me for her unexplained absence. What else could scare a Knight so?

It was almost impossible to see within the stables. The darkness had taken on form, filling the air between us. It was a physical thing, something that would protect me, if need be.

"You're not going to Canth, are you?"

That got her attention. She dropped her hand from the pen she was unlatching and I knew I'd said something as stupid as it was brave.

"Why do you say that?" Sir Ightham asked, no longer as dismissive as she had been.

"Because there aren't dragons in Canth, are there?" We both knew it wasn't the reason. "I saw the map you were looking at, and it was just of Felheim and Kastelir. Canth wasn't on it at all, so I thought..."

Sir Ightham brought her hands together. Her arms disturbed the darkness as her armour clattered against itself, so unlike the sound of metal I didn't trust my ears.

"Why might I have said I was going to Canth in the first place?" she asked.

"I don't know. Maybe you just wanted an excuse to leave, or maybe... maybe your *real* work's a secret. I don't... look, I'm really not going to

18

tell anyone about this, Sir."

"My real work," she repeated. She mulled the words over, satisfied with my reply, and pulled her horse's pen open with a creak. "And what would that be?"

"You're going to slay a dragon?"

It felt like a trick question. A Knight's work ever revolved around dragons, yet I doubted myself in the same instant.

"Quite," Sir Ightham said, accompanied by the sound of hooves.

She led her horse out of the pen with his reins in her fist and didn't ask me to step aside. I almost tripped over my feet to get out of their way. Sir Ightham climbed onto her horses' back, meaning to disappear forever.

There'd be an outrage in the morning and it'd be my fault.

"Wait, Sir!" I said before she could head off. "Let me come with you."

I blurted it out and felt my face redden as the words lingered in the air between us. Sir Ightham stared at me. She glanced at her horse, silently consulting with him, and he stared at me too.

"You'll need a squire, won't you?" In truth, I wasn't entirely sure what a squire *was*, but they always featured alongside Knights in all of Michael's better stories.

It took all my strength not to stare at the ground.

"Have you ever held a sword in your life?"

There was no amusement in it. Her voice was entirely flat, and she spoke in a way that said she already had her answer. Which didn't mean she wasn't silently demanding a reply.

"No, but..." I bit the inside of my cheek, not wanting my honesty to give her reason to charge off. "I know how to fight! I might not be able to use a sword, but I grew up wrestling wolves. Someone has to take care of the sheep, and that's always been my job."

I twisted my fingers in the hem of my shirt, ready to hoist it up at the first sign of scepticism. If Sir Ightham wanted war-wounds, I had plenty to show her. Gnarled, twisted scars covered the entirety of my torso, made infinitely worse by my early attempts at honing my necromancy. The wounds hadn't all washed away like those I'd earnt on the day of her arrival. They'd turned the colour of bruised, rotting fruit, but I would've let all the world see them if it meant proving myself to her.

Sir Ightham was a fighter, versed in slaying towering beasts. She'd see past the grotesque and understand the scars for what they were: proof that I'd thrown myself into the heat of a moment and come out victorious.

She said nothing.

My grip loosened.

None of it meant a thing to her. She'd spent her life slaying *dragons*. What did mere wolves matter to her?

Sir Ightham tugged on her horse's reins.

"Wait! Hold on, Sir!" I called, rushing after her. "It's alright if you don't take me with you. I won't tell anyone about this. But could you leave a note? Explain that you had to go, and that it was your choice. If you don't, they'll think I... they'll blame me. They already hate me enough."

Only then did Sir Ightham show real feeling. Irritation, put there by the fear that spilt into my voice. Her horse came to a halt before they'd had the chance to get anywhere.

"They all know what you are, do they not? And word has spread beyond this village, hasn't it?"

"I..." It wasn't the time to falter. "They know. Everyone, for miles around. It's why they won't trade with us anymore."

Like the day I had wandered into my village to find they knew the truth about me, I *knew* something was about to change. That my life would never again be what it had become: losing myself in the hills day after day, afraid, alone.

"Feed your horse bitterwillow," she said. "We've tens of miles to cover before sunrise and I have no more time to waste."

CHAPTER TWO

We'd started growing bitterwillow once it became apparent that no-body was going to replace the apothecary. My father didn't have the same knack for it, but Thane deemed it *good enough* for the villages' aches and pains. I shoved a handful of crisp red leaves into my pocket as I bolted into the stables, waking my horse.

Charley wasn't pleased to see me. In the time it took me to coax him out of his pen, Sir Ightham could've escaped the valley. I held out the leaves but couldn't tempt him into action. He sniffed my hand and swished his tail against the sides of the pen.

"Come on, boy," I pleaded with him. "I'll get you carrots at the first market we reach. Carrots, apples, whatever you want!"

Charley wasn't the fastest horse in the world. He wasn't even the fastest horse in the village. I could've taken another less reluctant, but he'd been with me since I was sixteen and always came through, even-tually. He ate the bitterwillow and clopped out into the night, grunting impatiently as I saddled him up.

The bitterwillow had been prepared for endurance and would give him energy enough to run for a few hours. I grabbed a little more on the way out, shoving the pain-killing stems into my pockets, wishing I'd brought a bag. Wishing I'd brought *anything.*

There wasn't a candle burning within my house, but I'd never make it to my room without each and every stair betraying me and waking half the village. If my father stopped me, if he asked me what I thought I was doing, I'd have to admit that I didn't know.

Sir Ightham had left, though she hadn't gone far. She was waiting at the foot of the hills beyond the farm, looking to cut around the woods. That was a small mercy in and of itself. Leaving the village was an in-comprehensible step, and I wasn't yet brave enough to push into the perpetual darkness between the trees.

The wolf from before would be there, flanked by its sturdier siblings, and my head filled with childhood tales of the pane that lurked within. I was ready for some level of adventure, but not the sort that involved giants tearing the flesh from my bones.

"Okay. Okay, I'm ready," I said to Sir Ightham, who hadn't taken the time to ask. Side by side on horseback though we were, she towered over me. Without a word, she set off along the path zigzagging back and forth, winding its way out of the valley. "Wait. Wait!"

Sir Ightham looked back without stopping, unwilling to tolerate another delay.

"It's quicker this way," I said, tilting my head towards the black of night. I might not have gone far in my life, but I knew all the hidden ways in and out of the valley, all the shortcuts that would save us miles. "The path's not on any map. Actually, I might've made it myself, but... it's quicker. Definitely quicker."

She followed my lead to make up for the time I'd already wasted. From the top of the valley, the village was much of nothing. Shadows claimed the streets and I couldn't pick out one building from the next. Not a single light struggled against the black. Sir Ightham wasn't the only one exhausted by the festivities.

It was much the same, towards the world unknown to me. I made out the shape of hills in the distance, trees wandering away from the edge of the wood, but clouds covered the moon and night fell across Felheim.

We turned away from my village, but my heart was trapped in the past. I'd stood at the foot of the path Sir Ightham was taking more than once, but I'd only ever stared down it. It'd never occurred to me that I could take a step forward and leave my old life.

Charley hesitated.

"I don't have any money," I said to Sir Ightham's back.

"If you aren't coming with me, leave," she replied. But that wasn't it. I wasn't having second thoughts, wasn't yet rational enough for that. I didn't want to be a burden. I didn't know what I could offer her and I wanted her to know that upfront, believing that I could say something to make her dismiss me when she already knew I was a necromancer.

"No, I just don't have any money," I said, catching up with her. "Or clothes, or food. I didn't have time to pack. I mean, I didn't expect to be doing this."

Sir Ightham pulled a bag from her shoulder, holding purpose out to me.

"Carry this."

I held both arms open but wasn't prepared for the weight of it. I almost toppled clean off Charley's back but didn't dare to complain. I slung the straps over my shoulders and something inside dug into my spine.

Sir Ightham hadn't been exaggerating when she said we had a long way to go before sunrise. The land evened out at the top of the valley and her horse set off at a speed I worried Charley wouldn't be able to match. We tore through dark hours and she didn't once glance back at me.

But she didn't try to lose me, either. I took that as a good sign.

I feared I was missing so much of the new world I'd never expected to see, but the darkness kept little from me. We passed open plains larger than my entire village, a river that reminded me how dry my mouth was, and an assortment of trees twisting themselves into terrifying shapes. I'd been out of my village for four hours and already concluded that the world repeated itself indefinitely.

But as the sun rose and colour trickled back into being, I realised I hadn't allowed myself to become excited. I was stepping into the world all of Michael's stories were born of. No one would know who I was, what I could do or what I'd done; I was *allowed* to be happy.

The morning dragged on. My father and brother would be up for breakfast, accompanied by an empty seat at the table. They wouldn't think much of it. I'd taken plenty of time to myself, those last few months.

Sunlight hit Sir Ightham's armour. It was as Michael had said. *White* really was the only way to describe it. It didn't hurt my eyes, not exactly, but it made me thoughtful when I already had far too much to think on. Hours must've been put into carving each link in her chainmail and the scales spreading across her pauldrons. The first thing they said about dragons in stories was that only dragon teeth could cut dragon-bone, and the smallest of those was the size of a fist.

"Where are we heading?" I said, breaking hours of silence. Sir Ightham made no reply, so I elaborated. "Not that it matters to me! I'd never been as far as Birchbridge until today and I *think* we passed that hours ago. I'm curious, that's all."

Sir Ightham nodded ahead.

After a beat she said, "You'll see."

I scowled at her helm but she was right.

The endless green of Felheim was broken up by grey intruding on the horizon. It wasn't the sky full of dark clouds set to burst. Rather, a wall I'd never seen the likes of rose before us. I'd thought Michael's tales

23

of towns to be exaggerated as everything else, but the settlement was *huge*. The stones of the wall must've taken five people each to get into place. And to think, I'd been so certain he'd romanticised his life with all the talk of the endless bustle within towns. It had seemed impossible that there could be so much life in the world, colours cast in a different shade.

The wall grew and grew but Sir Ightham turned sharply, leading us away from the hill the town was built upon. She took us to a scattering of trees and I kept my eyes on the town for as long as I could. Too soon it was out of sight but firmly within my mind.

"Aren't we going to the town?" I asked as Sir Ightham dismounted her horse. I remained on Charley, convinced this was my only chance to set foot in a settlement that wasn't my village. "It wouldn't have to be for long. Isn't there anything you need? I could get it for you, or—"

"Are you hungry?"

"... Yeah," I grumbled, admitting defeat.

It was for the best that I didn't give Sir Ightham any more reasons to be rid of me.

Perhaps she didn't want to face the inevitable crowds before breakfast. I couldn't think of anything worse than a rumbling stomach putting me at even more of a disadvantage.

Sir Ightham sat on the flat surface of a rock, armour making all manner of uncomfortable noises as she moved. I left Charley to get acquainted with her horse and sat before Sir Ightham in the dirt, finally getting a real look at her.

I did my best not to stare, instead stealing glimpses while pretending to dig dirt from under my nails with a loose rock. Luckily for me, she'd removed her helm and dropped it next to her. Daylight told me far more than the sharp shapes of the night had.

My mind hadn't formed the right impression of her. Armour notwithstanding, she didn't look like the Knight I'd imagined. I'd expected her to be as dark as the storm clouds Knights march against on their way to slay dragons – dragons being held accountable for foul weather, of course – but she was fairer than anyone I'd ever met.

Her long, blond hair was kept at such a length as a display of power and wealth, and her skin was pale enough to rival the dragon-bone she wore. She was older than me, perhaps by as much as a decade. I thought

24

it showed.

There were few white-skinned people this far south and I was certain she'd burn, even though the early spring sun lacked the power to thaw the ground beneath us. I was a descendant of the Myrosi people, dark brown skin common to most of Felheim, and with my short, messy hair, there were few similarities between us.

Her features might've been delicate on anyone else, yet the freckles scattered across her face, disappearing into her armour, weren't enough to stop there being something unnervingly hard about her. Even her eyes were hard, or as hard as blue eyes *could* be.

"Where are we now? What's the name of that town?" I asked.

"Eaglestone," she replied, rummaging through one of her bags.

"Eaglestone," I repeated, stealing a glance in its direction, hoping it had inched into sight while I wasn't looking.

Sir Ightham took a few parcels from her bag, and I thought she might be in a better mood for questions once breakfast was seen to. She didn't look at me as she unwrapped a pie, but didn't go out of her way to avoid eye contact, either. Knights must be in the habit of meeting and rescuing a lot of people. She wasn't obligated to pay any particular amount of attention to me.

She pulled a knife from her bag, unsheathed the dragon-bone blade and set about cutting up the pie. There was a carving along the blade and handle of a bird escaping flames. A phoenix, most likely. She scooped up a small slice of the pie and held it out to me with two fingers atop the crust. I cupped it between my hands, crumbs falling into my lap, and ate it as neatly as I could.

"Oh. This is one of Ms. Parson's pies, isn't it?" I said, belatedly remembering not to speak with a mouth full of food. Sir Ightham looked at me, but didn't nod or shake her head. I didn't need her to. "No one else can make a crust *this* good. She used to make me one every week, but, um..."

"But she discovered you were a necromancer?" Sir Ightham asked.

"Something like that. Now she won't even sell my brother one. She says she's too busy for baking lately, but..." I shrugged. "You know. Probably thought I was going to curse her."

"I'll never understand why people abandoned religion, only to cling to superstitions."

25

I enjoyed the pie for the first few seconds, but my mouth was so parched it was like swallowing handfuls of dirt. Sir Ightham had no such problem. I'd only been given a small portion in comparison to her, and she was doing an admirable job of devouring a mountain of food as she took liberal sips from the waterskin at her side.

She didn't speak to me again. She reached over and took one of the bags from my side. She didn't ask me to hand it over; she leant forward and snatched it up, and began searching through it with one hand. I needn't have been eager to see what she was looking for. She pulled out a scroll, quill and ink, and set about writing.

"Can I help?" I asked, feeling useless doing nothing but press my tongue to the roof of my mouth.

"Can you?" she asked without looking up.

Probably not.

I took in my surroundings for the umpteenth time: trees and grass, the town still out of sight. Sir Ightham wrote and wrote, and twice reached for more pie when there was nothing left on the crinkled brown paper. She looked up, giving me false hope, but did nothing but stare at my bare feet, brow furrowing as she continued to write.

"Hand me that bag," Sir Ightham finally said, nodding towards the larger, lighter of the two. I scrambled to pick it up, almost spilt its contents, and saw in her eyes that she regretted not reaching over and taking it without a word. "Turn around."

I swivelled on the spot and drew my knees to my chest. I didn't realise what was happening until I heard her huff, chainmail and dragon-bone plates coming away with a clatter. Intrigued by the sudden movement and strange sounds, Charley wandered away from Sir Ightham's horse. I reached up, putting a hand on his chest to stop him.

"Be patient," I whispered.

Charley whinnied, bowed his head to nudge me with his nose, and set about sulking.

"Turn back around," Sir Ightham said to let me know she was finished.

I'd endured tales of *the Knight* for so long I'd let myself believe her armour was part of her, carved from an extension of her own bones. Yet all that made her gleam was gone. The chainmail, helm, scaled boots and all else were piled at her feet, looking as strange without anyone filling them as Sir Ightham did dressed in leathers. A passing traveller might think a terrible creature's flesh had been torn away, bones left to collapse in on themselves.

The Sir Ightham from within the armour was but a memory. I stepped back, hand on my chin, and took in the sight of her. The leather coat, dark enough to make her pale skin paler, reached the back of her knees, where it was promptly met by a pair of boots. Black breeches were tucked neatly into them. Her white shirt was obscured by a leather chest piece, as tough as paper in comparison to what she was used to wearing.

"Well?" she asked, scrutinising me as I stared. It was hard not to look away, with the sharpness of her gaze. "How do I look?"

The question was to point, no ulterior motive flattened by her tone. She wasn't looking for a compliment. A woman like her never would've had to fish for one, even without the advantages of high society and the tremendous power she wielded.

"... Not very much like a Knight at all, Sir," I said, and it pleased her well enough.

She knelt down, gathered her armour and threw it carelessly into the bag her clothes had been in. I winced, wanting to tell her to be careful, but the armour was *dragon-bone*; she could've spent the day beating it against a rock without getting a scratch on it.

She swung the bag my way without any warning. I braced myself, caught it, and found it wasn't half as heavy as I was expecting.

"Come," she said, striding away with half the bags on her back. "You wished to see the town, didn't you?"

It didn't matter that she couldn't grasp what could possibly be so exciting about a town. I rushed after her, unable to feel the weight of the bags I'd gathered, full of too many questions to ask, too many fears to feel in earnest. I thought of all the things there were to be afraid of, the whispered warnings of pickpockets and pane and violent drunks, but none of it mattered. I was there with a Knight. A Knight who was taking a painfully leisurely stroll uphill, but a Knight nonetheless.

"When we reach the town," Sir Ightham began, "You aren't to call me *Sir*. Least of all *Sir Ightham*."

"Right. I bet everyone would want to meet a Knight, right? There'd be too much fuss," I said, deciding that must be it.

Not to mention the fact that Sir Ightham was supposedly on her way to Canth.

Sir Ightham looked down at me in surprise, but not in a good way.

"Exactly," she said.

The town rose higher and higher as we approached, a thousand tangled sounds reaching our ears, and I tugged on the straps of the bags, hoisting them higher on my back. Eaglestone had stood for hundreds of years and would be there for a hundred more. It wasn't going to crumble to dust on the hillside if I didn't charge towards it.

"What should I call you, then?"

Sir Ightham glanced at me, looking away just as quickly.

"Do not call me anything."

Something slipped through the cracks, something verging on disgust. Whatever her reasons for bringing me along, I was still nothing more or less than a necromancer. Of course she didn't want me addressing her.

I could've argued my worth to her. I could've argued my worth to the village over the last five months, but I hadn't. Instead, I let Eaglestone capture my attention, thoughts flowing outwards. Guards stood at the gate, some merely manning their stations, others greeting those who drifted into the city.

"Good morning, good morning!" a woman with a smile as sharp as her spearhead said to us. Sir Ightham marched into Eaglestone as though there were neither guards nor citizens around us, but I caught the guard's eye and grinned. "Welcome to Eaglestone!" she said to a man dragging a cart of turnips behind us.

Arriving early didn't make my first visit to a town any easier. I'd never seen the ocean, but I was suddenly caught in its currents, knocked back and forth by waves of bodies and foam. I knew I was short, but the crowd around me had formed solely to emphasise the fact, while Sir Ightham was able to lift her chin and make out her destination.

The buildings were tall, towering, poised to topple over and crush me. I couldn't take in the colours around me. The buzz of the crowd drew my attention, rendering all else grey, but something rose and swelled in my chest when I realised that of the hundreds of people, no one knew who I was. What I was. Nobody looked at me twice.

"It's... it's busy," I said, wanting to cling to Sir Ightham's arm, lest I was dragged out with the tide.

"Hardly," she said, tilting her head down a wide street. I inched close before she set off, certain a wave of people were bound to rush between us. "It'll be worse by midday."

A man as broad as an ox pushed past, catching my shoulder with the side of his arm. I'd done my best to weave between people and wasn't surprised to have knocked into someone. The man grunted, and the lack of apology carried more of an impact than the collision itself.

The street was twice as wide as my village's main road, and I kept my eyes fixed on Sir Ightham's back. Carts were pushed against buildings and people bellowed over one another, boasting that they had the best fruits and vegetables in all the town. In all of Felheim, even. I didn't stop to look. It would've left me dizzy with how much there was to take in.

It didn't take long to find Eaglestone's market. The open space was large enough to fit half the buildings of my village in, and was no less crowded than the entrance had been. At the height of my village's prosperity, twenty merchants from ten settlements came over twice a month, stalls and carts pressed up against their neighbour's, goods overlapping. In Eaglestone, there must've been a hundred stalls, each within their own allotted space, marked out with chalk on the ground.

I was torn every which way. Garments were draped on racks, dyed in colours I'd never seen, and vases, plates and casks of wine were set out on makeshift shelves. An endless array of fruit and vegetables filled deep trays, and meat hung from hooks, next to spices in corked jars. Jewellery glinted in the distance, and women haggled over weapons as though they were loaves of bread.

Sir Ightham made her way to a stall selling all manner of trinkets and inspected a number of items. She didn't greet the merchant eager to sell her what she already had her sight set on. The stall was covered in letter openers and paperweights, compasses and pocket watches, so many things that didn't interest me. My gaze skidded over the silvery surfaces and onto the crowd.

That was what mattered. The people churning down streets in their dozens. Each had their own business to attend to but had learnt to go along with the crowd, to be a part of a whole without getting their feet stepped on. My view was blocked by people cutting across me, but I could see enough. *More* than enough.

"S—" I began, but caught myself when Sir Ightham's head snapped around. She should've given me something else to call her, if she didn't want her title slipping from my tongue. "Is that... is that a pane?"

The marketplace drowned out the cries of merchants and blurred all conversations into one, but I lowered my voice. I pressed my fingers to my clammy palms. I couldn't see over people's heads but didn't need to: curved horns rose above the crowd, surrounded by a distinct sense of unease. Sir Ightham confirmed my fears with nothing like concern hastening her actions.

"It would appear so," she said, attention back on the array of compasses.

My heart pounded, fear creeping upon me like a building roll of thunder.

A pane had been to my village, when I was three. I didn't remember any of it and neither did Michael, no matter his claims to the contrary. It had come in the dead of night, snarling, half-starved, having to crouch to pound on doors, to demand to be let in. The villagers had gathered what they could to defend themselves, pitchforks and torches, but it was as threatening as facing a dragon with a shovel.

In the end, hunger won out. The pane made off into the fields and tore a flock of sheep to shreds with its tusks, more gruesomely than any wolf could think to, and had never been seen again. The village kept watch for a month, to be certain.

And now a pane roamed freely through Eaglestone. I hoped it wasn't hungry.

I hoped Michael was mistaken when he said they could smell fear.

"Very well. I'll take it," Sir Ightham said to the merchant. I'd missed the crossfire of bartering and kept one eye on the pane's steadily retreating horns as she reached for the leather pouch at her hip. A glint of gold pulled my attention from nearby monsters, but it wasn't a trick of the light. Sir Ightham really *was* paying with a mark.

It was a rare day that silver coins changed hands in my village. I'd never seen a gold one before.

The merchant tried to dig enough change out for her, flustered. In a display of either generosity or impatience, Sir Ightham held out a hand and told him it was fine. She swept a handful of coins off the stall and into her pocket, and the merchant protested, "No, please, that isn't even *half*—"

Sir Ightham bid him good day.

"I was careless. I left my compass in your village," Sir Ightham explained, tucking the new one into her top pocket. "Come. We'll find you something more suitable to wear."

"What's wrong with what I'm wearing?"

I already knew the answer. My clothes were Michael's patched up hand-me-downs, ill-fitting and wearing thin, but my mouth moved of its own accord while I scanned the market, trying to pinpoint the pane. The last thing I wanted was to blink and find it towering over me.

"You don't look fit to be my servant, much less a squire," Sir Ightham said bluntly. Neither irritated nor amused, she added, "Pay attention. The pane isn't going to eat you."

I was determined not to be any more of a burden, but I knew I wasn't the only one in Eaglestone made uncomfortable by the creature's presence. What did it *want*? Best not to find out, I reasoned.

We reached a row of clothing carts and Sir Ightham told me to pick something suitable. I waited for her guidance but it never came. There was too much on offer, styles that weren't familiar to me, fabrics the merchants assured me had been imported from Canth, and after a long, indecisive moment, I picked the plainest things I could find.

A loose white shirt, dark-green trousers and black boots. I burrowed a hole in the ground with my gaze as Sir Ightham paid for my things, though I knew money was of no consequence to her.

"We'll be covering the same distance again, before night falls," Sir Ightham said. "Will your horse manage?"

"I've still got plenty of bitterwillow."

"If you were to eat bitterwillow, you'd have no problem running to Benkor and back. Physically speaking," she said, holding out a hand to silence the man eagerly offering us a sample of wine. "Your body may not give into exhaustion, but your mind would."

"Um." I frowned, shuffling the boots in my arms. It took a moment to hit me: my horse. She was worried about my horse. I saw a flash of orange out the corner of my eye and caught up with myself. "No, no, Charley will be fine. He's tough! But listen. I promised him I'd get him carrots at the first market we came across."

"You promised your horse you'd buy him carrots?" Sir Ightham asked, lifting her brow. "Will he be affronted if you return from market without them?"

"Probably?"

"You've no money," she pointed out.

I thought that was the end of it, but Sir Ightham veered off to the side and made for the carrots that had jogged my memory. By the time I thought to hurry after her, she'd procured two dozen carrots, which she promptly dropped into my arms.

It wasn't until we were leaving Eaglestone that I could process it all. The smells faded, all the spices and cooked meats filling the market-place, trying to drown out the stench people were made of, replaced by the crisp morning air. The rest of the world was empty, endless plains broken up by nothing more than trees and rocks, while hundreds of people hid behind stone walls.

I smiled.

I'd done it. I'd really done it. I'd got out of my village and visited a town, a *real* town, and couldn't wait to tell Michael.

"Your village tells me you were deceitful," Sir Ightham said without easing herself into the conversation. "They tell me you lied, intentionally tricking them for seven years. That is a considerable length of time to pretend to be something less than you are. You can't be older than twenty-five."

I waited for her question, but it never came. She didn't care to be tactful and all things considered, I should've leapt at the chance to speak. I hadn't been given an opportunity to explain myself, and all my arguments went unspoken, festering in my mind for the deaf ears they would've fallen upon.

But I couldn't take the anger the village had incited within me out on Sir Ightham. There was nothing cruel in her voice, nothing beyond neutrality.

"Twenty-three," I said. "And it didn't start as a lie. I didn't want to trick anyone, didn't want to have to hide what I was. I realised I could heal people, so I did."

"Yet healing and necromancy are two distinct arts," Sir Ightham returned. "One purifies, one pushes death back."

"So?" I asked, shrugging. "I'm the only necromancer anyone seems to have met, and *I* don't see the point in acting like giving life and pushing away death are different things. Why should anyone else! I stopped people from dying, from being ill, fixed their broken bones, healed wounds. Where's the difference?"

Sir Ightham looked at me, thoughtful for the first time. I had to remind myself to keep moving, to put one foot in front of the other. Talking about necromancy made my head spin, and every ounce of sense in my body screamed at me to stop.

"Perhaps you're right. Perhaps it is not our place to make that judgement," she said.

"Everyone calls me a liar," I said, taking her remark as a victory. "But I did it to help them. To protect myself. And it's not like nobody else has never lied."

"Oh, no. Indeed it is not," Sir Ightham hummed.

As we reached the horses, I gathered the courage to ask, "They imprison necromancers in Thule, don't they?"

Sir Ightham patted her horse and Charley on the side of their necks as I placed the carrots on the ground and brushed imaginary dirt off my new clothes. I hoped I hadn't reminded Sir Ightham of something she'd forgotten.

"It is a good thing that we are neither in Thule nor heading towards Thule," she said, instantly winning Charley over with a carrot. "And I cannot say I have heard tell of a necromancer in Thule within my lifetime. Now: change."

I did as she ordered. I tugged my dirt-stained shirt off and clutched it to my chest as I fumbled into the new one. I didn't have the gall to tell Sir Ightham to turn around, but her back was to me as she acquainted herself with my horse. I tugged on my new trousers, certain someone wandering out of Eaglestone would catch sight of me, and put a boot on the wrong foot.

"Okay," I mumbled, curling my toes in my boots. I wasn't used to wearing anything on my feet, least of all stiff leather.

Sir Ightham turned around in her own time, idly raking her fingers through her horse's mane. I straightened when she set eyes on me, brightly asking, "How do I look?"

She arched her brow. I crouched down, scooped up my clothes, and draped them on a nearby bush, hoping someone in greater need of them than me might walk by.

"Not very much like a Knight at all," she said. I looked back at her but it was too late. She'd already climbed onto her horse, reins biting into her palms. "We've no more time to waste. Dragons aren't wont to wait around forever."

CHAPTER THREE

I could underestimate dragons.

Sir Ightham, while considerably taller than I was, was hardly a tower in and of herself and had taken down a handful of dragons on her own. They couldn't have been as large or fast as anyone claimed, even if they were undoubtedly dangerous. In my mind, the business of disposing of them was orderly: Sir Ightham would track down the beast and slay it, while I stayed at a safe distance, tending to the horses.

I couldn't shake the fear of pane so easily.

I was convinced the one from Eaglestone would follow us, and a woman on a cart had a few words of warning for us.

"You be careful now, girls," she said as a worn donkey pulled the creaking cart along. "Saw a couple of pane a few miles back."

From that moment, there was a pane lurking behind every tree and rock, no matter how impossible. I could finally take in my surroundings under the bright midday sun, but I was too busy searching for horns and claws and blood-stained tusks to appreciate any of it. Not that I missed much: Sir Ightham made a point of avoiding any and all settlements and I was treated to field after field.

Whenever Charley ran alongside her, she tugged on her horse's reins and pulled away from us. By late evening, we were in the depths of a forest. The sun had yet to be lured to cinders by the horizon, but there wasn't as much light as I would've liked. Shadows grew darker, longer, and tales of Queen Kouris rushed to the front of my mind.

It didn't matter that she'd been executed before I was born. Everyone knew that her ghost wandered the forests, severed head clutched in one enormous hand as she searched for the eyes that had been gorged from it; searching for any eyes she could claw out. It was a story, I told myself. Just a story, though why the pane would've been any different in death than she was in life was unclear.

Charley was starting to get skittish by the time we found a clearing to make camp in for the night. We'd only stopped to eat and drink throughout the long day, and Sir Ightham hadn't said a word to me since Eaglestone.

I saw to Charley, reassuring the both of us with a few forced, up-beat murmurs, and sat by the fire Sir Ightham had built. I wrapped my arms around myself and Sir Ightham kept her eyes on her writing.

"Do you think we're really going to run into one?"

Without looking up, Sir Ightham said, "Run into what?"

"A pane," I said. "That woman said she'd seen two, and there was one in Eaglestone. It could've come along this road..."

Sir Ightham put her quill on the ground and rubbed her temple.

"They."

"I'm sorry?"

"They. *They* could've come along this road," she said, scanning over the ink that had yet to dry. "He, she, they. Not *it*."

"Right," I decided to agree. "But it—*they* could've come this way, couldn't they?"

"Unlikely. Pane always travel alone, outside of their tribes," she said. She didn't put any effort into reassuring me. It was a side-effect of what she knew to be true. "I highly doubt the woman saw one pane, let alone two."

"So she was trying to scare us?"

I dropped my gaze when Sir Ightham did nothing beyond stare at me without blinking. There was a portion of food set out for me. I assumed it was mine, at any rate. There was a second, larger pile next to her, and she idly tore apart a piece of bread while contemplating my question. I pulled the food into my lap and pushed crumbling chunks of cheese into my mouth.

"I don't think she saw what she *thinks* she did. It happens. Either that, or she wanted some spark of excitement at our expense, after spending too long alone on the road," Sir Ightham said. "Pay no heed to the pane you saw in Eaglestone. After all, you know what they say about pane."

I knew *plenty* of things plenty of people said about pane, but most of those involved tearing flesh from bone. I was eager for an answer. Sir Ightham, as brief as she was, phrased things in a new way. I'd never heard of pane living in *tribes* before. In all the books Michael read to me, they lived in herds, like wild animals. Like the dragons they lived amongst.

"They never attack, even when provoked; they rarely defend, under such circumstances," she said plainly.

The scrawl of her quill across the parchment said she was done humouring me. I picked at my meal of bread and cheese, missing the morning's offering of pie, now that there was ample drink available. Sir

Ightham had pitied me enough to give me a spare waterskin and allowed me to fill it from a nearby river.

"But Queen Kouris—" I blurted out, pretending our conversation hadn't drawn to a close.

Sir Ightham's head snapped up. She wasn't frowning. Her expression had never been anything but even, but the fire made her eyes shine like steel in a forge.

"Queen Kouris? Don't tell me you're afraid of *ghosts*," she said. "Why should you concern yourself with what pane may or may not do? You're a necromancer. Push it from your mind."

Sir Ightham spoke the word easily, meaning to remind me of what I was over and over. She said it with the same overwhelming force my village's silence had roared with, and heat rushed to my face and throat as I fumbled with the implication that being ripped to shreds shouldn't bother me.

"Look, being able to heal doesn't mean that—"

"Go to sleep," she said.

My voice pulled taut before she cut me off. I did as she said.

I laid on my back and stubbornly kicked off my boots, scuffing the sides with the soles. All in all, Sir Ightham did little to sour my mood. There'd been a bitter taste in the back of my throat for months, and after a full night and day of travelling, clenching my jaw wasn't going to stop me falling asleep.

I dreamt of nothing, but slept soundly enough to convince my waking mind I was at home, safe in bed. It was dark when I awoke to something prodding my ribs, and the ground had yet to form beneath me. I blinked my eyes open, saw a figure looming above and started. I realised it was Sir Ightham as I scrambled back, realised I really *had* run away, and she didn't laugh.

"You slept for too long," was all she had to say.

Dawn was making a commendable effort to get started, but the sky wasn't tinged with enough light to be particularly useful. I reached blindly for my boots, pulling them on as I hopped over to Charley. The fire had been doused, charred wood and cinders thrown into the grove beyond, and I didn't feel as though I'd slept for more than five hours.

"Where to today?" I asked, confident I was mostly awake. I didn't care where we headed, so long as it wasn't into the maw of a dragon or pane. The previous day had introduced Eaglestone, and I couldn't shake the feeling that today would have greater things in store.

"Praxis."

"*Praxis?*" Even I knew where Praxis was. It teetered on the edge of Felheim, acting as a centre of trade and a gate in and out of Kastelir. "What's in Praxis?"

"Plenty of things."

"What's in Praxis that *we* care about?"

We might've been too strong a word to use. Sir Ightham gave her horse's reins a sharp tug and I followed them through the thicket of trees.

"I need somewhere to store my belongings. I'm certain you'll agree," she said. "And I am expecting a raven from a contact."

"Who? Someone helping with the dragon?"

"Someone helping with the dragon," Sir Ightham repeated. She came to an abrupt halt and I stopped as she did, wondering what I'd done wrong. The sound of feet against brittle twigs sent my concern elsewhere. "Say nothing," she whispered.

Light broke through the trees, matched by a cheerful whistling. My first instinct was to run and I didn't know why. We couldn't have been the only travellers making our way through the woods. Sir Ightham stood her ground. Having our horses sprint off would only draw more attention to us.

"Well, well," a man said, imbued with confidence, thanks to his four companion. "Up early, aren't you?"

I'd been so terrified of imaginary pane that I hadn't scared myself with the thought of running into bandits. The five of them were dressed in clothes I suspected weren't as fine as they first appeared, and they made a point of letting us know they had weapons.

The man who'd raised his voice, their self-proclaimed leader, drummed his fingers against the pommel of the sword resting against his hip.

"Good morning," Sir Ightham said. Two of the bandits behind her clumsily drew their swords. "Might I be of assistance?"

The woman who'd drawn her blade snorted a laugh. The leader scowled, thinking it no way to conduct business.

"That you can," he said. "Heard there was a Knight around these parts, and I reckon a Knight would have a wealth of treasure on 'em. Gold least of all. Don't suppose you've seen anything that could help the both of us, have you?"

"I don't suppose I have," Sir Ightham said, sounding sorry to admit it. "But a Knight, is it? What do they look like? I should like to meet them."

The bandit gave a dry laugh, not finding it funny at all. His companions slowly joined in the mockery. Sir Ightham dismounted her horse and passed the reins to me, drawing the bandits' attention my way for the first time.

"If yous can't help us on that front, ladies, would you be so kind as to leave those rather hefty bags on the ground?" the man said, met with a murmur of agreement from behind. "Jeb, if you'd be so good as to help 'em out..."

One of the bandits rushed forward, sword clasped between both hands. I'd climbed off Charley's back to better keep hold of his and Sir Ightham's horse's reins. Jeb took that to mean I was going to comply. Sir Ightham set the record straight by drawing her sword. She'd packed the dragon-bone one away but a steel blade was no less of a challenge. She swung it in her hand as though it was part of her arm, not something she could run clean through the bandit.

"Awful bold, ain't ya?" Jeb asked, ducking down low. Sir Ightham hadn't shown any intention of striking, but the bandit was under the impression that he'd formed a formidable fighting stance.

"I only wish to warn you of your folly," Sir Ightham said.

"Boss?" Jeb asked.

He'd let go of his sword with one hand and was trying to determine whether he'd lose any fingers if he snatched one of our bags.

"Oh, that's right, is it?" the leader mused. All of the bandits were holding their weapons out, while Sir Ightham stared at the blade of her sword, trying to glean something of her reflection. "Reckon you can cut your way through all of us?"

"If I must," Sir Ightham said. She held her stance and used the tip of her blade to point at the bandits one by one. "Your companion here – Jeb, wasn't it? – hasn't the good grace to hold his sword properly. Try it in the *other* hand, if you wish to land any blows. This young woman's blade has come loose in its hilt, meaning it isn't facing the direction her grasp suggests she's aiming for, and the gentleman by her side doesn't think anyone will notice how he trembles, so long as he stands back and lets the others look threatening. As for *you*, I've no doubt you *can* fight. But only so well as to appear intimidating to individuals caught unaware and ambushed in the middle of the woods."

Jeb clasped both hands around the hilt of his sword, sneering. The man Sir Ightham accused of cowardice was betrayed by his own torch. Flames licked the air, letting all see how red his face had turned. The leader responded with a snarl that fuelled his movements. He lunged forward and thrust his blade straight at Sir Ightham's throat.

I recoiled from a blow that didn't land. Sir Ightham took a swift step back, rendering the blade's reach ineffective. Hand balled into a fist behind her back, Sir Ightham brought her sword against the bandit's three times, forcing him to lose ground with each clatter of steel. It was the first time I'd see her fight, the first time I'd seen a *real* swordfight, but I knew she could've disarmed him with a single blow. She lashed out so as to startle the other bandits, lest they mimic their leader's movements.

"Well?" Sir Ightham asked, when she'd seen to it that he'd tripped over a root and slammed his elbow into a tree trunk.

"C'mon!" he spat. "Useless louts! Give us a hand already."

There was no strength in numbers. A wandering group of thieves could never compare to a dragon. Sir Ightham fought fluidly, ensuring it was over as quickly as it started. She weaved around their weapons, disarmed some and knocked others into trees, and didn't spill a single drop of blood.

I would've felt any wounds, had her sword struck anyone.

With her point proven, Sir Ightham lowered her blade. I feared the leader might've been humiliated enough to put his all into one final strike, but he wasn't so stubborn as to forfeit his life. He grunted for his companions to back down, and Sir Ightham watched them scamper into the woods.

I ran my fingers through my hair, forehead clammy, having managed to stay perfectly still. It may have been fear keeping me grounded, not courage, but the result was the same. My heart began to pound with the bandits gone, for I had time to imagine all that could've happened, but didn't.

Sir Ightham patted Charley between the eyes before climbing onto her own horse.

"They're gone," she said when I didn't move. "... Why are you smiling?"

"Because that was *incredible*!" I said, holding my hands out for emphasis. "You fought off *five* of them, all by yourself."

"They were bandits," she said, offended that I found the quarrel worthy of remark.

"They had swords!"

"So did I. Now, might we leave, before we're stumbled upon by more of the same?"

So much for paying her a compliment.

Another mile of woodland stood between us and open plains, and milky light covered the land by the time we weaved out way out of the trees. Sir Ightham's compass led us off a road as soon as we joined it, and we headed west, to the border. A wall stood between Felheim and Kastelir, but in my mind, it had been like that of a house, or the cobbled wall wrapped around the village, little more than waist-high where it hadn't crumbled completely.

But the wall that kept the Kastelirians out cast a shadow that covered half our Kingdom. Kastelir wasn't a decade older than I was, and had been split into four ever-warring territories before that. The wall had been a necessity for hundreds of years, and its age was evident in its stature. I craned my head to see the top, certain any clouds drifting by on a slight breeze would crash into it. It was worn by the elements and creeping vines had done what they could to scale the sides, but there were none who could say it didn't protect us.

I watched the wall until my neck ached. We didn't venture too close to any villages or towns, but I saw them from a distance. They looked like my village, only misplaced; dropped onto the side of a hill or strewn along a river, rather than nestled into a valley.

My fear of pane was replaced by a fear of bandits, and that fear was washed away by Sir Ightham's presence. We travelled for days that blurred into one another, exhausting my supply of bitterwillow, and only stopped to sleep or stretch our legs and eat. Sir Ightham said nothing and responded to questions that were barely worth asking with a grunt or shake of her head.

I didn't earn her attention, until I stepped over and tentatively brushed a hand against her horse's mane.

He leant into my touch, well behaved, but not beyond indulging himself in a little affection. Sir Ightham watched me like a hawk.

"What's his name?" I asked, scratching him behind the ears.

"Calais," she said after a cautious pause, unwilling to spill too many secrets at once.

"Nice to meet you, Calais," I said. He made the sort of noise that tended to mean *yes, but what are you going to feed me?* from Charley. "My horse is—"

"Charley. You already said."

She said nothing more but ran her fingertips across the diamond of white fur on Charley's forehead.

The wall curved with what I thought was the border, and it took me too long to realise that Praxis was built into the wall itself. From where we stood, leading our horses by the reins to get through the crowds, I couldn't see where Praxis ended. The horizon cut off prematurely, towers and spires pressing against the sky. There was more of a jump from Eaglestone to Praxis than there had been from my village to Eaglestone, and I'd convinced myself the whole world had come to gather within that town.

I was grateful for the clothes Sir Ightham had brought me, even if they were crumpled from sleep and riding. I flattened what creases I could as we approached the city, surrounded by a swathe of people finer than I'd imagined the nobles of Thule to be. Everyone's clothing was as vibrant as the city around them, and the stone of the streets gleamed as though a thousand pairs of boots didn't press down upon it every hour of the day.

I'd known that Praxis was wealthy, but wealth to me meant being able to choose what you ate for dinner. In Praxis, people were out for the sake of being outside, walking arm in arm with friends, chatting idly and showing off their purchases. The workers faded into the background, but even they were remarkable; they wore uniforms and donned hats as they stood in front of polished shopfronts, ever ready to open a door, or sat at the front of carriages, waiting for their next passenger to ferry around the city.

People pushed past, heels and canes clipping against the ground. I'd survived Eaglestone, pane and all, but my chest was too small for all I needed to fit within it. Sir Ightham put a hand on my shoulder to let me know I'd come to a stop and guided me forward. We took our horses to a stable by the gate and Sir Ightham paid no small fee to have them lodged there.

The bags were heavier than ever, what with the promise of finding somewhere to stow them. Sir Ightham cut across a river of a street, heading for a building that looked like all the others surrounding it. Everything in Praxis was made of precise angles, and buildings pressed perfectly together without being crammed and wedged into awkward spaces.

Sir Ightham knew the city as well as I'd expected her to.

The front doors were opened for us by guards. Or so I thought, from a first glance. Weapons hung from their belts and they wore a uniform, but it was unlike that of the guards I'd seen milling around Praxis or outside of Eaglestone. Sir Ightham gestured for me to head over to the counter, where I could see rows upon rows of safes the size of coffins through an iron gate.

"Can I be of assistance?" a woman asked.

She knew to speak to Sir Ightham, not me.

"I need to store two bags indefinitely," Sir Ightham said. "How much for, say, a year?"

The woman bowed her head, wordlessly apologising for the answer she was about to give.

"That would be a mark, I'm afraid. Fifty valts each, judging from the size."

Just to be safe, Sir Ightham slid three golden marks across the counter. It was such an unreasonable amount of money that I wanted to beg her to let me carry the bags, if it meant not throwing the coins away. Still, I placed the bags on the counter when Sir Ightham gestured for them.

One of the establishment's guards took a ring of keys from her hip and unlocked the gate. The bags were taken to a safe, and Sir Ightham was given a small silver key. Sir Ightham took it, thanked the woman for her help, and placed it on a chain around her neck.

We headed back into the city, each carrying a single, reasonable bag. One contained her dragon-bone armour, and I supposed the other was full of parchment for her letters, food, and whatever else we needed for the road.

"Where to now?" I asked. I assumed I wasn't to call her *Sir Ightham* in Praxis, either.

"We'll find rooms for the night," Sir Ightham said. "I've business to attend to."

I brightened at the thought. I had nothing against sleeping under the stars, having spent so many nights out in the hills, but I'd never had reason to sleep in a bed that wasn't my own. I'd been to the Marmalade Lodge a few times, when travellers who'd come in search of my aid couldn't make it to the apothecary's, but that was work. This was something different. Something new.

The city opened up as we reached a square, surrounded on all sides by cafés and taverns, tables and chairs spilling onto the patio. Statues stood in the centre, mounted on pedestals taller than I was, and I hurried over to get a better look.

A man and a woman towered over me, both of them fifteen feet tall. I rocked on the balls of my feet, grinning when I saw Sir Ightham out of the corner of my eye. She folded her arms across her chest, far from impressed or even interested, but I didn't let it dash my spirits.

"We're really in Praxis!"

There was more excitement in the word *Praxis* than there'd been in all of Eaglestone.

"We are," she agreed, not bothering to point out that we'd been in Praxis for close to half an hour.

"I never thought I'd come here. Never thought I'd go anywhere, really, but especially not here. I've heard so many stories about Praxis that I was starting to think it was just that. But look at it! It's bigger than my brother said it would be."

"And yet it has taken us a mere handful of days to reach. So much for stories," Sir Ightham muttered. "You'll soon see that the world is a lot bigger, a lot more *everything*, than can be gathered from books."

I wished Michael was there, just to see his jaw drop at the suggestions that books weren't the be all and end all of the human experience.

"Who are they?" I asked, pointing up at the figures.

"Read the plaque," Sir Ightham said, nodding towards it. She was rummaging through her bag in search of something. I didn't say anything. I kept looking at her, shoulders hunched. When she finally glanced up, she pressed her lips together tightly and said, "You can't read."

I nodded. It wasn't a question, but I nodded. Sir Ightham sounded irritated with herself for not piecing it together sooner and went back to searching through her bag. I kept my eyes fixed on her until she relented.

"King Garland and Queen Aren," Sir Ightham said. I brightened, enthusiasm for Praxis renewed, and she read the inscription out loud. *"Commissioned in 1477 by Liege Halka, to acknowledge the roles Their Highnesses played in ensuring the Territories' war never encroached on Felheim, never marred our way of life."*

My father had been a soldier, during the war that resulted in Kastelir. He'd told me how our rulers had promised to lend their aid to one territory, should another cross our borders, and none had been willing to take that risk. If we could slay dragons, we could crush them.

"Are there statues of the Princes and Princess, too?" I asked, glancing around.

"Why would there be? They were barely infants during the war."

"No, that's not what..." I said, laughing at myself. I leant closer to Sir Ightham, letting my voice drop to a whisper. "What are they like?"

Sir Ightham found what she was looking for – more parchment, surprise – and said, "What are who like?" barely bothering to follow the tenuous line of conversation.

I pointed at the statues and said, "You're a... *you know*, so you must know them."

"I suppose I must," she said, turning from the statues.

I hurried after her, pleading my case.

"Come on! Everything I've heard about them is from my brother, and you can't learn everything from books, right?"

I grinned at her, though she stared dead ahead.

We left the square by a narrow road was that was far from empty, surrounded by houses and apartments on all sides. Rows of washing were strung out on lines far above our heads and the flowers bursting from balconies were starting to bloom. Certain she wouldn't know peace until she answered me, Sir Ightham sighed, slowed her pace, and said, "They are neither as tall nor as stern as their statues make them out to be."

Those few words were invaluable to me. They were something for me to hold over Michael's head. A thousand other questions came to mind – did she know the Princes and Princess, how big was the castle, and could Thule *really* be bigger than Praxis? – but I knew better than to push my luck.

Instead, I said, "I'm glad we got rid of those bags. What was in them? A dragon?"

"Don't get too used to your newfound freedom. We'll need to stop for supplies at the next market. Additional food, some manner of pan, more bitterwillow. Can you remember all of that?"

Without it being written down, she meant.

"Food, pan, plants. Got it!" I said, sealing the information with a nod. "Anything you like in particular? How about Calais?"

"We eat most things," was her eventual reply. I didn't question her further. She was a Knight, likely trained to withstand all forms of torture; I wouldn't be able to force a preference between chicken and pork out of her.

"I'll get more carrots," I decided. "He liked those."

Sir Ightham didn't answer me, as was her way, and we strolled into what would've been the bad part of Praxis, if Praxis could be said to have a bad part. The houses around us were replaced by taverns, and doors and windows were thrown open to soak up the first hint of spring. A musician played piano in one and a patron drunk enough to mistake himself for a musician played in another, and the sounds entangled in the centre of the street until I couldn't tell who was playing badly.

Instead of looking around, I found my attention drawn to Sir Ightham. Her expression was as neutral as ever, and I wondered what it would take to pry a reaction out of her. I wondered how many questions I'd have to ask before she snapped and told me to shut up, rather than simply falling silent. Realising I'd stared for a second too long, I followed her gaze and saw what everyone was already aware of.

Outside a tavern, perched on a stool with plenty of empty seats around them, was a pane.

CHAPTER FOUR

Even seated, the pane was taller than me.

I couldn't say how the seat beneath it – *her* – hadn't been reduced to splinters, but it was far from the most pressing thing on my mind. I wanted to run, but my feet were stone and I couldn't part them from the cobbled street.

Pane had been overgrown humans with horns and fangs in my mind, but I saw how wrong I'd been. Thick tusks protruded from the pane's prominent lower jaw, each of them three inches long. Her skin was no darker than mine, but it looked more like soft, brown leather than flesh, and a ring of gold stood against the coal her eyes were made from.

Sir Ightham inclined her head respectfully towards the pane, and the pane's long, pointed ears stood up at the recognition.

The pane rose to her feet, strange as they were for being hoofed like a goat's but shaped like a wolf's, until there was no less than eight or nine foot of her, horns making her taller still. Sir Ightham barely reached halfway up the pane's chest. The pane bowed her head, offering a lazy sort of respect in return.

"Dragon-slayer," the pane said.

Her voice was unlike anything I'd heard before. It wasn't human, but it wasn't a growl, either. It was like gravel sifting through fingers, having been left out in the sun to trap heat.

I hadn't slipped up. I hadn't called Sir Ightham *Sir* since we'd been in Praxis, but the pane knew what she was, even without her dragon-bone armour. Being called a *dragon-slayer* might've been a compliment from a human, but from a pane it couldn't be anything less than a death sentence.

Sir Ightham was entirely unperturbed by the pane knowing who – or what – she was and said, "A good day to you, dragon-born."

The pane grinned. Her tusks were arrowheads, set to lodge in Sir Ightham's throat. I lost faith in the fact that I was a necromancer, for I could never negate the damage caused by a pane. But the pane didn't strike. That was all in my head. She did nothing beyond slip a hand between the tough leathers and the sash of bright orange cloth she wore, plucked out a letter with a great, clawed hand, and held it out to Sir Ightham.

"Been hearing some troubling rumours, lately," the pane said as Sir

Ightham took the letter. "But as they say, a burden shared..."

Sir Ightham scanned the letter. I couldn't imagine the pane writing, couldn't imagine her holding anything as small as a quill between her fingers. When she reached the end of the note, Sir Ightham's brow creased, and she read it for the second time. Certain she understood it, she folded it in two and tore it down the middle, over and over.

"Peculiar," Sir Ightham said.

The pane nodded gravely and fished something else from beneath her leathers. She clasped a chain in a fist, gold-silver pendant swaying too much for me to make out the design. It was gone in a flash, but Sir Ightham understood what she'd seen. She brought a hand to her mouth and ran her fingers across dry lips. The pane's ears twitched at the reaction she'd drawn out of her.

"What say you?"

Sir Ightham considered the question as though she had no choice in the matter. Whatever she'd read, whatever the pendant meant, affected her more than five bandits and their swords ever could. She set her jaw and tilted her head towards me.

"Give her your things," she said, pushing all of the pane's attention onto me.

I'd hardly been inconspicuous up until that point. I was right there, unable to back away, but now the pane was looking right at me. The corner of her mouth tugged upwards, revealing rows of fangs more subtle than her tusks, and I was so intent on not blinking, on not showing fear, that I missed her swing her bag off her back. It hit me square in the chest and my arms instinctively wrapped around it.

I didn't wince. I didn't breathe.

"This your servant?" the pane asked.

"This is my *squire*," Sir Ightham said. She was met with a moment of silence, before the pane let out a deep, hearty chuckle. Even Sir Ightham was amused by her own words. I dug my fingers into the pane's bag, hoisting it further into my arms.

"What's our first step to be?" the pane asked.

A few secrets scrawled onto a letter had earnt her a place within our group. That said, if Sir Ightham was willing to travel with a necromancer, why not add a pane into the mix?

"I'll take rooms for us at the *Rambler's Rest*," Sir Ightham said. The pane nodded, and Sir Ightham turned to me. "I trust you remember what we need from market."

I slung the pane's bag onto my back, meaning to use my arms to strengthen my protest, but Sir Ightham took the chance to slip a handful of silver coins into my hand. I clasped them tightly and Sir Ightham was gone before I could get a word out. She pushed a hole through the crowd and it closed behind her, leaving me alone with the pane and my thundering heart.

If Sir Ightham wanted to be rid of me, she could've sent me home.

I kept my head down as I considered my options. For the first time in months, being ignored was appealing. I couldn't run. The pane would reach out and grab the scruff of my collar, and the crowd would never let me back in. They'd made a well around the pane, not daring to walk too close to her, pace quickening as they passed.

Hoping the pane had business of her own to attend to didn't help. She crouched in front of me but it didn't put us close to eye-level. She tilted her head to catch my gaze. I was being rude, I knew I was. I would've had an easier time with it all if I could bring myself to acknowledge the pane, but I couldn't force myself to move. All I could think of was the pane who'd come to my village, Queen Kouris in the woods, and all the people who'd been ripped to shreds by hands like the one being waved in front of my face.

"Now, now. Was only teasing you, yrval," the pane said, returning to her full height. She reached out not to attack, but to pluck the bags from my back. The weight lifted, allowing my gaze to flicker up, but I couldn't move. She slung the bags onto her back with such ease they appeared empty. "Name's Rán."

"I'm R—" I stuttered. My tongue was too large for my mouth, too heavy, and I was in such a daze that I might as well have been struck across the back of the head. "Rowan, I'm..."

Talking was getting me nowhere. I'd forgotten how to wield my words and had to dig to remember my own name. Poor though it was, Rán didn't hold my introduction against me. She smiled in a way that thankfully didn't show too many of her teeth and immediately turned to leave.

Relief claimed me and immediately loosened its grasp. Rán was gone, but she'd left with Sir Ightham's dragon-bone armour. Horns or no

49

horns, I didn't think I'd come out of it in one piece if I went back to Sir Ightham empty-handed.

I did the most foolish thing I could think of.

I ran after the pane.

I soon learnt there was an advantage to walking with a pane: people got out of the way as quickly as they could. Rán walked at a comfortable pace, but I had to half-jog to match her stride.

"What's that dragon-slayer having you fetch?" she asked.

My words came automatically, loudly.

"Food, pans, bitterwillow."

I gripped the coins tightly, fifty valts in five and ten pieces, terrified one would slip through my grasp and roll along the street, lost under someone's boot or a stray cart. Worse still, I was afraid they'd lose their value simply by being in my possession. I was on the verge of making the coins sweat and focused on making sure I hadn't dropped any. It gave me an excuse not to look up, and up, at Rán.

"What kind of food are we looking for?" Rán asked, rubbing her chin. "Doubt that dragon-slayer has much in the way of taste. What about yourself, yrval?"

"I..."

It was no good. I couldn't get my brain and mouth to work together.

"Food, yrval. What are you in the mood for?" Rán went on cheerfully. "Could be pointing you in the direction of a pretty good fruit stall. When they say they're getting their goods from Canth, you can almost believe 'em. Tasty as anything, but not grown that far south. Got any favourites?"

"What?"

Rán tilted her head towards me and I caught the toe of my boot on a raised paving slab.

"Fruit. You humans are still eating that, aye? Apples, melons, pears. That sort of thing."

"Oranges," I blurted out. It didn't sound like a real world.

I couldn't even tell if it was the right answer.

"Not a bad choice," Rán mused. I was too confused by the thought of pane eating anything other than raw meat to offer up anything remotely intelligible. On Rán went, supporting the conversation without my help. It was a bizarrely welcome change from the past few days. "We'll stop off for fruit first. They sell some hefty joints of meat more or less opposite the stall. Should be enough to keep you and the dragon-slayer full for a few days. Haven't had any time to look into cheese or bread yet, so that'll be an adventure. Now, just to get this out there, I'm not in the habit of biting off heads, so the worst thing that's likely to happen if you relax is you feeling a lot better."

"I know!" I squeaked. Actually *squeaked*. But I didn't know. I was convinced my life was forfeit, but Rán made no effort to hold it against me.

"Ah. Can't go forgetting about those horses of yours. Best be stocking up on this and that for 'em, too."

A fear of squeaking for a second time stopped me asking how she knew about our horses, and rightly so. The market came into sight and I realised I'd been leeching paranoia from everyone we passed. Of course we had horses. How else would we be getting around?

I mumbled an agreement and a fairly accomplished nod. Rán led me to the promised fruits. Her assessment of *pretty good* had been woefully understated. I didn't recognise half of the selection spread out on the stall, all of them so relentlessly vibrant that the colours themselves may have been invented solely for them.

I wanted to get back to Sir Ightham and away from the pane as quickly as I could, and so played it safe. I grabbed an assortment of fruit I could name and didn't protest when Rán took those bags from me as well.

The young couple running the stall weren't as wary as the rest of Praxis seemed to be. They were pleased to see Rán, bright smiles backing up their cheer, and spoke a handful of words to Rán in what must've been her mother tongue. The cut of her grin said she was impressed, and she bowed deeply, leaving me to tip the merchants.

I'd been in Praxis for a matter of hours and already met a pane. If the couple worked there day in, day out, who knew what else they'd seen. Michael's stories often hinted at the furthest corners of Bosma, where giants who could knock a pane into the ground with a swing of their fists roamed, along with landscapes that would make the Bloodless Lands pale in comparison.

"Catch!" Rán said with a flick of her wrist. My reflexes were sharper than my mind and I grabbed the blur that sprung from her hand, albeit after stepping to the side and clipping my shoulder against a passer-by. He'd been walking with his head down, meaning to charge through the crowd like a bull, and turned to shoot me either a glare or harsh words. Upon seeing the company I was keeping, he resolved to quicken his pace.

I stared at the orange in my hand as though it was one of the strange spiked fruits from the stall, uncertain what to do with it.

I glanced up at Rán.

"You're welcome," she said, grinning.

I kept the orange in my hand as we dealt with the matter of meat, a field Rán claimed expertise in. She took a leg of lamb between her fingers and held it up for inspection. It would barely serve as a bite to her, let alone an entire meal. The merchants at that stall weren't as amiable as the fruit sellers had been. When Rán asked how much two legs would set us back, they looked at me and said, "It's four relds for two of them. Make that three. Can't sell 'em on now that they've been handled," with a sneer nobody missed.

Rán's pride was far from wounded, for she must've suffered worse. She'd suffered far worse in the depths of my mind that very day. I was a hypocrite: the way the man refused to speak to her, slighting her all the while, didn't sit well with me.

I took the meat at a discounted price without saying thank you, deciding that profit out of the merchant's pocket did something to alleviate his rudeness. Rán wrapped the meat and slung it under her arm, and I pierced the orange's peel with my thumbnail.

"Are people always that rude?" I asked as we ventured over to a promising rack of pans. It was the most coherent thing I'd managed to say since meeting her. "He wasn't just ignoring you. He was making a *point* of letting you know he was ignoring you. And you're... well, you're kind of..."

"Conspicuous?"

"... I was going to say huge," I admitted.

Rán slapped a hand against my back as she laughed. I tensed, but wasn't scared to death; I was growing braver by the second.

"Why do that? You weren't causing them any problems. You were a paying customer!"

Rán's expression had been animated from the moment I'd met her.

She'd only taken breaks from smiling to grin, fangs flashing under the midday sun, but her features evened out as she considered my question. She took my thoughts more seriously than she otherwise would because it was the first time I'd managed to speak freely around her. I was letting my guard down. I was treating her like a *person*.

"Pane don't go responding to words with anything other than quick wit. They're not gonna stir us to violence. Not with threats, not with insults. Not with actions. Some of you humans, you're just..." Rán paused, tapping her chin with a claw. "You're fond of making outsiders out of anyone a little different. And once you've got someone who's a *lot* different, well. Here we are. Let the lad waste his breath. I've been accused of worse than ruining a little meat."

"People scare too easily," I said, working an orange segment free. The number of pane I'd met who hadn't made a meal of me outweighed the number who had by a considerable amount, and I decided it was only right to treat her with an ounce of the warmth she was treating me.

Which wasn't to say I wasn't *terrified*.

Rán chuckled to herself and said, "You'll pull yourself together before you know it, yrval. Don't remember ever meeting a Myrosi sort who was so pale."

I knew better than most how it felt to have people jump to conclusions, and berated myself for having followed in the villagers' example just as soon as I wasn't the one being shunned. Being scared of Rán wasn't going to make me any less of a necromancer; I wasn't suddenly going to fit with the rest of humanity.

I popped the piece of orange into my mouth, pierced it with my teeth to make my smile orange, and tugged on Rán's cloak. The juice bled from the corners of my mouth and Rán let out a laugh so deep I thought she might knock the cooking pots from the stall they were precariously placed upon.

Placing a hand on my back with more care than I braced myself for, Rán said, "Don't reckon you're anything like that dragon-slayer. How'd you end up with the likes of her? Never known a squire to go around without at least a little armour on. Certainly never seen one who'd left their sword behind."

I chewed slowly on another orange segment and debated telling Rán the truth. A human wouldn't have taken kindly to it, but I had no idea

53

how the pane felt about *anything*. Beyond how they liked their steak, that was.

"I had a falling out with my village and needed to get out of there," I said.

Rán could pry the truth out of me, if she cared to.

"You had a falling out with an entire village?" Rán asked, mildly impressed. "Now, tell me. Exactly how does a friendly young woman like yourself go about achieving a feat of the sort?"

With the prompting of a second question, I found I was *eager* to tell her the truth. I'd either been caught in the act or fallen prey to vicious rumours in the past and had never been given the chance to actually *tell* someone before. And why not Rán, this mountain of a woman?

Perhaps I wanted to be honest for the first time in years. Perhaps I wanted to give her as much as a fright as she'd given me.

People were sure to be listening in on a pane's conversation, to have something to discuss over their dinner tables that night, so I pushed myself up on tiptoes. It didn't get me far. Seeing I had something of a secret to share with her, Rán leant down.

"Necromancy," I whispered into her pointed ear.

The word came out easily, leaving my nerves rawer for it.

Rán didn't flinch or shrink away from me, which did something to stop my heart from hammering in my chest, but unlike Sir Ightham, she had no problem showing what she was feeling. She furrowed her brow, bemused, and licked her upper lip with a long, thin tongue, searching for an appropriate response.

It wasn't until the word was out there, irretrievable, that I recalled the pane's role in the Necromancy War. Rán had assured me that a threat or insult wouldn't provoke her to violence, but her eyes could become icy whenever she looked at me.

To a necromancer, that would leave as much of a bruise.

"Heh," came her reply. She stood back up straight and said, "You humans sure are a peculiar lot."

Disappointment came rushing in along with relief. I'd hoped it would take Rán more than a moment to decide it didn't matter, for the years I'd spent terrified necromancy would take everything from me. I reminded myself that the pane weren't necromancers, weren't healers. She probably didn't understand what it truly meant.

54

"See that building with a red coat of paint? That's the inn we're meeting the dragon-slayer at," Rán said. "Go ahead. And don't be worrying, I won't be running off with your bags. Just saving your back the strain, is all."

I watched her horns rise above the crowd as she went on her way, not waiting for me to say goodbye. Strange how I felt more comfortable with a pane than without one. The city grew larger without Rán towering over me, and the crowds drew in closer. I hurried to the inn.

The *Rambler's Rest* was a wooden building placed between two stone ones, with more floors than could possibly be necessary. A sign hung above the door, a mediocre painting of a man sitting at a table, lit by only a single candle, and a tavern was built into the ground floor.

I headed there when I found the lobby empty, save for a woman working behind a counter who didn't look up from her book. The tavern smelled more of roasting meat than it did alcohol, and was better lit than the sign had led me to believe. I didn't spot Sir Ightham straight away and worried the man idly cleaning glasses for something to do would tell me to clear out.

I'd never spent much time in my village's tavern, outside of the Phoenix Festival and Winter's End. *Not got work to attend to, Rowan?* the patrons would ask cheerfully. Later, they'd tell Thane they were worried the drink and atmosphere might dampen my powers.

But nobody said anything. The barkeeper nodded at me and moved onto the next glass.

Sir Ightham was sat in a corner the candles didn't quite reach, one foot rested on an empty chair. She clasped a half-empty stein of ale between her hands and stared into the middle-distance, gaze fixed firmly on her thoughts. I was hesitant to interrupt her, but had nowhere else to go. I slowly stepped into her field of vision, not wanting her to lose track of what she was mulling over.

She brought her drink to her lips without saying a word.

"You left me with a pane," was the first thing I thought to say.

It wasn't the accusation I'd meant it to be. My fear had started to subside and I could let go of enough irrationality to not be angry about it. Sir Ightham took another sip of her ale, moved her boot from the chair and gestured to it.

"If we are to travel with her, you need to understand that your fears are baseless," she said as I took a seat. "I thought you of all people would know better than to be taken in by rumours. I suppose all is well between you now?"

"No one's been that nice to me in forever," I admitted. I was already ashamed of who I'd been a few hours ago. "She'll be here soon. She said she had some things of her own to attend to."

Sir Ightham nodded and I emptied the change onto the table. She raked the money towards herself, only setting down her stein to put it back in her pouch. She left a coin between us and inclined her head towards the bar.

I hurried over, greeted the barkeeper with too much of a smile, and didn't know what to ask for. He laughed under his breath and said he'd get me what my friend was drinking. My cheer had its downsides: the stein was full to the brim, ale threatening to slosh over the sides with every step I took.

By the time I returned to our table, Sir Ightham was back in her own world. I put my stein down and she returned to the moment, to the tavern, and fixed her eyes on the drink, not me.

"You know a lot about the pane. More than anyone I've ever met! Well, you know more things that are probably true," I said, trying to reclaim her attention. "Have you met any? Are there a lot in Thule?"

From my understanding of the capital, there wasn't much that couldn't be found within it.

"Some. It is close to the mountains, after all," Sir Ightham said, not interested in what she was saying. "I lived with them, for a time. Years and years ago."

"You lived with the pane? In the mountains?"

I forgot about keeping my drink still. Ale dripped down my knuckles.

"Mm," she hummed distantly, drumming her fingers against the edge of the table.

"Did you ever see the Bloodless Lands?" I asked in a whisper.

"Did I see the Bloodless Lands?" Sir Ightham repeated, raising an eyebrow. "Do you think I'd be sat here if I had?"

The mountain range and walls built between sloping peaks were the only things protecting us from the Bloodless Lands, but I wasn't certain how Sir Ightham could've avoided setting her eyes on a scar half a continent wide.

But it was as she'd said. She wouldn't be sat in front of me if she'd glanced into the Bloodless Lands for even a moment. Still, my curiosity was far from sated and I made a note to ask Rán later. Rán, who couldn't be from anywhere but the mountains and would do more than answer my questions with yet more questions.

"Did you hear from your contact?" I asked. I was surprised I hadn't found Sir Ightham poring over yet more letters. She didn't reply or use the distraction of her drink to hide behind, and I kept talking to stop the silence from closing in around us. "Everything's alright, isn't it? We'll be at the, um..."

"The dragon?" she asked, tilting her head towards me.

I lifted my glass and gulped down so much that my chest ached.

"Right. The... dragon."

"It'll be dangerous," Sir Ightham said, answering the question I'd yet to ask. It was probably written in my expression, for I'd never been good at keeping things below the surface. "Go back to your village, if you wish."

She propped her elbow on the table and her chin against her palm. There was no roughness to what she said. No spite, no annoyance. It was that lack of *anything* in her voice that got under my skin.

"Go back? I'm not—" Not scared? Of course I was scared. I was scared of taking a wrong turn, scared of losing a coin, scared of bandits and ghosts in the woods. Fear had lost its meaning, encompassing so many things. "I can't go back. It'll be like before."

No matter how far I'd come, it'd only taken a matter of days. It wasn't enough to change me, or change the villagers; I would still be a necromancer to them.

Sir Ightham's narrowed eyes flickered across my face, searching for *something* I'd no doubt she'd find.

"What *was* it like?" she asked. "What did you do? You had them fooled for seven long years. I do not yet know enough to condone or condemn it, but it is intriguing."

I shouldn't have answered her. I should've sent the questions back her way – what did she *think* I'd done? – but it was the first time she'd looked at me properly. It was the first time anyone had seen me in a long time, and she was the only one to care about the details, beyond the deceit.

"When I realised I was a... when I realised what I could do," I said, terrified of anyone overhearing us. Terrified of saying the word *necromancer* so often it was given more weight than Sir Ightham could tolerate. I wrapped my hands around my drink, glad of the shadowy corner we were sat in. "I went to the village elders. I said... I said that I could help them, and they smiled, and said of course I could! I was already a big help at the farm, already doing my bit by chasing wolves away. I insisted that no, *really*, I could heal, and I guess they found it funny. I was only fifteen, and we have to make our own entertainment in my village.

"Anyway, you met Thane, didn't you? His son was ill at the time. He'd eat bitterwillow, be fine for a day, and then come down with whatever it was again. I went to his house while Thane was busy talking things over for Winter's End with my father and fixed his son up. Word got around and before I knew it, people couldn't be nice enough to me."

I hesitated, needing to condense that turning point in my life, lest Sir Ightham grow bored.

"I, uh..."

"Take your time," she said, nodding encouragingly.

"You probably saw our apothecary's too, right? You saw how small it was. They gave me half of the shop, gave me a table to work on, and before I knew it, everyone was coming to our village. Some came all the way from Ironash. Apparently I only charged half the price that a healer twice as far away did, but I never really saw much of the money. Thane said I was renting the space in the apothecary's, that I was doing it for the village, so I only got a few relds a week. I gave most of it to my brother, so he could study outside the village and buy more books."

Sir Ightham's eyes were still fixed on me and her expression hadn't changed. I wondered what it would take to interest her, to impress her. More than my life story, apparently.

"I won't *make* you go back there," she said. The corners of my mouth twitched both because of what she'd said and what she hadn't. "You are, of course, welcome to leave whenever you choose. Should you wish to stay here, or in any other city, I will make the necessary arrangements."

"I don't want to stay here," I blurted out. Travelling with Sir Ightham meant heading towards dragons, but the thought of staying in Praxis, of sinking deeper into the maze of streets, made my stomach twist. There were too many people, and they were too close. They'd find out, sooner or later.

"Very well," Sir Ightham said.

It was of no consequence to her.

She sat back up as Rán came lumbering in.

A spike of fear rose in my gut at the sight of her, but I shook it off, determined to be better than all the people who'd forgotten what they were talking about in favour of gawking at her. I couldn't deny that she was a sight to see, ducking through the doorway and wrapping her hands around her horns to stop them scraping across the ceiling, knees bent as she went.

I greeted her with a smile and she returned it with more than twice the enthusiasm. She swiped a candle from a nearby table and frowned at the empty chair next to me. She pushed it to the side and sat cross-legged on the floor, leaving her little more than a head taller than me.

Horns not included, naturally.

"Put all our things in the room. The woman behind the counter was kind enough to show me to 'em," Rán explained. "What about you, dragon-slayer? Get the things you need from your contact?"

"My name is Ightham," she said, staring at her empty stein. "And I'm afraid not. There have been complications, meaning we'll have to head elsewhere."

"That so?"

I was too grateful for Sir Ightham taking me along to be bitter that Rán was privy to information I wasn't, but it was disheartening when Sir Ightham said, "Go order dinner for us. Choose whatever you please and get me the same. Rán?" to dismiss me.

Rán wasn't about to turn down a free meal.

"Steak. The biggest they have. Get three of four of 'em and make sure they're raw," she said.

One of my preconceptions about the pane had to be right.

I took a few coins, more of a servant than squire, and returned to the bar. I felt their eyes on my back as I went, and glanced back while the barkeeper was busy serving someone else. They were huddled over the table, talking in low whispers. It wasn't all out of paranoia. Half of the bar had left their own business and gossip behind in favour of staring at Rán without an ounce of subtlety.

"Back already, miss?" the barkeeper asked.

"I'd like..." There was a chalkboard behind him, smudged words scrawled across it. "Uhm..."

He came to my rescue and said, "Lot to choose from, isn't there? Well, can't speak for your tastes, miss, but personally, I'd say you can't go wrong with potatoes and a nice side of bacon."

"I'll take two," I said, and paused before saying, "This might be strange, but can we have a pile of steaks? Raw steaks. Three of four of them."

The barkeeper laughed and said, "If you've got the coin, our cook will be more than happy to save himself a little work."

I took another round of drinks back to the table. Sir Ightham and Rán had rushed through all they needed to say while I'd been gone, and a stiff silence wrapped around the table. Rán made her stein look like a thimble, and we tended to our drinks, pretending to be lost in thought.

It was Sir Ightham who brought life back to the conversation.

"Perhaps your questions about the Bloodless Lands would be better directed at Rán," she suggested.

It'd been my plan all along, but I felt foolish for demonstrating how little I really knew.

Rán's ears perked up and she said, "Oh? What's all this then?"

The words weren't hard to find, in the face of genuine curiosity.

"I was just wondering, that's all. If you'd ever seen them, seeing as they're so close to the mountains."

I'd never seen a mountain, but they had to be like rockier versions of hills, if not a little taller. Nothing that couldn't be conquered in a matter of minutes, especially with legs like Rán's.

"Reckon you'd be better served asking any other pane about that," Rán said. She'd gulped down her drink and was using her long, forked tongue to steal the last few drops from the bottom of stein. "Left this all behind when I was a young'un and headed off to Canth with a friend of mine. Human, as it happens. Reis. Good person. Think of the dragon-slayer here, only with red hair. Been friends with 'em for as long as I care to remember."

The Bloodless Lands were pushed from my mind. Fruit claiming to be from Canth was one thing, but meeting someone who'd actually *been* wasn't the sort of thing that happened. Canth was a strange land, semi-mythical for being as far across the Uncharted Sea as it was.

Michael had told me it'd take ten weeks on the Kingdom's finest ship to reach the sun-scorched land, but it was like heading into a different world. A dozen questions formed in my mind. Were there really as many pirates as they said? Was it true that phoenixes still lived there, that people still worshipped Isjin, and was it really so hot that you had to sleep the entire day away?

Rán saw my questions coming a mile off. Her eyes shone brighter than gold coins under candlelight and she told me that yes, there were pirates, yes, they worshipped the gods still, but the only phoenixes she'd ever seen were made of gold and silver. As for the heat, well. Sir Ightham wouldn't stand a chance with her fair skin.

"Lived in a pirate town, in fact. Port Mahon! Most welcoming place on the continent, providing you pull your own weight," Rán said. Dinner was brought over by a man far more skittish than the barkeeper. He placed Rán's plate on the edge of the table while standing as far from it as he could. The plate almost dipped towards the floor, but Rán placed a hand under it, saving her steaks. She ate them at her leisure, neglecting the knife and fork provided, and cut the meat to shreds on her tusks. "Reis is in charge down there. Now, they're not the *official* leader, Mahon's never been the place for that kind of order, but they grew into the role. People listen to 'em. *I* listen to them, if you'd believe it.

"Really?" I asked. I speared a stray chunk of potato with my fork but my hunger had been put aside in favour of conversation. "You let a human tell you what to do?"

Rán put a hand to her heart – where I assumed her heart was – and said "What? You think I'm stubborn and proud? Is that it?"

A week ago, if I'd been told I was going to have dinner with a pane, I never would've believed it. Had I been told I'd be making fun of them, I would've planned my own funeral.

"Just bossy," I said.

Rán rolled her eyes and snatched up another steak.

Sir Ightham finished her meal faster than I thought possible. She'd eaten as though she was the pane, and with her food and drink gone, she listened to us speak with her gaze fixed on me. It was distracting. I'd say something to Rán, only too happy to indulge each and every question I had, but be too aware of Sir Ightham staring at me to hear her answer. I tried to shake it off. Her thoughts were elsewhere, and she must have been staring *through* me.

"How about you, yrval?" I didn't know what the word meant and Sir Ightham arched her brow every time Rán said it, but there was a softness to it I didn't dislike. "Is this your first time in Praxis?"

"It's my first time almost anywhere," I told her. Her face tended to be more animated than most, but that got the biggest reaction yet out of her. Her ears folded back and she waited for me to continue. "We went to Eaglestone a few days ago, but before that, I'd always stayed in my village. Thane probably didn't want me to think there was much more to the world than our little marketplace."

Yet I could've spent a lifetime exploring all the hidden corners of Praxis alone. Rán had been to Canth and back, had undoubtedly travelled further still; to her, I had been trapped in a cage. Sitting there, surrounded by people who knew what I was and allowed me to speak, allowed me to move freely, made me feel as though I *had* been trapped. I was on the verge of saying something saccharine when Sir Ightham sunk against the bench, into the shadows.

Rán growled softly at the sight of a soldier standing in the doorway. He wasn't a guard, wasn't like those who milled around Eaglestone and Praxis. That much was clear, even by candlelight. He wore the royal family's crest on the front of his golden armour, and the barkeeper stopped what he was doing to speak to him.

"Go to Rán's room, collect our things, and leave the building," Sir Ightham said. Rán pulled a key from her pocket and slid it across the table. "Room three on the first floor. Don't run."

I took the key with shaking fingers. I wanted to question Sir Ightham but couldn't find my voice. I rose slowly and headed out of the tavern and into the inn, doing all I could not to look at the soldier. He couldn't hear my heart pounding but my eyes might give me away.

The lobby was brightly lit. It took me a moment to get my bearings, but numbers, if nothing else, were easy to recognise. I slipped the key into the door, unsteady fingers doing their best to betray me, and started when the lock clicked.

The room was plain, housing a bed too small for any pane to sleep in and a basin Rán's hands probably wouldn't fit in. The bags were placed on the bed and I scooped them up, one over each shoulder, and carried the rest in my arms.

I left the key in the lock and spared a glance at the tavern on my way out. Sir Ightham was gone, but Rán remained at the table. Leaving with a pane would've drawn too much attention to her, but nothing else made sense to me.

I understood Sir Ightham's need for privacy to work efficiently, but that did nothing to explain why she'd been scared out of an establishment by a Felheimish soldier.

I met two more on my way out: a woman no older than I was with an axe at her hip, and a red-headed man with a cloak draped around his shoulders, dragon-bone armour shining through. I almost walked straight into them and dropped my bags, but the man – the Knight – placed a hand atop them, steadied me, and said, "Careful now."

I stuttered my thanks and did my best to stare at the ground.

They didn't suspect a thing, but why would they? I rushed into the night, cold air washing away the lightness ale had brought with it, and couldn't see Sir Ightham anywhere.

Rán rounded the side of the building and saved me from the weight of the bags. She pressed a finger to her lips and I followed her through the streets, running to keep up with her, until we reached the stables.

Sir Ightham was already there, Charley and Calais by her side.

"Doesn't mean they know you're here," Rán said, patting Sir Ightham's back. "But it's better to be safe than sorry. What's the plan now, dragon-slayer?"

CHAPTER FIVE

Rán didn't have a horse of her own, but had no trouble keeping up with Charley and Calais.

She kept close to Sir Ightham's, arguing with her as we charged away from Praxis. I tugged Charley's reins, willing him to catch up with them, but it did no good. They spoke in a rough language I didn't understand. The words themselves were far from aggressive, despite them continually rebuking one another. They pointed in different directions, each convinced their plan was the one worth following.

It didn't matter that I couldn't understand them. Sir Ightham and Rán could've been speaking Mesomium and I wouldn't have taken any of it in. Sir Ightham was running from our soldiers, from another *Knight*, and I was more tired than I'd been in months. None of it made sense to me. The uneven road beneath us kept my body awake, but my mind drifted, wondering if she was a *Sir* at all.

She could've killed a Knight and stolen their armour. She was good enough for it. Perhaps I'd been wrong to trust her and Rán so easily. Perhaps Sir Ightham had chosen a pane to confide in for a reason, perhaps—

They stopped.

"What are we gonna do with this one?" Rán asked, tipping her head towards me.

Sir Ightham paused but I didn't try making out anything in her expression. The sun could've risen a handful of hours early and I still wouldn't have learnt anything.

"... She comes with us."

I already knew too much, or at least enough to help other people piece the whole picture together. That had to be it.

"Glad to hear it," Rán said. She placed her hands on her hips as she scanned the horizon in all directions and said, "We haven't been followed. Looks like we're at the mercy of your paranoia, dragon-slayer. What say we rest up for the night, though? The horses will appreciate it, if nothing else."

She must've had better vision than any human. I couldn't see anything but darkness around us.

Sir Ightham begrudgingly agreed. If she was fleeing the Felheimish army, it didn't matter which part of Felheim she ran to. I wasn't averse

64

to sleep, either. Things would make more sense in the morning. I'd caught flashes of what was happening and had misinterpreted the whole situation. Perhaps the man at the inn was the thief, not Sir Ightham.

No matter what doubts I had, I couldn't force myself out of the habit of using her title. Even inside my head.

We weren't further than half a mile from the wall. I only knew it was there because the stars were abruptly blotted out along the horizon. We headed away from it, where trees gathered. Trees for cover; trees for bandits to hide behind; trees for bandits to scamper up, once they realised we were with a pane.

The night was warm enough to forgo a fire and Rán settled down cheerfully, curled up on her side like a house cat. Sir Ightham towered over her and said, "I'll keep watch then, shall I," as I did my best to get comfortable on the ground. The thin grass couldn't live up to the bed I'd been promised, and every time I swept a stone away, I lured a twig out of the dirt and into my spine.

For all their arguing, Rán and Sir Ightham must've come to an agreement, even if that agreement was nothing more than leaving the matter until morning. Rán fell asleep within moments and Sir Ightham's presence became subdued, until there was no telling her apart from a shadow, or one of the trees surrounding us.

Excitement and fear faded within the two of them. They were used to this sort of life, yet my heart was in my throat, thoughts swirling until closing my eyes left me dizzy. I was exhausted but restless, starkly aware that I didn't fit into their world, and more than anything, aware I'd never fit into my old life, either.

I moved onto my front when I couldn't trick myself into falling asleep, and saw Sir Ightham sat on a tree stump with Calais sleeping close by. She turned something in her palm and a stray cloud deserted the moon, letting light glint against gold.

"Sir," I whispered. Her head snapped up, fingers tightening around the pendant. "What's happening? Are you in trouble?"

No answer. Not straight away. I waited for Sir Ightham to tell me to go back to sleep, but the longer she kept her silence, the more convinced I was the answer to that second question was *yes*.

"It's better you don't know," she murmured. "Safer, for the both of us."

Which did nothing to quell my curiosity.

"But that man at the inn was a Knight, too. Why did you run from him?"

"A Knight?" Sir Ightham asked, voice rising. Rán didn't stir. "You're certain there was a *Knight* there?"

"Sorry. I'm sorry. I should've said something earlier, but we were in such a hurry, and you and Rán were arguing, and..."

Sir Ightham didn't care for my excuses.

"What did he look like?"

"He was wearing dragon-bone armour under a cloak. That's how I knew," I said. "He was older than you. Forty, I think. White, red hair. I didn't really see more than that. I was trying to avoid eye contact..."

But what else did she need to hear? There were hardly hundreds of Knights in the Kingdom.

"Sir Luxon," she said in a way that made an insult of the title. "At least it wasn't one of the Mansels. If there is any kindness in the world, you will never have to meet either of them."

I thought that would be the end of it. Sir Ightham knew everything I had to share and had made it clear she wouldn't tell me anything in return, and once more I waited for her to tell me to sleep. But Sir Ightham moved from her tree trunk, took a few soft steps towards me, and sat cross-legged in the dirt.

"Your ancestors were from Myros, by the look of you. Mine were from Mesomia. A very long time ago, after Kondo-Kana's war, they worked together to create what would one day become Felheim," she said. For once, she sounded hesitant. She toyed with the pendant between her fingers and it dawned on me that she *wanted* to explain herself. She wanted me to listen. "But Felheim is not merely the ground beneath us or the cities we've founded. It isn't simply a place on a map. It you were to be given a choice between the dirt and stone of our Kingdom and the people themselves, which would you choose?"

The people of Felheim had only ever been kind to me when I was useful to them and had discarded me when they believed they knew what I was, but there was Sir Ightham: a stranger who'd taken me along and asked for nothing.

"The people, of course," I said.

It wasn't much of a choice at all.

Sir Ightham nodded and said no more. I had cast her as a murderer, a thief, simply because I didn't understand what was happening; because I did not understand *her*. I said nothing else, didn't utter an apology she wouldn't understand, because she clearly had no desire to discuss the matter any further.

Yet she didn't move away from me.

She might've wanted company while she kept watch. Refuge from her own thoughts. I reached out, gesturing to the pendant in her hand.

She hadn't been aware she was fiddling with it. It took her a moment to understand what my outstretched hand meant, and another for her to place the pendant in my palm.

It was a weighty thing. I tilted it this way and that, letting the moonlight hit the surface as I ran my thumbs across the metal. It was beautifully made with details enough to be made out in the dark; a silver phoenix was encased within a ring of gold. I frowned. It was just like her knife.

"Is this your family's sigil?" I asked.

Only the elders in my village had sigils worth speaking of, though Michael was determined to trace back our ancestry until he discovered a crest we could call our own.

"No. That was too obvious. Too recognisable. I thought it might give me an unfair advantage," Sir Ightham said. "This is of my own choosing."

"Oh," I said. I bit the inside of my mouth and handed it back to her. It didn't have to *mean* anything. Phoenixes were just phoenixes and there were a thousand reasons why a person would take one for their sigil. "... My brother said they were already making preparations for the Phoenix Festival, before you arrived. It's not for another two months, but it's all anyone's been talking about at market."

I was rambling.

Sir Ightham responded cautiously, saying, "It's to be expected. This year marks the fifteen-hundredth since the exodus."

Fifteen-hundred years since the Bloodless Lands were formed, since the end of the war. The festival wouldn't be any different, at its core. It would be bigger and louder, but nothing else about it would change: everyone would gather over food and drink, celebrating the fall of the necromancers, burnt to cinders by the phoenixes, and the end of Kondo-Kana, chased across the land and drowned in the sea.

"It doesn't have to mean what you think it does. I—" Sir Ightham started. I wanted her to tell me why else she'd chosen the phoenix for a sigil, but she only shook her head. "Come now. We're about to wake Rán. You ought to sleep."

I did as she said, but only because her voice wasn't hard. She hadn't turned me away because of my necromancy yet, and there may have been another explanation for the phoenix engraved on her knife, cast in gold and silver on her pendant.

I'd ask her at a better time, when we weren't running from the mere thought of Knights.

I awoke unable to tell when I'd closed my eyes. Rán crouched by my head, grinning toothily as she leant over me. I yelped, pushed myself away, and belatedly realised I wasn't scared of her anymore.

"That's one way to get you up," she said, holding out a hand. "Morning, yrval."

I clung to two of her fingers and she helped me to my feet without having to stand. She remained crouched as I stretched out, eyeing the food left atop one of Sir Ightham's bags.

"Where's Sir Ightham?" I said, snatching a piece of bread.

"Down by the river, I reckon," Rán said. "You might want to be taking a trip down there yourself, yrval. We've got a long trek ahead of us and you'd be wise to be making the most of this lull while it lasts. Who knows when the dragon-slayer's gonna go charging off again?"

I saw Sir Ightham in the distance the moment the words were out of Rán's throat and hurried to meet her halfway. It couldn't have been much later than six and I hadn't slept for particularly long, but it was that quiet, timeless part of the morning that promised peace, in spite of what the day might actually hold.

"Good morning," Sir Ightham said, once I was close enough to see that her hair was almost brown with the weight of water.

"Morning, Sir," I said with a nod. There was a wall of trees behind her, and I pointed in the direction she'd come from, saying, "Straight ahead for the river?"

"Don't take long," she said. "Ten minutes at most."

We carried on our separate ways but I didn't get far. I came to a halt and said, "Sir?" before I realised what I was doing. I would've shaken my head and said it was nothing, if not for her having stopped to look

68

around at me. "At the next town we visit, do you think you could... help me write a letter?"

I should've asked Rán, even if I couldn't imagine her hands forming words small enough to fit on a piece of parchment. Sir Ightham didn't scoff, didn't give me any reason to cringe at my own shortcomings.

She tilted her head towards the river and said, "If we have time to spare."

I ran the rest of the way. The shallow river barely reached my knees, but with the safety of trees and shrubs surrounding me, I stripped off quickly and plunged my face under the surface. I shook off as much water as I could, clothes draped across the safety of a large rock, and balled my shirt up to dry myself off. The sun would have to do the rest of the work. My short hair was soaked, sticking out every which way, and I sprinted back to camp, refusing to succumb to damp clothing.

"Off to Benkor, then," Rán said.

"Benkor?" I asked, but Rán was gone.

She pushed off on strong legs, launching herself in wide strides, and I matched Sir Ightham's pace. She wasn't going slowly by any means, but we weren't tearing across the country as we'd done for the last week. I was glad of it. The scenery wasn't any more interesting for having time to take the details in, but I appreciated my bones not being rattled around like the thoughts in my head.

"Wouldn't Calais take any more bitterwillow?" I asked, smiling down at him.

"Yes, but that's beyond the point. He has too much in his system; it won't have any effect for another few days," Sir Ightham said.

If only bitterwillow always worked and worked, if only the body never needed a rest from it; the world wouldn't need healers and I wouldn't be in this mess.

"Right," I said. I knew that. Of course I did. I'd spent seven years in an apothecary's and could prepare the plants in my sleep. "What Rán said about Benkor. Are we really going there?"

"We are."

Sir Ightham wasn't as talkative as she'd been the night before. The dark circles under her eyes told me Rán hadn't taken over the watch at any point, but I kept trying.

"But that's basically Kastelir, isn't it?" I asked. She looked at me, waiting for more of an explanation. "We had some traders from there, a couple of times. Everyone said that they probably weren't even Felheimish, just Kastelirians who'd come to Benkor, wanting to make money off us. They're always trying to bring the wall down, right?"

"Are they?" Sir Ightham asked.

They must've had a higher class of rumour in Thule, because *everyone* in my village knew all about Benkor. Soldiers and mercenaries alike had slipped through Benkor to sell themselves to the highest bidder, back when the territories were still warring, and a handful of decades weren't long enough to forge the fragmented pieces of centuries of strife into a *real* country. If the Kastelirians ever got to us, it'd be through Benkor.

"Yesterday morning you were convinced a pane would eat you," Sir Ightham said. "Do try thinking for yourself."

"But—"

Sir Ightham and Calais quickened their pace and sped off towards Rán.

I might've been wrong about the pane, or at least one of them, but there was ever word reaching the village about Kastelir's latest misfortune. A food shortage, a revolt, rebels trying to rend the country back into its former territories; monarchs being assassinated, or nearly assassinated.

But Sir Ightham was right. Benkor was still within Felheim and couldn't be blamed for the Kastelirians who slipped through its streets.

We travelled for hours at a time. Rán never seemed to tire. She'd stop to let us catch up, and though she charged ahead, she wasn't leading us.

"Can't say I know much of Felheim," she admitted, happy to let Sir Ightham's compass and a battered map do all the work.

As we wound around scattered villages and hamlets, I decided the monotony of riding was far better than the monotony of my old life. If I were in the village, I'd be sat at the same table, eating the same thing I did every morning, about to undertake the same chores I did every day. All in all, the fear of Knights coupled with the fear of the unknown was far less unsettling than the fear of my village finally getting the courage to lynch me.

"Ah! Look at that, the town of Doevon, as strong as it's always been,"

Rán said whenever a jumble of buildings came into sight, one hand held up to shield her eyes from the sun. "What say we take a little break there?"

"That's *Eltson*," Sir Ightham always corrected Rán, who winked at me. Sir Ightham must've known that Rán was making a mess of geography to rile her up, but she took the bait with an exasperated sigh every time. "No breaks until sundown," she always said.

Rán was the only one who wasn't exhausted by the time the sun set. We barely had to tug the horses' reins to make them stop. Sir Ightham rubbed her fingers against her eyes, trying to make bruises out of the dark shadows beneath them.

We'd come to a rugged, hilly area with sudden, rocky drops almost as tall as Rán was. It made for decent cover, along with a littering of trees. Sir Ightham spent a few minutes consulting her map.

"There's a lake, a quarter of a mile off. I'll fetch water and fish," she said. There was a note of finality in her words. She didn't want help refilling the waterskins, nor did she want anyone pointing out that we had food enough to last us another day. She said, "Go gather firewood," as she left and didn't wait for me to reply.

"That one always bossing you around, is she?" Rán asked, seeming smaller now that the ground had claimed our bags.

"I want to be useful," I said, but couldn't help but laugh. I'd spent most of the day forcing back a smile whenever Rán teased Sir Ightham and it was easier to relax when it was just the two of us.

"Come on, then," she said, crouching down. "I'd best be helping you out."

"You mean...?"

Rán reached over her shoulder, patting her back.

Her intent was clear but I still hesitated. I held out my hands and stepped towards her slowly, waiting for her to howl with laughter because I'd *really* tried to climb up her back. She grinned at me and said, "Hurry up. Don't wanna keep that dragon-slayer waiting, do we?"

I bundled my fingers in the orange cloth swathed around her shoulder and Rán hooked an arm under my knees, hoisting me high enough to wrap my arms around her trunk of a neck. She rushed to her full height quickly enough to make my head spin. I felt her throat rumble with fond laughter.

71

"Grab onto my horns if I go too fast," Rán said, and I didn't wait.

There was a strange texture to them. They were unlike bark or bone, and stronger than a ram's horns. I could feel grooves and scrapes under the pads of my thumbs, could see faint traces of patterns once carved into them, but they'd grown out with age.

Rán set off with a sprint, almost knocking me back with the force of it. I clung to her horns and didn't let go, even when I was confident I wouldn't be thrown to the ground. I peeked over the top of her head as she charged through the trees. When she'd said she'd help, she meant she'd do all of the work; she grabbed low-hanging branches as she bolted along, tore them from trees, and ducked down to scoop up any that had already fallen.

I laughed until it hurt, heart pounding with the speed of it all, and almost slammed my jaw against the back of Rán's head as she ground to a halt.

"Reckon that's more than enough," she said, jostling the wood in her arms. She didn't gesture for me to get down so I wrapped my arms loosely around her neck and buried my face in it as she wandered back to camp.

"I guess you can't tell me what you and Sir Ightham are up to, can you...?" I asked, inexplicably hopeful.

"You guess right, yrval," Rán said, flicking one of the sticks back and thwacking my forehead. "As much as I'd like to tell you, I'd like it even more if there was nothing to tell."

Disappointed though I was, I didn't want Sir Ightham to think I'd gone behind her back. Especially not after what she'd said last night.

Still, I couldn't help but ask, "Have you fought one before?" as we headed back to camp.

"Fought what?" she asked.

"A dragon," I said.

She'd called Sir Ightham *dragon-slayer* so many times that it ought to have been obvious.

"Dragon?" she said with a short, sharp laugh. "Who said anything about fighting dragons?"

Sir Ightham returned as we did, stopping me from questioning Rán further. Her sceptical look soon became a frown. She had a few fish roped together and held tightly in a fist, and had been expecting a roaring fire to greet her. Rán knelt, lowering me to the ground, and I became reacquainted with my own feet as she put the sticks down and Sir Ightham set about bundling them together.

She threw the largest fish in Rán's direction. Rán caught it in one hand and tore into it without any regard for the small bones. I watched from the corner of my eye, more intrigued than disgusted. I'd helped slaughter animals on our farm since I could wield a knife, but it was unsettling to see a creature go from something to nothing in a matter of moments.

I watched Sir Ightham push the remaining fish onto spits, and it occurred to me that she'd never said anything about fighting dragons. I'd come to that conclusion, and she'd done nothing but hum along with it. I folded my arms across my chest and she looked up from the fish she was cooking.

"You're really used to doing all of this?" I asked. It was better than accusing her of—*something*. Of letting me believe one thing and telling Rán a different tale altogether. "Cooking, I mean. Don't Knights have servants for everything?"

"I'm perfectly capable of preparing my own meals," she said. "Besides, it would hardly do to travel with a band of servants."

"Well," I said, settling down closer to Rán than her. "I'm more of a servant than squire, really."

Rán laughed at the cost of almost choking on her fish, and though Sir Ightham's eyes were fixed firmly on the fire, I did what I could not to smile. It was true, for all it mattered. I didn't mind. Running errands and carrying things was well suited to my current skillset.

Sir Ightham said nothing. I was surprised my fish didn't end up burnt.

"This *is* good," I said to appease her, wanting to lure her back into the conversation, but she wasn't even facing us. I hadn't been lying. The fish was as interestingly cooked as fish over an open fire could be, and hot food was the very thing to nudge me towards sleep.

I leant against Rán, picking small bones from between my teeth as she told me about the time a pirate raid had turned into an extensive fishing expedition, and found myself glancing over at Sir Ightham time and time again. She ate in quick, clean bites, wasting neither time nor food, and the moment she was done, she started rummaging through one of her bags.

I couldn't catch a glimpse of what she'd carried halfway across the country. It only took her a second to get to her feet with a sword in hand.

It wasn't the dragon-bone blade, and the one she'd used to fight off the bandits was at her hip.

"Why do you have two swords?" I asked.

"To fight with both hands," she said. "On your feet."

"What?" I'd just got comfortable against Rán. "Why?"

"It's your own doing. You said you were more servant than squire. We ought to fix that, if you're to travel with us."

Rán betrayed me. She shrugged, having no way to rebuke Sir Ightham's point, and nudged me. I ended up on my feet, if only to avoid being knocked over. I didn't have any choice but to go along with it.

Sir Ightham took me a short distance from the campfire, so the light could reach us without the fear of tripping over a bag or stepping into the flames.

Sir Ightham unsheathed the sword, not trusting me with that much, and held out the weapon, hilt-first. I reached out tentatively, frowned up at her, giving her a moment to realise this wasn't the best of ideas. Years spent swiping sticks in the air and pretending they were blades fresh from the forge had done nothing to hone my imaginary skull.

I wrapped both hands around the sword, trembling as I tensed my arms and strangled the hilt in my grasp. I focused on it so hard that an enemy could've run me through and I wouldn't have noticed straight away.

Once I was finally holding the sword steadily, Sir Ightham said, "It's a one-handed weapon."

She demonstrated with her own blade, pulling it from her hip and holding it out like a roll of parchment. I grumbled nonsense but refused to give up, and slowly freed the hilt from one hand. Sir Ightham held her sword in her left hand, but it didn't look comfortable to me.

I strained my wrist and the sword obeyed me. I didn't expect praise from Sir Ightham, but a nod of acknowledgement couldn't have been out of the question.

She took a step forward and knocked the sword clean out of my hand.

"Pick it up," Sir Ightham said. My entire body was on edge. The ringing of metal sent a shudder straight through me. Sir Ightham didn't let me gather my senses before the blade. "Your sword. Pick it up."

She gestured at it with her own blade. I ducked down to retrieve it, lest she lose the last of her patience and strike again. It went on and on: I held the sword out, Sir Ightham made a lightning-fast movement, and it was stolen from my grasp. Frustration didn't help. I told myself that I only had to hold the sword. I didn't need to swing it, didn't need to block, didn't need to worry about moving my feet or arms. Yet every time, Sir Ightham disarmed me without the slightest hint of effort.

"I'm not *getting* it," I half-growled, stubbornly stabbing the blade into the dirt and wiping my clammy palm on my trousers.

"It's been less than an hour," Sir Ightham said. "If you were getting it, I'd have to hang up my helm."

I wanted to scowl, but she was right. She hadn't decided to become a Knight a week before marching into my village.

I let my shoulders slump and picked my sword up for the thousandth time. If nothing else, I could hold it without it wobbling, more often than not.

"We'll continue another time," Sir Ightham said, returning her sword to its sheath and doing the same with mine.

"You want to continue?" I asked.

I was certain she'd only being trying to prove a point: I was better suited as a servant and ought to have that drilled into me, before I started thinking I really *was* her squire; something like that.

"I am a Knight. I would think you'd take instructions from me without questioning what I want and giving me a reason to change my mind," she said. She wasn't frowning; her expression wasn't as neutral as I was expecting it to be. She tipped her head forward and I supposed I ought to give it one more go.

Who knew; perhaps I'd be able to keep hold of a sword, one day.

Rán watched without judgement, without making any remarks, and had lost interest and fallen asleep by the time we returned to the fire. I smiled down at her, wondering if drifting off so easily was an ability all pane possessed, or if she'd worn herself out more than she'd let on.

With her sleeping, I took my chance to say, "Rán doesn't seem to think that there's a dragon," to Sir Ightham.

I wanted to bite back my words the moment I'd spoken them.

Sir Ightham was knelt on the ground, putting my sword away for the safety of me and all those around.

She faltered, and said, "There is always a dragon," as softly as she could.

"It's just that you never *said* there was a dragon. That was all me. I figured I put the words in your mouth, so I'm sorry if—"

She moved faster than her blade had. She rose in front of me, blocked the fire, and said, "There is *always* a dragon."

I wasn't certain how Rán was still sleeping. Sir Ightham's voice hadn't risen like that in all the time I'd known her, but I wasn't afraid of what she might say or do. I was only worried she might tremble.

Before I could act, Sir Ightham moved to the fire. I thought I should leave her be and settle down for the night but couldn't bring myself to move; I'd snap a stray twig underfoot and make her flinch.

She didn't remain by the fire for long. She fashioned a torch from one of the thicker sticks that had barely been touched by flames, and when she turned to me, I knew not moving had been the right thing to do. She held the torch high and titled her head towards our horses.

I followed Sir Ightham without a word. She might've wanted to show me something, but she made no effort to wait for me.

Calais roused easily, but I was met with resistance from Charley. By the time he was in any mood to move, Sir Ightham's torch was a dying speck of light in the distance, and for the dozenth time since leaving our village, I promised him I'd find some way to make it up to him.

Sir Ightham was trying to navigate by torchlight, map crumpled in one hand, compass pressed between her thumb and the torch.

The light caught her eyes. I didn't dare to ask where we were going. We travelled no more than a mile and a half, and in the darkness, our destination was no different to the rest of the landscape.

The torchlight didn't reveal much. I saw silhouettes I couldn't place against the backdrop of the night sky; the shapes were far from natural, some as tall as Sir Ightham, all of them formed from sharp edges. I drew closer to her and the ground became hard beneath my feet, like stone.

Sir Ightham knelt, lowered the torch, and revealed a scorched road. She moved the torch this way and that, turning the strange shapes into the remnants of buildings, stray walls and arching doorways. They were all smooth and cold under my fingertips, unable to have escaped the touch of flames.

I knew what it meant. Sir Ightham didn't need to say anything, but I understood. More than that, I *felt* what had happened. It wasn't the overwhelming emptiness of the place that struck me, wasn't the absence of sound, the ruined buildings, or even the gaping void left in lieu of those who'd once filled them. It was the presence of something else.

Death was there, lingering like a shroud drawn over the land. I tried not to breathe, tried to avoid drinking down the thick, inky darkness all around. It wasn't night. The sun hadn't been blotted out.

"Lanesborough," Sir Ightham told me. "Its population was nearing six hundred. There was little more than this when I arrived, though the ground was still warm. The dragon had already moved on."

My fingertips twitched against my palms. Something cracked under my skin; I was powerful, in spite of the way my stomach twisted in on itself, throat tightening at the stark understanding of what those people had been through. I would've become trapped in the roiling darkness of my thoughts, if not for the way I saw Sir Ightham's shoulders rise.

I felt, more clearly than I felt what lingered on after death, the way she took responsibility for this all upon herself.

"Sir..." I said softly, breaking myself out of my trance. I placed my fingertips against her elbow, and for a moment, she didn't move. For a moment, I thought I might be able to offer her some comfort.

She stepped back from me, torch held out as she headed back to her horse.

"There are always dragons, Rowan," she told me, and I shrank from her voice. "There are always dragons, and my work does not end."

CHAPTER SIX

Benkor was no smaller than Praxis. The city was endlessly cluttered for the way it was laid out, roads intersecting at awkward angles, buildings growing from one another, low bridges creating chaos on busy streets. It was built against the wall, not into it. Its perimeter was marked by houses pressed close together, but being protected from Kastelir was what really mattered.

The establishment we left Calais and Charley made me uncomfortable, but Sir Ightham promised the stablehand a substantial tip once we retrieved them. I trusted the inevitability of money would keep them safe.

Benkor, while not as refined as Praxis, would've awed me if it had been the first settlement Sir Ightham had taken me to. Being poorer than Praxis didn't mean the people lived in squalor. There was wealth to see.

For all that was said about Kastelir, the citizens of Benkor were far from displeased with their lot in life. People went about their business as they would anywhere, dragging carts to market, rushing between houses and stores, but the poor were hidden in plain sight. They cluttered the streets, crowded under bridges, and spilt from alleyways. Some held out hats and chipped bowls, begging for change. Those better off did all they could to pretend they hadn't seen them, but gave themselves away in increasing their pace.

I had nothing to offer and walked with my hands bundled in my pockets, head down. But not looking at them wasn't enough to banish them from my mind. Whatever they suffered seeped into the air, following me through busy streets, as though the shadow I'd felt last night had returned to claim me.

Sir Ightham led us straight to an inn. We'd passed three or four and I never did learn its name, or figure it out from the crudely drawn crown with faded gems on the sign.

The bell above the door chimed and the man behind the counter said, "Welcome," without looking up. He was busy writing across large, yellowing pages, and it wasn't until Rán's feet thudded against the floorboards that we really got his attention.

"Now, I won't be having any of that in here," he said, nostrils flared. "I won't put the other guests at risk."

I took a step closer to Rán. Sir Ightham drummed her fingertips on the edge of the counter.

"I believe I had letters directed here," she said calmly.

The man narrowed his gaze.

"What's the name?"

"Eden Westerdale."

He moved slowly towards the shelves where a dozen or so letters were stacked. He flicked through them, only glancing down for a split-second at a time, imagining Rán was on the verge of putting her horns through the window.

"That'll be two relds," he said. He didn't let go of the letter until Sir Ightham had slid a single coin across the counter.

Her usual careless generosity was nowhere to be found. She took the letters without another word and slammed the door behind us.

"The two of you could've stayed there," Rán said, once we were back on the street. A pane's patience was truly endless. I would've at least growled at the man, in Rán's place. "Could've found myself somewhere for the night."

"I'm fully aware of that," Sir Ightham said, tearing the letter open. "I do not wish to bestow patronage on such an establishment."

"Warms my hearts," Rán said, splaying a hand over her chest.

Sir Ightham scanned the letter and strode blindly down the street.

"Are we going to find somewhere else to stay?" I asked, convinced I'd never sleep in a bed again.

Sir Ightham didn't hear me.

"Not the news you were hoping for?" Rán asked.

"Not the documents I was expecting, no," she said. She began tearing the letter into presumably unreadable pieces, as was her wont. "But no matter. My contact will be with us tomorrow."

It was hard to glean anything from her features. She'd taken watch once we'd returned to camp the night before and I awoke to find her sat bolt upright, arms folded across her chest, head tipped forward. She'd started awake when I made the slightest sound and a flash of anger over-came her. It wasn't directed at me. Rather, she was frustrated with herself for falling asleep in the first place.

"I'm starting to think they're having you on," Rán said, cracking her knuckles.

Sir Ightham wasn't entirely convinced Rán was wrong. With a sigh that might've masked a yawn, she said, "We'd best find rooms for the night."

The next inn we came to unfortunately only had two small rooms available. Two *very* small rooms, the innkeeper had assured us. The third had a sign outside, covered in bright red letters that made Rán roll her eyes.

"It says *Establishment Suited To Humans Only*," Sir Ightham explained.

Rán snorted.

"Pretty nice way of saying *no pane*, aye?"

The innkeeper at the fourth inn we ventured into looked up, saw Rán, and said, "It'll be double the cost for you. Can't risk having any more of our ceilings scratched up."

It wasn't altogether unfounded. Rán ducked her way through the door and was standing doubled-over to avoid knocking her horns against anything.

Sir Ightham paid in full, distributed the keys, and I waited for soldiers and Knights to barge through the doors. When none came and Sir Ightham and Rán headed towards the stairs, I said, "What now?"

"Now you do as you please," Sir Ightham said. "The tavern across the street serves dinner from six, should you care to join us."

I gathered the courage to ask her to help me write a letter the moment she disappeared up the stairs. I resolved to ask her over dinner and silently hoped she'd get some sleep as I headed to my own room.

It was hardly extravagant. There was a bed and a basin, along with curtains that were a little dusty, but I didn't need much. Between the small window's rickety shutters, a clock tower rose from the heart of Benkor. It was barely three. I took my time washing by the basin, combed my hair into place with my fingers, and found it had only taken me to ten past the hour.

I fell down on the bed, immediately realised that it wasn't *my* bed, and the next thing I knew, I was halfway down the stairs. I pushed through the crowds, away from the inn, and didn't map the city in my mind as I went. I was following something. Colourless threads were woven into the air, tendrils no one else could grasp at, tugging me without having to sink their claws in.

The sun flowed through me. I didn't worry about the crowd swallowing me, didn't believe it was possible to ever become lost. Not when I was alive with purpose. I kept moving until I reached the shade of an arched stone bridge, all the sick and poor huddled beneath it.

I was no longer being guided; I was where I needed to be. The sounds of the city came back to me and I gripped the hem of my shirt with both hands, uncertain where to start. In the same way the wealthy walked past without sparing a glance at those with less than nothing, the people who made the dank, dark underside of the bridge their home didn't notice me. They didn't get their hopes up.

I couldn't stand there, waiting to be asked for help. After a few minutes of going unheard, unseen, I knelt by a woman cradling a baby in her arms.

"Excuse me, ma'am," I said, "What's wrong with your boy?"

The baby coughed, but the cry he let out rattled to nothing in his throat.

His head lolled back, glassy eyes dull beneath the bridge. His mother studied my face, needing to be certain I was talking to her. I didn't want to know how long it'd been since anyone had offered her so much as a stale crust of bread. She was surrounded by a sea of her kin and I was sorry to say that her son wasn't the worst off.

"He coughs, that's all he does. My boy, he won't sleep. Can't eat, even when I manage to get him something. You see all that's wrong, don't you?" Her throat tightened as she spoke. Desperation brought colour back to her face. "Do you have anything on you, miss? Any bitterwillow? Just a little would help, if only for the pain, if you could spare it..."

"Please," I murmured, putting a hand on hers when she reached out to take whatever I could offer. "Can I hold him? Just for a moment. That's all I'll need."

I didn't want to make any promises. I didn't want to lie. The woman went from thinking I meant to reject her to daring to hope for the first time in an age. If she hesitated, it was only to stop herself from believing what she thought to be impossible.

Slowly, she held the baby out to me and said, "Careful with him. He won't cry if she's distressed, hasn't in days, but you need to support his neck. It's only a weak thing."

I'd held plenty of newborns in the village but went about handling him more carefully than I needed to. There was no end to the child's ailments. I didn't need to hold him close to know that. The constant, rattling cough, his glassy, vacant eyes and the rot that had spread across the soles of his feet were hardly the worst of it.

But that didn't matter to me. I'd never needed to know the specifics to heal, to purge. Fixing a dozen things at once was as easy as fixing one.

"What's his name?" I asked, ghosting a hand across his face.

I had to bite the inside of my mouth to stop from smiling. This was it. This was the one thing I was good at, the one way I could *really* help people. There was no strain in it, not at first. I barely had to think about what I was doing, beyond healing.

Or not-healing.

"James," his mother whispered.

"Hello there, James," I said softly. I willed everything twisted inside of him to leave, banishing it with a thought. The coil of death loosened and fled, and that was it. I was done.

The change was absolute. James let out a cry that made his mother start, colour rushing back to his face, rot fading to nothing. He was wailing within seconds, writhing in my arms and flailing his limbs.

I handed him back to his mother with a laugh.

"Thank you, thank you!" she said with a smile and a sob. I placed a hand on her shoulder to let her know that it was alright, tearing her ailments from her in the same motion. "I wish I had something for you."

"It's fine," I reassured her as she searched for some treasure she'd overlooked. "I only wanted to help."

It was true. I'd been pulled towards them, shoved out of the inn by months of idle necromancy, but I'd only acted as I had because it was the right thing to do. I hadn't lied to them. I hadn't told the entire truth and had let the woman leap to her own conclusions, but I'd saved her son and couldn't force guilt to grip me, no matter how deep the deception ran.

No matter what the world wanted me to think of myself.

My actions hadn't gone unnoticed. A few people turned to watch for the sake of watching, and the moment they saw the change in James, they were shuffling nervously, saying, "Now, look here, miss," expecting me to demand their right arm in payment for fixing their left.

"I don't have anywhere to be until six," I said.

More and more people gathered around me, queueing and crowding all at once.

There was nothing I hadn't dealt with before, but I worked with a smile on my face. They'd managed to keep me tethered to the village for all those years because I *loved* what I did. The underside of the bridge wasn't all that different from the apothecary's. It was dim enough to mute my abilities and give me all the control I needed. The bright sun had always made me feel like I had rather too much power.

I didn't know if the same was true for healers, so I'd claimed to be squeamish. I said I couldn't stand the sight of blood and couldn't see myself ever becoming used to it, either. The villagers had only been too happy to board up the windows, forgetting I'd been helping chickens go from the coop to someone's plate since I was eight years old.

I didn't know if healers felt the aftereffects of what they'd fixed, either. The wounds I healed and diseases I cleansed echoed through me. It was like a whisper, at first, but after helping two dozen people under the bridge, it became a pounding in the back of my head, like the beating of the sun I was ignoring.

I hadn't been sick a day in my life and my necromancy wasn't plaguing me. It was exhausting, but I wasn't falling apart. On and on I went, long after the clock had tolled six, finding an ever-growing stream of those in need.

My head rang with notes of gratitude as I finally allowed myself to break away and head to the inn. I could still feel the palm prints of those who'd reached out to shake my hand. I walked in a sort of daze, body awash with poison while my blood itself was the antidote. They swirled together with every step I took, one burning out the other.

I got lost on my way back to the inn. Nobody stopped to ask if I needed help, because I was too far from the bridge I'd worked under for anyone to recognise me. People would be talking about me, though. They'd want to track down the healer who'd come out of nowhere.

I hoped we'd moved on before the rumours spread.

I reached the inn and got halfway up the stairs before realising we were meeting for dinner in the tavern across the street.

Sir Ightham and Rán were sat in the back corner, having found a bench sturdy enough to support a pane. They were talking about something that couldn't have been important, judging from the exaggerated gestures they were making with their hands and the empty steins on the table between them.

"It's half-seven," Sir Ightham said sternly.

"Was wondering where you'd got to," Rán said more warmly, using a foot to push a chair out for me.

I fell down more than I sat, and after a moment, remembered to say, "I was exploring the city."

"Did you get lost?" Sir Ightham asked.

"A bit," I admitted, slumping in my seat.

What was I feeling? The remnants of a broken leg, the ripples of whatever had been rotting people from the inside?

"We've already eaten," Sir Ightham said. "So you'll have to order yourself something."

"I'm not hungry."

I wasn't. I was full. Full of—*something.* Everything I'd torn out and pushed back was trapped within me, turning my blood to stone.

"Already eaten, yrval?" Rán asked, covering the sound of Sir Ightham almost knocking a half-empty stein over. "Seen a few vendors around here that half tempted me, even if they were charring their meat."

I shook my head. They waited for me to say something more, and when I had nothing to offer up, they resumed the conversation I'd interrupted. I didn't understand anything they were talking about, which mean it was probably a pane thing. Or a human thing I'd yet to stumble across.

I must've sat there for some time, for they both got through another two drinks before I recalled that there was a bed waiting for me.

"There we were, Canthian soldiers on our right, Ridgeth a few feet to our left. What are we supposed to be doing *but* jump the border," Rán was saying. Was this the start of a story or the end? "And then, the Canthian soldiers give each other this *look* and they—"

"And they shoot at you regardless," Sir Ightham finished for her.

Rán grinned and said, "Aye. We'll make a pirate out of you yet. But you've gotta believe me, you don't want gunpowder making it this far north. Nasty stuff. Like Canth ain't already enough of a mess."

"I'm going to bed," I said, chair scraping across the floor. I don't think I said it as abruptly as it felt, for neither Sir Ightham nor Rán did much more than turn from their conversation and bid me goodnight.

I slept for an hour or less. I might not have slept at all. I closed my eyes but was too aware of the room around me, the stairs creaking, the noise rising from the streets as taverns emptied. I sprang to my feet at the sound of a fist against my door and hurried to unbolt it, convinced it'd be knocked off its hinges if I didn't answer immediately.

Sir Ightham stood before me, corridor brought to life by a single candle, and leant ever so slightly against the doorframe.

"Here," she said, holding something out to me. I took it and felt the hard crust of a loaf in my hands. "Should you find yourself hungry throughout the night."

"Thank you," I said, more touched than confused by the gesture.

My stomach hadn't started to rumble yet and I must've been sleeping more deeply than I first thought for the act of someone bringing me bread to seem so bizarre.

She waved a dismissive hand as she headed unsteadily to her own room.

"Rán insisted upon it," she said.

I locked myself back in my room, bread left by my pillow. I slept soundly after that, sickly sensations under my skin replaced by nothing but exhaustion. When I awoke, I did my utmost to swallow the loaf whole.

I washed for the sake of something to do, but had no idea what was expected of me. Neither Sir Ightham nor Rán had given me any instructions, and the only plans I knew of revolved around meeting Sir Ightham's contact. Which could be taking place at sundown, for all I knew. I decided to explore the city in earnest, or at least the streets around the inn.

I stepped out into Benkor and the city hadn't changed. The poor and sick were still just that, huddled together en masse. No one was darting around, trying to find the elusive healer who'd cleansed so many yesterday. I couldn't have been the first to wander aimlessly and content myself with doing a good deed or two.

I wasn't the only one who'd decided to take an early morning stroll. Sir Ightham had left the inn moments before me and was quickly disappearing into the crowd. I set off after her, no longer bothering to excuse myself as I weaved through the city. When I caught up with her, I couldn't say why I'd been in such a hurry to see her.

"Good morning," I said brightly, amazed by what a night's sleep could do. "Where are you going?"

"Nowhere," she said. She didn't look at me, didn't break her gait to let me join her side in earnest. She only noticed the silence between us because I made no effort to fill it, and eventually said, "I'm taking a walk so as to wake up properly."

I stole a glance at her to see if there were dark circles smudged beneath her eyes again, but Sir Ightham was already looking my way. Our eyes met and I ended up staring at the pavement. She didn't tell me to leave, and that was all I needed. I carried on down the street with her, too conscious of her presence to take in my surroundings.

"Is Rán still sleeping?" I tried.

"I imagine so."

"Do they sleep a lot?" I kept at it. "The pane, I mean. More than humans?"

"They've been known to."

I was mustering up a third attempt, thinking I'd ask what it had been like to live with them, when a boy in a scruffy jacket walked up to us. We'd almost been bumped into a handful of times, but there was nothing accidental in the boy's actions.

I mistook him for her contact. He tilted his head in the direction he'd come from and said, "Morning. There's a gent over by the bakery who's wanting a word with you."

The boy carried on down the street, probably paid to run the errand. I dared to look back at Sir Ightham but she was as bemused by the situation as I was. The only thing that differed between us was the flicker of frustration in her features. Her jaw tightened and she marched down the street, towards the bakery.

I followed, not knowing how I could help or avoid hindering her, but didn't want to lose myself in the crowd.

There was a gap between the bakery and the house next to it, not quite deep enough to be called an alleyway. I recognised the man immediately.

"Ightham!" he greeted Sir Ightham cheerfully.

"Luxon," she replied calmly, but with no lack of spite in her voice. He wasn't wearing his armour, but his unusual red hair gave him away. "Well, whose doing was this? Who sent you?"

"Who *sent* me? Ightham, I'm wounded. Truly wounded. Can't I be here for the sake of my own curiosity? Can't I want to know if the rumours *are* true?" Luxon said, enjoying himself far too much. "Now, now. They don't often waste Knights on deserters, do they? I've got to say, Ightham, I thought you would've done a runner a long time ago. Back around..." he paused, scrunching up his face as he searched for the right word. "Back around the incident."

Sir Ightham wasn't taken in by anything he said

"Do you wish to fight? It would be your choice of weapon, naturally."

"I wish to fight," Sir Luxon said. I tried to work out how long it'd take me to run back to the inn, wake Rán, and lead her back there. "But I do not wish to lose. So, I suggest we keep talking."

"You're not here to take me back," Sir Ightham said slowly. "Yet you went to great lengths to track me down. What is it you want, Luxon?"

Sir Luxon leant against the wall, arms folded over his chest.

"Look, my dear Phoenix. You're making far too big a deal out of this. Knights flee all the time. Something about the inherent strain of being thrown against dragons every other week. Get out before they get you. Sound logic, really," Luxon said, nodding in agreement with himself. "Keep on running. Go to Kastelir or Canth, Agados or Ridgeth. Go to the Bloodless Lands for all I care. Take your wealth and your new friend – hello, there – and live in luxury. Just, ah. Remove yourself from the picture, as it were."

I sunk into myself when Sir Luxon acknowledge me and Sir Ightham's hand drifted to the side, forming a barrier between us.

"And are you aware *why* I left?" Sir Ightham asked after a moment's deliberation. As much as she didn't want me knowing what had driven her out of Thule, it couldn't go unasked.

Luxon shrugged.

"Like I said, the pressure and whatnot. I heard something about you moving away from the Knights, and if such a promotion were to exist and you weren't around to fill it..."

"Then your station rises," Sir Ightham said, finally understanding what it was all about.

She was relieved to realise it was rooted in greed. I relaxed a little, if only because Sir Luxon wasn't the enemy I'd imagined him to be. He hadn't brought soldiers along with him, hadn't struck out against Sir

87

Ightham, even though he'd been there and she hadn't known.

"Very well," Sir Ightham said. There was a reluctance in her voice, feigned to stop Sir Luxon from thinking he'd got what he wanted too easily. "What will you do now?"

Sir Ightham didn't offer her hand, but Sir Luxon reached for it and shook it heartily. Not wanting to react, Sir Ightham stared at him until he was quite done.

"It's back to Thule for me. It's simply a matter of waiting for His Highness to realise that you've truly retired," Luxon said. "You're all set. See yourself out of Felheim and do it *quickly*, Ightham. Otherwise your parents will send more and more search parties after you, and not all of them will be headed by individuals as ambitious as I am."

Sir Luxon bowed to both of us before leaving, not sparing a glance back as he lost himself in the crowd. I didn't dare to face Sir Ightham after all I'd heard, even if it had only created more questions for me. That didn't matter. Sir Ightham was in more trouble than I'd thought she was. She didn't strike me as a coward, as a deserter, and I knew well enough the sort of things a person could be made to run from.

"Rowan," she said slowly. Her fingers curled into fists at her side, as tight as her voice. "What you just witnessed: know that Luxon is not a man to be trusted, or to be taken light."

"I'm not going to—" *say anything*, but Sir Ightham didn't care to hear it. She waved a hand in the direction of the inn.

"Go to Rán. Her room is directly left of yours. Ensure she's awake and tell her to meet me at midday," she said, eyes burning a hole in the crowd. "She knows where."

Sir Ightham was gone before I could protest. I told myself she'd be fine. Sir Luxon had what he wanted, and had admitted himself that Sir Ightham could best him in a fight.

Rán's door was unlocked. There wasn't any need for a pane to bother with a key. Any intruding human would've tripped over themselves to get away. I almost did the same thing when I poked my head in and found her curled on her side, chest rising and falling. I reminded myself that she was Rán, that I knew her, and smothered the urge to back away from the slumbering mountain.

I nudged her shoulder to wake her up and it worked too well. She sat bolt upright and pulled me towards her. I put my hands on her shoulders for balance and her hands covered most of my back as she held me loosely. She tilted her head back and yawned, giving me a glimpse of more fangs than I thought possible to count.

"Always doing the dragon-slayer's dirty work, aren't you," she said, screwing her gold eyes shut and blinking to adjust to the onslaught of daylight. "What's the emergency now? Someone question her honour?"

"Actually..."

We were so close I could see the thin white scars marring her dark skin, could see my reflection in the stark black of her eyes. I could see the grain of her horns and hesitated not out of fear, but to appreciate how at ease I felt mere inches from her tusks.

Rán scratched behind a twitching ear as she waited for me to reply. I glanced away for a split second. Sir Ightham hadn't told me to hold my tongue, but if she wanted Rán to know what had happened, she could tell her herself.

"Something like that," I said. "Listen, I know you can't tell me what's happening, and I know it's supposed to be for my own good, but do you think I should be here?"

"That's a funny question, yrval," Rán said. "You're worried about what's going on, about any danger you might be imagining, when usu-ally, any person on this backward continent would be running from what they think you are. Makes me think you don't know the half of what your sort get up to."

"Wha—" I started, but Rán tapped a claw against my nose as she rose to her feet. She promptly bowed, curved horns grazing the ceiling even with her back arched.

"The dragon-slayer told me a little about you. Nothing too personal, mind," Rán went on to say as she reached for the orange sash bundled on her bed. "Just about you being cooped up in that village, pretending to be a healer. Reckon this is exactly where you're meant to be. You're gonna figure out a few things along the way."

My initial reaction was to say *Sir Ightham speaks about me—?* but I bit it back and said, "What do you know about people like me?"

"Not much," Rán admitted. She held her sash out, shaking it flat. "You're only the second I've met. Well, the second I've been aware of. But people aren't so pointlessly aggressive, down in Canth."

Rán paused, furrowing her brow as she wrapped the sash around the leathers she'd slept in.

"Scrap that. They're pointlessly aggressive alright. You ever tried living in a pirate town? But they've got their heads screwed on right about some things. If anything, necromancers are revered down there."

She was saying it to humour me. She must've been. Canth was still a myth to me, something from my brother's stories. It had no bearing on my life, and Rán was only trying to cheer me up. I said nothing in reply, ignoring the questions that were clawing at me, because how could everyone not hate and fear necromancers? I tugged Rán's arm and lead her out of the room.

We took our bags with us. A guest paused in the lobby, confused when the staircase groaned in protest of Rán's feet, and made himself scarce when he spotted a pane. The woman behind the counter kept her eyes on us, ensuring Rán's horns didn't reshape the doorway on the way out.

She didn't say she hoped we'd stay again.

"Everything okay down there?" Rán asked, dropping a hand on my head.

I was having trouble clawing my way free of the well of thoughts I'd tumbled into, but Rán's hand pulled me halfway out. I nodded at her, certain there'd be plenty of time for plenty of questions later. What had happened between Sirs Ightham and Luxon was far more pressing than necromancy.

"Sir Ightham said to meet her at noon," I said as we set off through the parting crowd. "She said you know where to go."

"That I do," Rán agreed. "Gives us a little time. Treat yourself to breakfast yet, yrval?"

"Something came up," I said, and Rán declared she knew the best place to go.

Not that she'd been to Benkor in some years, mind, but she was sure it must still be in business.

The place we eventually found ourselves at couldn't have been the establishment Rán spoke of, had it existed at all, but the food tasted better than any imaginary café could live up to. The owner greeted us with a smile and said, "Good timing. Just out the oven."

They held out a tray of freshly baked rolls and Rán skewed a few on her claws. I began to see that she was constantly stepping between two worlds: the one where she was a monster, carving her way through crowds and being turned away from shops and inns and taverns, and a smaller, quieter one where people greeted her warmly and she responded in kind.

If it was like that for the pane, a similar duality could exist for necromancers, even if it was across the Uncharted Sea and buried beneath a story.

We wandered through Benkor with our breakfast in hand. I kept an eye out for Sir Ightham, but quickly concluded Rán wasn't heading anywhere in particular. I stuck close to her side, walking along the sunny side of the street she favoured, and spotted a second pair of horns heading towards us.

"Oh!" I grabbed Rán's arm. Her pace slowed for all of a step and she returned to her rolls as though I'd pointed out nothing more than another human.

The second pane moved through the shadows, leaving as much of the street between himself and Rán as he could.

He was taller than she was, something I hadn't believed to be possible, but his horns weren't as long. They'd yet to start curving back and his skin was black, making the two pane look as different as Sir Ightham and I did.

Rán hurried me along. Neither of them looked at each other, despite the way the street buzzed with talk of two pane. Once he was out of sight, I said, "Why didn't you say hello?"

"Are you always saying hello to every human you pass?"

She wasn't annoyed, but she didn't look at me, either.

"No. But it's not as if I'm in a world of pane, and I've only run into one human in days!"

Rán shrugged.

"Those are the laws," she said in a way that made me think twice about asking any more questions.

I wrapped my arm around Rán's and leant against it as we carried on through the streets.

They were making preparations for the Phoenix Festival in a square we came across. There weren't any decorations out, nor was there any of the entertainment I was used to on display, but people sat behind tables covered in scrolls. Queues formed as people scribbled something down and left. I only realised it was for the Phoenix Festival because of the golden bird embroidered onto one of the cloths draped across a table.

If my village needed months to prepare for the fifteen-hundredth celebration, then Benkor had likely been making arrangements for twice as long. I thought back to the festival, to how cheerful everyone was to recall that the Necromancy War was over. Our ancestors had fled the Bloodless Lands and we'd shaken off the shackles of our neglectful gods. The necromancers were dead and gone, and Kondo-Kana had met her end at the bottom of the ocean.

I'd always laughed and sung along, because I was a healer and nobody ever questioned that.

"Do the pane celebrate as well?" I asked as we drifted close enough to overhear that they were taking volunteers to hang lights around the city.

"It's a human tradition, no doubting that," Rán huffed. "The same as most things. Remember what you want, omit what you wanna forget, and change whatever makes you look bad. The pane aren't about to be wasting their time on something of the sort."

"Right," I agreed with an unsteady laugh. It hadn't seemed ridiculous to me at the time. Michael had never questioned the truth of it, so I hadn't, either.

"Come now," Rán said, nudging me away from the festival preparations. "Let's go track down that dragon-slayer before she gets herself into any more trouble."

It wasn't yet noon, and we took the long way around to wherever we were going. Rán talked all the while, telling me how Benkor was the same as ever, once you looked past all that had changed, and read all the shop signs and notice boards out loud to me. I took in snippets of conversation, from complaints that the price of cheese was rising *again* to rumours that one of our Princes was set to marry, but always returned my attention to Rán.

I didn't forget all she'd said about Canth and necromancers, and I didn't manage to put thoughts of Sir Luxon or the Phoenix Festival out of my head, but it was easy to focus on other things in her company.

We looped around to the entrance of Benkor. I was in the middle of telling Rán a story she was enjoying far too much, considering it was about little more than wandering sheep when she nudged my shoulder and nodded towards Sir Ightham, by the stables.

I broke away from Rán, relieved nothing had happened in my absence, and hurried to join Sir Ightham.

Until I saw who she was with.

In the shadow of the stable, looking all too pleased with himself, stood my brother.

CHAPTER SEVEN

Betrayal was my first thought. Sir Ightham had only let me tag along because waiting for my brother to collect me was easier than prying me off herself. I marched over, meaning to declare that I wasn't going back with Michael, but faltered when he caught sight of me.

He started so much he almost tripped over backwards. If nothing else, he hadn't expected to run into me. He rushed over and hit me around the head with an open hand.

There was almost enough force behind it to make me blink.

"Rowan!" he exclaimed. "What the hell do you think you're doing out here? Do you have any idea how worried we've been? What are you playing at?"

Michael shook me in the middle of the street. I retaliated by kicking his shin and he hopped back, hissing.

"What am *I* doing here? What are *you* doing here?" I asked, throwing my hands out to the side as he made a fuss of his leg.

"I have a *reason* to be here, unlike some people," he said proudly. "I wanted to send Sir Ightham's things by raven, you know, but it seems that I was right in not trusting the mail. And a good thing it was! If I hadn't come here directly, who's to say what would've happened. Beyond dad and me assuming you'd met your end at the bottom of a ditch, a-any..."

Michael trailing off in the middle of a lecture was an event in and of itself. His gaze led to Rán, hovering over my shoulder.

"Collected another one, have we?" she asked, bowing down to put a hand on my shoulder. From the way his hands shook, I didn't think he was capable of absorbing anything we were saying. "Now, if you don't mind me saying, this one looks an awful lot like you, yrval."

"My brother," I explained, sighing. I might not have understood what Michael was doing there, but I could relish in the fact that he was scared and I wasn't. That I knew something and he didn't. "I don't know what he's doing here. When Sir Ightham said we were meeting a contact, I thought it'd be someone... important."

His face remained pale, but he came back to enough of his senses to snap out, "*Hey—!*"

He inched towards me and hissed, "That's a *pane*," in my ear.

"Her name is Rán," I said brightly, and Sir Ightham brought a hand to her forehead.

"That's enough," she said, tempering the situation. "Let us keep this brief: I asked Michael to come here as a necessity. I did not inform him of your presence, for it is none of my business, and he is merely here to deliver the documents necessary to cross into Kastelir."

"We're going to *Kastelir?*"

Michael was suddenly the least of my problems.

"You didn't know?" he asked cheerfully.

Sir Ightham remained stony-faced and Rán shrugged.

"Wait. Wait, we're going to Kastelir," I said, desperate to make sense of it. The wall behind Benkor became paper-thin, poised to let Kastelir rush through at any moment. "We're going to Kastelir and you didn't tell me."

"It didn't seem pertinent," Sir Ightham explained. "You hadn't left your village before, so I doubt you'll measure much of a difference between Eaglestone and any city Kastelir has to offer."

"It didn't seem... you didn't think it was important? We're going to *Kastelir* and, and..."

I was battling against panic and outrage while the others watched me struggle, perfectly calm. Rán knew the plan and Michael had evidently been aware that Sir Ightham was crossing the border for longer than I'd known her, by all accounts. The tips of my ears burnt red.

We were heading into a country in a perpetual state of discord, even during peacetime. My brother was involved in it all.

And it hadn't occurred to Sir Ightham that it might matter.

"Calm down," Michael said. He threw an arm around my shoulders and dragged me further and further from Rán. Sir Ightham was close enough for him to pretend to be brave. "You're getting yourself worked up over nothing, as per usual. Sir Ightham didn't mention Kastelir because it's of no concern to you! We'll head back home before there's too much of a fuss about your absence and let Sir Ightham continue her work without distraction."

I threw Michael's arm off. Benkor's buildings drew closer, dimming my vision.

"What? I'm not going back. Do you have any idea what will happen if I do? Do you have any idea of how they'll—"

"Yes, yes," Michael said, waving a hand. "It's terribly hard to be, ah, *as you are.* I've heard it a thousand times! I know it well enough to feel the extent on your behalf. But think of someone other than yourself for a moment. There's work to be done, and if you'd only make the effort to get on with things, you'd see that—"

My whole face burned, eyes stinging.

"Rowan is coming with me," Sir Ightham said sharply. "Should she still wish to, that is. I'm afraid I was remiss for not divulging our destination sooner."

I didn't know what to say. Happily, Michael didn't either.

No one wanted to argue with Sir Ightham. We stood there in awkward silence, not looking at one another. We'd behaved like children in front of her. Michael had snapped at me, acting as though dragging me back to the village was an inevitability, and I'd let myself get flustered and frustrated in the middle of the street.

"... I want to come with you," I mumbled at the floor.

Sir Ightham placed a hand on my shoulder. If I'd been wrong about the pane, I could be wrong about Kastelir, too.

"Clearly, there's been a lot of miscommunication and misunderstanding going on here," Rán said, stepping closer. Michael flinched. "Let's be taking a moment to sit down and explain as best we can."

We didn't sit down. According to Sir Ightham, there was no time for that, but we managed to talk as we collected our horses.

"Sir Ightham is *obviously* doing important work, so I've done what I could to help," Michael told me. A blind sort of faith made his words light. He had no idea what she was doing, either. "I let the surrounding villages and towns believe that she was on her way to Canth, and rushed to let the elders know I'd seen her off when she disappeared. That sort of thing. Kastelir was her real destination, of course, which is where I come in again. While Sir Ightham is no doubt skilled in a great number of things beyond dragon-slaying, I must admit that I have far more practice when it comes to forging certain documents."

He smiled at her and bowed his head as he spoke. Sir Ightham didn't take her eyes off the road ahead.

"But sensitive documents are rarely safe with ravens. Innkeepers probably make half their yearly income on blackmail alone! I thought it best to deliver the items in question, but I heard there were problems in Praxis. And so here we are, meeting in Benkor! I expect it's easier to cross the border here, anyway."

Michael was positively beaming. He took the sleeve of my new clothes between a thumb and two fingers and tutted.

"What about you, though. Running away in the night. I actually hiked up to the fields, thinking you'd fallen asleep tending to the sheep again. And all for nothing! Never thought you'd get the nerve to actually do it."

I'd done it and he hadn't; *that* was his real problem. He was devoid of a reason to finally make his way into the world.

"We ran into bandits," I told him, elbowing his ribs. "Five of them against Sir Ightham! Oh, and I have my own sword now. And what about Rán? You've been ignoring her all this time. Don't be rude, Michael."

Michael opened his mouth, not certain whether to start with bandits or blades, but his eyes betrayed him. He couldn't stop looking at Rán.

"Good day," he said.

Squeaking, apparently, ran in my family.

"You have my thanks," Sir Ightham said as we neared the gate to Kastelir. *Kastelir*! Her fingers covered her pouch as Michael, who'd grinned ear to ear at a hint of gratitude, waved a hand in front of him.

"Wait! You can't expect me to leave my little sister behind!" Michael said, clinging to me like an anchor. "It'd be a tad suspicious, don't you think, for a woman of your supposed standing to only take one servant on such a trip. Even if a pane *could* bow to a human, they would never serve one, which takes this, ah... which takes *Rán* out of the equation."

The guards idly watched us from a distance and I didn't want to jeopardise Sir Ightham's plans by fuming in the middle of the street. I took a deep breath, searching for the best way to explain that I didn't think it was a good idea, because... because what?

Because Michael had more experience out in the world than I did and had proven himself useful already?

Sir Ightham and Rán shared a few words in the language I didn't understand and came to the mutual agreement of a shrug.

"Hurry along," Sir Ightham said.

"Excellent!"

Michael clapped his hands together. With the way he was grinning, anyone would've been forgiven for thinking Sir Ightham had begged him to come along.

The documents he'd brought were proof of identity. I only had a vague notion of such a thing existing in the first place, but as I learnt at the gate, my Kingdom was eager to keep the Kastelirians out and curious when it came to those willingly choosing to leave. The papers were squinted over, while Rán's horns negated the need to fuss with any documents.

No one had to tell me to keep my mouth closed. I made myself as inconspicuous as I could, piecing together Sir Ightham's story as the guards questioned her. She was a wealthy trader from Thule, papers saying as much, by the name of Eden Westerdale. She was headed towards Riverhurst and the cities along the border to help redirect some of the trade from Praxis, through Benkor.

Michael and I were her servants. Michael chimed in to say he was the cook, though he'd never made the effort to prepare his own meals at home.

We were let through without too much hassle. The guards were more concerned with keeping people out than stopping them leave. It was on our heads if we wanted to venture into Kastelir. Michael and I dragged Sir Ightham and Rán's things through the gate to look the part.

I wasn't given a glimpse of Kastelir. The gate was a corridor of a building, and we were at the far end of it. Sir Ightham stopped on the way out, leaving Rán with our three horses, Michael's horse Patrick now numbering amongst them. She headed to a man sat behind the iron bars of a small window looking into a small room.

He grunted in greeting. Sir Ightham emptied her pouch onto the counter, gold ringing against stone, and said, "We need to exchange our money to the Kastelirian currency," for my benefit.

"Is it different?" I asked, pushing onto my tiptoes to watch the man reach through and gather the coins. It'd never occurred to me that Kastelir would use different coins. Money was money, to my understanding.

"It's mostly aesthetic. Look here."

She took one of the coins the man was counting. It looked like a mark, was just about the right size and colour, but she turned it in her palm, revealing a bear's head worked into the metal in place of the royal family's sigil. Sir Ightham pulled more coins aside and showed me the backs: there was a stag with flowing antlers, a tiger's head, and that of a dragon.

I studied the coins, taking in the way something so slight made so much of a difference, and knew I wasn't ready for Kastelir. Not that I had a choice. Sir Ightham collected her money, made ready to leave, and Rán led our horses away from Felheim. My feet followed in spite of my fears, and I saw Kastelir for the first time.

It was unremarkable.

Hills rose ahead of us, clusters of trees speckled the landscape, and the shapes of a few towns were scattered in the distance. I wasn't sure what I'd expected. The wall between Felheim and Kastelir was only a matter of metres thick. It wasn't enough to turn the land into mulch, make a swamp of the land and sear the sky red.

Still, I hadn't expected the transition to be so underwhelming.

I stepped away from the gate and tripped on a loose stone. Michael chuckled, patted my shoulder, and deigned to take the lead from Patrick's back.

Sir Ightham and Rán fell back, talking amongst themselves as we took the worn path to a town in the distance. They made no effort to whisper, and I picked out the words *Luxon* and *Thule* from their strange language.

I wasn't looking around for bandits and pane anymore. I was searching for something that would instantly make Kastelir feel distinct, a shock to my system that would make the fact that I'd left my country behind settle in. It wasn't that it was identical to every place I'd ever been, but Eaglestone had been different to my village, and Praxis was different to Benkor; there was nothing unique about the dissimilarities.

I'd grown up on tales of Kastelir's constant turmoil, stories where siblings were set against one another out in the fields, but Kastelir was whole. It wasn't the patched together pieces of four separate territories I'd let myself believe it was. It was open and wide and quiet. Beautiful in comparison to the wasteland I'd imagined.

Riverhurst was half a mile away, and had no walls built around it. Its perimeter was made of buildings pressed close together with plenty of gaps to squeeze or stroll through, and a wide road took us to the real entrance.

It was marked with a statue unlike that of the King and Queen I'd seen in Praxis. It wasn't built upon a pedestal, and there was little skill to speak of in its execution. It was made from weathered stone and depicted three people. Kastelir's rulers, I assumed. The remnants of a fourth figure confirmed it: a pair pane feet were the only part left intact.

Michael dismounted Patrick to scrutinise the statue.

"Queen Kidira, I'd wager. Although the height..." Two of the figures towered over Sir Ightham, while Queen Kidira was shorter than I was. "Probably emphasised here, as though the statue is some manner of joke. As for the others, King Jonas and King Atthis. Or the other way around. Neither of them are particular distinct from the other, though I've read they have widely differing heritages."

"He's a smart one," Rán said dryly.

Had someone other than a pane spoke, Michael would've found a way to look pleased with himself.

"He just reads a lot," I said, hopping off Charley.

"Yes, well..." came Michael's reply. He cleared his throat, and I vowed to tell him Rán was of no threat the moment it stopped being funny. "That, of course, leaves only Queen Kouris unaccounted for. Unaccounted for beyond the feet, that is. If the mob who did this had any sense of wit, they would've ceased their vandalism once they reached the shoulders."

Michael laughed enough for all of us at his joke, and it brought him back to himself. He cleared his throat again, only it wasn't out of a sense of discomfort, that time.

He was preparing for another of his tales.

"What a farce of a Kingdom! Their Queen married a pane and everyone acted as though nothing untoward had unfolded," he said.

"Michael, I don't think—"

He hushed me with a wave of his hand and set about straightening his collar.

"Towns such as this one are more than used to all manner of performers," he explained. It was the thought of him telling a story about Kastelir *in* Kastelir that troubled me, not the fact that he might have difficulty drawing a crowd. "And since Sir Ightham has been infinitely kind and allowed me to accompany her on her journey, I ought to repay her in whatever way I can."

Michael's stories were more of a gift to himself than anyone else, but I couldn't deny that he had a knack for it. He was tall and lean, taller than I was by a head and a half, but when he tangled himself up in one of his tales, his presence could fill any room or market square. People took notice, and he spoke as though he'd keep on talking whether he had an audience of one or one hundred.

Her perched himself on a cobbled step by a lamppost and lingered until a few passing Kastelirians turned their heads. Michael was animated when he spoke, but most of that sprang from his voice. He never acted out scenes, never did much more with his hands than push his words higher and higher.

"Long before the young, thriving Kingdom of Kastelir was forged through peace, four territories filled the map. For centuries, the only common ground they shared was that of the battlefield. When people speak of the War of the Territories, they mean to say *wars*. Rulers came and went, borders were redrawn time and time again, and treaties were created with the intention of being broken.

"For centuries, it had been considered a human war, until the pane Kouris forced the entirety of the continent to take notice. Pane claim to be peaceful. If this is the case, then Kouris was the exception that proved the rule. But nonetheless: there the territories were, teetering on the verge of signing the first genuine peace treaty in over two centuries, when Kouris came down from the mountains, a falcon emblazoned on her armour and a rabble of humans who'd fallen to her command at her heels."

I glanced skittishly at Rán, worried Michael's words might wound her. For the first time, I noticed a dragon emblem pinned to her leathers, along her collarbone. Rán was only distantly entertained by the story. History was history, and she had likely learnt plenty from the example set by Queen Kouris.

"Kouris was tall. Even amongst pane, she towered over her kin, as if trying to rival the dragons. Her horns were so long they curved back and scraped her shoulder blades, and her cheeks were scarred by her own tusks. Kouris marched through the northernmost territory, burning villages as she went, slaughtering those who challenged her as well as those who fled. She sharpened the bones of her victims into weapons, as if to scorn us for what we do to dragons; dragons who have razed our lands. But never before sucking the meat clean off them.

"Kouris had the skins of humans tanned and stretched, forced the survivors to scrawl falcons across them, that they might carry the grim emblems across the land. She marched through the territories with such determination, such ferocity, that those who had come together to unite the lands feared she had some plan to overthrow them. Or worse still, that she wished to continue the war indefinitely, for her own amusement.

"But when she stood before the Kings, simply Lord Jonas and the Warlord Atthis at the time, she did not draw her blade. She didn't bare her fangs any more than she had the misfortune of doing so naturally. She fell to her knees, horns scraping against the floor as she bowed.

"When they asked her what she wanted, she made no reply. She didn't understand a single word of Mesomium, and neither of the leaders knew what to do.

"There was a glint in her eye like a spark of dragon's breath, blood staining her teeth and armour, caught in her hair, mixed with the dirt smeared across her face. She shook, quite like a mad woman, and all in the room expected her to attack. And though the Kings Atthis and Jonas drew their blades, there was little need for it.

"Queen Kidira, merely twenty years old at the time, had recently arrived to sign the peace treaty. She wasted no time. She leapt upon the pane's back, struck her skull with the heel of her boot, and had her behind bars before Kouris could regain consciousness.

"She paid no heed to the way Kouris growled and snarled, rattling the iron bars of her prison, and met her with both sharp words and kindness. Kouris didn't understand what was said to her, of course, nor did Kidira understand what was being snapped in return, but in time, the two of them learnt from one another. Kidira never forgave Kouris for what she'd done, but took it upon herself to have Kouris brought back to what she believed were her true senses.

"The pane was fed and washed, and as the months passed, Kouris showed herself to be less and less of a savage beast. As if reflection was all she truly needed, Kouris slowly pieced herself back together, and the two began to speak of official matters. Peace was still out of reach. No matter how the leaders agreed it was the only path for them to take, the people found reasons to continue fighting amongst themselves. And Kouris, it turned out, was as skilled at nurturing peace as she was at manufacturing strife.

"Needless to say, in time Kouris was let out of her cage. She agreed to represent her territory, where the pane are numerous, and within three years, Kastelir was finally formed. The only objections to Kouris being crowned Queen were spoken of in disgruntled whispers, and for three long years, as the city of Isin grew around them, Kouris ruled alongside Kidira, Atthis, and Jonas.

"But note by note, the whispers became louder, until the roar of a mob found its way to the castle gates, pounding and pounding, demanding justice. For no matter the change she had been through, no matter all she'd accomplished, Queen Kouris had yet to answer for her crimes. It is said, though I do not know who first said as much, that Queen Kouris went to Queen Kidira in the night and asked her to steal away with her.

"When Kidira told Kouris that her duty was to her land, and that she could never betray it, Kouris understood what she had to do. And though she left the castle that very night, she did not run. She gave herself over to the mob, where she was put to death by beheading. But not before they took her eyes and fed them to falcons, as she had once done to all those who crossed her path.

"And thus Queen Kouris atoned for what she had done, forever leaving one of Kastelir's thrones empty, for no pane would ever take her place."

I breathed a sigh of relief. He'd changed the story. It wasn't the tale of a savage land, and the cast of characters weren't as senselessly brutal as Queen Kouris. He made everything softer for the audience, and it felt closer to the truth than anything I'd heard before.

He'd drawn a small crowd. Only a few were there to judge him. His accent gave him away, and one man muttered, "What do the Felheimish know about our history, anyway?" under his breath. Someone chimed in that we were always hiding away behind our wall. It didn't deter Michael, evident in the way he saw the story through and bowed when he finished.

"Cheerful," Sir Ightham said, enticing Michael to bow again.

"Read that in a book, did you?" Rán asked, amused. She'd earnt no shortage of wary glances from the audience. They were still watching her, wanting to know how she'd react.

Made bold by the scattered applause, Michael said, "Are you suggesting that I missed some details? Didn't do justice to the historical truth?"

"Invented most of the details, more like," Rán said with a chuckle. She couldn't have known the truth any better than Michael did, having grown up in Canth, but that didn't stop her teasing him.

She headed deeper into Riverhurst, having errands of her own to attend to, and Michael recovered from his prejudices enough to bolt off after her.

"My good pane, if I might have a moment of your time!" he called as he went, leaving me with the horses.

Sir Ightham and I saw them to the stables, and once they were secure, I followed Sir Ightham through Riverhurst. She didn't say where she was going, nor did she ask for my company, but after a few minutes I realised I'd been hovering for too long to make an abrupt departure. Sir Ightham didn't say anything, but neither did I.

I kept *thinking* of things to say, but they never reached my lips. She didn't care about anything that came to mind; didn't care that the weather had really warmed within the past few days, didn't care that I was taken aback by Michael's abrupt and bold presence; nor did she care about his story, or any of the remarks I could've made about the unfolding town.

She was distant and distracted, but that didn't make her cold. I wanted to tell her that she could confide in me about Luxon or anything else that troubled her, but could only stare at the pavement.

Sir Ightham stopped outside a small corner store with a dark red awning covering the doorway, but didn't enter. It was the chalkboard propped up outside that had caught her attention.

"Excuse me," Sir Ightham called through the doorway, to the man behind the counter. "Which Prince?"

The store was full of a dozen different vegetables, rows of bottled ale and stacks of newspapers, all kept cool and dim. A young boy shopping in the corner paused to look at Sir Ightham, and the shop owner pushed his glasses up to the bridge of his nose and said, "What's all this now?"

I wanted to take in the nuances of the Kastelirian accent, but before meeting Sir Ightham, I'd never considered that words could be spoken in a way that different from my own accent. The letters were rougher, perhaps, and some of the syllables might've been longer.

"Your sign says that a Felheimish Prince is to marry a Kastelirian noble. Did your source happen to say which Prince?"

The man hummed as she closed the tattered book he'd been reading around his thumb and said, "Something with an *A. Adam?*"

"Prince Alexander," Sir Ightham said briskly. "Thank you."

She turned on her heels and headed off as if she were tearing free of something. She moved with such force that I was left watching her charge down the street, until she came to a crossroad and stopped, looking left and right, left and right, not knowing which way to turn.

I took the opportunity to catch up with her.

Her hands were balled into fists, and I tentatively said, "Sir? Do you know the Prince?"

She pursed her lips together and held her head high. I didn't expect an answer, and when she tilted her head to the left, I thought that was to be the end of it. But she swerved off the street, towards a bench.

I took a seat next to her, watching the people of Riverhurst come and go as she did the same. Or stared straight ahead. I sat with my elbows propped on my knees, turning her way every few seconds. Part of me expected her to start shaking, but she never did.

"He is my brother," Sir Ightham eventually said, not turning to me.

"You have a brother?"

I was so startled by the thought of Sir Ightham having a life outside of Knighthood that the most obvious question was jilted out of my mind.

"I have two. Princes Alexander and Rylan," she said. "These past months, I have been away, and for longer still I have... I ought to have heard such news from Alex. Not a shopkeeper's scrawlings."

She tried to unbundle her fists and succeeded, for a few seconds. It wasn't anger or frustration that had moved her; she was upset. I'd done the right thing in hovering around her.

"Hold on. If they're Princes, that means—"

"I am a Knight. Let us leave it at that."

She was as stern as ever, deflecting my accusation of her royal blood like it was one of my questions about the weather, or where we were going. Confusion was written all over me, and it was enough to make Sir Ightham spill a few more words.

"When I was a matter of weeks old, I am told that my birth parents found themselves in a measure of trouble. My birth father was an adviser to one of the King's advisers, unhappy with his station in the court, and along with two accomplices, took untoward measures to increase his lot in life. When plans fell through, his partners fled to Canth and his wife had no interest in raising a child. I've been led to believe I wasn't the only child of theirs to end up in such a predicament.

"And so I was adopted by the royal family. Alex is my age, and Rylan a few years older."

"That means the King and Queen are—"

"The King is my King and the Queen is my Queen. The same as anyone."

I wanted to scream that they were her parents, that she was the *Princess of Felheim*, but she'd only cut me off again. I couldn't comprehend the enormity of the life Sir Ightham had led before coming to my village. The enormity of the life she was leaving behind. It wasn't just position and power she was discarding, but family, too.

The Princess of Felheim. I'd barely had the chance to accept that I was travelling with a Knight. She was right there, sitting on the bench with me. The Princess of Felheim! I wondered if I should spring to my feet and bow.

"I'm sorry about your brother," I eventually said. I shouldn't have been drawing attention to the things she wanted to keep inside. Not only was what she said important, but so was the fact that she'd chosen to tell *me*. She'd trusted me with something. "I don't know what's going on, and I'm not going to ask again. Don't worry! But I bet the Prince would understand. You can sort whatever this is out and still make it to the wedding, right?"

Sir Ightham tilted her head back, huffing a dry laugh.

I knitted my fingers together. There wasn't much I could say without making her feel worse.

"And yourself?"

She slumped in her seat and caught my eye.

"Huh?"

"What of your family? Beyond your brother, that is. He's happy to speak volumes on that topic himself."

I brought a hand to my mouth as I laughed, nose bumping my knuckles.

"You want to know about me? Really? You just told me that you grew up in a castle, that you're a... um..."

"You may use the word *Princess*, so long as you do not call me by the title," she said.

"A *Princess*, and I'm... I'm from a village in the middle of nowhere. You've *been* there. I bet they showed you everything worth seeing the first morning," I said, hating the way the tips of my ears burnt.

"I asked about you, not the village," Sir Ightham said. "Besides, I have spent my life surrounded by lords and ladies and lieges, politicians and captains, monarchs and diplomats. Who's to say I haven't tired of all that?"

Certainly not me.

I swivelled on the bench and sat facing her, cross-legged.

"Well, you already know my brother. Other than that, I only have my dad. He was the one who donated our best pig for your feast, by the way. I was so mad about it at the time," I said, having trouble sticking to the point when Sir Ightham was watching me so attentively. "He used to be a soldier, actually. He worked along the wall forever ago, before Michael and I were born, back when Kastelir wasn't Kastelir. He doesn't talk about it much. I've always known him as a farmer. My mother died when I was young. Not even a year old. I only know things about her because Michael tells me."

"I met your father," Sir Ightham said, contesting with recollections of dozens of villagers. "He said little to me, but what he did say was kind."

She returned her attention to the crowd, watching passers-by scurry back and forth, and added, "I should be sorry to have taken you away, had you not made your case so emphatically."

"Even if I wasn't..." I scratched the back of my head. "Anyway, even if I'd got along with everyone, you wouldn't have been taking me away from much. Look at this place! It's more than I ever imagined seeing in my life, and it's only one of a whole load of places we've been. If I were still at home, I'd just... I'd be up in my room or out in the fields, still scared of pane. Still scared of the *villagers*. I wouldn't have anyone new to talk to, either. I definitely wouldn't be talking to *you*."

I smiled and she tilted her head to see it.

"I never would've considered a place like this impressive, or even

107

remotely interested," she said, after I'd convinced myself that I'd said too much and Sir Ightham cared for none of it. "See? We are from very different worlds indeed. This makes for far better conversation than any ballroom gossip."

I wondered what they discussed in ballrooms. Dresses and suits and suitors, most likely, but I refrained from asking. For the first time since I'd met her, Sir Ightham was almost at peace. Dark marks remained beneath her eyes, but her shoulders slackened as she looked out onto Riverhurst, trying to see what I saw.

I didn't search for anything else to say. There was no gnawing urge to fill the silence.

The reprieve didn't last long. Sir Ightham would never let herself remain idle for more than a handful of minutes, but taking a moment to herself had done her good.

"Come," she said, getting up. "We'd best ensure that brother of yours doesn't have Rán at her wit's end."

I bounced to my feet and we headed out in search of Michael and Rán. Pane were convenient landmarks in and of themselves, and I wandered along without having to push myself onto tiptoes or squint. I was about to say something to Sir Ightham, something I hadn't rehearsed a dozen times over, when I caught sight of a woman struggling with her belongings on the other side of the street.

It was a quieter part of town. The street was empty enough that it became glaringly obvious when people went to great lengths to weave around the woman. She wasn't old but her face was weathered, and I expected she was carrying everything she owned, and did so every day.

It was her rot that demanded my attention.

It was rooted so deeply within her that she must've believed the weight of her bags was what caused her to ache so thoroughly.

"Excuse me," I said, jogging over. Her eyes flashed and I knew she'd mistaken me for a thief. "Can I help you?"

"... 'salright," she mumbled.

She tugged the straps of her bags, securing them on her back.

"Not with that," I said, hands clasped behind my back. Sir Ightham joined us, but I didn't let her presence distract me. "You're sick, aren't you?"

The woman narrowed her eyes, scared I might use the information against her. Her fingers tightened around her bag straps, and I reached out slowly, as I would to a lamb that had cornered itself in a panic.

"You're a healer?" the woman croaked. I didn't lie; I didn't have to. Before I could nod or shake my head, she said, "What do you want? Ain't got nothing here worth having."

"I don't want anything from you. Please," I said, ignoring the way Sir Ightham turned her back to us, either casting her gaze away from my necromancy or scouting out any onlookers.

The woman relented. Her calloused fingers brushed against mine and I drew all of the disease from deep within her. If Sir Ightham had feared I'd call attention to us, it was for nought. It happened in a heartbeat, unnoticeable to anyone but the pair of us, hands brushing together.

The woman blinked, seeing through clear eyes for the first time in years. Her features were worn as ever, but there as a brightness to them. Her thanks were made unsteady by confusion, and Sir Ightham didn't give the woman the time she needed to process what had happened.

"Here," she said, pressing coins into her open palm. "Please, find yourself somewhere to stay and have something to eat."

Her surface kindness was nothing but a way to get rid of the woman. Her thanks doubled, gratitude split between Sir Ightham and myself, but I wasn't given the chance to assure her it was fine. Sir Ightham marched me away as though from the scene of a crime, as stony-faced as she'd been when I first met her.

"What do you think you're doing?" she asked. Any warmth I'd heard in her tone had long since turned tepid. "*Anyone* could've seen what you did."

"So?" I ground to a halt, refusing to match her pace. "I healed that woman. That's all. She needed help and—"

"And *you* need to be more careful," Sir Ightham said. "This isn't your village. You can't make the same mistakes here."

Who was she to lecture me on carelessness, as though I hadn't lost everything when the village had found out what I really was?

"That woman was in pain, and now she's not. She was... her body was rotting, like bark, or, or..." My head swam with colours, flashes of what I'd felt upon ripping the disease out tumbling through me. I could never explain what I saw and tasted and *knew* around death and disease. "She's okay now. That's all that matters, right?"

"That's not all that matters," Sir Ightham said.

Of course. Of course she always knew better.

"What you wish to do is admirable, truly. But if you help one woman today, then tomorrow you will justify helping two, and word will spread. It will be like your village all over again, only the laws against necromancy are not so relaxed, here. You will not merely be forced into isolation."

Anger left me. Sir Ightham finished speaking and still I couldn't comprehend that her sharp words came from a place of concern.

"I kind of thought... once I left my village, you'd leave me behind somewhere, or I'd find a town I wanted to stay in, and I'd become a healer again," I mumbled. "I figured I'd get found out eventually, but I'd have made some money and could move on. I'm not really... I don't know what else to do. I'm not smart like Michael, I'm not a Knight, and I... I can't *not* do it. I don't know how it works! Just how it feels. And ignoring it, it's like, like it'd be worse than whatever anyone would do to a necromancer."

Sir Ightham stared at me. I looked at the pavement between her feet and she bowed to catch my eye, not straightening until I met her gaze.

"Running is no way to live," Sir Ightham said. We were both too aware that she spoke from experience. "I do not mean to chide you, Rowan. I do not wish to scorn what you do, but I do mean to protect you. Remember what I said earlier: the world is still open and new to you, and you must trust that there are things I *know* that you have yet to learn."

"Yeah," I said.

It was all I could manage. I swallowed the lump in my throat.

"Besides, it would not do for you to settle down somewhere," Sir Ightham continued, after the silence grew heavy around us. "I am in need of my squire, after all."

"No you aren't," I said, remembering how to grin.

I could barely hold a sword, but that didn't matter to her.

"Perhaps not," she said, smiling.

CHAPTER EIGHT

We left Riverhurst shortly after. Michael and Rán had gathered supplies for the journey ahead. Three weeks was the best estimate Sir Ightham and Rán could give us, at which Michael seized hold of the map, turned it this way and that, convinced that there *had* to be a quicker way.

Kastelir could've swallowed Felheim whole three times over. Our destination, Isin, was at the very heart of the country, marking the former meeting place of the territories.

The days were long and monotonous.

They blurred together but never seemed to roll on; all we did was ride and ride, avoiding cities and villages alike, while Sir Ightham looked over her shoulder, expecting something other than the wind at her heels. Her paranoia wore off on me. I couldn't sleep, for fear that Sir Luxon would be towering over me when I opened my eyes.

Michael told stories to pass the time, when he wasn't busy complaining about anything and everything, or begging Sir Ightham to let us stay at an inn for the night. We were grateful for the stories, if only have something other than the beating of hooves to listen to, but even his supply of tales began to dwindle.

Yet no matter how dull the days were, the evenings took on a life of their own. Once the horses were fed and the fire was burning, Sir Ightham would prepare dinner while Rán, Michael and I talked and talked, as though we hadn't spent an entire empty day together. We spoke of nothing of note. We told anecdotes from our childhood and Rán asked more questions than she answered, but it gave me something to look forward to throughout the day.

Sir Ightham didn't say much to me, after leaving Riverhurst. She spoke to Rán when necessity dictated and she answered Michael's questions as briefly as she could, but she was ever trapped in her own thoughts and what laid ahead.

When we needed to restock our supplies, Michael and I wandered to one of the solitary farms scattered across Kastelir. I'd gone with Rán once and never again after that. The owners caught sight of her from the window and bolted themselves inside.

"More lessons tonight, hm?" Michael asked as we headed down a hillside towards a lonely house caught between overgrown fields full of grazing sheep and horses. "Who knows, perhaps this time you'll manage to point the sword at Sir Ightham."

"At least she wants to teach me," I said, but it wasn't much of a defence. Sir Ightham insisted on drilling swordplay into me every night after dinner, and by some miracle, I wound up frustrated long before she did. Once I'd tried to swing the sword and ended up burying the blade inches into the soil.

"I've no interest in anything of the sort," Michael said, toying with the coins Sir Ightham had given him. I carried the bag to fill, but he preferred to handle the money. "For all the wolves you've wrestled, you'd think you'd have something of a knack for it. You'd have better luck trying to read again."

I elbowed him but he side-stepped it, chuckling to himself as I grunted. It was true that I was bad, but I was determined to improve. If only so Michael would shut up about it, and Sir Ightham wouldn't have wasted her time.

"Good evening. Terribly sorry if we've come at a bad time," Michael said when the farmer opened their front door. He liked to do all the talking, too. I did my best to look cheerful. "We were wondering if you might be willing to part with any food. Cheese, bread, meat. Anything you have! We're more than happy to pay double what you'd get at market."

The farmer rubbed their chin, glanced at the coins in Michael's hand, and said, "Not from around here, are you?"

Not that anyone was from around there. I'd hadn't seen so much as a barn in hours. Our accents never failed to give us away, and the Kastelirians looked at us as warily as I would've looked at a Kastelirian, back in Felheim.

"Indeed we aren't! But we have family a few day's ride from here. A couple of cousins," Michael said. It was a different story every time. "We underestimated how long it'd take and don't have nearly enough to tide us over."

The farmer grunted, which I took to mean *wait here.* They returned a few minutes later with slabs of meat and an armful of vegetables covered in dirt. We paid more than a fair price and had change to spare.

"You wouldn't happen to have any ale, would you? Wine? Anything would do," Michael asked, never satisfied with what we had.

"Not in this house, lad," the farmer said, clicking the door closed.

"Bah," Michael grumbled, trudging up the hill as I slung the bag of goods over my shoulder. "That's the third time I've been turned down. They *must* have it! They live on a farm in the middle of nowhere. What's there to do *but* drink?"

"Work?" I suggested. "Anyway, if there's nothing to do but drink, they're not going to want to share it with you, are they?"

"I suppose," Michael allowed, equally annoyed by me being right as he was at the lack of drink. I knew better than to expect him to let it rest, and sure enough, moments later he was saying, "You'd think I'd be allowed a modicum of comfort. Over the last week we've slept on a fine assortment of dirt and rocks. Tree roots, I've found, make for a particularly good night's rest. All this washing in rivers, not having a single wall around us for protection, let alone a roof, is downright barbaric. Sir Ightham could afford to put us up in a different inn each night, if she so chose. Now, I understand and respect that she has a plan she must stick to, but it does make one wonder... Still, she's a fine cook. You'll hear no complaints from me there."

For all he proclaimed to loathe our life of travelling, Michael had never shown any sign of turning back. He'd ride ahead of us, excited by the prospect of what was over the next hill, inevitably disappointed when there wasn't a bed awaiting him.

"What are we going to do once this is all over?" I asked. Our camp was in the distance, fire not yet lit. I could make out Rán and our horses, but Sir Ightham wasn't much more than a speck on the horizon. "Once we reach Isin and everything's done with."

"Who's to say? If it's merely an errand Sir Ightham is running, perhaps we'll have the pleasure of accompanying her back to Thule," he said. "More likely than not, however, Sir Ightham and Rán will leave to attend to other matters and it'll just be the two of us. We have to go home at some point, you realise. If only to see dad."

Michael had written to our father several times. I'd done my best to contribute, but whenever I asked Michael to write something, he put down far more than I'd dictated and would often screw up the parchment and start over again, distorting what I'd wanted to convey.

"Right," I said, wishing I'd never asked the question.

Thinking about any of it being over made my chest tighten. For all

113

of Felheim and Kastelir that I'd roamed through, I was convinced I'd snap straight back to my village the moment Sir Ightham and Rán were done with us. It didn't matter how far we'd come. If there were other options open to me, I was blind to them. I couldn't carve out my place in the world without my necromancy.

I shoved it out of my mind. Isin was still weeks away.

Sir Ightham and Rán pointedly weren't looking at one another. They sat on the ground, doing nothing; there wasn't even a fire to heat the pan for dinner.

"Oh dear," Michael said, unwilling to wade through an uncomfortable atmosphere. "Is everything alright? Didn't interrupt anything, did we?"

Rán growled dismissively. Sir Ightham took the change from Michael, pocketed it, and didn't ask what we'd managed to procure. I pulled a chunk of meat from the bag, hoping it would cheer Rán up. Not that she'd had to rely on us for food at any point. She was perfectly capable of hunting for herself, and had pounced on no small number of rabbits, goats, foxes and sheep. She got through more food than Michael, Sir Ightham and me put together.

She held out a hand and I sat by her side, leaning against her arched knee. She ran her claws through my short hair, using her other hand to make short work of what was supposed to be everyone's dinner.

"Rowan," Sir Ightham said, holding a sword in each hand.

I knew better than to ask if we could have dinner first.

I squeezed Rán's hand as I got to my feet. Sir Ightham wandered further from the camp than she tended to; I was usually the one trying to put distance between us and the others. I'd asked to practise somewhere out of sight the night after we'd crossed into Kastelir, behind a row of trees or over the crest of a hill, but Sir Ightham told me that if I was to use a sword when it mattered, I had to learn to deal with distractions.

"Is everything alright?" I asked, once we were out of earshot of even Rán's ears. "You didn't have an argument with Rán, did you?"

"It was nothing personal." Sir Ightham was more forthcoming than I'd expected her to be. "A disagreement about which route to take. The both of us have too much pride."

I took my sword, relieved that things should be back to normal in the morning. If nothing else, I'd grown accustomed to holding the blade. It

114

still felt unnatural between my fingers, but I'd learnt not to grip it so tightly my wrist ached with the strain.

I wasn't quite as proficient when it came to swinging the blade. Michael said something about imagining the sword as an extension of my arm, but to me, it was more of a growth than anything that belonged. I tried. No one could say I didn't try, but my movements were clunky and uncoordinated. Sir Ightham favoured her left hand when it came to swordplay and writing alike, and though I mimicked her, I had even less luck that way.

The sword was getting in my way. I couldn't find a balance between my body and the blade to throw against Sir Ightham. For the first time since I'd picked up a sword, Sir Ightham resigned to failure before I did.

"I don't understand why you aren't making progress," she said. To her, my inability to parry a blow was a reflection on her teaching, rather than my natural ineptitude. If her disagreement with Rán earlier had shortened her temper, I was glad of it. "Your brother tells me that you were never one to be antagonised, in your village. And you yourself said you were wont to wrestle wolves. Something that takes no small degree of skill, I'm sure."

"I'm glad my brother tells you these things," I grumbled, letting the sword fall to my side.

"How would you fight, had I not given you the sword?" Sir Ightham asked, sheathing her own blade.

I'd used whatever I could get my hands on to scare back wolves and foxes, but I didn't consider them actual weapons. Shovels, rakes and fallen branches weren't the sort of thing Knights wasted their time on.

"With my hands, I guess," I said, settling my sword in the grass. "Unless there was something lying around I could use."

"Very well," Sir Ightham said.

She fell into a stance that made me want to take wide strides back, and bundling my hands into fists was about all I could do. I might've been a necromancer, might've been able to heal from anything, but that didn't mean she couldn't hurt me.

But I'd wasted her time with swordplay and had to prove myself to her. Not to Michael and Rán, not even to myself. Sir Ightham was the one stood in front of me; Sir Ightham was the one I had to picture as a wolf, a snarling, hungry thing, teeth bared.

She was better than me. I knew she would be, but had thought she might go easy on me to see what I could do. She moved faster than my eyes could keep up with and didn't lunge as a wolf would. She caught me off-guard and saw me to the ground within seconds.

I sprang back to my feet, bruises healing before they could form, body thrumming with adrenaline. I circled her, wanting to use her height against her. It didn't work; she deflected the punches I threw, returned the strikes in kind, and didn't hesitate to knock me down over and over again.

But it was better than sword fighting. A whirlwind of motion surrounded me, yet no matter how heavy my breathing became, I saw through the moment, peeling it back layer by layer.

I got lucky.

Sir Ightham hit me in the ribs as I caught her nose with the heel of my palm. I struck too hard. Weeks of frustration forced Sir Ightham back, and she landed more gracefully against the grass than I'd ever managed to. She was surprised, not angry, when she caught my eye. Blood ran from her nose and she lifted a hand to wipe it away from her lips.

"Sorry," I blurted out, as though I hadn't been in her position a hundred times over. As though it hadn't been her idea. "I'm sorry, Sir."

"Claire," she said, holding out her hand to me. I took it and pulled her to her feet, staring blankly at her. "My name is Claire."

"Oh." Colour rose in my cheeks as she smiled. I stared at her, uncertain why I was faltering. It was hardly the first time I'd been entrusted with something as simple as a name. I belatedly realised I was still holding onto her hand and yanked my own back. "... I didn't break your nose, did I?"

"Far from it," Sir Ightham – *Claire* – said, dusting the front of her coat. "You are good, though. Undisciplined, but good. Perhaps your brother would have more luck with the sword."

"Or maybe we could melt it down and make another pan," I suggested.

So long as I never had to touch it again.

Claire let out a breathy laugh and said, "I am not certain why I didn't think of that."

116

A few nights later, we left the open fields in favour of forest. Kastelir as a whole was more open than Felheim, and the ground became rockier as we headed west. But there was a point, beyond a city Rán told me was famous for its baked almonds, where spring had gathered and left a rush of blossoming apple trees leading onto sturdy evergreens, mossy rocks surrounding a winding river.

The overgrowth worked in our favour and against it. While we were hidden from the elements and any passing travellers too curious for their own good, we wouldn't see anyone who was tracking us until it was too late. Claire, who I was easing myself out of the habit of thinking of as *Sir Ightham,* was as paranoid as I'd once been about the imaginary monsters pane weren't.

That evening, Rán had me patrol the area with her. Claire had nothing of importance to discuss with her, and stayed behind to do the cooking. I hurried along by Rán's side, amazed that horns and teeth could have ever frightened me.

"We're getting there, aren't we?" I asked, not bothering to look around in earnest when Rán was there to scare off any supposed assailants. "It's been *weeks!*"

I wondered how big Kastelir could be. How big Bosma was beyond that. We'd been walking and riding for so long I was convinced we should've wandered through Canth and Ridgeth alike, and stopped off in the Bloodless Lands on the way back. I was starting to suspect that we were going in circles. From a distance, one city looked like another, and I couldn't be expected to distinguish between every tree, rock and river.

"A week and a half," Rán said. "Reckon we've got as long to go again before we get near Isin. Not enjoying the company?"

I bumped my shoulder against her and wrapped an arm around one of hers.

I shouldn't have complained. I didn't *want* to reach Isin. It was the end of Claire and Rán's journey, but held no resolution for me. Time was slipping from my grasp and through my fingers. I silently willed the next week and a half to never end.

"Once we get to Isin, what are you going to do?" I asked. "Are you going to stay there? If there's anything you need help with..."

"Might stay. Might be heading back to Canth," Rán said.

"Depending on what?"

"Depending on who," she corrected me.

She carried on her way, snapping a branch as thick as my arm under-foot.

"Who?"

I jogged to catch up with her. She didn't know her own speed, some-times.

"Aye," she said, quickly moving on. "All clear. That should be keep-ing your dragon-slayer happy, unless she's worried about a few rabbits. Now, as for what you were saying, I don't want you to be worrying about anything, yrval. There'll be a place for you with me, if you want it."

I smiled at the ground and Rán placed a hand on the top of my head, ruffling my hair.

"I'd like to go to Canth. Or stay in Isin. Anywhere with you, really!" I said. "Oh—you said you knew another necromancer, didn't you? Is it Reis?"

The thought of travelling to Canth was hardly as pressing as the idea that I might one day meet another necromancer.

Chuckling, Rán said, "Nah. If Reis was a necromancer, reckon they'd still be in one piece."

"Um?"

"Lost a leg," Rán clarified. "Hm. That's assuming you lot can grow body parts back. What do you think?"

I held my hands in front of myself and said, "How am I supposed to know!"

"Heh. Guess that's one thing we won't be finding out."

We made our way back through the forest together, to the clearing where Claire and Michael were waiting for us. They were discussing something that went over my head, the use of repetition in some book or another, and dinner was just about ready.

"Any problems?" Claire asked, idly stirring the stew.

"No one's tracking you down," Rán said, falling to the ground and propping herself against a sturdy oak. "Don't be worrying, dragon-slayer. You're still the one doing the hunting."

Claire frowned and I saw her chest rise as she debated whether or not it was worth answering.

"A-anyway, Sir, I was wondering if you might've perused Singer's

Myrosi Compilation at any point..." Michael said jarringly loudly, heading off a confrontation that wouldn't have had any bite behind it.

Claire held Rán's gaze for a beat longer, and turned to Michael and said, "One of my favourites."

He brightened and went on a tirade about an age-old debate regarding historical accuracy. Michael ignored much of what was happening around us, though I knew he had his suspicions, and kept himself occupied with talk of books and the worlds they tried to encompass. He often attempted to learn more about Rán's language, even if the words didn't fit properly in his mouth. I'd gathered that it was called Svargan, but most of their impromptu lessons took place while Claire and I sparred.

Like that, with Claire ladling out stew and Rán letting me lean against her as Michael babbled on, I was sleepy enough to believe there was nothing bad in this at all. We were all travelling for the sake of travelling and would know what we were looking for once we found it.

Yet I couldn't help but notice that I knew less about Rán than I did about Claire, reserved as she was. Rán spoke openly about her adventures with Reis and her time in Canth, but her stories felt like Michael's tales; entertaining, but not about the speaker.

"How old are you?" I abruptly asked her, blowing on a spoonful of stew.

"How old do you think I am?" Rán bounced back, enjoying what had once been part of a deer. I assumed.

I hummed, looked between her, Michael and Claire, and the best guess I could make was, "A few years older than Claire?"

"And how old might the dragon-slayer be?"

I looked to Claire for an answer. Michael was eager for a response, as well. He'd learnt to hold back on some of the more prying questions he usually dealt out.

"Thirty-one," Claire said, realising everyone was waiting for her.

"Then I suppose I'm a few years older than that," Rán declared cheerfully, licking a streak of something off her palm.

Rán turned the conversation back to tales of Canth. All she'd say about Reis' missing leg was that it involved a woman by the name of Yin Zhou who held more power than any of us could fathom, and had resulted in a large amount of gold coming Reis' way. She told the story of a pirate named Tae, who had used her sword to pry people's teeth out of their heads yet sobbed the entire time she got her first tattoo.

I wondered how long it would take for Michael to repurpose Rán's stories and make them his own creations.

I drifted off with Rán's chest rising and falling beneath me, lulled to sleep by the thought of Isin not being the end. In truth, I was only irritated by Michael's constant complaints regarding our sleeping situation because I had an advantage. One night, Rán had seen me shuffling on the spot to get comfortable against the gnarled ground. She'd snatched me up in her arms and held me against her. Her chest was broad and tough, as though she wore armour beneath her leathers, but that armour was her skin itself.

I slept peacefully with one of her arms draped across my back.

Rán moved in her sleep. It wasn't unusual: she always had to rise to take over the night's watch from Claire. I stirred but never woke all the way. As large as she was, all teeth and claws and curved horns, Rán was surprisingly gentle. When the time came for her to stand guard, I was so deep in my dreams that the hard ground didn't bother me.

But that night, something disturbed me. A twig snapped beyond the border of my foggy dreams, and not loudly enough for Rán to have crushed it. Claire always moved as silently as a shadow. I doubted any of the horses were to blame, for they needed more sleep than the rest of us, which meant that Michael was causing a fuss.

I grumbled myself half awake, shuffling onto my side so I could hiss at him to be quiet, but it wasn't Michael stood above me.

A woman froze, eyes fixed on mine. I saw the shape of an axe against the backdrop of the fire's dying embers. There was no chance I could screw my eyes shut and pretend I hadn't seen her: the blade didn't gleam but it was headed for me regardless, swung swiftly in a strong, panicked bow.

My mind reeled but my body reacted. I scrambled through the dirt, grit and stones pressing into the heel of my palms, feet scoring ruts in the ground. The axe came down, embedding itself into a tree root instead of my skull.

My mouth wouldn't open. My jaw trembled, lodged in place, and I clawed at a tree trunk, desperate to hoist myself up.

But the rest of my body was shaking, too. The woman lifted her axe again, held it high above her head between both hands, and I held out an arm to shield myself.

For a single, solitary second, the woman didn't move. A statue stood over me in place of anything warm and yielding, axe and hands carved of the same stone.

Moonlight caught Claire's sword, pushed clean through the axe-woman's back.

I finally moved in a way that wasn't to tremble. I pushed myself into a sitting position and saw Claire standing behind her, eyes hard as steel and fixed on me.

She pulled her blade free. The woman whined, but no sound followed as she crumpled to the ground. She clawed desperately at her chest, trying to hold back the torrent of blood as it pooled from the twin wounds through her torso.

She gurgled on the blood that rushed between her teeth, convulsing on the floor. Life rattled its way out of her. Claire became a statue in the axewoman's place. She stared at me, bloodied sword in hand, and the pounding in my chest rose between my temples.

I tore my eyes away from her. A hundred miles away, Michael was ripped from his sleep and hopped around the camp, blurting out, "Rowan! Are you—? Is she—?". It faded into the distance. The gushing of blood slowed and the last few weak, falling beats of the axewoman's heart made the air thrum.

Something guided me.

Tendrils of black in the dark, wrapped around my wrists, leading my hands towards the wound.

"Rowan," Claire said sternly. "What are you doing?"

"She's bleeding out," I murmured, fingers slick as they slid under skin.

"She tried to kill you," she said, dropping her sword and stepping closer.

"*Tried*," I said.

It didn't matter if Claire wanted me to stop.

I'd already started.

The wound closed. Rent muscle knitted itself together, skin sealing shut as new blood filled the woman's veins, rushing into her heart, forcing it back into a rhythm. The wound echoed in my chest. My body buzzed as I worked and a jolt tore through me as I pushed death back, hands plunged into ice-cold water.

The axewoman writhed the whole time. She didn't stop moving once she was healed. Her breath came harshly as she choked on the blood left in the back of her throat, and I was drenched in all she'd been drained of, like the ground beneath us.

"Fuck. I—thank you," she whimpered into the dirt.

She must've thought I was a healer.

Michael clamped his hands on my shoulders and I came back to myself. I didn't realise I'd drifted, but he said, "It's done, it's done." Everything shifted back into focus. Claire stood in front of me, ready to hoist the woman to her feet, and the forest was full of sounds again. Leaves rustled and small creatures scurried through the undergrowth.

I sprang to my feet, clenching and unclenching my fists to ease the sharp stab of power out of my system, and watched as Claire picked her sword back up. The axewoman froze, terrified of what Claire would do next, making it easy for Claire to drag her through the dirt and pin her against a tree.

Michael remained by my side, fussing under his breath, far too jittery to make sense of anything.

And Rán was nowhere to be seen.

"Who sent you?" Claire demanded, pressing her forearm across the woman's collarbone.

She didn't answer. She wasn't holding her tongue. She might've swung her axe with the intention of killing me, but she was too frightened to speak. Her eyes were wide and watery, pleading for help, and I brought a hand between my ribs.

Claire gestured to one of Rán's bags.

"Rope," she said.

Michael almost tripped over himself in an effort to comply. He was doing all the panicking I hadn't had the chance to.

Claire tied the axewoman to the tree. She didn't struggle, but dug her heels into the ground when Claire began to pace in front of her.

"Now," Claire said, taking a deep breath. "We have no intention of hurting you. Not again. Whether or not you answer my questions, you shall remain here until such a time as someone comes to collect you, or happens upon you. Do you understand?"

Michael brought the fire back to life. The woman's uniform was unfamiliar, dark greys without an emblem or distinct patterning, but I started when light washed over her face.

"I know who she is," I blurted out. I'd been silent and motionless since Claire had dragged the axewoman away, and everyone turned my way. Narrowing her gaze, Claire stepped close to me. I got the hint and pushed myself onto tiptoes and whispered in her ear. "Remember when we had to run away from that tavern, and I'd seen Sir Luxon? She was with him."

"You're sure?" Claire asked, straightening.

"I am," I said.

Claire nodded to herself and headed back over to the woman.

"You know who I am, I see," Claire said.

"Yes," the woman said, one heel and then the next pushing into the dirt. "... Your Majesty."

It was far from cold, but I couldn't stop shaking. Wrapping my arms around myself did nothing to help.

"I understand how it is," Claire eventually said. "Luxon sent you here to assassinate me. The man always was a coward, and must've known you'd barely succeed in slowing me down, much less stop me. Your plan is made more tenuous still when my squire wakes up, spots you, and you make an attempt on her life. Yet she is far better than I can profess to be and opts to *save* your life."

The woman slumped against the tree and stared off to the side.

It wasn't the time for her to sulk.

She nodded her head and Michael breathed a gasp of surprise, getting himself into a state all over again.

"Why?" Claire asked.

"I... Queen Aren sent me. She said to follow Sir Luxon's orders, and..." The woman stopped, swallowing the lump in her throat. "Sir Luxon sent me here. You're right! He said he couldn't say why he was doing it. Just that the pressure had got to you, and you'd gone rogue and killed half a dozen citizens."

Michael stopped pacing behind me to cling to my arm, fingertips digging in.

"And you thought assassinating your Princess a good idea? An admirable career move?"

The woman shook her head, saying, "You're right. You're right! I was never going to be able to kill you, Sir Luxon must've known that. And I didn't *want* to. I was gonna warn you, but I freaked out, okay? *She* woke up, and I realised how bad it must look, wandering into your camp at night with an axe in my hand. And anyone you travel with must know how to fight, and, and..."

"That's enough," Claire said, silencing her.

The woman had gone from being terrified to frustrated.

"No, listen. Queen Aren, she said she was going to take care of my family, okay? It's been rough for my mums lately, and I figured, figured I couldn't be doing anything wrong if a Knight *and* a Queen were telling me to do it, and—"

The woman finally shut her mouth when Rán lumbered through the trees, pushing back low branches as she went.

She froze at the sight of the axe on the ground and the woman tied to the tree. Her keen eyes picked out the blood soaking my clothes and smearing my skin and she pieced it all together. She rushed over and I wanted nothing more than to sink against her chest.

"Yrval, what happened, are you—" she started, but Claire marched over and knocked her hands off my shoulders.

"Where were you?" Claire demanded. Her voice was not quiet. "You were supposed to be keeping watch."

"I—" Rán faltered. Claire advanced on her and she actually stepped back. "I had to get away for a moment, that's all..."

Her words were weak. Rán didn't have an excuse for her. Her gaze darted towards me, ears drooping. She thought she'd be safe.

Any other night and she would've been right.

"Not good enough," Claire snapped. She did a remarkable job of being more terrifying with her words than she had been with a blade in hand. "Look. Look what happened. Look what *could've* happened."

"I was..." Rán mumbled, snarling in frustration. She took a step towards Claire and growled something in Svargan.

Claire's face paled.

"Ah," she said.

Her face softened, though her frown did not fade. She splayed a hand against Rán's chest and kept it there, before pushing her back.

"Watch her. Pack our things," Claire ordered. "We need to move on."

Rán didn't reply. I desperately wanted her to wrap her arms around me so that I could tell her it was alright; this wasn't her fault.

Claire stopped me from inching towards her. She gestured for me to follow her deeper into the forest and I moved on legs too light to be my own. The fact that I'd nearly had an axe embedded in my skull did what it could to catch up with me, but I was distantly numb, as though I'd witnessed something I wasn't part of. Michael's fussing had barely grounded me and Rán's guilt was already distant, but Claire was something solid for me to focus on.

I followed her between trees growing so closely together that I couldn't imagine Rán navigating the forest, until we came to a lake that was barely deep enough to drown in. I stared at the dim surface, wondering why we'd stopped until I remembered the blood on my shirt, on my hands and arms.

And only then, alone with Claire in the depths of the forest, did I recall what the axewoman said.

That she'd been sent after Claire because she'd killed innocent people.

Claire met my gaze. She was a world away from being numb to what had happened, and the even nature of her expression slipped. Her face was almost something I didn't recognise, but I knew, as surely as I knew I could conquer death, that the axewoman had been lied to.

I expected Claire's words to be sharp, for her to reprimand me for what I'd done, yet she reached out to me.

"Rowan. Your eyes were..." she began softly, fingers pressing beneath my jaw. "When you saved that woman, your eyes were bright. Not eerily so, but it was... unusual."

Claire brushed her fingertips against my neck and that iciness in my chest twisted deeper.

"Clean yourself up," Claire said, abruptly retrieving her hand.

I worked my knuckles against my chest and Claire took a seat on the rock, back to the lake, sword draped across her lap. I couldn't wade into the water straight away. I was trembling worse than ever, seeing flashes of the axe each time I blinked, and my arms were wrapped too tightly around myself to get my shirt off.

Claire stared into the black of the forest, content to remain still unless I called for help. She wasn't going to see the scars that weren't scars

125

riddled across my body.

I pulled my shirt off and plunged it into the water along with the rest of my body. Any rage or fear I ought to have been at the mercy of fizzled away and my stomach grew heavy, filled with all the muck and mire bloated at the bottom of the late. I scrubbed my arms, washed the blood from between my fingers and cleaned my face and shoulders as best I could, sure I'd missed most of it.

All the while, Claire remained silent and still, staring and thinking.

I stopped shaking, but the water turned the night air cool against my skin. I wrung my shirt out and hooked an arm through the neck in my hurry to get it on. I noticed things around the lake I hadn't before. The deep, scraping croak of a frog, the buzz of crickets gathering where the grass grew high, up to our knees; a breeze idly trying to steal the leaves from their branches; the dank smell of moss and peat, where the water had forgotten how to take form without any rainfall in weeks.

I made my way to the rock and sat with my back against Claire's, not quite touching. My shirt was still far from dry.

"I'm sorry," Claire said. Whatever made me tremble had rushed out of my system and was doing all it could to creep into her voice. "I ought not to have been sleeping. Had I been awake—"

"It was Rán's turn to keep watch," I said quickly, turning to face her. In the dark, I could make out little more than the line of her jaw. "You already sleep less than you need to."

"That doesn't matter. You could've been killed," she said roughly, but the scorn was directed at herself.

"Claire..." I said, placing a hand on her shoulder. She tensed but didn't shrug me off. I kept my hand there, wondering how she could think that when she'd just witnessed what I could do. "I don't think I could've. I think I would've been okay. I would've healed."

My teeth dug into my lower lip. Surely she'd rise to her feet, now that I'd reminded her of what I was.

"You could've been *hurt*," she corrected herself.

There was no arguing with that.

A faint feeling of nausea webbed in the pit of my stomach, in my throat. The axewoman could've hurt me. She *would've* hurt me, had Claire not been there. For all the fear I had felt since leaving my village,

I thought it was just that: an unsettling sensation that would never become anything greater.

Heaving a sigh, Claire rested against me. Her back pressed against mine and I had no idea what to do with my hands. I bundled them in my lap, fingers digging between the creases of my wet trousers.

"You were right to let her live. I have killed before, both as a soldier and a Knight, but I have never done so in cold blood," Claire murmured. "Had I watched her die today when I knew what you were capable of, I wouldn't be able to answer for that. She was confused. Mislead. Queen Aren can be *very* convincing, even if the assassination plot was all Luxon's idea. My mother would not see me killed before she pried answers from me."

In spite of what she was saying, a sense of calm overcame me on our world of a rock. I tilted my head back, resting it where the curve of her neck met her shoulder, and felt safe enough to close my eyes. It wasn't much darker, for the stars barely broke through the canopy, but it let me imagine that we wouldn't return to camp to find a bloodied woman tied to a tree, her axe discarded by the fire.

"I wish you'd tell me more about yourself. I know there's a lot you can't talk about, but there must be some things you *want* to talk about," I said, hands relaxing. "About your family. Your life. About *you*. I'll listen to it all."

She didn't answer. She'd already said enough, but when she rose to her feet and nodded back towards the camp, I knew it wasn't a no.

CHAPTER NINE

Rán and Michael argued as they shoved pans into bags and loaded up the horses.

"What do you *mean* Agados is still viable?" Michael asked. "We have a would-be assassin tied to a tree! What part of this plan of yours is going smoothly?"

Rán grunted, jabbing a claw against his chest.

"Oh? And you're thinking that we have time to turn around and scamper off to Canth? We keep moving. There's nothing else for it."

Michael let out a frustrated snarl that rivalled Rán's and stomped off, mounting his horse and racing off into the night. The three of us followed, and the dark of the forest behind us enticed me to look back. I hoped the axewoman would be tied to the tree for hours to come, but not for *too* long. I hadn't saved her to let hunger and thirst claim her.

I couldn't make sense of Agados. I'd heard mention of it in passing, but didn't know whether it was a town, city or something more. The next time we stopped, as late in the evening as it had been early in the morning when we'd left, I asked Claire where it was. She took out her map of Asar and traced her finger along Kastelir, stopping when we reached a patch of land half the size of Felheim on the western edge of the continent.

"It's a small, wealthy country with a thriving trade," she explained, folding the map back up. "But hardly the most welcoming of places."

I didn't ask her why no one had mentioned it before, or why Michael was privy to a plan I wasn't. Three days later, I was glad of it. Rán made an off-hand comment about Isin creeping ever closer and I realised our destination hadn't changed. They'd only wanted the axewoman to overhear them and report back to Sir Luxon.

A little more than a fortnight into our journey, we were given no choice but to pass through a city. Orinhal had grown wealthy for the bridge crossing the ravine it boasted. The next crossing would've added another three days onto our journey. Claire took minutes to mull it over, and Rán rolled her eyes and said, "Come on, dragon-slayer. It's just one city and we'll be passing through in a matter of minutes."

Orinhal was a city of intricacies. It was built from white stone dragged from the bottom of the ravine, and each spire, arch and walkway had been treated as though they were a piece of art. Swirls and far-reaching patterns were carved into the stone, vines crept along carefully planned paths, and flowers bloomed from every window and lamppost. A tower in the centre of the city rose high above all else, bringing it all together, and I had no reason to doubt that the eagle adorning the peak was cast from gold.

"*Definitely* pre-Kastelirian architecture," Michael said, for all the Kastelirian architecture he hadn't seen. That was his way of calling it *old*. "Amazing that they managed to get *anything* done with all that senseless fighting, let alone something that's held up as well as all this. Look at that! Fantastic. Wait! Is that a *shrine*?"

I absent-mindedly followed his gaze, not expecting much. The shrine in our village was little more than a weathered rock people told stories about. Our gods had been left behind fifteen hundred years ago, and when those native to the lands south of the mountains saw that my ancestors weren't struck down for their heresy, religion had slowly fallen out of favour.

But what I saw was beautiful. The shrine was made of something different than the rest of the city. The stone was sandier and though meticulously carved, it had its own distinct shape. It had either been placed there long before or long after the rest of Orinhal had been built. It was no larger than my farmhouse, but the murals on the side stood out from a distance.

The creator Isjin with her burning eyes, arms spread out to encompass the world.

And scrawled across that: graffiti. I didn't need to be able to read to know that none of the words were kind.

"Some still revere Isjin," Claire explained. "There is one in Thule, as well. A little bigger, perhaps. The Priests attempt to preach at the castle, sometimes."

"I'd heard whisperings, but I'd never imagined," Michael murmured. "*Oh*. But I did once hear something about one of the Kings still worshipping the gods. It isn't a stretch to imagine that *Isin* was derived from the name of the creator."

"Really, now?" Rán asked. "Seems a little strange to me, for a human from around these parts. Now, everyone's always at the temples down in Canth, but I figured you were all heathens here."

129

Michael's face twisted into an expression of distaste. We were standing firmly within Kastelir, yet he was stuck in his stories, entirely unlike the rendition he'd told in Riverhurst.

Rán and Claire walked ahead, making it easier for us to guide our horses through the streets. I fell back and stood close to Michael. I hooked my arm around his and bumped against his side until he looked down at me, sighed, and said, "What is it?"

"That story you told in Riverhurst. The one about Queen Kouris. You changed it. Whenever you told it to me, you always said that... that they'd allied with Kouris to scare off anyone who might challenge them. You said that life wasn't much better once the territories were Kastelir, because how can a country thrive under four rulers with four different ways of life? Things like that," I said. Michael was pleased I'd paid enough attention to him to notice the discrepancies. "You changed it because of the audience."

"Indeed," he said, waiting for me to make an actual point.

"Why did you never do that for me? After you found out what I was, all the stories about..." I lowered my voice. "About Kondo-Kana and the Bloodless Lands were the same."

"*Ah.* Well, talking about Kastelirian history to Kastelirians is dangerous, don't you think? I'd hate to make assumptions and have an angry mob of a country after me. But when it comes to all else, the Bloodless Lands and the Necromancy War, that's too far in the past to offend anyone. Our ancestors might've been from Myros, might've had to leave their homeland behind, but we've been here for countless generations. As for Kondo-Kana..." He paused, smiling with one corner of his mouth. "Necromancer or not, you aren't like her. She played her part in the war and came to suffer for it. You're hardly about to annihilate half a continent, are you?"

He was right, but I wished he had stories about *nice* necromancers to tell. About good necromancers, necromancers who used their powers to wipe out plagues and bring back people's loved ones, and hadn't ever considered abusing their abilities.

As I turned it over in my mind, someone ahead of me cried out, "*Necromancer!*"

The word hit me as an angry, sickly sensation took root in the pit of my stomach, spreading to my throat. It didn't matter that no one had turned towards me. Who else could they be talking about?

Michael started but recovered quickly, placing a hand on the small of my back as he urged me along. Claire and Rán dropped back to flank me, but we were forced to a stop. A barricade of soldiers blocked the road, weapons at the ready, while their captain pounded on the bright red door of a neat house.

"What's happened?"

I tasted bile, and no one answered me. They didn't know any better than I did, but the cry of *necromancer* sent ripples through the fast-forming crowd.

"Open up!" the captain demanded. When there was no reply from within the house, she gestured for two of the soldiers either side of her to knock the door off its hinges. A struggle within followed a great thud, and they pulled a man out onto the street, grey-haired and ageing.

"I'm a healer, a *healer*, everyone knows that!" he protested.

The crowd took a step back, as though all gathered felt the same sickness twisting their stomachs.

The soldiers took no pity on him. He was gagged, wrists and ankles bound in ropes so that he could be moved without anyone touching him, and anything that was said was done so for the benefit of the crowd.

"You have been found guilty of the abhorrent practice of necromancy. In accordance with the laws set out by Her Highness Queen Kidira, you must burn to purify the city you have polluted."

The captain recited her scripted words sternly, and the man, the *necromancer*, was engulfed by a swarm of soldiers and gone within seconds. Everyone who'd witnessed the scene threw themselves into speculation and rumour. They lamented how terrible it was that one of *those* had been living amongst them for so many years, and who could say what poisons the necromancer had exploited their trust to plant?

But nobody asked why such a terrible creature with powers beyond reason hadn't fought his way free.

I saw myself.

Moments before, I'd been talking about necromancy with Michael. Had anyone overheard us, then—

Months ago, my village had discovered that my healing powers were stronger than they'd imagined, and they'd banished me to the hills. They could've done so much more, and perhaps they'd been planning to. But

131

all this time I'd thought that imprisonment was the worst of it. Claire had told me to be careful, but she'd never said they'd *kill* me for what I was.

Or maybe she'd tried to and I hadn't listened.

Whatever the case was, I ran.

The cry of *necromancer* echoed through my head. If it were said again, all of the deceit I carried within myself would be stripped away and they'd know what I was.

I charged through the crowd, bumping into people with enough force for them to yell at me. I broke away from the main street, tearing through quiet, forgotten roads, not stopping until I was forced to. I came to an abrupt halt in an alleyway, lungs protesting, and fell to my hands and knees.

I sucked down deep breaths and fell against the wall.

I wasn't crying. I very pointedly wasn't crying. My eyes burnt but the rest of me was cold. All I could think was that they were going to burn that man. They were going to tie him to a stake and it wouldn't be over in minutes. It wouldn't be over in *days*.

I'd hurt myself before. Caught myself while cutting up vegetables or been snapped at by a wolf, and I'd always healed over without thinking about it. There was no stopping it. The man, the necromancer, would be torched as his skin regrew time and time again. His lungs would force the smoke out but the pain wouldn't fade. It'd grow stronger and stronger as the fire grew hotter and hotter, and the speed of the flames would slowly overtake the speed of his necromancy.

I pressed the heels of my palms to my eyes, trying to breathe.

I rocked back and forth. When I finally focused on the alley wall, Claire was standing over me.

I flinched as she took a seat next to me and wrapped her arms around her bent knees.

"If I had known anything of the sort would happen..." she began.

I nodded over and over, letting her know there was no need for her to say anything else. She couldn't be blamed for bad timing.

I mirrored Claire's pose, rested my head in my arms and stared towards the end of the alley, away from her. There was nothing I could say. The sickly feeling had retreated when the necromancer was taken away, but my vision was warping. Sparks of colour blinked in and out along the blurred edges.

"How did it happen?" Claire asked quietly. "Should you wish to talk about it."

"Peter, he, ah..." I heard myself mumble. I wanted to talk about it. I wanted people to know that whatever they thought about me was wrong, but I'd never been asked. Michael found out on his own and my father had been subjected to the villager's twisted truth. "He was seven at the time. His parents were friends with my family. I mean, most people were friends with each other in the village, but they came over for dinner a few times a month, and Michael used to give Peter private lessons..."

The words came slowly. I kept pausing, swallowing lumps in my throat and finding my mouth too dry, but Claire was patient. She was listening.

"He was playing outside of the village, climbing the rocks like all the kids did. Me and Michael used to do the same thing. No one knows what happened, really. He slipped, or one of the other children pushed him. Either way, he cracked his head open. He was still alive when his parents brought him to me, but only just. He was dead by the time they put him on my table.

"They started crying, begging me to help, saying there must be *something* I could do. Whenever anyone died in that room, it was always the same. I always shook my head and said that I was so, so sorry, pretending I couldn't do anything. Once they *knew* the person they'd brought in was dead, that had to be the end of it. A few times I managed to bring people back, but I'd been alone with them, or... Or I was the only one who'd seen them slip away.

"But I looked at Peter and couldn't stop thinking about how unfair it was. He was *seven*. He didn't even have all his teeth and he was just lying there, *dead*. He wasn't going to spill his gravy when he came over to dinner again, or... Anyway, more than any of that, I couldn't stop thinking that it wasn't right. I could help him but I was making the choice not to.

"So I brought him back. His parents kept crying, only it was out of relief. They were so happy to have Peter back I thought they'd keep my secret," I said.

I exhaled shakily, having emptied myself in speaking those words out loud.

"But they didn't," Claire murmured.

I turned towards her, wondering if she'd be disappointed that after so many years, I'd given up pretending so easily.

No one had their suspicions. No one had dug to uncover what I was really doing.

I could've left Peter dead on the table and carried on as a healer.

I could've helped more people, but I'd thrown it all away.

Claire looked at me, quiet and understanding in her own way. She reached out to brush the hair out of my face and tucked it behind my ear.

"They didn't. I went back the next morning and the whole village was crowded outside of the apothecary's. At first I'd thought something had happened, that there'd been an outbreak nearby and everyone wanted to be safe. I remember laughing and saying I guessed I'd be working late that night, but..." I buried my mouth and nose back in my arms, staring ahead. "Everything was boarded up. No one said anything to me, and that was that."

I closed my eyes and was back in the apothecary's. Everything was so close: the warmth of the log fire, the sharp, sweet smell of bitterwillow being boiled; the grain of the table beneath my fingers; the door creaking as it swung to and fro, people poking their heads in to say *If you have a moment, Rowan, hear there's a few heading over from Ironash.*

"It won't be of much consolation, but I believe you did the right thing," Claire said. "There are few who can claim to have helped somebody so wholly, and at no small cost to themselves."

I leant back, gravitating towards Claire.

I was running from my village, from what I was, but Claire was running, too.

I pressed my forehead to her shoulder.

"Why did you bring me along?"

She hesitated. Her shoulders rose but she chose to be honest with me, as I had been with her.

"Word of what you were had already spread. People would not mistake it for mere rumour forever. There are those who would not be so kind as to turn you over to the authorities. Those who would use you for their own ends," Claire said.

It was enough to drag me from the depths of my past. I wanted to know who those people were and what she knew.

Michael and Rán tracked us down before I had the chance to ask.

"There you are!" Michael exclaimed. The redness of his face said he'd hurried all over Orinhal in search of me. "Nasty business, this. The sooner we're out of here the better."

Rán held out a hand and I took it. I felt raw for what I'd shared with Claire, but no longer numb or dizzy. I decided it was an improvement. Rán knelt down, put her hands on my shoulders, and asked over and over if I really was alright. It'd been like that ever since the night with the axewoman. There was no end to her apologies, no matter how I told her I knew she'd never intentionally do anything to hurt me. The tips of her ears drooped towards the ground in spite of that.

It was obvious how sorry she was. I couldn't hold it against her, even if Claire did.

Michael held out the paper bag he was carrying. I peeked inside and he dug out a scone for me. I was far from hungry but appreciated the gesture, and fared better for having something in my stomach as we crossed the ravine.

Michael had procured the alcohol he'd wanted for so long in Orinhal, but we didn't drink that night. Nobody brought up what had happened in the city, for there was nothing that could be said that wouldn't sour my mood all over again, and we turned in shortly after dinner, staring up at the stars when sleep didn't come to us.

Nor did we drink the night after, or the night after that. Since encountering the axewoman we'd covered more and more distance with every passing day, cutting our sleep short and pushing our horses on.

It was taking its toll on all of us.

Three days of drizzle followed. The sky faded from one shade of grey to another, and the closer we came to Isin, the more Rán withdrew from us. She often took the lead, but had never actively pulled away from us before. She had little to say to me and less to say to Michael and Claire.

She sat by the fire of a night, toying with a coin between her fingers. It was so dented and scratched that I could barely make out the tiger's head on the back. When she slept, she curled up with her back to me. I told myself it didn't mean she didn't want me to stay with her; she'd still take me to Canth.

When Claire said, "We ought to reach Isin tomorrow evening," as she cleared the dinner things away, Michael decided he'd had enough.

He took out the bottles that had weighed him down for days, held one in each hand, and said, "It's our last night together! Our last night like *this*, anyway. Now, I know that I've done my share of complaining about certain aspects of our situation, but that isn't to say I won't miss it. It's worth celebrating, isn't it?"

Drink was the last thing I wanted, but Rán snapped back to the present and snatched a bottle from him.

"Alright, alright," she growled. "But no making a toast, you hear?"

Rán downed half the bottle in one go, which made me think it was safe to sip on. I screwed my eyes shut the moment it touched my tongue and did my best not to choke on the taste. It was stronger than any wine I'd stolen a sip of.

Laughing, Michael said, "If you could read you'd have no problem. Look: *whisky*."

He tapped a finger against the label and took a mouthful from the second bottle. He wore a brave face but I knew it'd taken him by surprise, too.

Claire took the bottle from Michael. She wasn't in as much of a hurry as Rán, but she drank as though it was nothing stronger than ale. Michael did his best to keep up with her, but to his dismay, the alcohol didn't bring any life back to the conversation. He had fewer words to share than he usually did, and after no more than half an hour, fell into a heavy slumber.

I had enough to make my legs feel light, and Rán finished off all that remained. Claire sat on the other side of the fire, making a dent in the bottle Michael had given up on. I envied Michael his sleep, but the silence was too thick to settle down in.

Without a word to either of us, Claire got to her feet and headed away from camp, taking the bottle with her. I watched her go and hoped Rán would speak to me, now that we were practically alone. I shuffled to the side, brave enough to hook an arm around hers, and she didn't rebuff me.

Not straight away.

"That dragon-slayer can't handle her drink half as well as she thinks she can," Rán said idly. "Best be making sure she's alright."

I wanted to tell her Claire could take care of herself, but didn't want to endure her coming up with some other reason to be rid of me. I reclaimed my arm and pushed myself to my feet, steadier than I expected to be. Or else the alcohol hadn't been given the chance to catch up with me.

I found Claire a few minutes away from the camp, sat halfway down a gentle hill, and the cold night air made my head spin.

"Claire?" I said, squinting through the darkness. The grass was heavy with rain that hadn't quite stopped falling, making the dirt slick between my toes. "Is everything alright? Rán was worried."

"Mm."

She hadn't stopped drinking. I heard the whisky gulp as it plunged towards the neck of the bottle.

"It's getting muddier by the second. Come back to camp," I said.

Claire took another drink and spoke as though I wasn't there.

"Tomorrow, we arrive in Isin, and see if this has all been for nought."

I sat next to her, not bothered by the feel of damp grass through my clothing. It was like being back in the fields at home. Besides, for all I'd put them through, my clothes didn't look particularly new. I was having trouble telling dirt stains from bloodstains.

Claire handed me the bottle, actions far less steady than her words, and I took it, though I didn't want any more to drink.

"I'm sure it will be. It'll all work out! Whatever you and Rán are trying to do, well. There's no way you can't pull it off between you," I said. I wanted to be encouraging but didn't want to allude to how clueless I was; I didn't want her to tell me what she was doing because alcohol had caught her off-guard. "I know I'm not exactly built for any of this, but if I can do anything to help, I will. I promise."

Claire hummed and reclaimed the bottle. It took her a moment to realise she could drink from it.

"I used to have a good life, you know," she said.

All the comforts she'd once known were a memory she was running from. I couldn't say that it wouldn't always be like that, because I didn't know that it wouldn't.

"I made myself a Knight. In spite of my connections, my family, *I* did that. I made a home for myself, in a set of chambers overlooking Lake Lir. I spent years collecting art, making it mine. I had friends. I had Alex and Rylan, I had my brothers..." she said, dropping the bottle. I grabbed it before it could roll away. In a murmur she added, "I even had a fiancée, once."

I wrapped my fingers around the bottleneck. All the warmth brought on by the whisky was gone.

"Oh," I eventually said, when it occurred to me that I should say something. "... What happened?"

"Nothing involving *this*," she said, voice losing its edge. She put a hand to her forehead and brushed her hair out of her face, fingers tangling in it. "Dragons. That's all. It was years ago and there were dragons. A task I was assigned to did not go as planned. It cannot be said that I took it well. After that, she and I... Hm."

Without looking, she gestured to the bottle in my hands.

"I indulged in too much drink, perhaps. Focused on my work too hard after that. If you are asking what happened, what single factor is responsible for it all, then I am afraid that *I* happened."

I pressed my lips tightly together and let the bottle roll down the hillside, whisky soaking into the ground as it went. She needed someone other than me to comfort her, but I couldn't leave her there. I got to my feet, wrapped both arms around one of hers, and hoisted her off the ground.

"Come on. Let's get back to camp," I said, firmly enough to let her know that I wasn't going to return alone.

Claire moved surprisingly steadily, for all that she'd had to drink. We returned to camp and she laid down without any fuss. It was the first time I'd seen sleep claim her so quickly, and supposed that something good had to come out of Michael's plans. I settled down on my own side of the fire, glanced at Rán without saying anything, and trusted her to watch over us until morning.

Isin had been our goal for so long I'd forgotten it was a city made of moving parts. In my mind, it had become a fixed spot where *something* would happen. It could've been a tree stump or a dusty rock, for all it had mattered.

But as we drew closer, the roads became busier than Praxis or Benkor themselves had been. Claire changed into her dragon-bone armour a few miles from the city and swathed a long black coat around herself, helm nestled safely in one of the bags. Rán marched on, as sullen as she'd been for days.

There was a sense of finality in the air, of inevitable dread, and we waded through it until we reached the crest of a hill and Isin spilt out across the landscape like ink in water.

It forced a smile out of me. I saw the castle at the very heart of the city, surrounded by a moat so deep I could make out the faint edges of it from where I was. It was built from stone stained light blue, the same colour the sky finally was, now that the rain clouds had rolled on. The whole city spread out from that point; the castle was the seed, and the twisting streets and scattered towers had bloomed from it.

Praxis didn't compare. Nothing could.

Michael and I were the only ones eager to press forward, but we couldn't lead the way.

The city gates gave the impression of being greater than the wall along the border, and we had no idea where to head. Charley, Calais and Patrick were left on the city's outskirts and Michael and I did what we could to be patient. Michael caught sight of a store selling mathematical tools and almost leapt through the window as he pressed his face to the glass, but Rán tapped his shoulder and gestured for him to keep moving.

This was it. Isin, the heart of Kastelir. It was a city that had only stood for as long as the Kingdom had. The cobbled streets were barely worn down by the thousands of people who made their way around, and as we followed Rán's horns through the crowd, I didn't have the time to take in all that was around me.

There was too much and it was hitting me that this was it. This was the end; it was what Claire had been striving to reach, and the reason Rán had joined us.

We passed a dozen inns and Michael didn't make a single joke about staying in one. He was as curious as I was. We cut through the city. The castle rose over the shops and stacks of houses, coming into clear view. It wasn't until we were so close that I couldn't crane my neck back to see the top of it that I realised we were heading straight for it.

Stone bridges stretched from the castle, and arches and columns, interlaced with iron bars, ran around our side of the moat. From what I could see, there wasn't any need for them. Soldiers stood to attention at the end of each bridge and the unguarded edges led to a drop of some thirty feet, before reaching the water.

"Yrval," Rán said, falling back and smiling distantly at me. "I'm sorry. Truly, I am."

I wanted to smile but could only make the corners of my mouth twitch.

"You've already said that! I told you, it's fine. I'm fine."

But I knew she wasn't apologising for what had happened in the forest.

She approached the soldiers standing guard. They didn't react, didn't flinch or look at her. They were used to all manner of people approaching them and had learnt to ignore the monotony of the city, even when it came in pane-shape.

"Now, how's this..." Rán said, digging beneath her shirt.

Claire held out an arm to stop me from stepping forward and getting a better look at what she was doing. Still, I saw enough. She took out the pendant she'd shown Claire the day we'd met her, and it had the same effect on the guards: they paled and turned to one another, speechless.

Rán held the pendant out until they relented. The older of the pair took control and unlocked the gates.

They swung open and Rán stepped through.

"What just..." Michael mumbled, looking to Claire for an answer.

"Come with us or stay here," was all she said.

She marched after Rán and the soldier escorting her into the castle.

Michael hurried after them and I barely slipped through the gate before it was closed.

There were no railings on the bridge, nothing to stop me from tumbling over the edge. I was convinced I might fall in, until I was blinking my eyes, adjusting to the dim of the hallway. Colour came flooding back, and nobody wasted any time.

It didn't feel right but I had no choice but to go along with them, feet moving faster than I should've had the courage to do so. We were in a castle. We were in a castle in *Kastelir* and we'd been let in, no questions asked.

We sped through the castle with its wide windows, drinking in the last of the daylight, stepping beneath the high arches carved into the corridors. Miles above me, the ceilings burst into blossoms of interlocking patterns. None of it made any sense. We'd only just been out in the world, staring at Isin from a distance. I could've covered the castle with

140

my thumb, yet we were suddenly inside of it, being led through one doorway and then another.

None of the guards knew what to make of us, but the soldier who'd guided us from the bridge had the authority to keep going. Servants and scholars alike looked at us curiously, and when we reached the final door, carved from oak and reinforced by iron, Claire took the bag I'd forgotten I was carrying to retrieve her helm.

She was as sharp as she'd been the night we'd met. She was a world away from me again.

Rán pushed the doors open without knocking.

We stepped into the throne room. All four seats were empty, but a man stood behind them, looking out of the windows that took up the entirety of the back wall. The glass turned the light winter-blue as it washed over him.

He didn't need to wear a crown to make it known that he was a King.

He opened his mouth to calmly demand an explanation for our intrusion, but only managed to exhale. His eyes grew wide and his hands trembled. I realised Rán too had been trembling since we'd stepped into the castle.

"Atthis," she said in a low rumble of a whisper and stepped towards him.

"Gods..." he said, grasping the orange sash across her chest and letting her pull him close. He drew a breath and said softly, as though he thought the name often, if not always, "Kouris. It's you."

PART TWO

King Atthis was a sleek tower of a man, but nobody looked tall when a pane took them in their arms.

His hair was more white than grey, and green eyes shone against olive skin as Rán placed both hands on his back. She was humouring him. Any moment, she'd chuckle under her breath and tell King Atthis he was wrong; she was a pane, but she wasn't the ghost of a pane he'd once known.

Michael grabbed my arm. He stared ahead, not blinking, not breathing. Rán's eyes faded from gold to gleaming silver, hands engulfing King Atthis' shoulders, and Claire wouldn't look at me. Her shoulders tensed. All I saw was the sharp, smooth profile of her helm.

"You've brought company with you," King Atthis said, breaking away from the moment. He did Michael and me the courtesy of glancing our way, but his gaze settled on Claire and her dragon-bone armour. "You always were one for a dramatic entrance."

He kept a hand on the side of Rán's arm, afraid to let her wander, and she said, "A dragon-slayer from Felheim. Sir Ightham. Not how I envisioned making my return, I'll give you that."

She was going along with it.

I inhaled shakily, sure I was drowning. Water lapped within my chest, but the rest of the room was still, untouched by the turmoil.

"Rán," I said softly. "Why are you...?"

Her eyes met mine but she wasn't Rán.

Not anymore.

I saw her in disjointed pieces. Tusks jutting from her lower jaw, eyes that had darkened back to gold; claws pointing at the ground like blades held loosely in her hands; thick, tough skin, a mountain of muscle twisted around bone. I wanted to scrape it together, wanted to form a whole, but it was as though a book had been opened in front of me.

The words were shapes that meant nothing, drifting in and out of focus, ink smearing itself across creased pages. It made sense to the others. To Claire, to Michael. To King Atthis. I might not have been able to tell a letter from a word from a sentence from a paragraph, but I intrinsically *knew* what this book contained.

The story of Queen Kouris.

The pieces fell away, taking the illusion of Rán along with them.

"Why..." I mouthed again.

I was furious but muted. Terrified but far from cautious.

I tore my arm free of Michael's digging grip and moved towards the woman who wasn't Rán, deceiving myself as I went. She would kneel; she would fall to her knees and explain herself, make sense of it all, and I wouldn't flinch when she held her arms out to me.

Yet all Queen Kouris said was, "I think it'd be best if we had a little privacy, Atthis."

And because Queen Kouris had never really been Rán, she turned away from me. Half a dozen guards appeared when summoned, and a wall of bodies cut Michael and me off from the King, the Queen and the Knight. I wanted to lash out at them, armed with halberds and spears though they were, but it was no concern of theirs whether I went willingly or not.

The guards moved as a unit, jostling me out of the throne room when my feet decided to merge with the stone beneath. Michael was far more compliant than me, muttering, "Well now—Excuse me, do you think you might—Rowan, that's my *foot*," as we were led through the corridors, encased in a ring of clattering metal. King Atthis had given the guards some order I missed, for they moved cohesively, with purpose.

I couldn't pick out a landmark. The walls and windows were blocked by bodies, and the only way I could look was up. The ceilings domed wherever two corridors met, but we took so many twists and turns that I became too dizzy for anything I saw to be useful. And what would I have done, had I recalled the way back? Broken free of the custody of six guards and rushed back to confront Queen Kouris?

My eyes grew heavy at the thought. We finally stopped, but only for as long as it took to slide a key into a lock. The bolts groaned opened and we were unapologetically pushed into a room, door slammed shut behind us.

I beat my fists against the door, but the guards remained silent no matter how my hands stung, no matter how many times I shouted for them to, "Open up! *Open up!*"

"Rowan!" Michael scolded. He grabbed my shoulders and peeled me away from the door. One of the guards cleared their throat in the hallway. "Calm yourself a little, won't you? The guards are only doing their jobs!"

144

"Only doing their jobs?" I shoved him away. "They, they—they *locked* us away!"

"It's hardly a prison," Michael scoffed.

He opened his arms. I had to wait for the world to stop spinning to take it all in.

A low oak table stood in the centre of the room, curved legs carved to resemble arching lions, surrounded by armchairs and sofas draped in fabrics worth more than I could earn in a lifetime. Intricate iron lamps spilt from the walls, interspersed with paintings of unfamiliar land-scapes.

All of it meant nothing to me.

"How are you so calm? We were with *Queen Kouris* all this time, *the* Kouris, and Claire knew and didn't say anything, and..."

"Yes, yes," he said, flicking my forehead. "It's *marvellous*, isn't it?"

I couldn't believe him. I was trembling with more anger than fear, yet he couldn't stop grinning.

"We have the unique privilege of watching history unfold! Queen Kouris was believed to be dead for twenty-seven years, and yet here she is, alive and well. And, if I dare say so, scheming."

He couldn't believe his luck. I knew how self-centred he could be, but he'd finally outdone himself. He cared nothing for the betrayal, if he even perceived there'd been one to begin with, or the danger we'd been placed in. He didn't consider what we may have unwittingly been made accomplices in, either.

All that mattered was that we'd stumbled into something that had all the makings of a story.

"Claire knew," I mumbled, scrubbing my hands against my face.

"Sir Ightham knows *plenty* of things we aren't privy to. Don't take it so personally, Rowan. So you've had a few conversations with her," he said, shrugging as he fell into an armchair. "It's *boring* on the road. She indulges your curiosity for something to do. Don't assume she owes you anything because of it."

I groaned into my hands. I couldn't split the flash of anger flaring up within me between Rán, Claire and Michael, so I fell on the sofa and made a ball of myself. I pressed my knees to my chest and didn't care that my boots were leaving dirt stains across the fabric.

I didn't look at Michael. Couldn't. It was only a matter of time until my anger at him warped into a biting frustration with myself. If he could be calm and rational about this, why couldn't I? I forced all thoughts from my mind until the only thing weighing them down was a dense block of emptiness. Anything I focused on left my mind creaking, threatening to spill.

An hour passed and the key turned in the lock. I sprung bolt upright, plastered to the back of the sofa. Michael, attentive as ever, had been sitting that way for some time, and welcomed me back to the world outside my arms with a slight, skittish smile.

I'd been pounding on the door earlier. Now I wished it would never open.

The hinges didn't creak. Claire stepped through and closed it silently behind her.

She'd changed, but her body was no more relaxed for being stripped of the armour. Her shoulders and elbows jutted out from beneath her thin cotton shirt, body so wrought with tension I was certain she hadn't breathed for an hour or more. I wanted an explanation from her, if an explanation was worth anything at that point, but she didn't stand in front of me as a Knight, as someone of rank and power.

She clasped her hands behind her back and set her jaw. I looked at her and felt as though my stomach had been scoured from the inside.

She was waiting for me to say something, to shout at her.

I didn't disappoint her.

I was on my feet before I'd reassured myself the floor wasn't going to slide out beneath me, hands held out to fill the space between us, fingers grasping at nothing.

"You knew! All this time, you knew who we were with," I said. My voice was not loud, but it rushed out of me like a cold, dry wind. "Queen Kouris! And you let her come with us. You let me think that she was someone else, that I could trust *you*, even if you never told me why!"

"Rowan," Claire murmured, instinctively reaching out to me.

I took a swift step back. I was sick of people pushing and pulling me, grabbing my shoulders and arms to subdue me, to turn me away from whatever truth I was grasping for. Claire's eyes flashed. She straightened as best she could, and all the weight she'd shared with Rán returned to her shoulders, now Kouris was back in her castle.

"If I had thought you were in *any* danger, I would not have travelled with Rán. With Kouris," Claire said, regaining herself. "I would not have put all I have striven for these past months at risk. I would never allow harm to come to you, or Michael."

"But you let me near her!" I protested.

Michael rose to his feet and I screwed my eyes shut. I was back in the forest, hands clinging to Rán's horns as she charged along to the sound of my laughter, ducking to snatch firewood; not at all like the shambling ghost of a headless pane I'd grown up on tales of. She'd smiled. She'd laughed at my stories. She'd put her hands on me, and they were not grasping handfuls of thick, ropey hair while she cut through the night in search of eyes to replace her own mutilated ones. Her eyes were there, vibrant and beautiful, but... but *still...*

"She's *killed* people."

"As have I," Claire reminded me.

She tried to catch my eye as I stubbornly shook my head over and over.

"I just..."

I was on the verge of forcing my point into the air between us when Michael brazenly stepped forward, eager to override my words with his own.

"It's a little overwhelming, I won't deny that. But you have to admit you have a habit of overreacting at times like these. Really, Rowan! You've no concept of how to deal with stressful situations," Michael said. He nodded his head in deep contemplation of his own wisdom. "We ought to take a leaf out of Sir Ightham's book and think about the bigger picture. She's hardly concerned with herself, is she? Now, putting selfishness aside, if you—"

My face was red and my fists we shaking, but Claire saved me from hot, angry tears.

"*Michael*," she snapped. She pointed at an armchair and he fell into it like a house collapsing. "This is not some trifling matter. The return of Queen Kouris after twenty-seven years is not something one can *over*-react to. In the future, do not presume to speak for me."

If he could've sunk into the cushions, I never would've heard from him again. He folded his arms across his chest, so unused to apologising for his words that a Knight's authority merely sent him burrowing into a thickening gloom. A minute of stale silence crawled by, and when he muttered, "... Sorry," it was almost lost to the throat-clear he forced out half a second later.

Tensions spiked and fell flat. Claire perched on the edge of a sofa like a gargoyle sat vigil, and I slumped against the opposite side, pressing myself into the corner.

"I understand that the stories one grows up with stick in a person's mind, but the Kouris of your childhood tales is a tyrant who never existed. A ghost, no less," Claire said. "She was raised in a time of war, and none escape that without blood on their hands. I will not tell you to talk to her, much less forgive her, but know that her lies were a necessity."

How many of those had there been? Had she really travelled to Canth and lived as a pirate; was Reis a real person, and had any of their adventures ever happened? I thought of her arms around me, of how easily I'd fallen asleep against her chest. How blindly I'd trusted her to take me away.

I'd wanted nothing more than to remain by her side, and I hadn't even known who she was.

"You'll have questions. Should you not wish to speak with Kouris, I shall strive to answer them. But for now..." Claire paused, standing back up. "Dinner."

"Dinner?"

"The Kings have requested we join them."

Michael perked up at the prospect of dining with royalty, forgetting that Claire had shared meals with us for almost a month. I had no desire to face them, least of all around a table, but knew Claire had taken responsibility for both of us.

I couldn't put her at risk. Not after she'd come so far.

Dinner was hastily thrown together and the atmosphere was creased, jittery. One of the Kings must've put the whole affair into motion before thinking better of it.

The banquet hall we'd been escorted to was far greater than the scattered candles allowed us to perceive. A rich mahogany table stretched on endlessly, dipping into the darkness left and right of me. Candles stood in the centre, making the trays and plates and bowls of food into something out of a painting. All the luxury Michael had been harping on about for weeks was spread out before us, but our small party forced the hall to draw in on us.

Queen Kouris sat between Kings Atthis and Jonas. King Jonas was a bear of a man with a smile wrinkled into his face. He greeted us heartily but didn't keep his attention on us for long. He couldn't help but glance at Kouris every few seconds, glimpsing the past. Her chair was enormous, big enough for a pane and then some. I wondered whether they'd brought it in especially for her, or if it'd always been there, presiding over the joy and festivities of banquets and feasts like a tombstone.

"Well! The evening has certainly taken a turn for the bizarre. Had you told me this morning that I'd be dining with Kouris, not to mention a Felheimish Knight and her companions, I would've signed over the Kingdom to prove I didn't believe you," King Jonas said as I shovelled roast beef I had no intention of eating onto my plate. "Now, Sir Ightham—*ah*, or would you prefer *Princess*?"

"Ightham is fine," Claire assured him.

"Now, Sir Ightham and I have been introduced, but who might the two of you be?"

"Michael and Rowan Northwood, Your Highness," Michael managed in a single breath, gripping his cutlery to stop it from trembling.

"Northwood?" King Atthis interjected. He leant forward to scoop up a serving of boiled potatoes, thoughts elsewhere. He was on the cusp of irritation, meaning dinner had likely been King Jonas' idea, and his sudden contribution gave Michael reason to pause.

His eyes darted around as though he'd misspoken.

"Y-yes, Your Highness," he said.

King Atthis hummed, leant back in his seat, and dismissed his own enquiry with a wave.

The dull chime of cutlery against dishes emphasised the silence we'd lapsed into, and I dared to steal a glance at the woman who wasn't Rán. There was no food on her plate, but her fingers hovered over a knife. Nobody ate, because the Kings had yet to take a bite.

King Jonas showed mercy on Michael and speared a piece of potato onto his fork. Kouris didn't take kindly to the commencement of the meal.

"Kidira isn't here," she stated.

Neither King Jonas nor Atthis wanted to answer. They glanced at each other around Kouris and warily, King Atthis said, "You have missed her by two days. She went to Kyrindval on official business," busying himself with cutting beef into thin strips.

The corner of Kouris' mouth twitched.

"Then I will go to Kyrindval," she said, picking up the knife.

"I'm not certain that's the wisest course of ac—"

"I will go to Kyrindval," Kouris repeated softly, but buried the blade to its hilt in the only raw leg of meat sprawled across the table.

The candles flickered and everyone's appetite picked up. Claire and Michael ate more than their fair share, gulping down goblets of wine as they chewed and chewed instead of speaking. The Kings shovelled food into their mouths, wanting to swallow the sticky pulp of the atmosphere. All in the most refined manner possible, of course.

I mushed a criss-cross of asparagus with my fork but couldn't eat it. The others were so busy avoiding eye contact that I found myself staring openly at Kouris. For a woman who'd waited twenty-seven years to get home, the prospect of having to wait mere days to see Queen Kidira twisted her features and darkened her eyes.

Good. Let Kouris suffer, if only because of her own impatience. Wherever Kyrindval was, I hoped the ground would shake and topple it into the sea, into the Bloodless Lands, far beyond Kouris' reach. Not that it mattered: if my blood burnt with betrayal born of the weeks I'd known her, there was no way Queen Kidira would bring herself to forgive Kouris.

I wanted to scream that Queen Kidira wouldn't want to see her. It'd been twenty-seven years; it'd be better for everyone if she went back to Canth.

King Jonas cleared his throat, sending the roar of my thoughts rushing into the crevices of my mind.

"Although her daughter is here, should you wish to meet her."

He said it cautiously. Best to broach the subject in the company of others to temper Kouris' reaction. King Atthis' knuckles whitened around his cutlery and Michael scraped his knife across his plate.

There Kouris was, an insect full of her own venom, but something inside of her had torn. She was burning from within.

Yet I couldn't bring myself to feel vindicated.

I recognised the look on her face. It was the same one she'd worn when she'd returned to camp and found me drenched in an assassin's blood. She excused herself so quietly that I barely caught the string of words as they slipped between her fangs. Her chair scraped across the floor. No one told her to stay. She disappeared, taken by the darkness, leaving a well of silence where she'd once sat.

I stared at my plate as everyone continued to eat. The colours blurred together, the greens of string beans blending with the red of peppers and the rich browns of meat. I forced down the urge to charge after her. It was nothing but bile in my throat. Kouris might've stepped into the shadows, but Rán had disappeared long before that.

"Well!" King Jonas said abruptly, trying to laugh away what happened. "Dragon slaying, is it?"

"It is, Your Highness," Claire said with a bow of her head, and poured herself another glass of wine.

"Splendid! Well, not so much the trouble with the, ah, razings, but the beasts themselves. Terrifying creatures, I hear," he said, nodding his head. "And what of you? Seen many dragons in your time?"

It wasn't until then that I realised what the Kastelirians thought of our dragon problem. To them, they were common as rodents and no more of a pest; it was a novel business, ripe for storytelling, with the potential for adventure.

"I-I'm afraid not, Your Highness," Michael managed. "We're from a village some twenty miles from the coast, and as I've no doubt you know, dragons don't dare to venture too close to the ocean. I've read that they can smell the salt on the wind from great distances and are terrified of being doused."

"Is that so?" King Jonas replied, almost disappointed.

King Atthis watched unblinking as King Jonas's attention returned to Claire. Without Kouris there, the cogs of conversation slowly fell into place, turning smoothly with every question posed and answer delivered.

"If I might ask, Sir, how many dragons have you defeated?"

King Jonas' interest in the subject was genuine, not merely polite, and Michael's confidence began to build.

Claire took a sip of her wine and said, "I have only encountered nine, thus far. The fact that I sit before you is evidence enough that I came out victorious."

Only nine dragons? I stopped staring at my plate and focused wholly on the others. Strange. I'd imagined Claire being sent to fight at least one a week; it was the sort of thing she could do in her sleep, by that point.

"*Only* nine. Don't sell yourself short, Sir!" Michael chimed in. "Few of your predecessors have slain so many. Even the Sir Priorys, who pioneered the art of dragon-slaying and worked together for decades, only took down two-dozen in their lifetimes. And that was over two-hundred years ago, when the territories' last stint of peace collapsed and... oh, well, that is to say, before the territories were united by the rigidity of Kastelir. A-anyway, it was a long time ago, before techniques were refined. You could very well outdo them both!"

He recovered from his blunder with a puff of air that made him sound winded. He rendered the deaths of two-dozen dragons as something altogether unremarkable. Claire, sat amongst us as Sir Ightham, had single-handedly slain ferocious beasts. All else was a series of dusty, fast-fading numbers.

"Really? I must admit I've only read about such matters in books. I've never had the chance to discuss them with any Felheimers," King Jonas mused, far from offended by Michael's retelling of Kastelir's past.

They continued discussing Knights who'd come before Sir Ightham while I pushed food around my plate. King Atthis didn't contribute to the discussion, and despite the film of irritation that clung to his features, Michael's heavy-handedness wasn't to blame. King Atthis glanced at the empty seat next to him once a minute, like clockwork, and barely touched more of his meal than I did. I caught his eye and he raised his brow in mute sympathy.

"I expect there was a reason you came all this way, Sir Ightham," he said, cutting Michael and King Jonas off mid-conversation.

All attention turned to Claire. She placed her hands flat on the table and pointedly looked between Michael and me. King Atthis waved his hand and had us cleared away like so many dirtied dishes.

"The guest rooms on the next level," he said to the guards who stepped out of the shadows, and I regretted not having done more than chew a lettuce leaf for appearances' sake.

"Thank you. Thank you for dinner and your time, Your Highnesses," Michael said, placing his cutlery across his plate as he rose to his feet. I nodded, hoping I seemed as enthusiastic in my agreement.

"*Well*," Michael exhaled as we were ushered out of the dining hall. His shoulders relaxed as though his latest performance had gone off without a hitch. "No one's ever going to believe what just happened."

Had we not recently lost Rán, I might've been able to see the Kings as more than just people and be as awed as Michael was.

I turned back, wanting to catch sight of Claire, but the candles lent me little aid.

The guards had no reason to crowd around us this time, but it was so late not much more of the castle was revealed to me. It was all arching shadows and dark alcoves, torches flickering and not carrying the light far.

We were taken up a spiralling staircase of stone and I grazed my fingertips across the walls until we reached a floor less travelled. The corridor was narrower, but by no means narrow. Paintings lined the walls, paintings I couldn't make out much more of than the vague shapes of faces, and a dark blue carpet sprang beneath the soles of my boots.

"Here we are," one of the guards said halfway down a corridor, pushing a door to. A short distance on, Michael was taken to a room of his own. "If there's anything you need, let us know."

Moonlight hit the window, and under the soft, eerie glow, I found a drawer full of candles and matches. I didn't light enough for the entire chamber. It was enormous, draped in shadow and wealth beyond anything I'd experienced. The bed stood like an island in the centre of the room, curtains hiding the mattress, blankets and all else, and made it into a room of its own.

There were armchairs in one corner, as fine as the ones in the first room we'd been locked in, and I crouched by the table between the chairs, leafing through the supplies set out. There was everything I needed to make blends of tea I'd never heard of, as well as a stack of sugary biscuits.

I took one and nibbled on it as I explored the rest of the room. There was a bookcase twice my height, brimming with books bound in leather, titles embossed in gold and silver on the spines. If Michael's room were anything like mine, he wouldn't so much as think of sleeping tonight.

A mirror and basin stood next to a painting of what I assumed was an important point in Kastelir's creation, though I recognised none of the figures in it. Beyond that, there was space. More space than I knew what to do with. I glanced around, ran across the room, and dove through the curtains and onto the bed.

The mattress gave beneath me, sinking to accommodate my weight, so soft I thought it might swallow me whole. In an instant, the impact of sleeping on the hard ground caught up with me, and I sunk my fingers into the pillow, forgiving Michael for all the whining he'd done.

I drifted in and out of sleep for what felt like a week, but when I bolted upright, I knew it couldn't have been more than a few hours. A knocking at the door woke me, and when I didn't move, it sounded again. It didn't seem as loud, once I was fully awake.

It couldn't have been Kouris.

It definitely couldn't have been Rán.

I poked my head between the curtains, having forgotten the room beyond the bed, and scrambled over to the door, opening it an inch. I didn't know who I was expecting. The Kings never would've bothered with me in person. Under the slowly fading candlelight, I saw Claire in the dark of the corridor and hurried to pull the door wide.

"Is something wrong?" I asked.

She stepped into the room and looked around as though she wasn't entirely certain how she'd got there.

"No..." she mumbled, bringing a hand to her forehead. "Perhaps."

She wasn't avoiding the question. She didn't want to leave me in the dark. She genuinely didn't know how to answer. She stood there, lips slightly parted, and everything about her was heavy, from the way her shoulders slumped to the darkness beneath her eyes. I placed a hand between her shoulder blades, thinking words might not reach her, and pointed to one of the armchairs.

Claire moved clunkily into the seat, convinced she was confined to her armour or something more rigid. I hovered for a moment, and busied myself with pouring a glass of water from the pitcher by the basin.

I returned, placed it on the table in front of her, and she said, "I apologise," rubbing the heel of her palm beneath her eye. "I appear to be tired."

"It's alright, Claire. You're allowed to sleep," I reassured her. "Did you... Did the Kings hear you out? That's what you came for, isn't it?"

"They listened, but I do not know if it will stir them into action. Kouris is with me, but..." Claire paused. She brought the glass to her lips without taking a sip. "They will not act either way, until they have consulted with Queen Kidira."

154

I shoved a nearby armchair so its arm pressed against the side of Claire's chair. I fell against the cushions and Claire kept her eyes fixed on me, though they threatened to stay closed each time she blinked.

"Are you going to Kering... something? The place King Atthis was talking about?"

"Kyrindval," Claire said. "And I am. I do not wish to delay my meeting with Queen Kidira, and Kouris has agreed to wait until sunrise to leave."

I tucked my knees against my chest. I didn't have the energy to be angry at Claire for not telling me about Kouris. I ought to have been angry at Kouris for lying to me. Claire had far more to worry about than what I did and didn't know, and was likely only allowed to remain within the castle because of Kouris. She'd needed her to get this far, and she needed her to secure her position.

I couldn't compromise that.

"Where is Kyrindval?" I asked, sounding out the name slowly. "What's there for the Queen, anyway?"

"Kyrindval is in the mountains. It's one of the larger pane tribes. There are some nineteen-hundred residents, I believe," she explained, drinking in earnest. I wondered if the wine from dinner was taking its toll on her. "From my understanding, Kastelir was formed on the basis that there would always be a pane on the throne. But none would take the position, after Kouris, and thus Queen Kidira consults with various tribes on relevant matters."

The only lasting impression I had of Queen Kidira was as the woman who'd ordered the death of a necromancer, but the thought of a pane tribe, of anything so close to the Bloodless Lands, quelled any of the gaping discomfort I could've felt.

"How far away is it?"

"It should take a week to reach," Claire told me. Without missing a beat, she said, "Do you wish to come?"

I froze. It had to be a trick question. Claire rested her head against her propped up palm, eyes closed, and I knew that nonsense had escaped her lips on the way to falling asleep. I was convinced she'd come to tell me she was leaving, and that I was to stay there, in that room, keeping to myself and not saying anything to anyone.

When I didn't answer, Claire kept on talking, eyes still closed.

"I suppose this is the part where I tell you you're to stay. You ask me to come, I say no; you ask me again, I mull it over and grudgingly say yes. I thought I'd save us both the trouble," she said.

I nodded, even if she couldn't see it.

"Does this mean we have to bring Michael?" I asked. "We'll never hear the end of it if we go to a place like that without him."

Claire forced her eyes open and squinted at the low flame burning above the last inch of wax. She tried to sit up straight and succeeded the second time, gripping one of the arms for support.

"I suppose we'll have to, lest the Kings fail to overlook his next slight," Claire said. Just as I thought she was about to stand and excuse herself, she slumped back into the chair, bit the back of her hand and murmured, "I am—there is much to do, and yet..."

I left my seat and crouched in front of her to meet her gaze. She continued to stare into the middle distance as I placed my hands on her knees. As gently as I knew how, I said, "You should sleep, Claire."

She was doing all she could to bite back her secrets and I wasn't going to pry. I was there and she knew that; I didn't need to say as much.

"I might..." she began, eyes flickering to the darkness beyond the window. "I might stay here."

"Here?"

I didn't give her time to rethink it. I hopped to my feet and gestured to the bed. The blankets were a little crumpled and there was a dip in a pillow, but it was still good. Better than sleeping outside, where she'd force herself to keep watch; worlds better than not sleeping at all.

"I'll be fine here," she said, patting the arm of the chair. I hesitated, about to say something else, and she pointed towards the bed. "Go on. Please."

There was no arguing with her. Any sleep was an improvement over no sleep, and with the exhaustion washing over her, she'd barely feel the armchair beneath her.

"Goodnight, Claire," I said as I headed towards the bed. She nodded in reply, disappearing into the darkness as I snuffed the candles out between my finger and thumb.

CHAPTER ELEVEN

I awoke, still in Kastelir. Still in Isin, in the castle. Night hadn't given up entirely, but the first signs of sunlight on the horizon did what they could to push through the curtains. I threw them aside and found the room empty. I assured myself that Claire was preparing for the road ahead of us, and wasted no time washing at the basin and heading off to collect Michael.

The guards posted outside my room didn't cross their spears when I stepped through the doorway. I lingered for a moment and one of them said, "Know where you're off to, miss?"

I pointed to Michael's room. They were content to let me make my own way there, but I felt their eyes follow me.

Knocking didn't get me anywhere. I pushed the door open and found exactly what I'd expected. My brother had pulled near-enough every book off the shelves and made a fort around himself. He sat on the floor, surrounded by candles, and hadn't slept at all. He'd finally been given the bed he'd dreamt of, yet he'd spent all night poring over bulky texts.

His shoulders hunched as he leant over something with a red cover, and he didn't acknowledge my presence.

"Michael, we're—"

"*Shhh!*"

He waved a hand, knocking my words out of the air. I folded my arms over my chest and waited for him to be done with the page he was on, but he kept reading. I cleared my throat and he scowled at the page.

"Take a moment to appreciate this, would you? It makes everything I've read before sound like it was scrawled by an infant. Listen."

He thumbed back to the start of whatever marvel he was reading, and I took the opportunity to interrupt him.

"We're going to Kyrindval!"

That got him to tear his eyes off the page. His expression leapt between excitement and caution, and I was frustrated with myself, uncertain what had possessed me to invite him along.

"And how do you know that?" he asked, carefully placing the book down as he rose to his feet. Either he already knew what and where it was, or had read up on it throughout the night.

"Claire told me," I said. He raised his brow. Claire's word was no good if I was the one paraphrasing it to him. "She came to see me after dinner. She said that she's going with... She's going to speak to Queen Kidira."

If nothing else, he wanted to believe me. He snapped books shut, pushed them onto shelves, and shoved as many as he could fit into his bag.

"If you're winding me up..." he muttered as he hurried to get himself ready, though I could tell he was dying to burst at the seams with talk of *Kyrindval this, Kyrindval that, can you really believe we're going?*

"You ought to be careful, you know," he said, hoisting his bag onto his back and downing a glass of water. I stared at him blankly, and after a long-suffering sigh, he was kind enough to explain himself. "*Sir Ightham*. She's a Knight, and what's more, she's our Princess. The very least you ought to be calling her is *Sir*. Surely that level of decorum isn't beyond your grasp. We might not be in Felheim any longer, but it's all the more reason to go about this properly. You're toeing a fine line. Don't jeopardise our place here by stepping out of bounds."

"What?" My hands were too clammy to form fists. "She *told* me her name. She wants me to call her Claire! And besides, I'm the one who got you invited to Kyrindval!"

Michael shook his head.

"Yes, you got our village all manner of prosperity, too, and look how *that* turned out. This may all be rather informal, but don't delude yourself into thinking there is a permanence in any of this. Enjoy it for what it is," he said. "Sir Ightham would've brought me along with or without your suggestion. Leaving a Felheimer alone in a Kastelirian castle? Unthinkable! Well, which way are we headed?"

He opened the door and peered out into the corridor. I shoved him out of the way, having no real answer for him, and caught sight of Claire outside my door, about to knock. Claire, not *Sir Ightham*. I scowled at Michael's back. He hadn't seen the way she'd looked at me when she shared her name with me.

I briefly contemplated rushing over and asking if Michael could stay behind after all, but couldn't think of a way to phrase it without sounding petty. Siblings squabbled, I reminded myself. It was just Michael being Michael.

"Good morning, Claire," I said brightly.

She narrowed her gaze and said, "Good morning, Rowan."

She was back in her long coat and leathers, holding a pile of neatly folded clothing in her arms.

"I found you these," she said, handing them to me.

I took the clothes, shuffled back into my room, and parted with what I'd been wearing. All the signs of travel were there, from frayed hems to worn patches, and though the bloodstains had turned a dark, coppery brown, there was no mistaking them for anything but bloodstains. And to think, I'd dined with the Kings dressed like that.

"Do you have everything you need?" Claire asked as I stepped back into the corridor.

I thought it a strange question, for I'd never had anything to pack, but belatedly realised she was asking if I *wanted* anything from her.

Smiling, I said, "I have everything. Thank you."

Michael was painfully cheerful as we made our way through the castle, having apparently become an expert on its architecture overnight. He was certain that this corridor was in some style or another, that there was a significance to this and that painting, but I couldn't tell if we were in a new part of the castle or taking corridors we'd already traversed.

I saw Isin through the pale blue windows, all dark shapes against the rising sun, and when we stepped out of the castle, we were taken to a bridge unlike the one we'd crossed the day before.

I could see the one we'd previously taken, or one that looked like it. It crossed the moat at its highest point, while the one we took dipped down, close to the water.

"Quite a brilliant design! Eight sides, leaving a bridge to represent each of the former territories, and four entrances for servants and whatnot," Michael hummed, breezing past the guards and towards our horses.

I was surprised to see Charley, but Claire tilted her head towards me and said, "I had them sent for last night."

I wrapped my arms around Charley's neck, letting him knock his head against my chest in greeting. Kouris towered over us, and though I'd known she'd be there, for a moment, I'd thought I was walking over to Rán.

"Spent the night in the royal stables, did you?" I asked Charley, mussing his mane. I spoke more loudly than I needed to, determined to let Kouris know that I wouldn't keep silent around her; I wasn't going to

159

make myself small, unnoticeable, in her presence. "I know, I know. I never expected us to end up somewhere like this, either. But I hope you're rested, boy. We've got another week of travelling ahead of us."

Guards gathered to usher us across the servants' bridge, and once we reached Isin, we were on our own. I didn't know what they'd been told about Kouris, whether it was the truth or not, and I didn't care. She rushed ahead, wanting to escape the city before the day started in earnest, but I followed Claire's lead.

Kouris being there was inconsequential.

That's what I had to believe.

Isin stirred around us. Windows were thrown open as the city came to life, and though it would grow colder as we headed north, it was unseasonably warm, that morning. Mersa had become Far, and once we'd reached Isin, we'd slipped into the first few days of Etha. Less than a month stood between the Phoenix Festival and us.

I couldn't imagine how the city would change in our absence. How bright it would become, all golden banners thrown from windows and lanterns left to burn through the night, as people remembered all our ancestors had lost, fifteen hundred years ago.

Nothing but open space awaited us outside of Isin. The road leading away from the city was wide and well-travelled, and served us admirably for the better part of the first day. The land north of the capital became wiry and rugged, browns taking over as grass grew in sparse patches and the trees inched further and further apart.

I was determined not to let Kouris' presence hinder me, but it did. Of course it did. I couldn't risk looking at her for fear I'd never look away. My head ached as I clenched my jaw, determined to focus on the landscape changing around us.

Claire was more of herself than she'd been in weeks for the few hours or sleep she'd been granted. She said nothing to Kouris, but she made no point of ignoring her; she said little to any of us. When our horses slowed to a stop for the night, it was Michael who passed the first few words her way. Michael who'd been terrified of her, of all pane, not long ago.

"Ah, Kouris. That is *Queen Kouris*, Your Highness," he began, voice low. "I should like to formally apologise for the story I told in Riverhurst. No doubt it was riddled with inaccuracies. Not to mention highly insensitive."

Kouris grunted, shrugging the bulk of our bags off her shoulders.

"Kouris will do," she muttered. "And there's no need to be apologising. Reckon I should've spoken up a long time ago."

Her gaze stuck fast to me. I stared at the ground and broke down sticks for firewood.

But Kouris wouldn't let it be. She kept trying to talk to me, as though there had been something true between us, something worth salvaging. "Yrval, would you—" she'd start, wanting me to pass the waterskin, but the words died in her throat when I looked at her. She'd snap open the ribcage of whatever unfortunate goat or deer she'd hunted down for dinner and miserably gorge herself on it.

She was truly Queen Kouris, with blood staining her fingers and fangs. She was the woman who'd marched through the territories like a plague, using her claws to carve out the eyes of any who crossed her path.

On the morning of our fourth day on the road, which felt like our fourth week for all the silence lodged between us, I awoke early and found Claire already up, taking care of the horses. She'd brought a brush with her and was working the tangles out of Calais' mane, murmuring softly to him as she worked. Next to him, Charley was beaming, looking prim and proper. He only lifted his head from the offering of apples on the ground to knock his nose against Claire's elbow.

"Good morning," I said to all three of them. Patrick was dozing, and from the look of the sun, we had plenty of time to spare before heading towards the mountains I thought would never come into view.

Claire put the brush down and took Calais' muzzle in her hands, using her thumbs to ensure there wasn't anything caught between his teeth. His tail swished back and forth as he patiently endured his checkup, and he shook his mane out once he was free of Claire's grasp.

"I'm going fishing," Claire said, crouching by the bags and taking out the rod she'd been making use of. "Come, if you wish."

As had been the way throughout the first leg of our journey through Kastelir, we hadn't cut through any settlements, when it could be avoided. The villages and towns there were sturdy looking things, and much of the surrounding area was the home of various mining operations for iron and coal.

The river was nestled in a valley, and from the markings in the soil, had likely been twice as wide in the autumn, when the rains were relentless. The banks were dry, and I sat in the dirt, yawning as Claire cast out the fishing line.

"Do you like fishing?" I asked as she seated herself next to me, neglecting the rock a few feet away. "It's not like we're hurting for food at the moment."

"It's a distraction."

"And that's not an answer."

She looked at me and then the river, as though she might've missed a fish tugging at the line in the second she'd glanced away.

"Yes," came her eventual answer. "I suppose."

Thinking the conversation might gather momentum, I didn't miss a beat before asking another question. I hadn't been able to talk to her, those past few days, with Kouris and Michael around.

"What's the biggest fish you've ever caught?"

She let go of her rod, rested it against her drawn together knees and held out both arms so wide I might as well have asked how big a young child was. I raised my brow, cautious of being impressed.

"... Really?"

I squinted at her and she dropped her hands, huffing a syllable of a laugh into her lap.

"What else do you like?" She stared at the river. I couldn't tell whether she was searching for something to share with me, or if I'd overstepped my bounds, as Michael had said. "Other than horses, that is. That's pretty obvious. Charley's always been a bit skittish. He never really grew out of being that way as a foal, I guess, and sometimes he gets frightened by new people. But he's always been comfortable around you. Horses know when people are going to treat them properly, I think."

Claire hummed, letting me assume I was right, and stared at the village downriver. I followed her gaze, and the longer I stared at the windmill at the centre of it all, the more convinced I became that I could hear the blades creaking as they turned in the breeze.

"Not just horses. I am fond of all animals, honestly. Ravens, dogs, cats. I have had many companions throughout my life. Hunting, swimming, cooking, I..." she murmured, exhaling shakily as she reduced

162

herself to a list. Her hands were shaking and barely settled when she wrapped them around the fishing rod.

"Claire," I said softly. Her eyes were clouded, distant. How had I never noticed it before? Her nerves had been on edge all this time, anxiety poorly concealed by her taciturn silence.

I took a chance and covered one of her hands with mine.

Her eyes flashed, meeting mine, and instead of pulling her hands back or scolding me, she said, "When Rylan and I were much younger, we would spend the warmer summer days by Lake Lir. Alex would never come with us. He was convinced something once tried to grab his ankle, and after that, he'd only ever go out on the water on a row boat."

I squeezed her hand, and she hummed, no worse for wear for having dredged up the memories.

I was about to summon a story of my own, but Michael appeared at the top of the valley and called down to us.

"There you two are! Get anything for breakfast?"

I yanked my hand back and Claire reeled in the line. Michael glowered at me as I marched up the hill, but so long as I was by Claire's side, he wouldn't risk saying anything.

Claire pored over a map with Kouris, ensuring we were still on track.

"You keep talking to her," I said to Michael, eyes fixed on Kouris. "Why?"

"Why? Because I think we ought to give her a chance, that's why. Think of all we knew to be true about the pane before we ever met one. I've no doubt the truths of the tale of Queen Kouris are few and far between."

He joined Kouris and Claire for breakfast, making an effort to divide his time between both of them. If he'd ever made a good point in his life, that was it, but I was determined to cling to the belief that Kouris had murdered because she'd enjoyed it, and convinced myself it was the sum total of all the betrayal I felt.

The further north we travelled, the fewer settlements there were to avoid. Much of the Old North was untouched, and certainly untraveled. The few dirt paths we stumbled upon were overgrown, and the lack of towns and villages on the horizon made the land seem deserted, or at least emptied; even the soil was recovering from Queen Kouris' descent from the mountains, decades on.

And now we were taking the same route, in reverse.

The mountains came into view as soon as light seeped into the sky, nestling the early morning sun between their slopes and slicing it strangely. With each step we took towards them, I became less and less capable of comprehending what was in front of us. Claire assured me that we wouldn't be close until late evening, yet I could already *see* them, great, jagged teeth rising from the horizon. Surely there couldn't have been more than an hour between them and us.

As we rode on, I began to understand why no one had set foot in the Bloodless Lands in fifteen hundred years. We drew closer and the mountains grew taller; they rose with the sun, great stone giants slowly waking after an eternity of sleep, stretching out to snatch the clouds wrapping around them. I didn't trust the ground. I craned my neck up and up to make out more of the mountains and felt myself rushing towards the summits. If they could rise and rise, I was bound to fall upwards.

"Whereabouts is Kyrindval?" I asked. I saw nothing resembling a path and doubted we'd have much luck scaling the sheer sides. "Is it at the bottom or between the gaps?"

Our surroundings became lusher around the mountains, and greens blossomed back into life. Settlements cropped up across the fertile land, and I expected – hoped – the pane way of life was much the same.

Michael snorted a laugh.

"Around halfway up," Claire informed me.

"*Halfway?*"

I gripped Charley's reins too tightly. He slowed to a stop and the others were far ahead by the time I concluded there was no turning back now.

"We'll lead the horses from here," Claire said.

For the first mile, I was lulled into a false sense of security.

A hidden path wound around the mountain, no steeper than the valley I'd grown up in. It'd be time-consuming, but there wasn't much more to it. The well-travelled path was as wide and the incline was forgiving, and I saw cart tracks in the soft dirt. I was far agiler than they were.

"And leave them here," Claire concluded, once I was looking forward to seeing Kyrindval.

We'd reached a small but serviceable plateau, home to all the long grass Charley could ever wish for, along with a stream trickling down from the mountain. Beyond that, I couldn't see where *we* were supposed to head. I warily tied his reins to a low branch and saw a mess of footprints leading into a tangle of blackberry bushes. Kouris pushed the overgrowth back, and I saw a low fence with a sign hammered into one of the posts, overgrown with ivy.

I supposed it said something like *To Kyrindval* or *Turn Back Now*. Michael hurried after Kouris, scaling the fence as though it were a castle wall, and Claire made me go ahead of her. I understood why when I got to the other side.

That part of the mountain was far drier, path made of dust and broken stone. The path was considerably narrower, and I took my first uncertain steps with my shoulder to a rock-face. There was no gentle incline awaiting me this time. I wanted to claw the ground in front of me so I didn't slide backwards. Every step caused loose stones to shift beneath my feet.

"How do people get up here?" I asked Claire, hoping she'd say *Who knows, perhaps you'd better stay here.*

"The humans who use this route to trade with the pane often live in the mountains themselves, or at least scale them regularly. It'll get worse before we reach Kyrindval, I promise you that," she said, showcasing, for the first time, her unique ability to say the exact opposite of what I wanted to hear. "These paths were made by the pane. They have no such trouble."

She pointed towards Kouris, who was coming into her own. Those strange feet of hers were serving her well. She moved as though striding through an open field, clawed toes digging into the traitorous path beneath. At times, she'd forgo taking it altogether, gripping to the harsh mountainside and finding purchase in the tiniest of crags.

"This is—it's..." Michael said, taking a deep breath. He'd been taking a lot of those since setting off along the path, and his face was tinged green. Mirroring my own, no doubt. "Well, we'll be there soon, won't we!"

It took hours. I slipped more than once, but didn't do much more than hit my knee on the ground and dislodge my heart into my throat. Claire reached out each time, placing her hand on the back of my elbow until I was on my feet.

165

I was too focused on not falling to my death while refusing to acknowledge how far there was to fall. I didn't think to look for the Bloodless Lands. My head might've been spinning, but we hadn't made a full loop of the mountain; I couldn't have missed anything.

I didn't catch sight of the walls, either, but supposed the mountains there had been forged so close together that nothing could get between them, anyway.

"Here it is. Home," Kouris murmured to herself.

For all the years she'd been gone, it hadn't slipped away.

Kyrindval unfolded in my mind as a dusty plateau covered in a sparse littering of animal-hide tents, but I'd done the tribe as much of a disservice as I had the pane.

It was enormous. It rivalled Isin itself. Kyrindval was an entire world hidden away in the mountains; there were log cabins bigger than barns, bigger than anything I'd ever seen that wasn't a castle. They were strewn around twisting, slate paths, and pane filled the streets. Dozens of them. *Hundreds* of them.

They went about their business, fixing fence posts the height of doors, carrying buckets of water I could've bathed in, and trading furniture at store fronts. I soon learnt Kouris wasn't particularly tall for a pane. An arch of dragon-bone stood at the entrance of the village, and as we passed through, I was convinced it had changed me in some way. It had cut my height in half; I was surrounded by things I knew, things I recognised, yet I was out of proportion with the entirety of the world.

How absurd the rest of Bosma must be to the pane. How it must all seem like a model of Kyrindval, made for children.

We passed two butchers and a bakery, a store selling shirts as large as blankets, and even a library. Nobody stared at Kouris. For once, their eyes were fixed on the rest of us. On the humans. The pane, infinitely varied with their curved horns, looked on us with more kindness than any human ever would a pane. We weren't novelties, not quite, but some would stop their conversations to turn towards us. They didn't stare. They nodded their heads in greeting, or lifted their brows.

Kouris moved too quickly for me to wave at the pane who took the time to smile at me, and Claire didn't fall a step behind.

"Amazing. Look at that! Some kind of... fire pit?" Michael murmured. "A communal meeting area, perhaps?"

166

The building we stopped in front of was larger than the others, in the same way a castle was larger than a cottage. The great lodge had doors taller than any pane could have need for, taller than any pane standing on a pane's shoulders could have need for, made from thick wood and decorated with carvings of dragons and pane alike. Some were the size of my fist, while others were far greater in stature than any pane we'd come across.

"This'll be it," Kouris said, lifting a hand to knock. "The old meeting hall..."

Claire stood by her side and Michael peered around them, suddenly able to see through wood. All the time passed in the world and Kouris didn't knock. She didn't wrap her hand around a handle carved in the fashion of a dragon's tail until Claire placed a hand on her arm and murmured something.

With a heave, two smaller doors opened. I hadn't noticed them, until that point. They were seamlessly carved into the towering doors, dragon tails and pane horns jutting out as they were drawn to Kouris' chest.

Inside, statues of pane decorated the hall, close to the rafters miles above. Dragon-bone was used in place of their horns and claws, made brilliant by scattered torchlight. A single table had been dragged into the centre of the room, higher and longer than the one the Kings used to host feasts.

Four pane and two humans were gathered around the table. A dark woman with her hair worked into dreadlocks sat at the table, eyes fixed on one of the scrolls a pane was pointing to, and I knew she couldn't be anyone but Queen Kidira. I thought I'd never be able to take my eyes off her. My gaze was anchored there by the weight of what Kouris felt.

I blinked and the spell was broken.

"This is a private meeting. If you would be so kind as to leave," the oldest of the pane said, Mesomium perfectly pronounced. It was the sight of humans that put them on edge, and their gaze only briefly flickered over Kouris. They didn't recognise her at all.

Queen Kidira lifted her head, expression severe. She wouldn't be as polite as the pane.

The woman behind her, broad-shouldered and tall enough to rival a pane, was far more relaxed than anyone else in the hall. An axe hung at her hip, but from what I could tell, she'd forgotten it was there. The thick scars lining her face told me she'd had no qualms about protecting people in the past. The pane hurried to pull their scrolls and books into tight piles, protecting whatever secrets Queen Kidira had been studying. She wasn't dressed to fit her station, for there was no crown atop her head and her clothes were plain, and the woman behind her wasn't wearing anything resembling a Kastelirian uniform.

She stepped away from the table, arms spread out in half a shrug.

"My friend here, they are offering good advice, and they are offering it for free!" the woman said. "You are being smart, yes, and turning back. We are appreciating this very much."

Queen Kidira rose to her feet as she spoke, moving as though the statues above were pulling at strings. Kouris tore forward, a shadow carved free from the soles holding it down, and it was only Claire's hand held in front of me that told me I'd tried to move as well.

Kouris could've engulfed Queen Kidira. Instead, she fell to her knees, knocking dust free from the rafters. She bowed her head so low that her horns scraped across the floorboards, and neither the pane nor the woman who'd been standing guard knew what to make of it. We remained as still as the statues above, save for Queen Kidira, whose fingers betrayed her.

She reached out a hand, not believing her eyes, but didn't dare to touch Kouris, lest the contact cause her to fade. My nails pressed crescents into my palms and I silently willed Kidira to move. Not for Kouris' sake, but her own. When she neither breathed nor spoke, Kouris at last looked up.

Kneeling though she was, Kouris was still taller than Queen Kidira. She held out a hand, as terrified to move as Queen Kidira was. Eventually, Kouris' palm found her face, fingers trembling, unable to believe that Queen Kidira was really there; unable to believe that it had been so easy; or that it hadn't been easy at all, but that she'd finally found her, in the end.

Kouris' golden eyes gleamed, but Kidira's were made of stone. Her expression was carved of much the same. Finally letting out a shaky breath, Queen Kidira wrapped her fingers around the back of Kouris' wrist. Unblinking, Queen Kidira shook her head over and over, lips parting, though words refused to come to her, at first.

Until an ember that had never quite gone out rose up, roaring behind her ribs.

"*Leave*," she said darkly, and even the statues flinched.

CHAPTER TWELVE

Kouris' fingers curled towards her palm.

"Leave, *leave*," Queen Kidira repeated as she took steps away from Kouris, and though Kouris rose to follow her, her gaze had become steel, or ice.

All Kouris saw was her own reflection and she could do nothing but shrink from it. She stared at the ground, awaiting some admonishment, expecting a reprimand, a lecture, to fill the gap left by years lost to a lie. Queen Kidira froze, unable to move until Kouris did, and finally shook because of it.

Still, Kouris refused to leave.

"You are *dead*," Queen Kidira said through grit teeth.

Kouris held out her hands, bartering for peace, and said, "Yet I stand before you. I am here, and I—"

"And you are twenty-seven years too late."

Queen Kidira fell into her seat as though there was nothing left inside of her but bones. The woman, her guard, was the first of us who dared to move, but she didn't rush for her weapon. She knelt before Queen Kidira, hands on her knees.

"My Queen," she murmured in her thick accent, knowing that the meaning of words would escape Queen Kidira, shaken to the core as she was. Queen Kidira stared at the tabletop, though the scroll she'd been focused on was no longer there.

Her guard placed a hand on her cheek, turning her head towards her. For a moment, Queen Kidira showed the slightest sign of weakness; she leant into the touch, eyes almost closing; but it was only a moment. She recomposed herself in an instant. Her guard shot to her feet and sauntered our way, but the pane with the long, curved horns stepped in front of her.

"Kouris," they said, finally recognising her. Any softness in their eyes was drowned out by remembrance. "You aren't welcome here. You know that, Kouris."

"Now, Zentha," Kouris said, caging a growl behind her fangs. "I'm not here to start any trouble..."

She wasn't lying. She didn't have the strength to form a fist, let alone throw it at anyone.

170

"Leave. Leave the tribe," Zentha said, no small amount of force behind their words.

The growl escaped her. With one last look at Queen Kidira, she thundered out of the lodge, doors bursting open and slamming in their frame. My heart raced, desperate to keep up with her.

I forced myself to stay still.

It wasn't my fault. It couldn't be. No matter how much I'd wanted Kouris to hurt, to suffer, I couldn't have caused this. Kouris was the only one to blame. Kouris was finally paying for the deceit she'd sown. The thought should've strengthened me, but it didn't.

Silence battled with confusion as we stood there, echoes dying down. Claire stepped forward, meaning to approach Queen Kidira, but her guard took a swift step to the side and blocked her path.

"I apologise for being here at such a time, I truly do, but I have come to speak with Queen Kidira."

The guard placed both hands on her hips and squinted at Claire. The scars riddling her face cut across the bridge of her nose, the line of her jaw and the corner of her mouth, but they didn't mar her brown skin. If anything, they made her more of herself. Under any other circumstances, she would've been smiling brightly.

"How is it that you are knowing where my Queen is, hm?" she asked, lifting her brow. "And who are you thinking you are! You are barging in, and you are not even knocking."

"Again, I can only apologise. My name is Ightham, and—"

"Ah!" The woman snapped her fingers, pleased that all the pieces in front of her were slotting together so neatly. "Sir Ightham of Thule, yes, of course, I am hearing of you. The accent, it is giving you away. You are not as tall as they are saying, but you are living up to all other descriptions! I am hardly being prepared. But you are doing such remarkable work, yes. We are meeting under these circumstances, and it is a shame."

"Indeed," Claire managed after a moment. Michael nudged me in the side, wanting me to see the confusion scrawled across his face, but I kept my eyes on Claire. She hesitated before making a guess of her own. "Commander Ayad, perhaps?"

"No, no. You are leaving behind the title, as I am knowing you are fond of doing, Princess, and you are calling me Akela. This is fine," the

Commander said, shaking Claire's hand. "Now that we are knowing we know each other, I am needing to know how and why you are being here. Otherwise, I am having to pick up my axe, and I am thinking you are better at slaying dragons than facing Commanders, yes, Ightham?"

Akela said it as warmly as anyone could issue a threat, and Claire knew there was no malice behind it.

"We are here with permission of the Kings," she said, dropping her hand to the sword at her side. She unhooked it from her belt and handed the whole thing, blade and sheath, to Akela. She confiscated it without taking her eyes off Claire. "There are important matters to discuss, but I understand that the Queen will likely be here for several days. It might be wise to reconvene at a more convenient time."

Akela inspected Claire's sword, half drew it and admired the metalwork, and handed it back to her. For whatever reason, she'd decided Claire was trustworthy.

Her axe remained at her hip and what passed between them was lost to me. The pounding between my temples grew and grew, and I couldn't accept that they were going to entangle themselves with whatever news Claire had brought; that they were going to move on without blinking and pretend Kouris hadn't just stood before Queen Kidira for the first time in twenty-seven years.

"I've got to..." I murmured, but no one was listening.

I didn't know what I had to do, beyond running. Michael called out, "Hey, where do you think—" but I shouldered the door open, losing his words to the pulse of Kyrindval. Kouris was already out of sight, and it wasn't until I was frantically looking for one pane amongst dozens that it occurred to me I'd left for her.

She'd said she wasn't there to cause trouble, and she'd been true to her word. I found her outside Kyrindval, through the dragon-bone arch, slumped in the long grass. Her eyes were grey as ash and a pallor had overtaken her, the likes of which I'd only ever seen paired with the cold sweat of a raging fever.

I didn't stop until I was in front of her, stood squarely between her feet. She sat with her legs in front of her, arms folded across her knees, putting us on the same level. She looked at me but didn't react. She'd been trying to get me to talk to her all week, but her ears didn't twitch, and she barely blinked. She looked at me as though she was still Rán,

172

and I didn't want to forgive her.

But I didn't want to hold my tongue for any longer.

"You left her," I said, unable to tell if I was aching for Kouris or Queen Kidira. "You left her for a really, *really* long time. I haven't been *alive* for that long. What did you think would happen?"

My words didn't wound Kouris. After all that had unravelled in the great lodge, nothing could. I wanted the answers, I desperately did, and her lips twitched into something that wasn't a smile. She must've imagined seeing Queen Kidira hundreds and thousands of times over, but it'd never played out like that in her head.

"She was young when I met her. Just turned twenty, actually. Three and a bit years later, we were married. We were happy. We had our country and we had each other. But—" Kouris drew in a breath, crinkling her nose. "Three years after that, I was gone. And look at her now! She is grown. She is more of a Queen than ever, and she has a daughter. She has her life, her Kingdom. Maybe I never should've come marching back like this."

I wrapped my arms around myself as she spoke, fingers gripping and twisting the fabric of my sleeves.

"Why? Why did you do it?"

I didn't understand, and I wouldn't understand no matter what Kouris told me. Still, I needed to make sense of someone running halfway across Bosma to leave behind the person they loved the most.

"Because more than anything, Kidira loves Kastelir. Her blood's in the ground. It's part of the soil, holding everything together. Say I came wandering back here, say everyone knew that I hadn't faced my punishment. What do you reckon would be happening to Kastelir? Now, it's not exactly the most stable of countries at the moment. It's teething. You can't imagine what it was like back when it was newly forged, yrval. Before Isin was much more than an idea. The people would've become restless. We would've plunged straight back into war."

She couldn't have known that. There had to have been another way around it. She could've *told* Queen Kidira she was alive, could've come back not as a Queen, but just another pane. She could've—

I flushed the thoughts from my mind and bit the inside of my mouth. One look at her told me that if she could've done any of that, she would've.

I fell in the grass next to her. I sat close enough for my shoulder to bump her elbow, and though I told myself this was Queen Kouris, the person who'd pried eyes from their sockets, I couldn't force fear to spike in my chest.

"... How old *are* you?"

Kouris let out a sharp breath through her nose.

Definitely not a few years older than Claire.

"Fifty-eight. Still plenty young, for a pane," Kouris explained. "You saw Zentha in there, aye? They must be coming up on three-hundred now, and that's hardly pushing it. It'll be a good century before my horns start spiralling back like that."

I couldn't imagine anyone living that long. Even with the aid of a healer, a human wasn't likely to make it beyond two hundred. The body just stopped, eventually, in spite of anything pushed into it, anything ripped out.

"What about your family? Are they down there?"

I pulled my knees to my chest, chin propped atop them. It felt *right* talking to Kouris, even if everything that had unfolded clung to us like grime, and we were far from smiling.

"My family? Nah, yrval. You need to stop thinking like a human," she told me. "All this business with parents and siblings and cousins. We don't have anything like it. Don't need it, either. The entire tribe looks after the hatchlings. That's the only way it can work with us. We don't exactly, ah..."

Kouris licked her upper lip, brow furrowed as she searched for the words. I perked up, eagerly waiting for her to continue.

"Now, it's my understanding that humans carry on their legacy in pairs," she said, clearing her throat. "But the pane, we're needing only ourselves."

"I... Okay?"

I knew how childbirth worked. I'd watched over a few of the riskier ones back in the village and helped birth plenty of lambs and calves, and though I didn't understand everything Kouris was saying, I distinctly didn't want to ask any more questions.

We stared down at Kyrindval, at the life within the fields surrounding it, bustling with crops taller than any we'd ever grown in my village, gentle slopes covered in goats and deer. The buildings were all relatively

174

low, none of them having more than one floor, and from a distance, I could see that the great lodge was shaped like a claw. The cabins closest to it were the oldest, the stone of the street dark and worn, while those around the edge of Kyrindval were still being built, roofless or without walls, making the tribe greater still.

I looked upon Kyrindval for the first time, took in the twists and turns of the streets as though they'd always been there, but when Kouris took in the tribe, she saw how it, like her, had changed over the past thirty years.

"Yrval, listen..." Kouris started in a low rumble.

"Don't," I said softly.

If she apologised again, I'd have to tell her it was alright, because I felt bad for what had happened with Queen Kidira.

Kouris let the view reclaim her. After long minutes spent separating unfamiliar streets from ones she'd wandered down, she said, "Wanna see something?"

"See what?"

Kouris was exiled from the village and I'd taken in all I could get out of the fields. That alone was enough to pique my interest.

"You'll have to be following me," she said, hoisting herself to her feet.

She set off, intent on reaching her destination with or without my company. I could only stare at Kyrindval for so long. I hopped to my feet and jogged to catch up with her. Even at a leisurely pace, without crowds to wade through, Kouris was a struggle to keep up with.

"What is it?" I asked, unimpressed with the field we were trundling through. There were goats around us, tended to by a handful of pane wearing streams of white cloth around their leathers. They waved to me and squinted at Kouris, but otherwise let us pass unnoticed. "You won't get into trouble, will you?"

"Don't reckon so," Kouris said, colour returning to her face. "It's only Kyrindval itself I'm not welcome in. The rest of this land, that's belonging to the dragons."

Dragons.

I'd trekked to the mountains the pane lived in, but hadn't spared a thought for any dragons. I'd dismissed the notion of them altogether, along with all other vicious rumours about the pane, but I saw where

175

Kouris was headed. One of the lower mountain peaks came to a stop a hundred feet above us, and Kouris led me right to it.

An entrance was carved into the rock, an arch covered in dragon-bone, and while I was willing to be a distraction, if a distraction was what Kouris needed, I wasn't prepared to make bait of myself.

"There are dragons in there," I said, slowing to a stop. "You brought me here to see *dragons*."

"Don't be worrying yourself, yrval," she said, waiting for my feet to work again. "I'm sure they've already eaten today."

My bones did their utmost to rattle their way free of my body as something other than Kouris' grim reassurance drew me towards the cave, through an entrance high enough for any pane.

I expected darkness and was met with fire. The whole mountain had been hollowed out by dragon's breath, walls glossy like water frozen mid-stream, ledges left behind to roost on. Fires burnt brightly on some, and sunlight streamed in through what had once been the summit. There were no shadows for me to hide in. I saw the dragons and the dragons saw me.

There was no comprehending the size of them. My mind struggled to compare them to a house, a barn, a mountain, but these were living, moving creatures, scales glinting in the light as they breathed in and out, in and out, most of them dozing happily. A few peered down at me, and I saw their fangs without them having to bare them. They could've snapped their teeth and swallowed me whole.

"Kouris..." I breathed. I flailed my arm blindly behind me and she held out a hand, letting me squeeze it.

Dragons. I was standing inside a mountain, surrounded by dragons, and Claire had *slain* these beasts. They'd ravaged our country, razing entire cities to the ground, and now they were blinking eyes bigger than my head at me.

"Easy now," Kouris murmured, slowly crouching beside me. "When it comes down to it, they're animals, same as any other. Same as you and me. Treat them with a little respect and don't go sticking your arm in their mouths and you should be fine. Now, you see the big one up there?"

Kouris pointed to the largest of the ledges, where a dragon bigger than the others was rested, jaw propped up against its front legs. Its wings spread around it like a cloak, and it could've flicked any of the other dragons out of the air, no matter how immense they were. Sturdy horns curved back, shaped like a pane's but as white as Claire's armour, and each one of its purple scales served as a shield.

"That'd be the fhord. The leader, in a tribe such as this one," she explained, then gestured to the other dragons that had begun to stir with curiosity. "As for these, they're the kraau. Wherever you go, they're always making up the majority of any tribe. Reckon that's what you humans think of when you think *dragons*."

Truth be told, when I heard the word *dragons*, I expected something horrific. I'd pictured them as ungainly beasts, jagged teeth jutting out over lipless mouths, red eyes glowing; scales dripping with ooze, a stench that would thicken in my throat; but the kraau were nothing short of remarkable.

They were rich orange in colour, with long, thin bodies cloaked in wings that stretched from their shoulders to tails. Like the fhord, they were neat looking creatures, each scale placed as deliberately as the design of Claire's armour was meticulous. They, too, had long, curved white horns, as well as a spike longer than my arm at the tip of their tail.

There was no shortage of fangs and claws about the cave. Their teeth made Kouris' look blunt, and I thought that if Claire could take down creatures that exuded strength in their idle moments, she was either stronger or faster than a dragon, or something else it was not.

I wondered if I'd ever looked at her properly before.

"And *here*..." Kouris whispered, drawing my attention back to the ground.

I couldn't see anything other than kraau, at first. Bones from the dragons' last meal clattered behind a pile of rocks, and I caught a flash of swamp-green. A tail swished out and Kouris brought a finger to her lips, signalling for me to be very, very quiet.

I knelt down. I didn't know why I made myself smaller around the dragons, but I did. Slowly enough that I could've mistaken it for a boulder, the dragon came into view. It was far smaller than a kraau; if not for its wings, it would've been smaller than Charley. Its legs were short, body low to the ground, and it moved like a lizard, twisting towards us.

I squeezed Kouris' hand so tightly I would've broken a human's, but

I didn't turn and flee. I didn't want Claire to know that I'd run from a dragon. It crawled closer, scales speckled, and wrapped its long tongue around my wrist.

I started, but I wasn't scared. The creature was as timid as the lambs back home. I let go of Kouris and carefully placed a hand on the dragon's snout, watching as its nostrils flared.

"And this here is a yrval," Kouris said softly. "They aren't very strong and you're not gonna see 'em fly all that high, but their flames burn the hottest. They could breathe in the sun, if they wanted to."

I smiled as I grazed my nails across the yrval's scales and by some twist of fate, my nerves outlasted a dragon's.

Outside the cave, once my heartbeat was no longer deafening me, I said, "Is living so close to dragons really safe? Aren't they always attacking Kyrindval?"

"Not exactly. See, that's a problem you lot are only having in Felheim," Kouris explained. "Here the dragons and pane have to get along. We make use of their teeth once they're dead, but we're not about to pry 'em out of their jaws. So we take care of the dragons, if they ever fall ill, and make sure there's plenty of food around for 'em. It's all about give and take."

"Use them for *what*?"

"Take a tour of the tribe, some time," Kouris said, patting me on the shoulder.

I didn't flinch.

I stayed with her that night, in the hills outside of Kyrindval.

She told me to head back, that the pane would ensure I had somewhere to stay, but I wouldn't allow myself to go. I sat on the opposite side of the fire, cooked some of the goat meat she'd procured, and didn't say much of anything before exhaustion claimed me.

As darkness fell, the windows in Kyrindval began to glow, and at the heart of the tribe, a fire burnt in a deep pit. The pane trickled out of their homes, greeting each other in the streets and heading to the fire pit, where they sat in a circle. I wondered if we'd come during a festival, for many of the pane were clearly prepared for *something*, and Kouris said, "This happens every night, more or less. Once work is done, the pane get together and put on shows. Singing, dancing. Bit of poetry or a play, sometimes. They even bring new dishes around, from time to time."

I couldn't make out much of what was happening, from where we sat. My eyes were heavy, adrenaline leaving my body and reminding me how much my legs ached. I was half-asleep before I thought to curl up in the grass.

The sun had been up for hours by the time I joined it. Well-rested, I stretched out and headed back to Kyrindval without much more than a hint of a wave in Kouris' direction. On the way, I came across a group of younger pane. They were all taller than I was, but I doubted they were much older than eight or nine. Their horns had yet to start growing and their tusks barely touched their upper lips. A few of them were brave enough to wave at me, but immediately became bashful when I waved back.

"Thank you! Oh, and good morning," I said as they scrambled to let me pass. They didn't understand Mesomium, but my meaning was clear enough.

I started to notice patterns. The pane all wore a swathe of colour over their leathers, and I took it to be some manner of uniform. The three pane carving wood for furniture donned a dark green, and those in the butchers wore a soft, light red. The colours ran from the lodges, too, banners draped across awnings and hanging from windows.

Outside the great lodge, where I thought I'd have the most luck finding the others, one of the most amazing things I'd ever witnessed was happening.

Four pane had gathered and Michael stood amongst them, *listening* as they spoke. The pane went on talking for five, six minutes, stumbling over their words and injecting long pauses into the conversation, and not once did Michael speak over them or presume to fill the missing words. He was enthralled. He didn't notice me approach until the tale the pane were sharing with him was over and he had heartily thanked them for the information.

"Rowan! There you are! You can't begin to imagine how much the pane have to share, or how willing they are to do so," he said brightly, hooking an arm around mine. I wanted to ask where Claire was, but he was in such high spirits it wasn't worth interrupting him. "Look here. See all the animals carved above doorways? All the coloured banners? The pane don't have families as we do. Something about, ah, self-contained reproduction. Rather, they choose sigils of their own, as well as

179

colours, and sift from lodge to lodge with one of the same markings, until they find a comfortable home. Amazing, isn't it? Could you imagine turning up at our baker's house because you shared a sigil and not being asked what you thought you were doing, dragging all your things in?"

"The pane are a lot friendlier than we are," I hummed. "I think the colours have something to do with work? I saw a lot of pane working together, and they were all wearing the same coloured cloth."

"Oh, hm. Perhaps," Michael allowed. He wasn't as interested in speculation when it wasn't coming from a pane. "Had breakfast yet? They gave me... *something*, something baked, and I think you'd like it."

"Not yet." I took my chance to ask, "Have you seen Claire?"

"She's probably busy, you know," he said, releasing my arm. I lifted my brow and he sighed, gesturing vaguely to one of the nearby lodges. "But I believe she spent the night over there. Still, Rowan. Let her get on with her work, alright? She came here for a reason."

I thanked him all too cheerfully and rushed off, not giving him the chance to lecture me further. Claire would tell me if she was busy. All I wanted was to let her know I hadn't toppled off a mountain or been snapped up by a dragon.

And perhaps ask if she wanted to get breakfast.

The lodge was a lot more intimidating once I was in front of it. I had to push down hard to scale the steps, and the door handle was level with my head. I hesitated, not knowing the words to explain I'd got the wrong lodge, should a pane answer, and gathered the courage to knock.

No one answered.

I knocked again and it was much the same. I had more luck with the handle. The door swung open, revealing a wide hallway. A handful of fur cloaks were hung from pegs by the door, and I took tentative steps inside, glancing into open rooms as I went.

There was a table that could've seated a dozen humans in the kitchen, and the counters were covered in baskets of unwashed vegetables bigger than any I'd seen before. The other rooms contained more gigantic furniture; sofas bigger than the bed I'd slept in at Isin, bunk beds that would be like climbing a tree to get atop; all of them swamped with furs, tables cluttered with cups the size of bowls.

The pane who lived there were gone for the day, and I took my chance with the closed door.

I knocked and Claire answered with words I didn't understand.

"It's me," I called. "Sorry."

There was a shuffling from within and Claire hurried to the door.

"Rowan," she said, looking over me to ensure I was still in one piece. "Did you spend the night with Kouris?"

"I did. I'm sorry I rushed off like that. I don't know what came over me. I just... well, you had important things to do, so I guess it doesn't matter."

"Someone ought to have been with Kouris. Had I not thought you safe with her, I would've looked for you," Claire assured me. I bit my tongue, not yet bold enough to mention the dragons. "I have important matters to tend to today, as well."

"Oh. Right. Sorry, I thought you did. I just wanted to let you know I hadn't gone anywhere," I rushed to explain, stepping back out of her way.

Claire hummed, straightening out her sleeves.

"I'm free until midday," she added. "Have you had breakfast yet?"

I shook my head and did my utmost not to trip over my feet on the way to the pantry.

"The pane said I was to help myself. I'll be certain to reimburse them before we leave."

Probably tenfold, knowing Claire.

She rummaged around the shelves. They were too high for her to comfortably reach, but she didn't let that stop her. She pushed herself onto tiptoes, put one hand on the edge of a lower shelf, and hoisted herself up high enough to grab what she wanted.

I'd been dreading the prospect of chairs as tall as I was, but Claire had no intention of staying in the lodge. She wrested an empty basket from one of the cupboards along the floor, filled it with rolls the size of my head and cut great slices from a wheel of cheese so large she had to put all her weight on the knife to break through the rind.

"What?" she asked when I grinned at her and the basket.

"Nothing. Nothing!" I said, propping the door open for her as we left. "I wasn't expecting to go on a picnic. That's all."

Claire frowned at the enormous basket filling the width of her arms.

"It's nice out. It seems a shame to waste it," she muttered. "Would you rather eat indoors?"

Claire was seconds away from putting the basket down and embarking on a quick meal in the corridor, so I rushed out of the cabin and lured her into the sunlight.

She was right. It would've been a shame to waste the morning inside. It wasn't as warm as it'd been in Isin, but the atmosphere more than made up for that. The bustle of Kyrindval served as a constant, relaxing background noise, and friendly faces knocked the last of the morning chill out of the air.

As we strolled through the tribe, Claire pointed here and there, saying, "This is where the apothecaries work. There aren't healers amongst the pane, leaving them to rely solely on bitterwillow," – "One of the schools, though they only gather a few times a week," – "A library. Your brother will be pleased." I'd no doubt I'd forget what was where within minutes, but I listened intently, looking at Claire more than I did the buildings.

Something about her was lighter, now that we were in Kyrindval. Perhaps Queen Kidira had been willing to hear her out.

We stopped on the edge of the tribe, where a crescent of steps was carved into a hillside. Claire sat down, and the steps served as seats. They arched around a flat, paved area, and Claire was too busy attending to breakfast to explain its purpose. I would've been sorry for the tour to end, had I not been ignoring the way hunger dug its claws into my stomach for the better part of half an hour.

"Was it like this?" I asked, taking a slice of the bread Claire had carved from a roll using a knife verging on the size of a short sword. "The pane tribe you stayed in, that is."

Claire popped a crumb of cheese into her mouth before slicing a generous portion free.

"As similar as Eaglestone and Praxis are to one another," she settled on.

A handful of younger pane crept up on us. Their leader, a girl with the first signs of a right horn showing, inched her way to the steps. I raised a hand to wave and they shrieked, scattering like ants. It wouldn't be long until they towered over us, but I wondered what stories pane were raised on; whether they flinched at the thought of humans, ever-warring, ever turning on each other.

"Why did you go there?" I asked through a mouthful of bread. The

182

crust was so thick my jaw instantly ached, and I tried to swallow too much at once. "Were you studying the dragons?"

"Not quite," Claire said. She wasn't struggling with her food. Then again, she had experience. "I had a very... *sheltered* upbringing, in many senses of the word. Whatever I needed or wanted was mine. I never had to worry about there being enough to eat, or somewhere safe to sleep. The King and Queen decided that I ought to experience something of a more rugged way of life, to make me a better... What is it?"

"That's not it," I said, squinting at her. Claire had a habit of carefully selecting her words and holding back as much as she could, but she was burying the truth even deeper than ever, this time. "That's not why you went to stay with the pane, is it? You're not telling me something."

Claire tightened her jaw, tore off a chunk of bread, but didn't bring it to her lips. I went on chewing my breakfast, legs crossed, and kept my eyes fixed on Claire until she continued.

"Fine," she huffed. "I was sent there to instil myself with a sense of discipline."

"Really? *You*?"

Claire pressed two fingers to her temple, more determined to defend herself than she had been before.

"I was raised alongside two Princes. I grew up in a castle, my every whim catered to. I thought I could do as I pleased, entertain women indiscriminately, and drink mindlessly. I was *nineteen*," she protested.

I laughed into my breakfast, and it was worse than anything I could've said in reply.

"I doubt you were much better at that age," Claire grumbled.

"That was only four years ago for me! Besides, I was *working*. I was far too busy putting people back together to get myself into trouble. If I wasn't healing, I was helping out in the fields. I didn't have time to, um. Do any of *those* things," I said cheerfully.

I caught sight of the impossibly large village around me and grew giddy with the realisation that this was my life now. I'd brought up my past and for the first time, I hadn't found a reason to grimace.

"You must've got into some manner of trouble before that," Claire said, thinking it impossible for there to have only ever been one abrupt, all-consuming trouble in my life.

And because she was genuinely interested, I said, "I got bit by a wolf, once. I got bit by wolves all the time, actually, but the first time it happened, I nearly lost half my torso."

"Really?" She was more curious, now. Less demanding. "How does one accomplish such a feat?"

"Well!" I pivoted to face her in earnest, breakfast lying forgotten in my lap. "There are always wolves around farms, right? There's a forest at the top of the valley, so wolves are always sneaking in, no matter how many fences we put up. They always find a way around them, or under them. My dad used to hire people from the village to patrol around, but they only ever scared them back. They weren't getting rid of them. So one day I figured that I'd start fighting them off."

"You thought you could fight wolves?" Claire asked, raising an eyebrow. "How old were you?"

"You thought you could slay dragons," I returned. She nodded, conceding the point. "Anyway, I was twelve, and it seemed like a good idea at the time! So I made myself a spear out of a rake handle with a kitchen knife tied to the end and patrolled the edge of the farm. I waited for hours, but no wolves showed up. Michael came over, dragged me back home for dinner, and didn't even ask what I was doing."

I was talking with my hands. I was saying too much, stretching the story too thin, I was sure of it. Michael was the storyteller, not me, but Claire was listening and I found it hard to make myself fall silent.

"It took a few nights, but a wolf showed up. I thought it would circle me, trying to work out whether or not I was worth eating, but it started growling straight away. So I, I just *lunged*, and I think I hit the wolf! But it was moving too quickly and the knife came off, so then I, sort of..."

I was grinning and wincing at the same time, if such a thing was possible.

"Sort of got bit. A lot. Luckily my dad and another villager were out patrolling and turned up in time, but it was before I figured out what I could do, and there was a lot of blood, a lot of *everything*, and bitterwillow could only help so much."

Despite the years that had stretched out between me and that moment, a shudder ran through me. I shook it off, regaining my footing.

"Back then, it was the most exciting thing that'd happened in the village. I'm not really sure, but I think it might've triggered my powers. Maybe." I lowered my voice to confide in Claire. The fact that she'd let me speak without talking over me made me bolder than I ought to have been. "I didn't heal fast, not like I do now, but it was faster than it should've been. I mean, I probably should've died. That's how bad it was. And then one thing led to another, and I started putting lambs back together. Healing them made me think I could help myself. I tried to get rid of the scars left by the wolf, because they pretty much take up most of my body, but it doesn't work like that. It doesn't work on old wounds. They're already healed over, so I just made them look *weird*. All red and yellow and raised."

I let out a breath, tale winding to a close, and Claire said nothing. I bit the inside of my mouth and looked away. I'd said too much. It'd been fine when I was talking about the wolf, but just because Claire knew I was a necromancer didn't mean she needed to hear about it. I was dizzy. I'd never had the opportunity to tell anyone that before, and I'd rushed and stumbled over the first chance I had.

After a moment, Claire bowed her head to catch my eye.

"May I see?" she asked.

Her tone was gentle, but I wrapped my arms around my waist, gripping the edges of my shirt.

I hadn't meant to, but I was convinced she could trace the scars right through it. No one had seen them before. They weren't even scars, not really. I'd twisted them beyond recognition, and they rose from my stomach and chest like strips of rotting fruit, dark and grotesque, wholly irremovable.

Claire sat in front of me, and there wasn't a part of her that could be described as anything less than beautiful.

When I gave no reply, she pressed her fingers to the side of my arm and said, "Never mind. I shouldn't have asked."

She smiled at me warmly, and only then did my arms fall slack against my sides.

"How old were you when you finally beat back a wolf?" she asked, roping me back into the conversation.

"Fourteen," I told her. "I'd figured out a few things by then."

"I didn't kill a dragon until I was twenty-six," she returned. "You have me beat there."

We finished our breakfast and spent the rest of the morning idly wandering through Kyrindval, distracted by curious pane. When the

185

time came for Claire to meet with Queen Kidira, she handed me a few coins and asked me to see that the horses were fed. The challenge of scaling my way back down and around the mountain was less prominent than dealing with a language barrier, and if not for the threat of horses going unattended, I might not have gathered the courage to step into one of the shops.

Once I was through the door, there weren't any problems. It was exactly like a human shop, though the vegetables there were bigger than any I'd seen for sale at market, and I communicated with the shopkeeper through a series of laughs and hand gestures. I left with a grin on my face, arms full of carrots and confidence.

I'd ask Kouris to head down the mountain with me. I'd ask her why she'd done what she'd done, and to tell me her side of the story.

I reached the dragon-bone gate, but she was nowhere to be seen. I put the carrots down by the remnants of our fire from the night before, and though hours passed, she didn't return. My resolve weakened. I convinced myself I didn't want to hear what she had to say, dismissed her truth before I'd heard it, and left the carrots by the ashes, hoping she'd know what to do with them.

CHAPTER THIRTEEN

I awoke to the sound of Commander Akela roaring with laughter.

I'd been welcomed into the same cabin as Claire, given a bed big enough to lose myself in, and food enough to send me into a deep, dreamless slumber. I bolted upright at the sudden noise, hopped out of bed and opened the door, not yet awake enough to compose myself.

I poked my head into the corridor, hair all askew, and saw what all the commotion was about.

Commander Akela wasn't alone. She'd escorted Queen Kidira, presumably to speak with Claire; Claire who was dressed in the clothing of a pane. I understood why Akela was laughing, but didn't dare to smirk around Queen Kidira.

Claire wore tough leathers with a swathe of sky-blue cloth draped over her shoulder, crossing her hip, feet bare. She straightened her collar, pointedly not looking at Akela.

"You are telling me, you are not thinking of returning to Isin like this, yes?" Akela asked, not feeling the slightest need to compose herself in front of her Queen. "And where are you finding one that is fitting so well?"

"I dressed like this for *years*," Claire returned, pushing irritation down for the sake of the current company. "It was presented to me by Zentha. I'm surprised you weren't asked to wear one."

"Hah! They are liking me enough as I am, Ightham," Akela declared. "The pane, they are having a good eye."

Claire said nothing more and Akela followed her gaze. I didn't get the chance to slip back into my room. The three of them stared at me, Queen Kidira stared *through* me, and so I said, "Good morning," mussing my hair back into place.

"Northwood!" Akela boomed. "Your timing, it is being more than perfect! Ightham and Queen Kidira, they are going for a walk, they are talking about—" She paused, waving a hand to banish boredom. "They are talking about important, official things, and I am following them like an infant dog. You are coming with us, yes?"

A glance at Akela made it impossible to believe she had any ulterior motives. Her smile was fierce without being intrusive, and she was asking me to join them for my sake more than the sake of company.

"Um." I looked to Claire for my answer. For all I knew, those *important, official things* were the very matters she didn't want me overhearing.

Claire, in turn, looked to Queen Kidira for an answer. If there were ever two people entirely opposite in demeanour, it was Akela and Queen Kidira; the Queen barely glanced at me, and could not muster the force of will necessary to regard me as some mild irritation. She was not the woman she'd been yesterday. Whatever softened in her at the sight of Kouris was as stone once more.

"If the Commander insists upon it," was her eventual, grudging reply.

Claire headed out with Queen Kidira and I thought better of staying behind, having troubled her so. I was glad Akela trailed behind with me. I barely knew how to compose myself around Claire, let alone royalty who embraced their titles.

It wasn't as pleasant as it had been the morning before. Grey skies filled the air with a constant drizzle, and the pane were less lively, less enthused by all there was to do. Fewer of them wandered the streets but Queen Kidira had no such desire to retreat inside. We headed away from the cabins, through rain-soaked streets, and though we walked leisurely, Queen Kidira never went anywhere without purpose.

"You are looking at them, yes? Queen Kidira, she is bringing me here, she is saying it is a nice thing that we are doing together, and now she is leaving me out!" Akela said. I needn't have worried about hearing something I shouldn't. The pair of them were speaking Svargan, voices hushed. "At least we are both being left out together. I am glad I am not the only one being so confused. Mesomium, it is difficult enough for me already! I am knowing what I am good at, and Svargan is not being one of those things."

"I hadn't *met* a pane until six weeks ago," I said. "The only word I know is yrval."

Akela rubbed her chin.

"For some reason, I am being certain that *harva* is meaning *foot*. Do not ask me why, it is just seeming right."

As we walked towards the edge of Kyrindval, it occurred to me that Queen Kidira had learnt Svargan from Kouris. I wanted the thought to stir something within me, but it didn't. After all the venom that had coursed through my veins upon learning that Kouris had deceived me for a matter of weeks, I didn't understand how Queen Kidira could be so calm, so still, without being unfeeling.

"You are a Felheimish, like Ightham, yes?" Akela asked. "I am thinking this is good. She is coming all this way, and she is having a companion for the travelling. But if I am being honest, and I always am, it is surprising that the Kings are letting you leave the castle."

I wondered if we would've had to go through Akela first, had she been in the capital when we arrived.

"I think Claire was surprised, too. We only got as far as we did because of..." I lowered my voice and tilted my head towards the outskirts of Kyrindval. "Kouris. They probably wouldn't have let Claire *in* without her."

"Hmm," Akela breathed, eyes narrowing. There was a darkness to her expression that hadn't ghosted across Queen Kidira's face, as though Akela felt all of the anger she ought to have in her place. "Perhaps this is being true."

"What about you?" I asked, dragging the topic away from Kouris. "Your accent is a lot thicker than anything I've heard before. I can understand you, but..."

"My accent, my words, they are rough, yes!" Akela said, instantly perking up. "Where I am coming from, it is close to the border. So close that I am stepping out of my house and sometimes I am walking into Agados by accident. My family, my neighbours, we are not speaking Mesomium. All I am knowing is Agadian. The first time I am in Isin, perhaps I am knowing one hundred of the words. Ten years later and I am much, much better. But I am not thinking I am wanting to learn another language yet."

"Much better," I agreed. "I'd like to learn some Svargan, though. I feel like I should at least be able to say thank you in their language, after they've been so welcoming."

"Ah, little Northwood," Akela said, patting my shoulder. "Already, I am liking you!"

"How'd you know my name, anyway?" I asked, grinning.

"I am being very good at my job and making sure I am knowing of all that is threatening Queen Kidira," she explained. "But you are not worrying! I am speaking with Ightham and she is assuring me that your head, it is fine if it is staying on your shoulders."

The hollowed-out mountain Kouris had taken me to laid ahead. Claire and Queen Kidira had gained a considerable lead, but Akela and I caught up with them as they navigated the rockier terrain. Their conversation died down and didn't gather speed when the ground flattened out and they were able to pull away, either. They were both deep in thought, busy mulling something over.

"Are we going to see the dragons?" My question was meant for Akela, but Claire looked over her shoulder and furrowed her brow to demand an explanation. "... I went there yesterday."

"You went into the dragon's cave?" Claire asked, stopping on the spot. Queen Kidira barely broke her gait and Akela glanced back at me as she caught up with her. "What were you thinking? Anything could've happened, Rowan."

"But it didn't! Obviously," I rushed to reassure her. "It's not like I knew where I was going. I, um..."

I trailed off too late.

Claire knew exactly what was about to tumble from my lips, and though it didn't need to be said, Queen Kidira turned back and muttered, "Kouris took her there."

Claire, Akela and I were each uncomfortable in our own distinct ways, but Queen Kidira spoke of Kouris as though she'd been late for dinner, or forgotten to pick something up from market.

"We aren't visiting the dragons," Claire said, and returned to Queen Kidira's side.

Perhaps I ought to have stayed behind, or spent the day with Michael.

"Queen Kidira, she is having important work to do, and there is much of it," Akela whispered, leaning towards me. "Now, I am thinking we are gathering numbers. It is not *sounding* exciting, but soon you are seeing!"

Akela slung an arm around my shoulders and I wondered what, exactly, needed to be counted. A fence of felled trees and dragon-bone ran in a circle ahead of us, enclosing a patch of land too small to rightly be called a field. It was as tall as the tallest pane, with pane stationed around it.

Few of them stood to attention. They sat atop rocks, reading, napping. Some played cards, and one reached out with a crook, shooing a goat who wandered over with us. It bleated out its indignation and sprang off.

"What's in there?" I asked Claire. It hardly had the makings of a royal vault, but the pane who leapt to their feet at the sight of us *were* holding staves. "Something valuable?"

"In a sense," Claire said. She made it sound as though I was as close to the truth as the mountains in the distance. Within sight, but still out of reach. "What do you suppose the pane might hoard?"

"Well..." What if the dragons had burrowed deep enough into the mountains to uncover a vein of gold, or bright coloured gems caught between rocks? But why would they bring it out into the open where any magpie could catch a glimpse of it? Better to leave precious stones and metals with the dragons, where no passing merchant of spices or greed would be tempted to take a handful. "I have no idea."

"Akela! Queen Kidira!" one of the pane boomed. They towered over their companion, horns already spiralling back. "And new little friends!"

Akela broke away from my side and jogged over.

"Kravt!" she said, echoing their cheer. "I am seeing you again and it is being good! It is being months, yes?"

"Too long," Kravt agreed, bowing their head to Queen Kidira and letting me and Claire see all their fangs when they smiled our way. "Little friends, good morning."

Kravt was taller than any pane I'd met before, dark skin making their fangs gleam. They dressed in gold, like all pane around the fence, and greeted us with a cheerful smile. Kravt's companion wasn't so forthcoming. They remained slouched, digging the end of their staff into the dirt and staring vacantly into the distance.

"Good morning!" I replied, watching Queen Kidira and Akela slip through the gate.

Claire tipped her head and Kravt said, "What a time we have had! Already yesterday there is another little friend. They are visiting us. I am thinking, hm. Hair, eyes. Both the same," they said, gesturing towards me. "Then, perhaps...?"

"Michael!" I caught on after enough vague gesturing. The other pane rolled their eyes, despite going to great lengths to pretend they weren't listening. "That's my brother, Michael."

Kravt rubbed their chin.

"Michael, yes. Michael is very..."

There were any number of ways to complete the sentence, but Kravt had something particular in mind. They snapped their fingers, searching for the word. When they came up blank, they leant over to their companion and murmured something in Svargan.

The other pane huffed.

"*Curious*," they translated, eyes fixed on the pane playing cards.

"Curious! Very curious." Kravt dragged their companion closer and wrapped an arm around their shoulders. "This one, I am sorry for. Most unwelcoming! I am thinking, if we are little friends, Ayr is like my brother, or sister, hm?"

Ayr snarled, elbowing Kravt in the side. They chuckled, letting out a note deep enough to fill the gaps between the mountains.

"You get on well enough for it," I said, earning a sharp look from Ayr. "I'm Rowan, by the way. And I'm not really sure why I'm here."

"Ightham," Claire said, by way of introducing herself. "I was accompanying Queen Kidira and thought I might show my friend the *sca-isjin*."

Ayr ducked out of Kravt's grasp and straightened out the front of their shirt.

"It's always the same. You visitors come up here, wanting to nose around. None of you thinking about the damage you might do," they said, batting Kravt's hand away when they reached for them a second time. "Just here to gawk, then you'll go back to your flatlands and shun us all over again."

I wanted to say it wasn't true, that neither Claire nor myself would turn our backs on the pane, but Ayr was justified in what they said. Claire said something in Svargan that did nothing to temper them, and I knew that assuring Ayr that *I* wasn't like that was the wrong thing to do.

Enough humans were to make it a problem.

I'd thought exactly as the rest of us did, until a few weeks ago.

"Ayr, look. These little friends, they... *your* feet are bigger. They will crush nothing. Come," Kravt said, pushing the gate to and ushering us inside. "It is fine. Go, please."

I took an uneasy step forward, but Ayr didn't stop us. They didn't look at us as we stepped into the *sca-isjin*. It wasn't any easier to work out what it was, once we were inside. The field was laid out in a grid, dirt paths surrounding patches of grass with giant stone bulbs protruding from the ground.

Watering cans the size of my torso were scattered along the edges, and above, a net protected the bizarre garden from passing birds and threw a criss-cross of shadows over us. Three pane worked within the *sca-isjin*, one of them with stubs of horns no longer than my finger. They crowded around Queen Kidira, who heard each one of them out, and I followed Claire, wondering when it would start making sense to me.

"I don't get it," I said, staring at one of the stone bulbs until my vision blurred. "Why do the pane have a garden full of rocks?"

Claire took some amusement in my frustration and crouched in front of one of the rocks, waiting for me to do the same. It was far from small. If I tried, I would've barely been able to wrap my arms around it. It was intricately decorated in the same way leaves and bark were. The patterns flowed and swirled, not caring where they came from or where they ended.

"It's not a rock. It's a... we don't have a word for it, because we don't need one," Claire explained. "Think of it like a hen sitting on a nest, keeping the eggs warm."

She'd already lost me.

"They come from dragon teeth. There are seeds, of a sort, inside. They grow into these protective shells. Pane eggs are notoriously difficult to hatch. They're soft-shelled, and barely any of them hatch without some manner of protection."

I stood up, stepped back, and immediately stopped myself, lest I wander into another of the—whatever they were.

"Pane," I said. "You're telling me that they're *growing* pane in here?"

"*Hatching*," she corrected me. "The pane have always had a meaningful relationship with the dragons. Scripture states that they were once part of the same creature."

I opened my mouth, closed it, and frowned at the not-rocks.

There was a pane in there. Right now, there was a pane growing inside one of the rocky shells, no bigger than a newborn goat. I became convinced they were going to burst open at any moment, and out a pane hatchling would stumble, covered in a thick, slimy layer of something I didn't recognise.

"Kouris said, um..." I made a shaky effort to understand how it worked. "She said that pane don't need a partner?"

I scratched the back of my neck, glancing away, but Claire wasn't fazed by the question.

"Correct. They dislodge eggs on a yearly basis, regardless of any activity, or lack thereof."

"Dislodge eggs...?"

"From their throats," she clarified.

I stared at her, wide-eyed. She laughed awkwardly under her breath as it dawned on her that it was a strange topic to be discussing.

"The night Kouris wasn't there. The night with the axewoman. She was... well."

"Oh. *Oh.* I guess she had an excuse, then."

I hadn't blinked in a solid minute. Claire got to her feet and said, "Imagine how strange and unsightly the pane must find what humans do to continue their legacies."

Mercifully, Claire said no more. There was no way my face could've turned any redder.

We continued wandering through the *sca-isjin*, and I remained close to her side, not wanting to risk knocking one of the stone-like shells over. Their roots ran deep, but to me, they were precariously perched in the dirt, eggs in and of themselves.

"Ightham! Come, come, I am needing you to translate," Akela called from the other side of the *sca-isjin*.

Queen Kidira had taken to pacing the length of the strange garden, but Akela was surrounded by pane who didn't understand a word she was saying. Claire obliged, heading over to help Akela with a quick glance my way.

Averting my gaze did nothing to stop Queen Kidira coming closer. I didn't dare to step away, to start circling the *sca-isjin* of my own accord.

"You're friends with Kouris, then?" she asked after spending an unnecessary amount of time staring at me.

All I could think of was the soldier who'd dragged the necromancer from his home, and how she'd claimed it was by decree of Queen Kidira. I was convinced she'd see right through me, convinced she'd *know*. My throat closed up. All I could do was nod weakly.

"If not for her, I wouldn't have to have handle such matters." At best, Queen Kidira was vaguely irritated. "I would be in Isin, attending to a host of other problems."

I wanted to assure her that she was doing important work, because someone had to ensure the pane were being heard, but she knew that.

She knew the worth of what she was doing, else she'd never have left the castle.

Instead, I blurted out, "Kouris, she's really—"

Thankfully, Queen Kidira's stare pierced through me, turning the words to dust in my mouth.

She turned away and continued pacing the garden, hardly concerned with me at all. I hurried to cross the *sca-isjin*, and said, "I'm going to find Michael," to Claire.

She nodded, and Akela said, "Northwood! Later, you are coming back, and I am buying you a drink that is knocking out a dragon!"

I waved goodbye to Akela, keeping my head low as I passed the Queen, and made my way back to Kyrindval. As much as I'd wanted to stay with Claire, I succumbed to a palpable sort of unease around Queen Kidira. No matter what else Michael might've been, being around him was familiar and safe.

I found him at the centre of Kyrindval, surrounded by pane, young and old. Time and time again, he'd started project after project, book after book, but I'd never seen him so utterly enthralled. The pane were talking about their surroundings, their routines, and still Michael couldn't take in enough of what they were saying. I weaved through the crowd of pane and took my place next to him, glad to see him so focused, for once.

"Ah! This is Rowan," he said, pleased to see me. "She's my younger sister."

Or just pleased to have something unusual to show off to the pane.

There was a general murmur and nodding of heads, and I smiled at everyone in the crowd.

"We were just on our way to the amphitheatre, actually," he said, urging the party along.

"The what?" I asked.

"The *what*," he repeated, scoffing. "The amphitheatre, Rowan. Goodness. The pane recognise the word and half of them can't speak Mesomium."

I followed my brother, feeling foolish for not knowing what an amphitheatre was once we reached it. It was the crescent of steps Claire and I had had breakfast in the morning before. Not that I understood its purpose much better for knowing its name. All we did was sit around and talk, not getting much use out of it at all.

The group broke apart and reformed, pane leaving to go about their business, others joining us. We were taken to a tavern with chairs large enough for me and Michael to comfortably share and treated to mugs of ale I could've drowned in. The rest of the day was taken up by endless sight-seeing. We ended up at the library, where Michael decided he needed to know each and every book by name and feel.

He stared at the pages, frustrated that the words meant nothing to him, and a few of the pane translated passages here and there.

At sundown, I got it into my head that I might be allowed to call it a day and head back to the cabin, but Michael grabbed the scruff of my collar when he saw me drifting away.

"Where do you think you're going? You've missed the last two nights of entertainment! They were incredible, by the way. Kouris can last another night without you. Come on. To the fire pit!" he declared, tugging me along.

The fire was already burning, light thrown in all directions, making the shadows of pane like those of mountains. Seating was far from formal. The pane gathered in groups around the fire pit, leaving an empty ring around the edge of it to give the performers room. I thought better of cutting through it, and stepped carefully between the pane. Sat as they were, many were the same height as me, though I still had to push myself onto tiptoes to see properly.

Michael found a place for himself by a few of the pane he'd met that morning, and I looked around not because I was uncomfortable approaching anyone, but because I knew I'd be welcome in whatever spot I chose. Akela sat on the other side of the fire, laughing into a stein the size of her head, and I was so focused on picking Queen Kidira out of the crowd that I missed Claire waving at me, at first.

The pane next to her shuffled to the side. There wasn't much of me to squeeze between them, but I wrapped my arms around my knees so that I didn't take up too much space. Claire's shoulder pressed to mine and she didn't seem to mind it. Being close to her was all I needed to know she was happier than she'd been in a long time, dressed in pane clothing and sat in the heart of Kyrindval. She must've had fond memories of her time in the mountains.

"You hurried off earlier," she said. "Was something the matter?"

There was a buzz of conversation around the fire pit. We weren't supposed to be paying attention to anything, yet.

"No, no. It's just..." I glanced around before I spoke. I couldn't see Queen Kidira, but she'd have been with Akela, if she was there at all. "The Queen. I don't really know how to act around her. After everything with Orinhal, as well as Kouris..."

I rested my chin on my knees and stared into the fire. Claire kept her eyes on me. She didn't say anything, and I felt a strange sensation in my chest, like my heart was gravel and I was fighting to keep it clumped together. I'd gone from having everyone know what I was to my secret being kept by a select few.

If they willed it, it would sift through their fingers, easy as that.

Claire said nothing about necromancy. I knew she couldn't, but her silence on the subject left me sore. I was at odds with how happy I'd been to see her, moments ago.

"You should speak to Kouris about this all. You're letting yourself be taken in by stories of a mythical figure based on her, when she has never once held tales of the Bloodless Lands against you. She is rather fond of you, you realise," Claire said. After a moment, she leant close and added, "*Yrval.*"

"I don't..." I turned away from the fire and saw that Claire was smiling. "I don't know what that means. I know what an yrval *is*, but I still don't get it."

There was a rumble of, "Ah, yes, excuse, little friends," as two pane stepped over us to get to their friends, and the pane beside me got to his feet and rushed after them. There was a space in the crowd but I didn't shuffle over.

"Darling," Claire said, after a thoughtful pause.

"What?"

"Yrval. It's used as an endearment," she explained. "In this context, *darling* might be considered a faithful translation."

I thought back to the way Claire had scrutinised us when she saw Kouris and me talking in the tavern and I bowed my head forward, laughing softly. It didn't feel right. Claire and I were surrounded by half of Kyrindval, yet Kouris wasn't allowed to fill the empty space next to me. I'd spent months ostracised by my village and now I was on the other side of it.

None of the pane were monsters. None of them were hateful. Their lives carried on without Kouris; nothing revolved around her absence.

I wondered how much of it had been in my head. How little the people truly thought of me, when I was exiled to my farmhouse.

"Rán... *Kouris* was the first person who was nice to me in a really, really long time. I'd forgotten that people wouldn't just think I was a thing, a shell for my powers, or... It even took you a while to warm up to me, and I don't think my brother's all that nice at all," I said, realisation coming to me as I spoke the words. "But everything she did, all the people she killed. I grew up hearing about it, everyone did. I don't know how I can just talk to her after that, like everything's fine."

"The Phoenix Festival will be upon us soon. I expect we'll be in Isin, by then, and that you'll hear no shortage of tales about Kondo-Kana and all the necromancers who plagued Myros, laying waste to the land north of the mountains," Claire said in a low voice. "And I have no doubt that you have spent your whole life hearing stories about some necromancer or another, and how they were responsible for some disease a decade back. You know better than to believe those stories, Rowan. Speak with Kouris. She is not a headless ghost, roaming the forest by your house. She is your friend. There are only wolves in the woods, and I know you have dealt with plenty of those before."

She placed a hand on my shoulder and squeezed it. If not for the barricade of pane around me, I would've rushed out of Kyrindval and into the night, in desperate search of Kouris.

The chatter around the fire pit died down as five pane got to their feet and stood at the edge of the fire. All eyes turned towards them as they huddled together, mumbling amongst themselves, nudging each other and nodding towards the crowd. One of them finally relented and stepped forward, saying, "Um. I see many little friends, and we hope you will enjoy, even if you are not understanding."

They switched back to Svargan and exuded confidence. They were actors, and they put on a show the likes of which I'd never seen. There'd been a few performances in my village around the festivals, but never like this. The pane didn't stay still. They circled the fire, voices booming as they went around and around, sending the crowd into fits of laughter. The movement was suited for the stage, and certainly one way to stop people from squabbling over the best seats.

I didn't understand a word of what was being said, but the pane's energy was infectious. I sat there with a smile on my face, laughing breathily at their exaggerated movements.

A song followed the play, upbeat and unaccompanied by instruments. A recital followed, some sort poem, and though the pane speaking wound around the fire, it wasn't of as much interest to me as the previous acts. It left more of an impression on those who understood Svargan. The pane absorbed the words with a quiet awe, and Claire's attention was so focused on the speaker that I stopped stealing glances her way and looked at her plainly.

I searched her face for the poem's meaning. Firelight washed over her, making faint shadows darker and lighting up her eyes, and I didn't realise that the sky had shifted from dark blue to black, until I traced the edge of her profile against it. The performance stopped, but I was oblivious to the patter of applause that followed.

Claire turned to me, too quickly for me to look away. She lifted her brow and hummed. Not accusingly, not as if she wanted to know what I was doing, staring so unabashedly, but as if I had asked her a question and she hadn't heard it.

I opened my mouth, pre-empting what I wanted to say, but no words followed. It belatedly occurred to me that we'd been listening to poetry in a language I didn't understand and I could've asked Claire to translate, or give me the gist. It was too late, by then. I looked back towards the stage, face warmer than it should've been, and didn't dare take my eyes off it, lest Claire was still looking at me.

A pane ran over and saved me from myself.

He spoke to Claire quickly and enthusiastically. She held out her hands, shook her head, and said what I assumed was *no, no*. The surrounding pane overheard and hurried to the first pane's side. Soon enough, four pane were trying to convince Claire to do *something*. She was far from distressed. She was flustered, if anything, teetering on the verge of relenting.

One of the pane turned to me and said something. When I stared at her blankly, she said, "Little friend! Tell this one she should perform!"

Claire looked at me, pleading, and I betrayed her.

"I think you should do it," I said.

Whatever *it* was.

199

Claire narrowed her gaze and used one hand to push off the ground. "Very well," she said coolly.

The pane cheered.

I couldn't bite back a grin as Claire headed to the fire. The pane who'd first approached her was to be her opponent. They shook hands and spoke for a moment, and two other pane rushed over with weapons. They were large, even for a pane. Claire was handed a wooden sword as tall as she was, and she gripped the hilt with both hands, testing the weight.

The swords were beautifully made, with flowing patterns carved into the blade, making them lighter. I wondered how Claire was supposed to win against a man four foot taller than her, but when they started moving, I saw that it wasn't a fight at all.

Claire and the pane were light on their feet, moving in set rhythms around the fire. They brought their blades together, each strike letting out a hollow *lock* of a sound, and the pane murmured and clapped at certain moves, though I had no idea how any of it was scored. They moved around the fire, and Claire would step backwards and lunge forward, claiming the lead.

The whole performance was far more nuanced than I could discern in the few minutes it lasted, and though I understood little of it, I took plenty away in watching Claire.

The crowd swelled with applause when it came to an abrupt end, and Akela cheered from the other side of the fire. Claire returned her wooden sword to the pane and shook the hand of her opponent. She hurried back to my side, trying and failing to look stern.

"He was rather skilled," she said. "I haven't practised in years."

"If that's what you were trying to teach me with that tiny sword you had, you're a much better performer than you are a teacher, Sir," I said.

"Careful," she returned, brow arched. "You presume to be too familiar."

It already seemed absurd that she had once been nothing beyond *Sir Ightham* to me. I wanted to wrap my arm around hers, to lean close. I wanted to say something, but I couldn't pick the right words from my flurry of thoughts.

Instead, I said, "Why do they keep calling us *little friends*?"

"Because we are little and they wish to be our friends," Claire said flatly. It took me long seconds to realise she was making a joke. "They translated their word for humans rather literally. The fact that they still do so is a testament to their patience, really."

Despite what I'd seen, the next performance, if it could be classed as such, was my favourite. A young pane dragged over a pot half his height, and began handing out bowls the size of the sort I was used to. I was confused by them not being big enough to fit my head in, until I realised that the boy was merely giving out samples. It wasn't supposed to be a meal in and of itself.

"Dragon-tail soup!" he said brightly, ladling a serving into my bowl and moving swiftly around the crowd.

I blinked at the soup and Claire said, "Don't worry. There isn't any dragon in it. It's all vegetables. A poor translation, though it is a clever play on words in Svargan."

I took her word for it. The soup smelled wonderful, but before I could so much as blow on it, Kravt came lumbering over.

"Careful, careful!" they said, lowering themselves onto the ground next to me. "It is hot, you will burn."

They finished their soup off in a sip, and my serving sloshed in the bottom of the bowl, threatening to spill.

Kravt was far from inconsiderate. They simply weren't used to being around humans.

"There is, hm. A contest! A contest next week. This boy, he is gaining favour with free, ah. Gifts," Kravt explained, lapping what remained in the bowl with their forked tongue. "All week, they are doing this. I do not mind."

I brought the bowl to my lips and was beyond grateful it hadn't been spilt. It was brimming with spices I'd never tasted before, and a single drop was thrumming with more flavour than any meal I'd ever sat down to. My eyes watered a little, and I hoped the soup would have the same effect on Claire.

I hoped she'd forget whatever her journey was about and stay in Kyr-indval until the contest took place. Surely they'd benefit from the judgement of a human palate.

Claire and Kravt chatted in a mixture of Mesomium and Svargan as all those around the fire got to taste the soup. The bowls were cleared away with a clatter, and another singer took the stage. I meant to press my hands to the ground and lean back, but my palm touched the edge of Claire's fingers. I pulled it back as though I'd touched the flames themselves, but before I could mouth so much as a *sorry*, Claire took hold of my hand.

She placed it on the ground but didn't pull her own hand away.

I felt as though the soup was still in my throat, burning on the way down. The music pounded in my ears and I gathered the courage to glance at her. She stared ahead, watching the pane sing, but I could've sworn I saw her smile.

I dredged up the courage I didn't know I had and turned my hand, so I could press our palms together. The fire roared and the song rose, and mercifully, Claire said nothing.

The pane finished, bowed, and Claire pulled her hand away to clap.

It took me a moment to remember how to do the same.

"Queen Kidira intends to return to Isin tomorrow. Should you wish to speak with Kouris, you'll have an early start," Claire said, rising to her feet. "Kravt. It was good to see you."

Kravt waved an easy goodbye and I made my way out of the crowd with as few disturbances as I could. Claire wasn't waiting for me.

I ran to catch up with her. I dug my hands into my pockets, not knowing what else to do with them.

"Is it really like this every night?" I asked Claire as we drifted through the dark streets.

Most of the cabins had their curtains pulled to, and what little light bled through couldn't content with the starlight.

"Most nights. You ought to see a pane tribe in the midst of a festival."

Whatever hurry Claire was in was forgotten. I was aware of how slowly we were walking, and it didn't bother me, though I half expected Michael to leap out of the shadows and scold me for daring to place my hand in a Knight's.

Claire was thoughtful, but not distant. When she spoke, I got the impression that it wasn't what she'd wanted to say. But her words were warm and I hadn't pried them out of her. It was enough for me.

"The story you told me about the wolf reminded me of something. My brothers and I were taught to use a sword from the moment we could hold one, and I supposed Alex and I thought having the best teachers in the Kingdom meant that we were invincible," Claire said. She turned down a street that wasn't the most direct route back to the cabin. "When we were eleven, Alex and I took our swords and decided that nothing within the royal forest was a match for us."

"What happened?"

"We were arrogant, and there were bears," Claire said. "But there were healers in the castle, and it could've ended much worse. Most of our wounds were to our egos. Rylan took the blame, actually. Our father was furious with us, but Rylan claimed that it was his fault. He hadn't been looking after us properly."

Claire's mind wandered back, but nothing like sadness or anger rose to the surface. It was as though she'd convinced herself that this was her first time amongst the pane all over again, and that she was going to march down the mountains, back to Thule. Back to her family.

We moved on in silence, winding our way back to the lodge. Claire stopped in front of it and looked at me like she was waiting for something. My pockets were empty and I had nothing to give. I balled my hands into fists, only relaxing to tug the hem of my shirt.

"I am glad you came to Kyrindval," she said, tucking my hair behind my ears. "I have not been able to speak of such things for longer than I care to remember."

"Oh," I said. My brain provided absolutely nothing more coherent than that.

The cabin lingered in the corner of my eye, but I couldn't comprehend how I'd take steps towards it. How I'd take steps away from Claire. I brought one of my hands up, fiddling with the hair she'd just neatened, but it wasn't enough of a distraction. Claire was still looking at me.

I wished we were around the fire. I wished there were pane all around us, and that I didn't want to do what my brother had accused me of. Overstepping lines. Rising above my station.

"Claire," I started, lifting my head. I wanted to prematurely apologise, to make some excuse and disappear back into the cabin.

She placed both hands on my cheeks and I would've trembled, if I could've.

My heart pounded. It was a strong, solid thing, echoing in my chest, not about to crumble.

Claire bowed down to kiss me. It was only light, only brief, but I wanted to cling to her and never let go.

"Goodnight, Rowan," she said, and stepped back.

She didn't linger for any longer. She headed into the cabin, door swinging shut behind her, as I stood in the street, not yet daring to smile.

CHAPTER FOURTEEN

Sleep came easily, but damp realisation worked its way in when I awoke. I laid in bed and stared at the ceiling. I wasn't the first one up. Chairs scraped across the kitchen floor, and feet too heavy to be Claire's thumped through the corridor. I had two options. Either I hid away in my room, leaving Claire to inevitably seek me out, or I snuck out and risked running into her.

I swung my legs over the edge of the bed and took my chances. I'd have to see Claire eventually, no matter what happened, and I'd be braver later in the day.

Probably.

I eased the door open an inch, peered out and set off, determined to talk to Kouris before we were on the road. Before Queen Kidira was ever-present. I was light on my feet but not fast enough. Farsa, the woman in charge of the cabin I was staying in, stuck her head into the corridor and glowered at me until I dragged my feet into the kitchen.

"Sneaking out without a good breakfast, hm?" Farsa asked. A handful of younger pane lived with her, making some of the old chairs she'd dragged out easier to climb into. "What good is having human company if I don't get to cook meat for once!"

"Sorry," I said, lifting the enormous pitcher from the centre of the table and pouring myself enough water to wash in. "I was in a hurry to see a friend. I didn't want to trouble you."

"Pshh!" She dismissed the notion along with the sizzle of bacon. The two smaller pane huddled at the opposite end of the table crinkled their noses, unused to the smell. "Your friend already left. Said she had to speak with that Queen Kidira."

I didn't tell Farsa I'd meant Kouris. Claire wouldn't be joining us for breakfast, and my shoulders relaxed at the thought. I was very aware that I didn't want to avoid Claire; that wasn't it at all. I wanted to spare her the discomfort of seeing me.

Surely she'd made some mistake last night. As much as I'd wanted to kiss her, wanted her to kiss me, I couldn't come to terms with the prospect that it might be the same for her. She'd had too much ale at lunch, or some of the stranger spices in the soup had got to her. That had to be it.

Farsa scraped bacon onto a plate and gently tapped the backs of the pane who were staring, mouths agape. She said something I expected was intended to relax them, but their eyes widened. Farsa sighed and I ate as quickly as I could without distressing the young pane.

"The pane should really try cooked meat," I said, chewing through the last mouthful. Farsa scoffed playfully and after a moment's consideration, I said, "After we start eating it raw. That's a fair deal, right?"

There was a step in front the sink, so the younger pane could help with chores. I climbed it, but Farsa grabbed the plate from me and said, "Go, go. Find your friend, now that your stomach's full."

I thanked Farsa and waved to the younger pane, met with blank faces as I rushed out. Deciding that our horses would want breakfast as well, I bought more carrots and headed out in search of Kouris. She'd wandered but hadn't gone far; a pile of bones had been licked clean and left by the ashes of a fire, and I only had to wait a few minutes for her to appear over the crest of a hill.

She jogged over at the sight of me, as if I'd only be there if there were something amiss. When it became clear that there wasn't anything wrong, she reached for the carrots without a word.

I pulled them to my chest and stepped back. I ground my teeth together, bringing about the start of a headache.

I hadn't thought this through.

I'd assumed I'd be brave, because Claire believed I could be.

"If you're planning on taking those down yourself, yrval, you might be wanting a guide," Kouris said.

I nodded firmly and let her set off first. Two days ago, I'd been able to talk to her, but there I was, rooted to the spot.

The trek down the mountain was worse than the journey up. It was difficult not to look down when we were heading that way, and at some points, the path was so steep I was certain I'd tumble straight down. My feet slid on the rocky path, and I kept my hand pressed to the side of the mountain where I could, heart in my throat. Kouris walked ahead of me, feet perfectly adapted for the terrain, and moved slowly, that I might crash into her if I fell.

Once we reached the horses, I crouched down and buried my head in my arms. Charley wandered over, bumped his muzzle against the top of my head and sniffed, concerned. I groaned, and that was enough for him. He knocked my arms back and went for the carrots.

Kouris chuckled and I grumbled, "Stop it. I'm used to climbing trees, not mountains."

"No judgement from me, yrval," she said. "Those feet of yours weren't made for this life."

I tended to Charley, Calais and Patrick, and told them they wouldn't have to be there for more than a few hours. It was vital they knew Queen Kidira was travelling back to Isin. Vital I said so loudly enough for Kouris to overhear. She left me to fuss over the horses, giving me all the time in the world to speak up.

The words didn't come.

"Back to Kyrindval, aye?" she said, when I gave Charley one last pat and murmured my goodbyes.

I tilted my head back to take in the mountain we were about to climb and said, "Higher. I want to go higher."

The Bloodless Lands rested over the range. Blood pounded in my ears at the thought, some part of me being drawn closer and closer.

Kouris didn't ask if I was sure about that. Her ears flattened against her head and she said, "Alright, yrval. Reckon I know just the place."

Scaling the path back up the mountain was no more fun the second time, but I was less resistant to the idea of being caught by Kouris, should I stumble. She walked behind me, directing me on, but our path only altered when the last turn came into sight.

"Here," Kouris said, pointing to a sheer rock face. I thought she was making fun of me, until she started pointing out the hand-holds, the protruding rocks I could dig my toes against.

"Don't be worrying yourself. I'll be right behind you," she promised.

Well.

I was the one who'd wanted to go higher.

Climbing the side of a mountain was nothing like climbing a tree. I couldn't wrap my arms around it; I could only press flat against it, having to stop for minutes at a time with every step I took, every time I grasped a rock and it came loose. Kouris was endlessly patient, but having her beneath me didn't reassure me as it should've. I kept picturing myself falling back and knocking her off the rock face, onto the hard ground below.

You're a necromancer, I told myself. You'll be *fine*.

Treating injury and agony as a frivolous thing didn't spur me on as it ought to have.

When I reached up and felt a cluster of grass beneath my hand instead of more jagged rock, I scrambled up the last few feet as though possessed, certain the mountain would choose that very moment to tip over.

I crawled over the edge, clung to clumps of grass, and let out a long, shaky breath.

Kouris poked her head over the ledge, arms folded in the grass, still pressed to the mountain face.

The area she'd brought me to was hardly expansive. My bed back at the cabin was bigger, and the view was about as good. All I could see was the same side of a mountain I'd been able to see from the path.

"We're not there yet," Kouris said, abating my disappointment.

She pointed to yet another rock face, and I immediately regretted wanting to get a better view. I stepped forward, determined to keep going, and only then did I see what she'd been gesturing towards. Behind the shrubs and ivy was a gap in the mountain, big enough for a pane to crawl through, but not much more accommodating than that.

I reasoned that a dark, ominous tunnel through a mountain was better than another climb, and so I stepped in, doing what I could to ignore the spider webs that brushed against my face and the scratch of scurrying insects. Light wasn't far off. There was a second, smaller ledge at the end of the tunnel, and the whole landscape opened up before my eyes.

We were perched along the inside of a ring of mountains, edges sloping down, down, to a lake that looked to me like an ocean should. It went on forever, reflecting the whole of the sky, and the surface shattered when dragons flew out. Kraau shot in and out of the water, no bigger than dragonflies from that distance, and speared fish on the ends of their tails.

I couldn't bring myself to be disappointed that the Bloodless Lands were out of sight, sheltered by yet more mountains.

"Remember that being a lot easier to crawl through the last time I was here," Kouris said, grunting as she straightened, rubbing the curve of her horns. "Here we are. Not so bad, aye?"

I shook my head and clung to Kouris' arm as I slowly sat down, legs hanging over the edge.

"I thought dragons were scared of water," I said, watching a dozen of them soar through the sky, throwing out rings of fire and darting through them before they faded into nothing. They were actually making a game of it. "I thought that's why they didn't go south. Because they can smell the sea."

"Humans are always saying the strangest things," Kouris said.

As we watched the dragons hunt and play, scales gleaming from hundreds of feet away, I picked out other pane tribes amongst the mountains. There were those smaller than Kyrindval and ones far larger, and I knew Kouris had spent her youth doing this very thing.

"Why did you do it?" I asked, now that there was nowhere for me to run.

Kouris didn't act as though she didn't know exactly what I meant.

"You've never lived through a time of war, yrval. If you lot thought praying to the gods did any good these days, I'd do just that, if it meant you never have to," she said solemnly. "What you need to be understanding is that there's blood on all of our hands. Me and Kidira. Jonas and Atthis. Our armies, our enemies. No one came out of that looking good.

"I wish I could tell you that I wasn't like the other pane, growing up. That the elders always knew there was something off about me, and I'd stared into the Bloodless Lands for too long and was never the same after that. Truth is, I was just like anyone else. Spent a lot of my time working as a tailor, if you'd believe it.

"But the war, it wasn't just a human war. They were killing us, yrval. Picking us off because they could unite their soldiers in fear of us, and take us out without retaliation. None one fought back. It's just not in our nature.

"I was begging Zentha to do something. Asking them to let us gather enough forces for a defence, if nothing else. To round up the pane who were travelling far from the mountains and bring 'em home. Ever since people fled the Bloodless Lands, we've been losing our territory, bit by bit. The humans still go on and on about what our dead were forced to do in the Necromancy War, and back then, it was worse than ever. They got so confused about what they were fighting for that they wanted to wipe us out. Thought we were their enemy, if we wouldn't side with 'em.

"Like they weren't terrified of dead pane and dragons rising against them.

"So I did what I had to, yrval. I marched down from the mountains and took matters into my own hands. I protected the pane, herding them back to the mountains. Letting the humans know that *I* would fight back, even if none of the others did. It took months, but it happened. I started gaining a following. Human followers, at that. I don't know if they thought having a pane at the front of an army would scare off the other territories, or if they were just that desperate, but before I knew it, I was a leader.

"I did what I thought was best. I went to Kidira, Jonas and Atthis. I didn't speak a word of Mesomium at the time, not really, so I surrendered. Handed myself over. Let 'em know that I didn't want to fight anymore, and trusted that they'd feel the same."

Kouris kept her eyes on me as she spoke, but I stared at the lake. It wasn't one of Michael's stories. It wasn't another tale about the ruthless Queen Kouris; this was the truth. *Her* truth, if nothing else."

"You killed people," I said. "Didn't you?"

"Aye, I did." Kouris didn't miss a beat. I'd expected excuses, but she let her agreement linger in the air between us. "Never anyone that wasn't standing against us, though. And gods, I never made banners out of human skin, never clawed anyone's eyes out. Never *ate* anyone. Those stories were the doing of the other territories. How better than to smear the name of the north? They drifted down through Felheim, and you lot really got some strange ideas into your heads."

What did I expect? For her to tell me that no blood had been spilt throughout a time of war? Even I wasn't naïve enough to believe that the battles had been easy for Kouris, simply because she'd won. It wasn't the killing that created a void between us. Claire had killed, she'd told me as much herself, and my father had been a soldier; I'd allowed people to die on my table, people I could've saved with a thought.

It was the lying. I'd let myself get close to someone for the first time in an age, and she'd ripped that trust away from me. I'd *wanted* to believe in the legend built up around Queen Kouris, to convince myself there was nothing more to the betrayal I felt.

But she wasn't the monster from my childhood stories. She wasn't parchment and ink, wasn't a rushed whisper. I wrapped my arms around her and she was flesh and blood. She bowed her head, kissing my forehead, and she was warm.

"I should get back to Kyrindval," I murmured. "Queen Kidira wants to go back to Isin."

I gripped one of Kouris' horns, ensuring I didn't slip as I got to my feet. I went through the tunnel and scrambled onto Kouris' back on the other side. She near enough walked down the rock face I'd struggled to climb and barely had to use her arms for balance.

I remained on her back until Kyrindval was in sight. I was just in time: Queen Kidira was making ready to leave, along with Akela and Claire. Kouris lowered me to the ground, waiting a short distance away as I jogged over to the pane who'd gathered to see us off.

"I'm glad you took my advice," Claire said when I joined them. She wasn't particularly short with me, nor did she avoid looking at me. "We're waiting on your brother."

The pane were eager to offer us all sorts of supplies for our journey, none of which Queen Kidira considered politely declining. She gestured for everything on offer to be handing over to Akela, who ended up with a mountain of meat, fruit and bread in her arms.

"My Queen, I am thinking they are following the example I am setting and liking you too much!" she grumbled through a grin, whistling out a *phew* when Claire shook one of our empty bags open.

There was no sign of Michael. Queen Kidira silently blamed me for his tardiness, but I told myself she was only staring at me because her only other option was to look at Kouris. Claire frowned at Kyrindval, and the pane were in danger of running out of parting pleasantries.

Queen Kidira was on the verge of opening her mouth when Michael came skidding over.

"I know, I know, I'm running late!" he blurted out. "But I was thinking: I can't leave yet."

"You can't leave yet?" I asked.

Michael's shoulders rose, irritated by the interruption, and he proceeded to talk to Claire as though she'd asked him the question.

"I feel as though I'm finally doing something. Or as if I *could* finally be doing something. There's so much for me to learn here! I could write something of importance, rather than spend my life echoing other people's stories," he said. "I've found a few pane willing to take me in.

They're a very generous people, you know."

"I'm not certain I can simply leave you here," Claire said, though she looked as though she was considering it.

"It won't be forever. Queen Kidira, Your Majesty, I believe a few representatives will be heading to Isin in the near future...?" Queen Kidira didn't answer him. He continued regardless. "I'll come back with them. Have them take me straight to the castle. What do you say, Sir?"

"Rowan?" Claire asked, giving me the final say.

My brother started projects and abandoned them as quickly as he found something new to move onto. For all he'd learnt and tried to teach me, I'd never seen him *care* about something so much.

If we made him come back to Isin, we'd never hear the end of it.

He scoffed at the notion of his fate being in my hands and I said, "We'd have to drag you back, wouldn't we?"

It was decided. Michael beamed, thanked Claire heartily, and told her he'd never have got this far, if not for her. He threw an arm around my shoulders and shoved his bag into my arms.

"I probably shouldn't have taken these. See that they get back to the castle, won't you? And keep out of trouble, Rowan. You aren't going to have me watching your back for a while, you know."

I slung my bag over my shoulder and considered telling him that I'd kissed Claire.

He waved us off before I got a word out. I wound my way back down the mountain for the second time that day, wishing I'd stayed with the horses. Patrick whinnied when we left him behind, clomping his hooves against the ground as a pane who'd accompanied us down tried to lead him up to Kyrindval. It took some kind words from the pane, but Patrick reluctantly followed him to a second path.

Queen Kidira and Akela's horses were brought down the same way.

"There's another way up?" I asked Kouris in a whisper.

"That there is. Much easier for the horses, but it takes a few more hours," she replied in a low voice, lest Queen Kidira overhead her.

Kouris took the lead. She was always in Queen Kidira's sight, but they both acted as though the other was a ghost; as though only they could see each other, and so were unable to acknowledge one another, for fear of how it would seem to us.

The journey back to Isin was going to be a long one.

Over the days that followed, we didn't always move as a group, though we were never more than half a mile apart. I stuck close to Kouris' heels and Claire drifted between Akela and Queen Kidira and us, intent on watching over everyone. The further south we travelled the warmer it became, but Claire's face darkened as though we were charging into storm clouds.

"Being in Kyrindval was like being in another world," she said, one evening over dinner. I understood the implication behind her words and couldn't pretend to be happy about all we were leaving behind.

I spent that night by Kouris' side, not saying anything as I stared into the darkness.

Between Claire returning to reality and Queen Kidira and Kouris making it impossible for the five of us to slip into conversation, comfortable or otherwise, I couldn't wait to be back in Isin, locked away in the castle. Akela made a few enthusiastic attempts to rope me into conversation, and while we sat in silence, she would idly remark about the weather or sunset to Queen Kidira.

She never answered, but always listened.

Restless, Kouris took the books from my bag and scrutinised the covers.

"Hm. *Geometry in the Architectural Age.* Ugh. *Charting the Uncharted Sea.* Probably stole the manuscript from some poor Canthian pirate. Oh, this is looking more promising. *The Complete History of Kastelir*," she muttered to herself, because talking to no one in particular around the fire was permitted. "Let's see what I missed out on."

I hoped she'd read out loud, but only had the remnants of my dinner for entertainment. Isin was three days over the horizon, and I found myself envious of Michael. Perhaps I would've been wise to stay behind with him.

"Hmph. Three pages in and I'm already finding a mistake," Kouris muttered to herself.

Not wanting to leave the words hanging awkwardly in the air, Claire said, "What is it?"

Kouris cleared her throat, scanned the page once more, and read aloud.

"*As we near the thirtieth anniversary, this author suggests reflecting on the last major celebration,* and so on and so on, *and on the twenty-fifth*

213

anniversary of Kastelir's founding, a memorial service was led by Kouris. Correct me if I'm wrong, but I'd been gone for twenty-two years, by that point."

Claire hummed, unable to offer an explanation, and Akela cleared her throat on the other side of the fire. We all looked at her, but it was Queen Kidira who spoke.

"There is no mistake," she said plainly. "Kouris is the name of my daughter."

The fire crackled, wood twisting with heat. Queen Kidira stared straight through the flames, daring Kouris to blink. All she could do was snap the book shut in her hand. I couldn't bring myself to look at her, but I heard her shift uncomfortably, cracking her knuckles, searching for *something* to say. She eventually stood, sinking soundlessly into the shadows.

I should've gone to her, of course I should've, but I hesitated and lost my chance. Claire followed her, and when I dared to glance back, I saw that she'd placed a hand on Kouris' chest and was offering her more words than I would've been able to.

"She ought to be back from Thule by now," Queen Kidira said to Akela. "Do you know when she was due to arrive?"

"Actually, Lady Kouris, she is returning home three days before we are leaving Isin," Akela said. "But you are very busy, yes, and she is having much to be catching up on, so it is not surprising when you are not running into her."

Queen Kidira poked her empty bowl with her fork.

"I do not trust them. They spend centuries behind their wall, intent on ignoring our existence, and suddenly, they wish to marry my daughter off to some *Prince*," Queen Kidira said, as though there were none so despicable in all of society. "I would not abide it, but... do you think she seems happy?"

"Very much, yes! Every time she is returning or reading a letter, she is always beaming, and saying how good it is being for Kastelir. If they are planning something, I am going over and I am sticking my axe in their heads, yes?"

Queen Kidira stopped staring at her hands and looked up at Akela.

"Indeed."

I was glad Claire was with Kouris. She knew her brother was marrying a noble, but I doubted she knew it was Queen Kidira's daughter. Enough had already come out that evening.

A merchant passed us, a day from the city, and we bought a wheel of cheese for the sake of getting rid of him. The roads became busier and there were fewer overgrown paths to take, but we often went for hours without coming across another person.

I saw hints of Isin on the horizon under the early morning light, and found myself smiling for the first time in almost a week. I soon thought better of it. The trip back from Kyrindval would've been completely intolerable, if not for Akela, and the pull of Isin was dragging us all down, spirits dulled by what would unfold once we reached the capital. Not knowing what to expect or why Claire had been forced to flee through Kastelir did nothing to keep an ebbing sense of dread at bay.

I rode ahead, a short distance behind Kouris, and saw a figure in the distance. A man on horseback charged along the path, draped in a cloak. It was unseasonable enough to catch my attention. He galloped straight past Kouris, having no reason to look twice, and I made ready to nod my head politely, should he wish me a good morning.

I caught his eye as he charged along the road.

Sir Luxon's horse came to a clamouring stop, only to double back around me. I couldn't keep moving; his ivory horse blocked the path, and there was no pretending that I hadn't recognised him, no rushing off and luring him away from Claire.

"You!" Luxon's voice was loud, authoritative, exhaustion mixed with relief. "Where's Ightham? Didn't get bored of you already, did she?"

Kouris' ears didn't fail her. She skidded to a halt and made her way over, slowly enough that Luxon was content to keep his eyes on me.

Yes, I wanted to say. *She went on without me and headed to Agados.* I knew it was futile, but I wanted to say something, *anything*, that would let Claire know I'd done everything I could to protect her.

Dragon-bone armour gleamed beneath his cloak. I wasn't surprised Sir Luxon had gone back on his word.

"I..."

"*Well?*" he snapped.

"Is there a problem here?" Kouris asked.

"Stay out of this, pane," he said, waving her off like a persistent insect. Any momentary irritation was soon quelled by the sight of Claire in the distance. Akela and Queen Kidira were too far behind to be seen, but Sir Luxon was ecstatic in the face of being outnumbered three-to-one.

Jittery, almost.

"Ightham!" he roared when she charged over to us. "Ightham, do you have any idea how long it's taken me to find you? How little I've slept, how much bitterwillow I've had to chew on! I've shown your face to half the poor sods in this hell-hole of a Kingdom."

Claire met him with a hard glare and I inched back as Calais stepped between my horse and Luxon's.

"I thought you were returning to Thule to take on a new role," Claire said.

"Here's the thing. I have new orders. From your dear brother, this time. The one with his head on his shoulders," Luxon said, making a mess of his horse's mane with one hand. "When it became clear you weren't returning, your father offered the mysterious promotion to Prince Rylan, who decided you were... Oh, who cares what you're doing, Phoenix! Just come back, would you? All will be forgiven."

"Pretend you never stumbled across me," Claire said.

"Nice try. I'm only going to ask once, for old times' sake."

Claire was bemused by the prospect of these old times, and did little but regard Luxon with a mixture of scepticism and pity.

"And should I refuse?"

Sir Luxon opened his cloak and rapped an armoured fist against his breastplate.

Kouris grunted. Luxon chuckled, having convinced himself that Claire's terror was real, no matter how deeply buried, and I concluded I was panicking for the three of us. It didn't matter that Claire was better with her blade than Luxon; his sword was carved from dragon-bone, and she'd never be able to break through his armour.

"I'm not returning to Thule, Luxon. Not yet. I certainly don't have any intention of letting you drag my corpse back," Claire told him. "You do realise that this was never going to end well for you, don't you? What did you think would happen if you took my head back to my father?"

Luxon hummed, dismounted his horse, and let his cloak fall to the ground. His armour was different to Claire's, bulkier, with long, curved spikes jutting from the elbows and scales worked into the greaves.

"Need any help with this one?" Kouris offered.

"Like the pane have figured out how to defend themselves yet," he scoffed. No wonder he didn't feel threatened. He thought of Kouris as a creature of peace, like the rest of her kind. "Come, Ightham. Don't give up all you have. The leniency you've been afforded thus far has been tremendous. After your last little episode, I would've thought you'd be kept on a very short leash indeed. Yet here you are! Throwing it all away!"

Claire left Calais' back, having no choice but to accept Luxon's challenge. In the distance, Queen Kidira and Akela veered off the path. It wouldn't do for the Queen of Kastelir to become involved in an altercation between two Felheimish Knights.

Claire drew her sword. Luxon gripped his blade and swung it easily.

"Go back to Thule," Claire said, giving him one last chance. "Go to the King. Tell him I was nowhere to be found."

"After all the trouble I've been through? I've already lost a perfectly good axewoman to this ridiculous pursuit, as well as who knows how many months."

It was decided. Luxon lashed out with his sword, faster than I'd believed he'd be able to move, bravado backed up by skill. It was nothing like watching Claire fight off the bandits. She moved with a focus born of knowing exactly what her opponent was capable of.

Luxon lunged and Claire stepped to the side, dodging blow after blow without raising her sword to meet Luxon's. I gripped Charley's reins tightly, desperate for Kouris to intervene. She watched them fight like a hawk, and I knew she'd step in the moment she had to.

"You'll have to fight back eventually, Phoenix," Luxon said.

His dragon-bone armour clattered as he moved, and Claire had no choice but to lift her sword to parry his blow. The steel whined and I understood why she'd gone to such lengths to measure her movements. Luxon's sword made a dent in her own, marring the metal like a tooth knocked from a mouth.

They huffed and heaved their weapons apart.

"I'll cut it in two, next time," Luxon declared, swinging again. Blindly, almost. For the fun of it.

Claire blocked the attack, bringing her sword up with force. Dragon-bone sunk into steel and Claire twisted the hilt of her sword, prying Luxon's blade out of his hand. He made a grasp for it, but caught the air. The dragon-bone sword skidded across the dirt, entirely unscathed.

Claire placed a foot atop it and pointed her sword at Luxon's throat.

She'd won. The tangle of veins gripping my heart loosened and I blinked my eyes dry.

"If I were you, Luxon, I would remain *incredibly* still. I know how that armour is put together, and you were too arrogant to wear a helm," Claire said in a low, controlled voice. There was nothing celebratory in her tone, nothing that suggested this was a victory of any sort. She kicked the dragon-bone sword across the dirt and Kouris knelt, claiming it for her own.

"Not a bad piece," she mused, testing it in her hand like a dagger.

"Ightham, Ightham," Luxon said, sobering. "There's no need for this. What if I say you were right? I came to Kastelir and didn't catch so much as a glimpse of you. Say I heard of someone matching your description heading south, across the Uncharted Sea."

Luxon was disarmed, sword at his throat, but was far from begging for his life. He took Claire's advice, not moving other than to blink and speak, but believed he was in a position to be bargaining.

"Rowan. We ought to have rope left," Claire said.

I jumped off Charley's back and tore through the bags, certain that if Luxon escaped now, it would be on me. There was a serviceable amount of rope left, though I doubted we were going to leave him tied to a tree.

I took careful steps forward and hooked the rope over the arm Claire was holding out. Having discerned that we hadn't been bested, Akela and Queen Kidira made their way over to us as Claire took slow steps towards Luxon, sword edging closer and closer to his throat.

He silently admitted defeat. He hadn't considered a pane a challenge and had barely acknowledged me at all, but Akela's axe was a beacon at her hip. His shoulders slumped and he crossed his wrists behind his back.

Claire gripped him by the shoulder and turned him towards her. She sheathed her blade and wound the rope around his wrists, tugging on each end to tighten it.

Luxon moved.

He didn't reach for Claire's sword. A single step would've put it out of reach. Instead, he thrust his elbows back, dragon-bone spikes puncturing Claire's leather armour and tearing ruts from her stomach to sternum, digging in deep.

Kouris lunged forward. She sunk Luxon's sword into his throat and down, down into his chest, and all I could hear was the pounding of hooves as Akela and Queen Kidira were upon us. Someone spoke, someone shouted, but it was buzz drowned out by the pounding between my temples.

Luxon was dead, dragon-bone armour streaked with torrents of red. The shadow of death was upon him, coiling deep within the pulpy mess of his organs. It was a fine mist that no one else saw, staining the air, letting me know it could be mine; I could draw it deep into my chest if I so desired and exhale nothing but light.

I could close his throat and make his heart beat again, if I chose to.

It didn't speak to me in a mocking voice. It wasn't cruel or hungry, but thrummed through me like a gentle song I knew without hearing. I was overwhelmed by how much it wanted to yield to me, and I wanted so very much to reach out, to press my hands against Luxon's throat, but, but—

Claire.

She was doubled over, forehead scraping the ground as she clung to her bloodied stomach with both arms. That shadow if mist wasn't upon her yet, but it had taken notice. Blood poured out of her, leaving room for death to seep in.

I fell to the ground next to her, eyes stinging, burning, too hot and bright to be filled with tears. Everything slowed down. My fingers twitched with long-idle power and I knew I could do this. I knew I could save her. I placed a hand on Claire's shoulder, eased her back, and I wasn't afraid.

Her face was white and damp, blood caught between her teeth, but for all the fear that washed over her, her eyes were harder than I'd ever known them to be.

I held out a hand to heal her and Claire, torn to shreds, unable to speak for the blood that rushed into her throat, pushed me away.

CHAPTER FIFTEEN

Akela and Kouris did what I couldn't.

I'd been in a trance until Claire knocked me back, seeing layers of life and death press tightly together instead of my surroundings. No one wasted as much time as I did. Kouris ripped her sash off, knelt by Claire's side and pressed it to her stomach. Akela pushed handfuls of bitterwillow into Claire's mouth, forcefully working her jaw when she gurgled on the blood in her throat.

But all the bitterwillow in the world wouldn't close her wound.

Kouris took Claire into her arms and held her tightly as she began to convulse.

"I'll get her back to Isin, yrval," she said, and turned to Akela. "Sort this mess out."

Kouris set off faster than I'd ever seen her move. I never would've caught up with her on Felheim's fastest horse.

I trembled as Akela stepped over to Luxon's body, frowning at it like a stain on the carpet. She placed a boot on the back of his shoulder and wrenched the dragon-bone blade free from his throat. Kouris hadn't used a jot of restraint. It was stained red from hilt to tip, dripping into the dry dirt.

Akela held the sword away from herself and admired it grimly.

"One Felheimish Knight will soon be in the process of bleeding to death in my castle, and another is dead on the ground," Queen Kidira said, brimming with more sympathy for the land beneath her feet than Claire. "Dispose of the body, but keep the armour. It'd be too easily identified."

Akela sunk the sword into the grass but almost toppled over when the hard ground swallowed it with ease. Queen Kidira paced back and forth, keeping vigil.

"We should... we have to follow them, Claire, she's..." I rambled, teeth chattering.

"You will stay here. What can you do for the Knight that a healer cannot?" Kidira said. "Help Akela. Dispose of whatever's in those bags and pack the armour away."

What good was I to Akela, when Claire was fixed in my mind's eye, torn to shreds; being carried through the bustle of Isin, life trailing behind her; reaching the healers too late, and what good would they be to her?

I knelt down not to help, but because my legs were light, unwilling to support me. Luxon's armour would wash clean and none would know what truly happened to him. Not his friends, his family. Not the King and Queen, or those who looked up to the man.

I pressed the pads of my fingers to the edge of the armour, thinking it might stir something deep within me, but I could only stare blankly.

"Northwood, do not be worrying. I am understanding that there is being so much blood, but Ightham, she is fine." Akela offered a smile that wasn't too bright. "Isin, it is not far, but there are many healers, yes?"

Healers, in the city. In the castle, most likely. Had I seen them? Had they seen me?

I gathered up piece after piece of armour, packed it into the bags, and discarded our remaining food. The sooner we were done, the sooner we'd be back in Isin; if the healers were unable to act, it wouldn't be too late for me. It wasn't a race against time. I could save Claire, no matter how she'd looked at me when there was so much more to fear than necromancy.

With Luxon stripped of any proof he'd ever been a Knight, Akela hoisted up his corpse and slung it over her horse.

"The river Ista is half a mile west," Queen Kidira said, making an order of a statement. I hooked the bags on Calais' saddle and led him from Charley's back.

The river Ista started as a trickle in the mountains and was wide and fast flowing by the time it reached Isin, where it served as the city's main water source. The rush of water filled the air, churning over the rocks that hadn't been worn away, and Luxon's body hit the bank with a sickly thud.

"His face," Queen Kidira said, staring at him without going to the effort of sneering. "It's still recognisable."

With a grim nod, Akela's hand moved to her axe.

"Northwood," she murmured. "You are wanting to turn away, yes?"

I turned my back to the river and heard a single, focused crack of her axe. All I could think was *it's not too late, it's not too late*. Time wasn't of the essence. I was the only force that factored into the equation.

Luxon's body hit the water. Queen Kidira watched, wanting to be

221

certain the river would take it, and made for Isin without another word.

The pulse of the city was resistant to three riders, and passing through the gates put us further than ever from the castle. Our horses were caught amidst a sea of bodies, none of them willing to step aside to clear the way for us. Queen Kidira had no intention of using her status to force her way to the castle, and we zigzagged through the crowd, stepping into the gaps the moment they formed.

We passed through the city square, having more luck gathering something akin to space in the open, paved area, but the crowd in the centre was far more volatile than the rest of Isin. It hadn't formed by chance, made up of individuals tending to their own business and idly drifting together; it was a roiling, roaring thing, contained by guards, more exasperated than on edge.

I only caught brief bursts of what they were yelling, but the crowd swelled with applause each time someone spoke. "Said there'd be change, but—" "... thirty years already!" "—didn't vote for them, and..." "—an empty throne!" Neither Akela nor Queen Kidira acknowledged the turmoil, and the moment we were out of the square, any curiosity or interest slipped my mind.

All I could think of was the castle and Claire within it.

The guards wasted no time opening the gates, recognising Queen Kidira while the citizens hadn't bothered to look up and see who was sat astride the horse blocking their path. We thundered across the bridge, leaving our horses with the handful of guards who immediately flocked to attend to Queen Kidira. Akela assumed responsibility for the bags of armour, and I followed them through the arching double doors held open to us, down the corridor and towards a chamber, not knowing where else to go.

"—and for gods' sake, send out a party to rendezvous with the Queen," I heard King Atthis snap from outside the room.

"Calm yourself, Atthis," Queen Kidira said as she marched in. I peered through the doorway and stepped back when the guards came tumbling out, dismissed with a wave of Queen Kidira's hand. "There was only one assailant, and he was dealt with efficiently."

"*Efficiently?*" King Atthis spat back. Any relief he'd experienced at the sight of Queen Kidira, safe and unscathed, boiled over, back into frustration. "Not minutes ago, I received word that Kouris had brought a Felheimer to our castle, torn to ribbons. No, not just a Felheimer. The *Princess of Felheim*! Not efficiently enough, I'd wager. I know you insist on travelling inconspicuously, but you need to take more company along than Commander Ayad. The pair of you distract one another."

Queen Kidira ignored the remark and had Akela place the bags on one of the chairs. The room was used as a study of sorts, with an arch of bookcases surrounding a desk.

"I am *fine*," Queen Kidira said, patting him on the side of his arm. "Akela has procured a set of dragon-bone armour, as well as a blade. Take a look and calm yourself. We've much to discuss. Find me once you've settled down."

Queen Kidira caught Akela's eye on the way out and left without another word. Grumbling to himself, King Atthis fumbled with the straps of the bag, letting out a heavy breath and turning to the side when blood on bone was the first thing he saw. There was more annoyance than disgust scrawled across his features, and I tugged Akela's sleeve, wanting, needing, to be out of there.

"Your Highness?" Akela began. She cleared her throat and stood straighter. She wasn't as easy around King Atthis as had been around the Queen. She was far from timid; simply more formal. "Ightham, the Knight. Where is she now?"

King Atthis took a handkerchief from one of the desk draws and used it to safely grip the edge of the armour, rummaging through the bags as though they held Luxon's bones themselves.

"Back in her chamber, I expect," he said after a moment's consideration. "Ask Ocari where they housed her. Go, go. You're dismissed, Commander. But do not think we won't be discussing this at length later."

Back in her chamber.

Claire was back in her chamber which meant she was safe. She was *alive*.

The news didn't wear the tension in my body away. Nothing would, until I'd seen Claire for myself. Akela backed out of the room with a brief, practised bow, and King Atthis was too busy inspecting the armour to see me make a mess of doing the same.

"What am I telling you?" Akela said, door swinging shut behind her. She patted my shoulder and steered me down the corridor, in search of

Ocari. "Ightham, she is fine. Back in her chamber, yes. Maybe she is taking a bath!"

I smiled at the thought while Akela was looking at me, and it didn't take us long to find Ocari. They were the head of the castle's staff, responsible for handling every matter without a political edge in the castle, and never not busy. Akela stuck close to their heels as they marched from the servants' living quarters to one of the pantries, checking off this-and-that from a list, issuing orders as they answered our questions.

"Our Felheimish guest. Sure, I remember her. Had to send out a team to scrub down one of the bridges, and who knows if we'll ever get the stains out of the carpet. Sent her up a fresh set of clothing a few minutes back," Ocari told us, more aware of what was happening in the castle than King Atthis himself. "I assigned her to the northern wing, in Lord What's-his-face's old chamber. There'll be no mercy for whoever's moved her if she's not still there, though."

Akela clapped her hands together, grinning as she bowed her head.

"Ocari, as ever, you are being most helpful! Without you, this castle, it is a slum."

Ocari rolled their eyes, nudging Akela in the side.

"Get out of here, you. I've still got plenty of work to do."

The number of waves and bashful smiles Akela garnered on her way through the castle told me exactly how well-liked she was. She moved freely through the castle, taking countless sharp turns through narrow passageways, never once having to pause to get her bearings.

The corridor boasting Claire's chamber was far more polished than the one mine and Michael's room rested along. It was placed on the third or fourth floor, and one wall was dedicated to stained glass windows in shades of blue, drinking in the sight of Isin sprawling towards the hills.

Once I was at the door of Claire's room, I couldn't bring myself to knock.

She wouldn't want to see me. She'd pushed me away because of what I was, what I was capable of. My necromancy was suddenly a stark reality she couldn't resign to the back of her mind.

I didn't move. Akela knocked for me.

"If you are needing anything, anything at all, you are telling any guard and they are finding me. Yes?" Akela said, leaving me to face the consequences.

From within the chamber, a voice said, "Come in."

Claire's voice. She was alive, she was safe, able to speak. Albeit bluntly.

That's all I needed to know. All I'd come for.

Yet it wasn't enough.

I pushed the door open. Claire's chamber was far bigger than the one I'd stayed in, complete with a room leading off it, but the details were lost to me. My eyes fell on Claire and remained there. Claire, draped in a clean white shirt, without a trace of blood or pain anywhere on her. A bottle of wine sat on the table next to her armchair, barely touched, and Claire rose to her feet at the sight of me.

I couldn't account for what I was seeing. Couldn't find any correlation between this Claire, whole and safe, and the Claire who'd fallen to her knees, gripping her wounds and sucking panicked breaths through her bloodied teeth. I couldn't accept what had happened, because a power that wasn't mine had been evoked; a power I didn't trust to save her, but had.

"Oh, dammit," I mumbled, wiping the corner of my eye with the heel of my palm.

I'd given myself a headache gritting my teeth, and didn't realise my shoulders were shaking until Claire placed her hands on them. I looked at her, eyes wide and searching, but couldn't find a hint of what I'd seen in her eyes earlier. She was just Claire once more. She was looking at me, seeing me, and there wasn't a trace of disgust in her gaze.

I pressed my hand to her stomach, through the thin cotton of her shirt, and found her skin smooth and unscathed when I curled my fingers towards her.

"I thought..." The words rose up thick and fast, and I breathed deeply, trying to hold my tears back. "That the healers wouldn't be fast enough, or..."

"I'm fine, Rowan," Claire said softly, moving one of her hands to the side of my neck, thumb brushing against the edge of my jaw.

"I'm a *necromancer*, Claire. I'm not supposed to be scared of death, of people dying. *You* are. You should be scared of death, not of *me*," I blurted out. All the anger I was convinced would boil over, allowing me to snap at Claire, seeped deeper and deeper into my bones.

225

I was the only one it stung.

Claire pulled me closer and I wrapped my arms tightly around her waist, face buried against her collarbone. I had thought Claire to be calm, but her heart bruised the inside of her ribs, breath coming heavily. She was only quiet and composed, nothing more. How pathetic it was that she'd been gut like a fish and I was the one taking comfort from her.

"I was not scared of you," she said, pressing her nose to the top of my head. "I was scared *for* you. I have told you before that you cannot afford to use your powers, no matter the circumstances."

"I could've closed the wound before they saw. Could've said I was a healer..."

"It wouldn't have worked, Rowan. Say you managed to fool Queen Kidira, what then? She would have you work as a healer within the castle, amongst *real* healers. Do you think they would remain oblivious for long? You know Kastelir's rules. They would take you, Rowan, and they would burn you."

Her hold tightened as she spoke, as though there'd been space between us. I saw how cruel I'd truly been. Claire had been scared and I'd done her a disservice when all she wished to do was protect me. And at such a cost. I should've done more than freeze up when my necromancy was forced back. I should've acted as Kouris and Akela had, should've gripped her hand and told her she was going to be alright.

It was selfish, I knew it was, but I was relieved to have her in my arms.

I inched back, looked up at her, and wanted to voice everything I was feeling more than thinking.

But all I could say was, "You could've *died.*"

"I know," she told me, hand on my cheek. "But I took my chances, and I am fine."

Had she died, I wouldn't have let her stay that way. I would've ripped death from her so cleanly that it would shudder at the thought of ever returning, consequences be damned. They could place me in irons, they could tie me to the stake, but I would've found a way to escape. And though I was foolish enough to believe it at that moment, I wasn't foolish enough to say it out loud.

I kissed Claire, that time. My fists bundled against the collar of her shirt and I pulled her close. The moment I pressed my mouth to hers, I

226

knew it had happened before, knew that it had been real. She didn't just let me kiss her. She returned the kiss in earnest, hands on the small of my back, and without breaking away, I mumbled, "I need to know what's happening, Claire," against her lips.

She pressed her forehead to mine, nodding and nodding, and cupped my cheeks with both hands as she kissed me.

I waited for the truth to spill out of her, but was met with nothing but a knock at the door.

Claire let out a frustrated breath that brushed across my face and stepped back, calling out, "It's open."

She regained her composure in a second but I was flustered, scratching the back of my neck and doing what I could to fade into the background.

It wasn't anyone I recognised. A guard nodded in greeting and said, "Their Highnesses require your presence immediately."

Queen Kidira hadn't wasted any time in imploring them to hear Claire out again. Claire didn't delay. She saw her chance and seized it, following the guard out with little more than a tilt of her head in my direction.

I was left with her dragon-bone armour for company, propped on display, cold and empty.

I corked the wine, but found little more in the way of distracting myself. Head buzzing, I braved the castle alone, no real destination in mind. I wanted to find Kouris, but she was likely with Claire, and I didn't dare to ask any of the servants or guards where she was. I had no idea who knew she was Queen Kouris, and I didn't want to ask where this-or-that pane was, lest I accidentally reveal too much.

The castle was home to hundreds, and the spiralling staircases I took downwards led to endless kitchens and pantries, cellars full of wine barrels, bottles kept locked behind bars. I expected to be stopped at every turn, but the servants were too busy to notice me and the guards took me for a servant.

I rushed through music rooms that could've swallowed my entire house, avoided trampling rugs crafted with more care than Claire's armour, boots caked with dirt and blood from the trip to Kyrindval, and found Kouris in a courtyard.

A pond rested in the centre, surrounded by stone tigers snarling at the water, and lords and ladies and lieges wandered amongst the orange daylilies and black dahlias planted in neat rows. Most of them turned on their heels upon spotting a pane, promptly remembering they had other matters to attend to.

I approached from a balcony a level up and leant against the stone railing until Kouris noticed me. Her ears perked up as she headed over, looking up at me, for once. There was no need to ask if I'd found Claire. She smiled up at me and held her arms out.

"You want me to jump?" I asked, lifting my brow. "I'm sure there's a safer way down."

"Aye, but finding the right staircase could take *minutes*," Kouris pointed out. "It's hardly a mountain you're leaping down, now is it?"

The nobles who'd steered clear of Kouris stopped to watch from the columns surrounding the courtyard, and I didn't hesitate a moment longer. I swung a leg over the stone railing, sat on the edge, and let myself drop into Kouris' arms. She caught me with a playful *oof* and gave me a squeeze before setting me down.

"Thanks," I said, taking her hand and leading her to the pond. "Thanks for getting Claire back in time. I don't think any of the horses could've managed it."

"She's a tough one, she is," Kouris said, perching next to me on the edge of the pond. "Reckon that dragon-slayer's seen much worse than all of that. Shame about Luxon, though. We could've learnt a thing or two from him. Akela tells me that's all taken care of."

"Yeah, it's... it's been taken care of," I agreed.

I trailed my fingers through the clear water, watching the koi scatter as I leant against one of the stone tigers. Kouris watched me from the corner of her eye but said nothing, giving me time to reflect on how exhausted I was. I closed my eyes, listening to the din of the castle beyond, and decided I wouldn't stand again, unless I was heading back to my bed.

Luxon was gone and Claire was safe, and I was on the verge of finding out what had set this all into motion.

It did nothing to settle me. There was something else there, something lingering in my blind spot.

"What's on your mind, yrval?"

I opened one eye, intent on shaking my head and telling her I was tired, but curiosity got the better of me.

"I could've saved her," I said. "Right there. You wouldn't have had to run back to Isin, she wouldn't have had to be in pain for all that time. I could've saved Luxon, too."

Kouris hummed. I'd hardly given her anything to disagree with.

"You say that nobody cares about this sort of thing in Canth. That it's a *good* thing. So why? Why can't I help people?"

Even as I spoke, I knew it wasn't as simple as all that. What I really wanted to know was why it had become so complicated.

"Now, in Canth, they're having plenty of problems. The new Queen is a good one, but she's dealing with a country full of pirates and poverty. There's only one problem they've never had, and that's a war with necromancers," Kouris explained. "They call us heathens. Reckon we never should've abandoned our gods. And necromancers, they're considered Isjin's own. Sons or Daughters or Children of Isjin, they're called. The people in Canth, they never suffered like your ancestors did. There was no exodus. Entire countries weren't wiped out."

Everything I knew about Isjin was limited to the tales told during the Phoenix Festival, and most of those revolved around how much better off we were without her. The suggestion that she had some sort of fondness for necromancers didn't sit well with me. Where had she been when I'd needed to believe I was something other than a host for dark forces?

"But why can't they just learn to change their minds?" I asked, hands balled into fists. "I used to be scared of pane, of you, but... I'm not going to hurt anyone."

Kouris chuckled far from unkindly.

"Sometimes, yrval, I reckon you don't know how powerful you are."

"Healers are powerful!" I said, belatedly remembering how to keep my voice down. "They can basically do everything I can. They can even stop pain. *I* can't do that. Or I haven't figured it out yet, anyway."

"Aye, healers are powerful, but here's the thing: they have limits. Sometimes they're not quick enough, sometimes not skilled enough. Sometimes they've pushed a disease out too many times and the body adapts. Point is: they have limits and everyone knows what they are. Everyone knows that they're not the be all and end all of power. But you..." Kouris smiled in a way that made her tusks seem longer and pressed a hand to my cheek. "Yrval, you could do near enough anything you wanted. A human, now, even with the best healer on Bosma, they're going to be living two hundred years at the very most. But you, you won't have seen a drop of your life in that time. A necromancer can bring theirself back, can bring anyone back. No matter what. Even if they've been gone for days, weeks. Months. Even if they've had their eyes carved out and their head cut clean off."

The walls of the courtyard drew in closer, forcing my ribs to press too tightly to hold air in my chest. The implication behind what she'd said clung in the air, and she stared at me, unblinking, expression screaming that she'd wanted to voice it for a long, long time.

"Kouris..." I whispered, moving onto my knees, hands finding her throat.

She tilted her head back and I felt it. It wasn't a scar running across her flesh but something deeper than all that. It rushed through her like a wind howling through a canyon, calling out to me. It was there, it was there. How had I missed it?

"Yrval," Kouris said softly, fingers wrapping around my wrists. "We'll be drawing attention. Come on."

Questions knotted inside of me, a string of why-why-why, and I followed her out of the courtyard, through twisting corridors, as soundless as a forgotten spirit. My surroundings blurred around me, and all I could focus on was the power trapped in Kouris' core. Power that wasn't mine, but was so familiar I might as well have pressed my fingers against a mirror, rather than her throat.

The door rattled in its frame behind us, sunlight glaring through the windows. I blinked bright, scattered colours out of my eyes and watched my room take form around me. Kouris crouched in the corner, shoulders slumping, having been held up by secrets for years.

"Why didn't you say anything?" I said, standing between her knees and placing my hands on her cheeks. "Why did you let everyone believe you'd just run away?"

"Didn't like to be causing a fuss," she said, lips twitching into a smile, eyes grey as stone. "Better not to be... you're understanding how it is, I'm sure."

Best not to bring necromancy into it. Would the Kings look at her as they did, if they'd known she'd faced the guillotine? Or would they blame necromancy for changing her, rather than the decades spent in Canth?

I dragged her over to the bed. The curtains caught on her horns, but there was room enough for us both. She fell against the mattress and I pressed myself close to her side, doing all I could to refrain from clawing out everything she knew about necromancers.

"What happened?" I asked, head rested on her outstretched arm. "What really happened? If you don't mind talking about it."

"It's been too long for me to really mind. Just makes me thoughtful, that's all," Kouris said, eyes flitting left and right as she searched for a place to start. "For a while, I was running from the mob. Always intended to go to them, but I was scared. Seemed like a noble enough thought when I left the castle, atoning for all the hurt I'd caused, but once I was out there, once they were hunting me down, I couldn't help but run. I even considered running away to Canth...

"Well, not all of the stories were nonsense. You know what happened next. And as for the necromancer, his name was Iseul. Good lad. A decade older than you are now, maybe. He was the town taxidermist. They were gonna have him take my horns and send 'em back to Kastelir, serving as a sort of proof.

"Only he had his own ideas. He knew he couldn't just bring me back and let me roam around Kastelir, both for my sake and the country's. So he took me, body, head, horns and all, and off we went on a boat, all the way across the Uncharted Sea. Didn't bring me back until we were on solid ground, though. Turns out packing a little bitterwillow around a body stops it from going too far to rot."

She was calm as she spoke. Her chest rose and fell evenly and her voice didn't tremble, yet all I could think of was how scared she must've been. Knelt at the guillotine, feeling time in its entirety for how little there was left; knowing beyond knowing that it was all about to end; hearing the blade set loose, falling, falling.

And then waking up a world away, body bound together after so long. I wanted to know what she'd seen beyond this life, whether she'd seen the Forest Within the Forest, but didn't dare ask, lest there'd been nothing at all.

People did their best to forget that we only knew about the world beyond this one because of necromancers.

231

"Why don't you tell Queen Kidira? She thinks you just left her and started a new life. But if she knew, she might not be so angry," I said, and Kouris shook her head as I spoke.

"I stayed away for twenty-seven years. That's about all that matters. What difference would any of it make? Don't reckon I deserve her forgiveness, anyway."

Whatever had drawn Kouris back was more powerful than the love she had for Queen Kidira, and her plans running parallel with Claire's, if they didn't entwine, was the only thing that stopped me from asking wat it was. There was no need for Kouris to punish herself any more than Queen Kidira already was, and I hoped that she'd come to understand that, in time.

I hoped that in time, I'd see why she'd entrusted her affection to Queen Kidira in the first place.

"Iseul, is he...?"

It was too much to wish for, but I had to know.

"He worked off his debt in Canth and got back on a ship to Kastelir, a few years in," Kouris said. "Never heard another word from him. Sorry, yrval."

Then I was still alone.

The two of us laid there, reflecting on all Kouris had said. The difference between healers and necromancers, especially. Without having to close my eyes, I was able to see inside of myself for the first time; there was something burning deep, deep down in the black. So deep that the light barely sparked. It was an anchor, keeping me fixed there, in Bosma, made of something more solid than ageless mountains, tree roots twisting deeper than the ocean.

Everyone else was fleeting. There was a light within them, but it wasn't what they were. They were bound to Bosma by a tether; a tether anyone could cut, but only I could join the frayed ends back together.

"I'm going to live forever, aren't I?" I asked Kouris.

I understood what people intrinsically knew when faced with a necromancer: that I was not like them.

"Now, don't be getting too upset about it. I know I'm going to be living for a long, long time, but that's no reason to fret," Kouris said, poking my side with a crooked finger.

"How long *do* pane live?" I asked, turning onto my front.

"I said Zentha was about three hundred, aye? Over in Jorjang, I hear there's a pane who's pushing six-hundred. That's about the only remarkable thing there. Tiny tribe. Barely even two dozen of them. As for pane in general, well. Despite how I might be skewing your perspective, we're a pretty laid back people. We take our time with things. If we're ignoring any accidents, any human interference, I reckon five hundred is about the average. Though I'm told a dozen centuries back, a woman by the name of Borya made it to eight hundred, near enough. Not sure if I'm willing to believe that, though."

Moments ago, I'd tussled with the prospect of eternity, but that had the benefit of being an abstract idea. It was more comforting than the thought of being burnt, or drowning in the ocean, dashed to pieces against the rocks. Numbers like *four hundred* and *eight hundred* were too big for me to digest, and I could only think how *young* Kouris was. Perhaps twenty-seven years hadn't felt very long to her.

I didn't have it in me to ask anything more about the pane, no matter how valuable a distraction it might've been. I was exhausted to the point of apathy. It had all been too much. Luxon's death, what had happened to Claire, and now this. The truth about Kouris and myself. It'd feel real in the morning, but for now, it fell about me like a fog, swamping my thoughts with a constant thrum of grey.

Even kissing Claire felt distant.

Kouris understood my need to lapse into silence. She pulled me close, hands on my back, and sleep came to me before the sun had the chance to consider setting.

233

CHAPTER SIXTEEN

Kouris left early in the morning.

I felt her rise but didn't stir for more than a second, caught up in dreams as I was. I dreamt of Luxon, black mist rising from his body, slowly taking form, eyes burning like the moon. I dreamt of waking, of drifting through corridors, and coming so close to the truth Claire had promised me that I *almost* knew what it was.

Sleep didn't leave me rested, but I awoke to find I was still myself, arms and legs intact. The suffocating extent to which I'd felt my powers had drained away, already distant.

I was still rubbing the sleep out of my eyes when someone knocked at the door. I poked my head through the curtains and called for them to come in. Claire stepped into the room and held the door open for a servant. He placed a breakfast big enough for a pane on one of the low tables and left with a bow in Claire's direction and a few silver coins in his hand.

"I wasn't certain how comfortable you were issuing orders to the servants. Nor was I certain what you wanted for breakfast," Claire said, glancing at the assortment of bread, cooked meats, fruit and cheese. "Evidently."

I grinned from ear to ear. Sleep had replenished my appetite, but I promptly forgot all about food when Claire ducked beneath the curtains and perched on the edge of the bed.

Kyrindval had worn away some of the dark marks beneath her eyes, but Isin was determined to put them back. I wanted to wrap my arms around her and pull her onto the bed, but I knew she wouldn't be there for long. There was always something Claire had to do, always for someone other than herself.

"Are you alright?" I tried, and she turned her head towards me slowly, having not heard me at all. "Is everything okay?"

She nodded without meaning it. I shuffled across the bed and leant against her back.

"I am just..." she started. "It is..."

Claire let out a long, heavy breath, and I said nothing, giving her time to gather her thoughts.

"You will understand soon. I've no doubt of that. There is to be a meeting at midday, in the Cardinal Hall, where we will finally decide what is to be done. Kouris has ensured you'll be granted access."

I buried my forehead between her shoulder blades and nodded. My arms slipped from beneath the blankets and around her waist, and she leant against me, not needing to say anything more. She covered my hand with one of hers, and I lifted my head to see her glancing back at me. She bit her lower lip, on the verge of saying something more, but it was no good.

Claire was back on her feet before I realised I'd let go of her. I fought with the blankets and jumped out of bed, but she was halfway out the door.

"There are matters I must discuss with Kouris," she said.

I fell down on the sofa and glared at the mountain of food as though it was responsible for everything that had led Claire to Kastelir. She hadn't come to my room to bring me breakfast and let me know I was welcome at the meeting; she'd come to me for a reason. She'd been on the cusp of admitting she needed someone to support her, if only for a moment, and I hadn't been able to keep her in the room.

I tore through the food, taking my frustration out with my teeth, washed by the basin, and found clean clothing in one of the dressers. It more or less fit.

From the window, Isin was remarkably peaceful in its bustle. It was difficult to believe that anyone had reason to be angry, much less reason to band together about whatever I'd half-witnessed yesterday.

The clock tower opposite my window said that midday was hours away, but I wasn't taking any chances. I made for the larger rooms I'd happened across yesterday, but headed too far down, ending up by the cellars. I took the nearest staircase and had far better luck in a more open part of the castle, corridors full of courtiers and scholars drifting this way and that.

Less than a day ago, I'd been terrified a guard was going to grab me by the scruff of my collar and march me back to my room. Today, I'd barely been wandering for ten minutes when I walked into a King.

King Jonas stepped out of a chamber, surrounded by a slew of advisers waving parchment at him, trying to get his seal on some documents of great urgency, each bartering for a moment, just a moment, of his time. He waved a hand to silence them and said, "Good people, I appreciate your enthusiasm and dedication, but I shall not be returning to business until this afternoon. If you would be so kind as to give me some space..."

King Jonas caught my eye. His advisers followed his gaze, making me feel as though I should apologise for daring to stand within eyeshot of the King.

He rushed forward, forest-green cloak billowing behind him.

"Rowan! Goodness, I heard about the trouble on your return journey," he said, taking one of my hands between his. "I'm glad to see you safe. Never before have we experienced a problem of the sort on the way to or from Kyrindval, I assure you."

"I, um..."

His greeting was a world away from King Atthis', and I began to understand how the rulers of Kastelir balanced each other out. King Jonas had no one other than disgruntled advisers to put on a show for, but his concern was genuine. All I could think was that I'd been entrusted to return the books Michal had borrowed without permission, but had no idea where my bag was.

"No one saw it coming," I settled on.

Most of those encircling us scattered, attending to their own business when our conversation led to nothing of interest.

"Kouris tells me you're to join us in discussing matters today," he said, voice flitting from one serious tone to another. "Terrible business, that, but I'm convinced a solution can be reached."

King Jonas operated under the impression that I knew exactly what was going on, and I nodded mutely, not wishing to contradict him.

"I was trying to find the meeting hall, Your Highness," I said. "But I keep ending up in the pantries. Can you tell me where to go?"

"I can do better than that, dear," he said cheerfully, turning on his heels and taking wide, brisk strides down the corridor.

"Your Highness, I, it's fine, honestly!" I said, hurrying after him. "I'll be able to find my own way. You don't have to take me all the way there."

"Nonsense! I've plenty of time before I'm due anywhere. Besides, it saves me from having to deal with yet more poignant advice and endless account books."

There was no telling a King to stop. I dared to walk by his side, far from oblivious to the looks I was drawing, the sudden curiosity sparking in the faces of those we passed. The clean clothes did nothing to mask my station in life, sorely out of place amongst the nobility who spent hours styling and restyling their hair, swapping silver chains out for gold ones until they found something to match their carefully chosen outfits.

"Have you seen much of the city?" King Jonas asked.

"Not much, Your Highness. Only what I passed on the way in and out. Although yesterday, I think there was something going on in one of the squares. People were shouting, and not in the way they usually do at market. Or after too many drinks."

The last part earnt a laugh, and he said, "Kastelir is still young, I'm afraid. Isin deals with the brunt of it. It's nothing that won't blow over in a day or two, if that."

I took him at his word and focused on remembering the path there. It was either three lefts and a right, or two lefts and two rights; regardless, I had to pass under an archway with a bear carved into one of the columns, and head down a corridor lined with paintings of Kastelir's landscapes.

Our destination was a great courtyard, littered with stone benches and finely crafted topiary. It was likely the largest in the castle, and probably at its very centre. A dragon arched its back in one corner, opposite a stag with antlers rivalling its wingspan, while a bear and tiger claimed the other two corners for their own.

"Thank you for the company, Rowan," King Jonas said, pointing to the hefty looking doors we were to meet behind later. "This is where I leave you, for the time being. I shan't be gone for long."

"Thank you, Your Highness. You really didn't have to."

But King Jonas thought nothing of it. He left with a nod of his head, forgiving me for bowing awkwardly. The scholars taking advantage of the clear weather were too busy reading and writing and frowning to notice me, and the gardeners were similarly occupied.

It was surreal. I'd gone from my farmland of a prison, all the way through Kastelir, to the mountains and back, and a King remembered my name. A King had spoken with me, walked with me. I was starting to lose track of the royalty I knew. It wouldn't feel real until it was all over. Until I was back in my kitchen, telling my father all of the things I could never get across in a letter.

I sat down, deciding there was no rule against claiming a bench for my own, and Akela caught my eye from across the courtyard. The incident with Luxon had done nothing to stop her smiling enough for the whole castle, but the thought of the blade thrust in his throat turned my stomach. Either that or eating so much for breakfast had been unwise: I was light-headed enough that I found myself gripping the edge of the bench, and a strange, sickly feeling thickened in my throat.

Akela wasn't alone. A noblewoman stood by her side, wearing a sky-blue dress with such intricate patterns embroidered on it in darker thread that mapping them out would've caused my head to spin all the more. She was no more than a few years older than I was, if that, tall, and very slender. Her sandy-blonde hair was tucked behind her ears, top layer worked into two braids, and the fact that she was smiling came as no surprise.

It was hard not to, in Akela's company.

"You must be Rowan! Goodness, it's nice to meet you," she said brightly, offering me her hand.

I took it, but she saw the confusion creased into my features.

"I'm sorry! It was awfully rude of me to accost you like that. Especially when I have you at such a disadvantage! It's simply that the Commander was telling me about our Felheimish guests, and, well, you don't *quite* match the description of Sir Ightham or..." the woman paused to lower her voice. "Queen Kouris, which left me with but one guess."

Belatedly realising she was still shaking my hand, she let go, and Akela cleared her throat.

"Oh! You'll have to forgive me. It seems I've misplaced my manners today. My name is Kouris. It's a pleasure to meet you, dear."

"Oh, you're—" I began, making more of a mess of bowing than before. "It's nice to meet you, Your Highness."

Akela and Kouris – the human Kouris – glanced at one another, bemused, and Kouris broke out into laughter softer than Akela's.

"No, no. My, we aren't *quite* so similar to Felheim, dear. My mother might be a Queen, but that doesn't make me a Princess, or anything of the sort," Kouris said, charmed by my blunder. "Our rulers are voted onto the throne. That was the theoretical basis for Kastelir, at least, but my mother and uncles always find reasons to extend their reign indefinitely, and... oh, you aren't concerned with that. My point is, Kouris will do. Lady Kouris, officially, but that's rather formal, don't you think?"

"Then it's nice to meet you... Kouris?"

She frowned.

"Yes, I do see how that would be bizarre for you. Goodness, I'm usually the first and only Kouris people have ever met. This is new for me, as well." She hummed thoughtfully. "How's this: my middle name is Katja. I believe the woman who gave birth to me insisted that my mother keep it as some part of my name, though I was never given the sentimental details. I shouldn't imagine that I'd be averse to you calling me that, if you wish. What do you think?"

"It's a nice name," I said, feeling a lot better. The sickness was still there, but it was pushed down by good company.

"I'm glad you think so! I do so apologise if I don't respond to it immediately. It's nothing against you dear, trust me," she said. "Oh! Yes, I wanted to ask if you lived anywhere near Thule. I was just visiting my fiancé, you see, and wondered if you might be familiar with the area."

Had I been born in Thule, there was no way I'd recognise any of the places Katja had been. Akela might've told her my name, might've described what I looked like, but Katja had yet to grasp my station.

"I'm from the south of Felheim. Benkor and Praxis are the closest I've been to Thule, and that wasn't even a few months ago," I said.

Katja was a little disappointed, but it soon dawned on her that it'd be far more interesting to talk about places she'd never been.

"I'm certain you're more than a little busy at the moment, goodness knows we all are, but might I trouble you for your company, sometime? I'd love to know more about Felheim. Especially if I'm to marry a Felheimer! It only seems smart, don't you think? Sadly, we've had little contact with your Kingdom. This whole marriage situation is taking everyone by surprise. Me most of all."

I felt oddly qualified to answer any questions she might have, already able to predict what they might be. Had I ever seen a dragon? How often had my village been attacked? Did we have many pane? How many Knights had I met, other than Sir Ightham? What did the Felheimish think of Kastelirians?

Katja had a light, easy way about her, and I found myself readily agreeing.

"It wouldn't be any trouble at all, if you don't mind hearing about farms and sheep, because that's all I really know," I said.

Katja laughed under her breath, uncertain whether I was joking or not.

"This is where I leave you, Commander," she said to Akela, who bowed deeply. "Do ask my mother to stop by my apartment this evening, should she get the chance to."

Katja reiterated that it was nice to have met me and made herself scarce, heading towards a group of wealthy scholars, none of whom were dressed half as nicely as she was. Akela rocked on the balls of her feet, watching her go, and dropped onto the bench next to me.

The sickness subsided soon after, and Akela fiddled with the cuffs of her armour as she hummed under her breath. Distracted though she was, Akela did a commendable job of remaining as upbeat as she'd always been, when an axe wasn't in her hand. Her thoughts revolved around the upcoming meeting, and I glanced around for something to talk about, to take both our minds off it.

Akela was still in her armour, though not officially on duty, judging by the way she was idling in the courtyard. Brown leather plates covered dark blue mesh and chains, proudly displaying scuffs and scratches across it. It was far more beaten than anything any of the guards wore, bearing three red stripes on the left shoulder.

"What does this mean?" I asked, tapping the stripes. "I've not seen them on the guards' uniforms."

"Hah! I should not be thinking so. These stripes, they are only for those who are fighting, yes? Not just standing in the castle, holding spears, becoming part of the furniture," Akela said, eager to indulge me. "The colours, they are ferocity! Well, Their Highnesses, they are saying they are for rank, and I am saying, these are the same things, yes? Grey for the footman, yellow for the lieutenants, orange for the captains – I am missing some, I am not remembering every rank – and for me, because I am being the Commander – *The* Commander, with the big *t*, you are hearing this – I am wearing red.

"And the stripes, they are time. Three years, six, nine. It is being two more years and I am getting another. Impressive, yes?"

I'd met no shortage of impressive people since leaving my village, but that did nothing to render Akela's accomplishments anything less than remarkable. In all of Michael's stories, the leaders of mighty armies had been far older than Akela appeared to be. She was around Claire's age, though she had more wear to show for the years, and I understood Claire being a Knight at her age. There were no ranks to climb; either you had what it took to slay dragons or you didn't.

"It is normal to rise through the ranks so quickly?" I asked, once I'd found the right way to phrase my question.

"Not at all!" Akela declared. "The last Commander, she is working for King Jonas for eighteen years before finally, she is the Commander. But you are wanting to know my secret, yes? Queen Kidira, she is liking me very much."

Through some intervention of the gods who'd abandoned us, I managed to stop myself from saying *Does Queen Kidira actually like anyone?*

"No, no. I am joking, only joking. Mostly. Actually, it is being many years ago and I am being on the battlefield, and I am saving King Atthis' son. This boy, he is being excellent with the strategies, but he is no warrior. I am finally showing how good I am! So the King, he is getting his son back, he is being in one piece, and I am being promoted. Everyone is happy.

"Except the man I am defeating. He is having an axe between his eyes and not laughing about it at all."

No matter how macabre the topic, Akela forced a breathy laugh out of me. I could see her thriving on the battlefield, lifting her troops' spirits without shying away from the reality of things, always fighting on the frontlines, in the thick of the action. It was almost as if she'd been born a few decades too late, with the war long over.

"Wait. You saved King Atthis' son from *who*?" I asked.

"Hm?"

"You said you saved King Atthis' son in a battle, but Kastelir hasn't attacked Felheim *ever*, and I don't think Agados is big enough to go to war with a Kingdom like this one. I'd never even heard of it before! So who were you fighting?"

"Ah, you are knowing how it is. Sometimes, we are having pirates from Canth sail up, and they are taking whatever it is they are wanting from the ports. And Kastelir, it is only a young country. We are still having problems. Well, I am thinking Felheim is still having problems, yes? Some, they are wishing that the territories are returning, because if they are not fighting, they are not happy. Sometimes, there are problems," Akela said, concluding her point with a shrug.

I doubted enough pirates made it to Kastelir to evoke the wrath of an entire army. In some ways, Kastelir was as I'd always imagined it. The shift in Akela's expression told me that it went deeper than people merely fighting amongst themselves for the fun of it. Knowing better than to push the subject, I waited patiently for the Kings and Queen to arrive, promising myself that I'd finally speak to Claire properly, once I knew what had kept her awake for so very long.

The Kings Atthis and Jonas arrived with little fanfare. Two guards pushed the doors open and Akela jumped to her feet, following the guards inside. I hesitated, not moving until I saw Kouris and Claire trailing behind. I walked ahead of them, lest they promptly change their minds and tell me to turn back.

The room wasn't as large as I'd expected, but it was grander. An eight-sided table sat in the centre, with chairs that felt like thrones at four of the sides. The seat reserved for Kouris was more than big enough for her, finials of wooden horns flowing from the sides of the crestrail. King Atthis sat opposite her, his own seat similarly decorated with a crown of antlers.

To see the Kings look at Kouris was to know her seat had been empty for a very, very long time.

There were smaller chairs along the other four edges, and Claire took her place next to Kouris, while Akela sat by the empty chair Queen Kidira was to fill. I moved to Kouris' other side, seeing the whole of Kastelir spread out before me as I sat.

The table was a map in and of itself, carved from wood, rivers filled with meticulously sanded glass. Hills rose and fell along the uneven surface, and the settlements, from Riverhurst to Isin, were cast in miniature. Mountains ran across the edges Kouris, Claire and I sat along, and deep lines divided the map into quarters, marking the former territories.

King Atthis drummed his fingers on the edge of the table, certain it was a waste of time. The rest of us sat in silence, waiting for Queen Kidira to arrive. Akela shot to her feet when the Queen pushed the doors open and took a seat without glancing in her direction.

Akela cleared her throat and stood straighter, chest pushed out.

"Do take a seat, Commander," Queen Kidira said dryly.

Akela bowed too formally to be taken seriously and fell back into her chair.

I thought that would set things into motion, but everyone merely looked at each other, uncertain where to start. Eventually, King Atthis sighed, tilting his head towards Claire.

"Well, Knight?"

The back legs of Claire's chair scraped uncomfortably against the floor as she stood.

"Your Majesties," she said, greeting the room. "Commander."

"Are you quite recovered, Sir Ightham?" King Jonas took the time to ask.

"I am, Your Highness. Thanks to the healers within the castle," she said. She took a breath and moved on. "I am here to petition you for your assistance. This time with the support of both Queen Kouris and Queen Kidira."

"*Queen* Kouris is pushing it a little, don't you think?" Atthis said, pressing two fingers to his temple. "She's spent the last few decades living as a pirate on the other side of the globe. Don't plead your case too hard, Ightham. It's unbecoming."

Kouris shot King Atthis a look so cold that he lifted both of his hands and relented without another word.

"Then I come here with the support of Queen Kidira, and that of my friend, Kouris," she corrected herself. "I would ask that Kastelir lends its forces to liberate the people of Felheim."

"From?" King Atthis asked, well aware of the answer.

"From a ruling class that no longer has a sense of perspective when it comes to the safety of its people and borders," Claire said bluntly.

"*No,*" King Atthis returned. "You would not merely have us dethrone your King and Queen. And that, Knight, would already be asking too much. What you want is for us to blindly charge into the maw of a dragon."

Had anyone been under the impression I knew what was happening, it was soon dispelled. I tried to keep my expression neutral and build a sense of the whole problem from the scraps that were being thrown around, but at the mention of dragons, I turned to Claire, confusion lighting up my face. She kept her eyes fixed on King Atthis, not once looking my way.

"I am not asking anything of the sort, Your Highness, I simply wi—"

"You wish to make threats against Kastelir in the guise of a warning, to cajole us into aiding your mutiny."

Would that I could've brought my fist to the table and snapped at the King to let Claire speak. Luckily, King Jonas handled it far more sensitively than I would've, and Kouris leant back in her seat, letting out a growl of a breath.

"Atthis, we are never going to get anywhere if you refuse to hear her out. I am as sceptical as you are, my friend, but I am hardly pushing my fingers in my ears and waiting for it to all blow over," he said. "Sir. If you would continue."

King Atthis propped his chin on his palm, granting Claire permission to speak with a wave of his hand.

"I am not here to betray Felheim. Nothing could be further from the truth. I have spent my entire life serving Felheim, and in coming here, I serve it still. As a people, we have always been proud of the peace within our Kingdom, and our history of avoiding conflicts with larger, stronger nations; both Kastelir and the territories before. However, I cannot abide the methods that have been employed to shape the country, or what is likely to become of Felheim and Kastelir both," Claire said.

I was grasping to make sense of it all, but there wasn't enough. I was out of my depth, while everyone in the room listened, understanding every word of it.

King Atthis continued to look unimpressed. King Jonas took it in, if nothing else, and it was impossible to tell what Queen Kidira was thinking. Even if Claire supposedly had her support.

"Your Highness. Might I ask you a question?"

"You might," King Atthis said.

"What reason do dragons have to acknowledge borders set by humans? Dragons reside along the entire mountain range, yet Agados and Kastelir remain safe, while Felheim is plagued by a dozen attacks a year. Why might this be?"

King Atthis shrugged in what I was certain was a very Kingly fashion.

"And a question to all of you. In the time of the territories, the borders never remained fixed for long. The leaders were ever stealing land from one another, expanding their own territories, and going so far as to claim portions of what was once Agados. Yet no attempts were ever made on Felheim. Why?"

244

Queen Kidira took the question when the Kings only frowned.

"By the time each of us came into power in our respective territories, it had long since been established that we would not be able to rule a land plagued by dragons. It would simply not be worth it," she said.

"Exactly. You must believe what I am telling you. You must heed this warning, even if you will not lend me your aid," Claire said. "The first dragon fell to the Priorys the same year this land crumbled into territories, leading to a two-hundred and forty-seven-year string of dragon attacks. During which time Felheim has not once been threatened by outside forces. The dragons *are* being manipulated to sacrifice a few for the greater good of the country."

There are always dragons, Claire had told me, stood on the ashes of what had once been a village. The dragons around Kyrindval tore through my mind, curled up, peaceful, diving into the lake and playing. She was right. I instinctively knew that Claire was right. If the Kings would not believe her, I would.

I was desperate for her to turn my way and catch my eye for half a second. I wanted her to know that I was there for her, if Kastelir was not; I would not doubt her, whatever little that meant.

But she did not look.

"And how does one manipulate a dragon?" King Atthis asked, picking apart her words as though it was one of Michael's particularly tedious stories.

"By *abusing* it," Kouris said, slamming her open palm on the edge of the table. The mountains almost toppled. "Atthis, I swear to Isjin, I love you in a way that makes me think I might be understanding what a brother is, but you're doing everything you can to test my patience. How do you *think* they're manipulating dragons? The same way people are forcing their dogs to tear each other to pieces. Mistreat 'em enough and they'll spend their whole lives terrified. The moment you let 'em fly free, aye, they're gonna burn down the first thing they see.

"The dragon are my kin, Atthis. I'm dragon-born. In the mountain, the pane, we're always looking after the dragons. We know how they work, what makes 'em sick, and how to make them better. The Felheimish are twisting that. They're taking us, forcing us to turn against our own. So don't be sitting there, *bored*, when I should be all the proof you're needing. Twenty-seven years I've been gone, Atthis, and *this* is what finally brings me back. Never thought I'd return, but the moment I found out what was happening, I was on a boat before I could blink."

Queen Kidira watched Kouris as she spoke, and didn't flinch at the clear implication that nothing else could've brought her back to Kastelir.

Atthis rose to his feet, not about to leave Kouris unchallenged.

"You think I'm bored by all of this, Kouris? You think I am so stubborn that I am ignoring very clear facts laid out in front of me? I am being cautious. For thirty years, I have done everything in my power to stop Kastelir from slipping back into another war, a civil war, and gods know it hasn't been easy. Gods know we could've used you around," he said. "What am I to do for this Knight, for Felheim, when I can barely do enough for my own Kingdom? If we take on Felheim, we will fall. If we leave Felheim as it is, there is a chance that Kastelir will become all that it ought to be."

"You're protecting the *humans*. If they were the ones being made to do this, being taken from their homes, you wouldn't be sitting there and humming over doing nothing."

"I have always cared for the pane, Kouris. All Kastelirians are my people, whether they have horns or not."

Growling, Kouris said, "You can't be doing that. Can't be pretending you care about all pane because you care about me, and leaving it at that. We're facing a lot more problems than looking different, Atthis, and you know we aren't treated the same. No matter what promises were made when we founded Kastelir."

The tumult that followed was more futile than the cry preceding a dragon attack. King Atthis and Kouris engaged in a repetitive back-and-forth that led nowhere, while King Jonas kept interjecting, trying to appease them both. Akela offered up a suggestion, but was immediately dismissed; King Atthis and Kouris were interested in nothing beyond yelling at each other.

"That's enough," Queen Kidira said. She didn't raise her voice but the room fell silent. "Sir Ightham. There is something you aren't sharing with us."

Claire's jaw was clamped tight. Had anyone but Queen Kidira addressed her, she would've fought to keep silent.

"I do not... I was not given the details," Claire started uneasily. "I have been led to believe that necromancy is involved."

No wonder she'd refused to look my way.

"Necromancy!" King Atthis declared. It was the last straw. "All of this information you so generous bring us; King Garland simply told you, did he?"

"Yes, Your Highness," Claire said, voice drowned out by the blood pounding in my ears.

"The King is your father, correct?"

"Correct, Your Highness."

"And you were to take over in his stead?"

"Yes, Your Highness."

"Yet you insist we call you *Knight*, or *Sir*. You hide your true title, ashamed of being the Princess of a land you claim to serve."

"Ashamed?" Claire asked in a whisper. "Of course I am ashamed. Of course I am sickened by the thought of what my family has done."

Necromancy was involved. Was that the reason Claire had taken me from my village? My nails scraped the underside of the table, and Kouris reached over, squeezing my hand to stop it from trembling. I couldn't show weakness.

Not in front of Queen Kidira.

But Queen Kidira wasn't concerned with me.

She got to her feet, determined to bring about a resolution.

"See, Atthis? Sir Ightham has no need to resort to deception or force to claim the throne. A sacrifice of this magnitude can only strengthen her case. The pane have been warning us for years. They may not understand what's happening, but they know that the dragons in Felheim are not acting as they ought to. Jonas. I expect you've come around," she stated, to which he nodded. "You have little choice at this point, Atthis. It is three against one. We are not going to attack Felheim. Do not think I would allow my country to make such a foolish move. But we are not going to allow ourselves to ignore the issue simply because we already have enough to deal with."

"I am thinking," Akela added, "If we are having a problem outside of Kastelir, perhaps it is bringing the people together, yes?"

Silence held the room in an uneasy grip, and King Atthis held up both hands, scowling as he spoke.

"Very well. I concede," he said, making ready to leave. "But know that I shall not agree to anything that allows another Felheimer, soldier,

Knight, or peasant, to set foot on our land with ill intent. Ightham, with me. I've more I need to know on this matter."

The scraping of chair legs against stone followed, meeting concluded, and everyone left to attend to other business. I didn't move. I didn't believe that anything else on Bosma could be worth paying heed to, after what I'd learnt.

Claire had spent her entire life believing she was doing the right thing, putting her life in danger to slay dragons and protect the people, but she'd only ever been lied to. She'd only moved as our monarchy had dictated, and she wasn't saving anyone. Not really.

All she did was act in the way a dragon's abrupt end could be explained.

CHAPTER SEVENTEEN

Nausea returned as soon as I left the chamber.

The midday sun stung my eyes. I lifted a hand, shielding them. The castle wasn't in ruins. Dragons hadn't swept down, sensing the truth slip free hundreds of miles away, and their breath hadn't turned the sky red. All those in the courtyard carried on as though nothing had changed, because it hadn't.

Nothing Claire had said was new.

It was the way things had been for hundreds of years, and my knowing did nothing to disrupt the balance of either Kastelir or Felheim.

Katja had either lingered or returned to the courtyard. The Kings were gone, Claire and Kouris along with them, but Katja had caught her mother's attention.

"I will be by later," Queen Kidira promised. "And if you are to go into the city, take Akela."

"Mother! The Commander is... Goodness, it's right there in the title, isn't it? She isn't a babysitter," Katja protested.

"Go with Akela or I shall have a dozen guards accompany you," Queen Kidira said. "It is not about *babysitting*. It is about avoiding any unrest."

"If the Commander is with me, who will follow you around?" Katja muttered, but Queen Kidira was gone. There was no arguing with her.

"You are not wanting the pleasure of my company?" Akela asked. "I am knowing people willing to start wars to be seeing me."

"Commander! It isn't that. You know I hate to inconvenience you so," Katja said. Catching sight of me, she said, "Rowan, dear, are you alright? You look terribly pale."

The next thing I knew, I was sat on a bench with Katja fussing over me. A glass of water appeared from somewhere, and I sipped it to appease her, not wanting her to worry. Katja placed the back of her hand on my forehead, more contemplative than concerned. Letting her search for a hint of a fever was a better option than explaining I hadn't been ill a day in my life.

"You *feel* fine," Katja concluded.

"Perhaps all Northwood is needing is some fresh air. Come! Together, we are going into Isin," Akela decided.

"I'm not sure I should..."

Akela didn't listen. She hooked an arm around mine and hoisted me to my feet.

"Northwood, you are needing a distraction," Akela said. "And if you are not coming, then Lady Kouris, she is fussing, she is not going to Isin, and everyone's plans, they are ruined! Are you wanting to ruin everyone's plans?"

Conceding that I didn't, I let Akela guide me out of the courtyard and through the castle, hands on my shoulders. We moved freely over the upper bridges, gates held open by guards, and moved in companionable silence through the city. Akela drifted behind us, keeping watch, and Katja linked her arm with mine, delighted by every blooming flower and flowing banner we passed.

She tugged my arm, steering me this way and that, in no hurry to reach her destination. She slowed to look in every shop window, and took in each detail of Isin as though it was her first visit that wasn't marred by urgency or anxiety. I could've believed it. Everything in Isin was so new that a mountain could've stood there the day before, carved into the shape of a city overnight.

"Oh! Already preparing for the Phoenix Festival, I see," Katja commented, and not as brightly as I'd expected her to. She stopped to look at red and orange bunting zigzagging above our heads, hanging from window to window. "I suppose it's barely weeks away now, is it?"

The corner of her mouth tugged into a frown. She continued on her way, distracted. She didn't take in the boxes of fire-red flowers lining the wide, bustling streets, and half-heartedly apologised under her breath whenever anyone bumped into her.

Much of Isin was lost on me. I was preoccupied with Katja waiting for me to say something to drag her out of her thoughts, but was made reluctant by believing I had nothing of worth to offer her. We went on like that for excruciating minutes until, out of the blue, I realised that I *did* have something to share with her.

No wonder she'd sought me out as she had.

"Did you want to know something about Kouris?" I asked.

Katja furrowed her brow, taking a second to realise I wasn't talking about her.

"Goodness, no! I should think I hardly have anything more to learn about Queen Kouris," she said, laughing. "I have spent my life raised on tales of the woman who helped found this country, who did more good in six years than most did in a lifetime; who marched so very bravely to her death. I'm almost sorry to see my mother proven so woefully wrong. My mother who, I have on good authority, will not so much as *look* at Queen Kouris."

As though Queen Kidira needed defending, I said, "Kouris *was* gone for twenty-seven years."

"All the more reason not to waste any time!" Katja declared. "But if you must tell me about somebody, dear, I'd much rather you told me about yourself."

"About me?"

I didn't want to be defensive, but there was only one part of me that had ever been of interest to anyone.

"Only if you wouldn't mind, of course," she was quick to add. "I shouldn't like to make you uncomfortable, Rowan. I've always been told I'm too curious for my own good. You see, it's simply that Uncle Jonas told me all about Queen Kouris' return, as well as the arrival of the Princess-turned-dragon-slayer, Sir Ightham. And then he mentioned a third traveller. Not a warrior of any renown, not even a noble. Someone much more *ordinary* than that. If I might be so bold as to guess, you are the daughter of a smith, or perhaps a farmer? And despite the conditions of your birth, you uplifted yourself high enough to become the chosen companion of a Knight and a Queen thought dead for close to thirty years. That's certainly something, don't you think?"

I would've been no less comfortable, had Katja accused me of being a necromancer there and then.

Her tone was light, pleasant, but to hear her sum up the last few months of my life in such a way made it sound unbelievable. Accusatory, even. My old life, my life as a healer, was beginning to feel like a story from one of Michael's less riveting books. I'd tricked myself into believing that my life was supposed to be dull, uneventful; I was supposed to be trapped in that kitchen, cold stone tiles beneath my feet, until the day I died.

Katja was right. It was *something.* I couldn't appreciate it as she did, because I'd lived each moment. Seconds passed one after another, and I was there because I had kept going, one step at a time. I tried to trace the path backwards, tried to remember a time when Claire wouldn't look at me, much less talk to me, and found I couldn't account for all that had changed between us.

I didn't want to, either. I was much fonder of the present, dragons and all.

"I'm a farmer. Was a farmer," I said, supposing Katja deserved an answer. "My father bought the farm long before me and Michael were born. That's my brother, by the way. He was travelling with us, but he's in Kyrindval now. It's a long story, and I think he'd rather tell it himself. But we raised all kinds of things. Cows, sheep, pigs. Crops too, of course. The farm will be mine and Michael's, one day. And, um. That's about all."

"That's it?" Katja asked, disappointed by my brevity. Unfortunately for her, there was no way for me to go into details without leaving a hole of seven years in my story. "Well, I shall hardly blame you for being so modest. After all, we've only just met, haven't we? That said, I do so hope we came become good friends, Rowan, and that in time, you'll feel more comfortable talking about yourself."

I scratched the back of my neck, mumbled some sort of agreement, and Katja beamed, tugging me down yet another side road.

I hadn't paid attention to where we were heading, and it wasn't until the smooth surface of the road turned to cobble that I lifted my head to see how dramatically our surroundings had changed. I glanced back to ensure Isin was still behind us, around us, worried we'd wandered into another settlement altogether.

The street breathed more history than any part of Isin had any real claim to. There were shops on both sides of us, all varied in shape and size, with apartments above their foggy glass windows. All the buildings leant towards one another, making the narrow street narrower, and the peeling paint around wooden window frames served as a sign of character, not neglect.

"You look rightly bemused, dear," Katja said, chuckling to herself. "I doubt most in Isin know this place even exists. A crying shame, honestly, but I must admit that it's all the better for me. There's nowhere more peaceful. Especially not within the castle."

The few people occupying the street strolled at their leisure, nodding in greeting and tipping their hats at one another. There were no signs of the Phoenix Festival encroaching onto this part of the city; no sign that something as trivial as time had touched it in decades.

Katja led me to the patio of a corner café, where Akela hurried over to pull our chairs out for us. She claimed a seat of her own a few tables back and waved at the woman behind the counter, who brought out a bottle of ale for her and tea for Katja. Katja was sure I'd better have water, lest I come over dizzy again, and soon enough a glass was between my hands, lemon spliced on the rim.

"Do you know, this is my favourite place in the city. My favourite place in the country," Katja said, closing her eyes and breathing in the crisp spring air. I couldn't help but mimic her. It was far less stuffy in this misplaced part of the world. "I even have a small apartment here. Right there, above the bakery. This is the true heart of Isin. Not the castle, as the Kings and Queens would have you believe. They'd let you think that Isin sprung up overnight, buildings fully-furnished and all.

"Isin, of course, means *creation* in Myrosi, but the city is more an act of... restoration, shall we say? Its foundations are a dozen smaller settlements, many of which have been paved over and forgotten. But this small segment of the city was once a town in its own right. Autíra wasn't very large, population perhaps nudging eight-hundred, but it was very *old*, and it withstood everything the territories had to throw against it. But—I'm rambling, aren't I? Do excuse me, dear. You didn't come for an impromptu history lesson!"

My ability to endure impromptu history lessons was legendary, having spent twenty-three years in Michael's presence. Katja had a charm he lacked. She spoke to impart her love of the place, rather than to impress me with her accumulated knowledge.

She lifted the tea to her lips, watching me over the rim of her cup, and I said, "I don't mind. Everything's been happening so quickly lately that it's nice to be able to sit down and just look around."

I did so as I spoke, watching a tortoiseshell cat twist its way around the legs of a woman struggling to carry three loaves of bread. If Katja thought this part of the city was peaceful, she ought to have spent a week in my village.

"Looking forward to the Phoenix Festival, are you?" Katja asked, putting her tea down. "Prince Alexander tells me it's much the same, over in Felheim."

"I think it's going to be a lot bigger than anything I've seen before," I said, answering as non-committally as I could.

Katja hummed flatly. It wasn't the answer she'd wanted. I probably hadn't been enthusiastic enough for her. She picked her tea back up but didn't drink any of it, and kept her eyes fixed on me, something clearly burning the tip of her tongue. After the third round of putting her tea down and picking it up, she leant forward and let her words tumble out in a single breath.

"I'm not certain I like it. The Phoenix Festival, that is. Now, I'm aware this is practically treason, but I don't think it's *right*. Everyone's hearts are in the right place, I've no doubt of that, and I see nothing wrong with celebrating the end of a war and the start of a new life, a new culture, south of the mountains. But, oh, I can't help but think we're all a little misguided. Turning against a whole group because of the actions of one. Actions that have been lost to time and rewritten over and over.

"Every year we gather to mock them, to sing songs of thanks that the phoenixes burnt out the last of them, and act as though they no longer number amongst us. As though they aren't simply healers who surpassed the limitations wrongly imposed upon them. And who are we thanking? Certainly not the gods we abandoned!

"It doesn't sit well with me, I'm afraid. There's so much that's truly good, so much that's truly worth celebrating instead. Don't you agree?"

If we hadn't abandoned our gods, I might've prayed to Isjin and asked her to turn Katja's eyes from me. My pulse was racing. Surely she'd notice; surely she'd *feel* it.

She hadn't used the word necromancer, but her meaning was as clear as the cloudless sky above us. I'd spent my life participating in the Phoenix Festival, singing songs to mock the ashes of my dead kin, but I'd never been able to put what bothered me so deeply about it into words. Why I felt my skin crawl for days afterwards.

Katja meant what she said, but anything more than a shrug of my shoulders would give me away.

"I guess," I mumbled.

Katja was hardly thrilled with my answer. She finished the last of her tea, cup and spoon placed neatly on the saucer, and I downed the rest of my water in large gulps, certain we'd be leaving soon. I was a novelty to Katja, and hadn't proven myself to be as interesting as she was expecting. There was nothing profound about a barefooted, simple life, no farm-bred wisdom I had to pass along.

I fidgeted, making Katja think I wanted to leave.

"I'm sorry if I've bored you with my nonsense. I do hope you aren't still feeling under the weather. I had thought getting a moment of peace here might help you," she said. "As I said, I do so love this place, and I tend to be a little too eager to share it. It has a rather rich history, you know."

I'd been rude. Katja had gone out of her way to help me, and I'd only offered up grumbling agreement and shrugs.

"It does?" I asked.

"Oh, most certainly! Years back, I found some records that suggested a hamlet stood on this spot, some hundreds of years before Autíra was built. *Esarion*, it was called, population twenty-four. But that isn't the interesting part. For seven hundred years before that, the land beneath us went untouched. It was said to have been cursed. Do you know why?"

Katja placed her elbows on the table and entwined her fingers. I inched forward, arms bumping the edge of the table.

"It is said that Kondo-Kana passed through," Katja said. I didn't freeze up; there was heat rushing through me yet. "There are plenty of accounts of her leaving Myros, but they slowly dry up as she travelled south. They stop altogether, once she reached this part of the continent. It was a farm at the time, or something of the sort. Oh, well. That is to say, the last report that doesn't pertain to her unfortunate end at sea."

Katja spoke of Kondo-Kana with as much ease as she spoke of Autíra. How was I supposed to respond? To nod along, to murmur that it was interesting? My eyes were drawn to the cobbled street, as though the stones were about to slip away from one another, light spilling out of the cracks, revealing the bones of Kondo-Kana herself. Washed out of the ocean and onto the dirt, under Esarion, Autíra, Isin, propped up for all to see, proving I wasn't the only necromancer in the world.

How could I respond without betraying myself?

The woman who'd brought our drinks saved me. She collected the empty glass and cup, making me jump, and Katja said, "I must apologise, Rowan, but I've allowed time to slip away from me. I've business to attend to. Dreary stuff, honestly. I'd much rather spend the afternoon here, but that'll have to wait for another time! Shall we?"

Katja bid me farewell once we'd crossed the bridge leading to the castle doors, and said she'd like to see me again. I returned the sentiment as eagerly as I knew how, certain I'd be braver once I knew her better. It might take weeks, months, but I was determined to let her know I wasn't like the rest of people in Isin, in Kastelir and Felheim. I didn't blindly condemn the necromancers, either.

She left to attend to business that wouldn't interest me. There were guards in every corner of the castle to watch over her, and Akela was relinquished from her rather uncommanderly duties.

She folded her arms across her chest and looked at me expectantly. I didn't tell her to leave, or that I was sure she had more important matters to attend to, because I was glad of her company. Akela wouldn't have any problem excusing herself without much more than a slap on the back and an *I am going now, yes, goodbye!*

"Do you always do everything Queen Kidira tells you to?" I asked as we headed much of nowhere around the outside of the castle, walking along the edge of the moat. "Even if it's babysitting?"

"Of course! Of course I am doing what my Queen is commanding of me," Akela said, placing her hand across her chest, wounded by the mere suggestion that she might not always follow orders. "If the Queen is telling me to jump to the bottom of this moat, then I am jumping to the bottom of this moat. Why am I doing this? Because Queen Kidira, she is always having a plan. She is always knowing more than anyone else. Probably, there is an assassin, and they are lurking, and I am knocking them over the head and taking all the credit. You are seeing? My Queen, she is being most generous."

I half expected Akela to dive off the edge to prove her point and was half disappointed when she didn't. There was no guardrail along the edge of the moat, and I inched over to peer down. They must've dug out the moat to have enough stone to build the castle. The water had to be deep, or no one would ever survive the fall.

"Besides, I am not babysitting! I am *guarding*, yes? And Lady Kouris, I am not minding spending time with her. When I am first coming to Isin, Lady Kouris, she is, hm, fifteen, I am thinking this is right. For many years I am knowing her! Of all my moves, this is being the smartest. I am thinking, one day she is going to be Queen, and she will be remembering her loyal bodyguard then, yes?"

I turned on my heels and smirked at her. Akela grabbed my shoulder, lest I spontaneously lose all balance and topple backwards.

"So you have a plan," I said, stepping towards the castle to stop her from fretting. "And here I was, thinking you did it all out of the goodness of your heart."

Placing herself squarely between me and the moat, Akela elbowed me in the side, causing me to veer off course and crush the leaves of an innocent shrub.

"I am doing it for Queen Kidira, yes, and so it is always being from my heart," Akela said, and it was her final word on the matter. "Hm. I am thinking, your Ightham, she is still talking with the Kings. Is there somewhere you are wanting to go? Personally, I am being minutes away from my pillow, I am already tasting it, and I am not wanting to leave you here, where you are falling off the edge and crushing your skull like sparrow's egg."

"My—" I bit the inside of my mouth and started over. The mention of Claire and the Kings brought the midday meeting rushing back to me, and the reminder that it was as real as it was unpleasant. Drowning myself in the life of Isin and the quiet of what Autíra had once been did nothing to change the workings of the world. "Could you show me where the stables are? I have no idea where my horse is."

"Of course, of course!"

Akela stuck close to my side, convinced I was going to fall into the moat, and led me around the castle. There were few twists and turns to take. A great lawn spread out beyond a colonnade, littered with gazebos, with a thicket of trees along the far side, hiding the wall that ran around the castle.

The guards strolling around the perimeter had the best patrol in the city. They spent their day in the sun, occasionally nodding to the nobles enjoying their endless leisure time, never having to touch their weapons. They straightened at the sight of Akela and quickened their pace. She chuckled and led me past the young men enjoying half a dozen types of delicate cakes as they spoke over one another about some artist I'd never heard of.

The stables were nicer than my house. Nicer than any house in my village, Thane's manor on the hill included. Nicer than most of the buildings I'd seen in Praxis, honestly. They were made from stone painted white and gold, decorated with a frieze of stampeding horses. With all the stablehands the crown employed, it didn't smell like as much of a stable as it ought to have.

It was big enough for dozens of horses but hardly fitting for an army. These were the horses of the Kings and Queen Kidira, of the nobility and wealthy guests. And of me, it seemed.

"Thank you," I said, waving Akela off. "You've definitely earnt a nap."

She bowed to me as she walked backwards, pivoting on the spot and whistling as she headed for her chambers.

The back of the stable was built into the wall of the castle, meaning light didn't reach it as well it ought to have. I headed through the rows of pens, smiling at the horses and patting the friendlier looking ones on their foreheads.

I stopped by a foal curled up by its mother and it wobbled over to me, curiously sniffing my open hand and shrinking away when my fingers twitched.

Not wanting to give the foal a fright or earn the scorn of one of the stablehands, I hurried over to Charley. He was exactly where I'd expected him to be, in one of the less desirable pens at the back. Not that he minded. The hay he'd been given likely tasted better than any food I'd ever eaten.

"Hey, boy. Keeping Calais company, are you?" I asked, rubbing my fingers between his ears. He let out a non-committal grunt and Calais, in the slightly better-lit pen next to him, gave me an enthusiastic bump on the shoulder with his muzzle. "Sorry about running off yesterday. It's been a crazy few days, boy. A crazy few months! You're lucky you're a horse and don't have to worry about anything but eating and running."

He swished his tail in agreement and bowed his head to get to more hay.

I was about to say something more when a voice escaped the shadows and made me jump out of my skin.

"You left this," Claire said.

I swallowed my heart back down and turned towards her. She was sat on a hay bale to the side, holding my bag between her hands. I should've looked around more carefully before talking to my horse, but embarrassment wasn't my first reaction. It didn't even come to mind.

I looked at her and wanted nothing more than to make it *better*. But what could I do that a Knight, two Queens, two Kings and an army couldn't? Still, for a moment, our eyes met and it was enough that I knew.

It was enough that she no longer had to hide the truth from me.

I stepped towards her, taking my bag from her. I sat on a hay bale opposite her, back against Charley's pen.

"I'm sorry," was all I could say.

"Sorry?"

She wasn't scathing about it. She was exhausted, head tilted against the wall, and her words came out dryly. I'd do better, I'd told myself; I'd make sure Claire knew she had someone to talk to, someone who wouldn't question or doubt the truth behind her words.

I wanted nothing more than to bury my face in my hands and absorb how wrong it all was, but I couldn't crumble. Not in front of Claire. I couldn't take comfort from her when she had none left to give. She'd lived with this for months and she'd continued to fight.

She'd been alone for so much of it.

I scraped together a fraction of the strength she had and tried again.

"I'm sorry, Claire. I'm sorry that you've had to give up your home and your family, and I'm sorry you've been burdened with all this. I'm sorry you've had to keep secrets for so long. I know it's not the same, I'm not pretending it is, but I know how that feels. I just..." I paused, staring at my lap. "I think you're really brave. And I know that probably doesn't mean anything, but I see how tired you always are, how much you do, and I want to help you. I know I can't slay dragons, but I'm here and I know. That's something, right?"

She closed her eyes as I spoke. Her expression didn't shift, but I knew she was listening. I could still see bloodstains that weren't there on the front of her shirt, and she felt whispers of the wound echoing through her. The healers had taken it away too easily for her body to believe it was truly gone.

"Mm," she eventually agreed.

"Do you think you could... Do you want to tell me how you found out, Claire?" I asked, trying not to plead with her. I wanted her to speak freely, openly. I didn't want to push her. "I can't get my head around it. I thought you were keeping it from me because of what I am, but I was being selfish. I wanted to believe that it was about me, and not that it was awful."

Claire opened an eye, let out a breath that caused her shoulders to slump, and looked around. Satisfied that no one was within earshot, she sat with her lips parted, no words coming to her.

I gave her all the time she needed.

"How I found out? King Garland summoned me one day and told me. In quite plain terms," she said, laughing flatly. "He claimed that I had been raised for it. Rylan, Alexander and myself. I had thought, at first, that he merely meant for matters of succession, and I was not terribly surprised. Alex is a good man, a kind man, but he does not have the will of a ruler. He was happier out of the running. Rylan, however... I never wanted the throne, though it was not my place to deny it, but Rylan did. We started to grow apart, over recent years, when it became evident the King would be forced to choose between us.

"But that was only part of it. He said I was to learn the ways of our Kingdom and told me it all. He told me about the dragons, the planned attacks. It is somewhat amusing, when you think about it. The King brought me up with this one role in mind, trusted me freely, and here I am. A traitor to family and country both."

She knitted her fingers together and tilted her head forward. Her chin bumped against her knuckles and I knew that no matter what I told her, she'd never stop thinking of herself in such cold, clear-cut terms.

"What happened?" I asked. She wanted to talk and I didn't want to give her reason to stop. "What did you do when you found out?"

"I accepted. I told King Garland I was honoured he'd chosen me, and that I would serve the realm faithfully. And I did, for a time. Five months. I lasted five months, trying to claw at what information I could. But my initiation was slow. I barely learnt more than I'd been told that first day, and my duties as a Knight continued. The far-off succession was not yet official, and for a time, things were almost normal. Or at the very least, routine.

"But the last time I was sent to slay a dragon, I paused. I looked at it, truly looked at it, and didn't allow myself to be blinded by anger, desperate to seek vengeance for the lives that had been stolen. I looked at the dragon and saw that it was scared. Confused. It barely knew what it was doing, yet I slew it regardless."

"I put my sword through its lower jaw and ran. I fled, like a coward, into the war-torn arms of Kastelir, barely forming a plan as I went."

Placing my bag by my side, I got to my feet and stood between Claire's knees. I met her gaze, hands on her shoulders, and ached to say something that would bring her the slightest jot to relief. I wrapped my arms around her and pulled her close. With the hay bale as low as it was, she buried her face against my stomach.

"You're not a coward, Claire. I used to be scared of pane, remember? Now that's cowardly. But you, you've been brave through this all. Against bandits and Knights, across a foreign country. Even when you were hurt, you were still brave. You protected me from myself," I murmured, hoping she felt my words more than she heard them. "And you've given up so much. Don't you realise what you just said? You were going to be Queen, Claire. The Queen of Felheim! And you gave that up, because you knew what they were doing wasn't right. You might've betrayed the King, but he's just one man. He isn't the country. Isn't the people. You haven't betrayed Felheim. You're fighting for it, even now."

Her arms tightened around me and I let my fingers trail through the tips of her hair. All that mattered was that I had Claire close, not some future Queen.

"You're sweet," she mumbled into my shirt. "And I am tired. So very tired of all this, Rowan. There are always dragons, no matter where I go, and I find myself wishing that Rylan had been chosen. I believe he would've dealt with this far better than I."

I made no reply, letting her voice her thoughts out loud. I was grateful it'd taken me this long to learn the truth; she wouldn't have opened herself up to me weeks ago, even if she had to pry the words from between her teeth.

I had no intention of moving from that spot until she let go of me, and her grasp remained tight around my waist. I tilted my head forward, kissing her hairline, knowing I should give her the time to turn her thoughts over. But knowing did nothing to stop the questions from churning inside of me.

"Claire. What you said about necromancers," I said, hoping it would be enough.

"I know nothing more than what I told the Kings and Queen Kidira," she said, looking up at me. "I did not wish to tell them as much. I learnt nothing more. I can only guess that it bears some similarity to the way

Kondo-Kana manipulated dead dragons to her own ends during the war. All I was told was that there was a necromancer, or necromancers."

"Is that why you agreed to bring me along?"

"No. Yes. Perhaps," Claire said. "You were a nuisance, that night. You were hardly the first to try following me, but you were the first to brazenly admit to being a necromancer. Word would eventually spread further than the cluster of villages in the south and reach Thule. I didn't know what King Garland would do with the knowledge, but I do know that necromancers are beyond rare. You are the first I have ever knowingly met, or heard of anyone meeting.

"I expected you to follow me for a time and ultimately take up residence in Praxis or Benkor. I planned to leave you with no small amount of gold and hope you would be safe, should the King send scouts to track you down."

For the first time in my life, I was grateful for my necromancy. I had risen the dead, given people life anew, but this was the first time that a slow trickle of guilt didn't crawl through my veins.

I brushed Claire's hair out of her face, tucking it behind her ears.

"Should the worst happen, know that I will not let them take you, Rowan," she said firmly, eyes losing the tired haze that had claimed them.

"They have an army," I pointed out.

"What of it? I have slain dragons. People in plate armour present me with no cause for concern."

"They have Akela."

"... Then perhaps we will run all the way across the border."

I laughed and Claire's arms dropped from around my waist, disappointment negated when her hands found my hips. She was not yet smiling but her face had softened, and there was nothing in the world that mattered beyond the fact that she'd meant what she'd said.

I thought I might have the courage to bow my head and kiss her, but the sound of boots against the stone floor caused me to move faster than I ever had in my life.

Akela hadn't claimed the nap she deserved. She marched into the stables, axe at her hip, so far from smiling that she looked like a stranger. There were half a dozen guards behind her, fingers twitching in anticipation of drawing their weapons.

"Northwood. Ightham. You are being here all along, yes?"

Her eyes fixed on Claire. Barely any time had passed since she'd last seen me; I wasn't the one drawing her suspicion.

"We have," Claire answered, not rising to her feet.

"I am giving you this chance because I am liking you both. I am thinking you are both very smart, yes? You are coming with me and you are not saying a word," Akela said. "We are going to the castle and we are talking. You are understanding?"

I nodded my head more than I needed to, but Claire chose to push her luck.

"We're talking now, aren't we? Call off your guards, take a seat, and we can have all the conversation you desire. As you might well have noticed, neither of us are armed. You have us at a disadvantage."

"I am not asking again, Ightham," Akela said.

The guards stepped forward in unison.

Only then did Claire stand. She put a hand in front of me and drew the guards' attention towards herself.

"Tell me, Akela," Claire said in a low, even voice, as she stepped towards her. "Whatever misunderstanding has arisen, I assure you, we can clear it up between the three of us. There's no need for this."

Claire finally pushed her far enough. I caught Akela's eye and realised it wasn't anger burning there. It was something else, something familiar; something I'd seen time and time again in the apothecary's, when I hadn't been allowed to act quickly enough.

"King Jonas, he is murdered," Akela hissed through grit teeth. "And you are coming with me, Ightham."

PART THREE

Akela concluded every sentence by crashing her fists against the table in front of us, and I started every time. Claire didn't blink, let alone flinch. She felt no need to prove her innocence to anyone. She answered Akela's questions as briefly as she could and leant back in her chair, arms folded across her chest.

Akela had taken us to the least welcoming room in the castle. The low ceiling made her seem taller and closer, and the window, despite barely being big enough to look out of, had an iron bar running through the centre. The one table in the room slanted to the side, and the chairs we'd been pushed into were less comfortable than the bare stone floor.

"Ightham, you are stopping this. You are not saying *yes* or *no* and leaving it at that. I am needing you to explain things," Akela said.

Her frustration at Claire scored lines across her forehead. I didn't understand how Claire hadn't found herself locked in a cell, key thrown into the moat.

"I should hardly think you need me to repeat myself again," Claire said. "I've answered every question you've bombarded me with. Do you honestly believe Rowan or I murdered your King? You – *we* – ought to be out there, aiding with the investigation."

"*No.*" Akela slammed both fists down, table rattling on uneven legs. "I am not thinking you are responsible, or that Northwood is being capable of such a thing. But you are both being from Felheim, yes? And if I am clearing you, then Queen Kidira, she is trusting me. I am needing to be certain. I am needing to be *more* than certain. Are you understanding this?"

If it were up to me, we would've poured out every ounce of information Akela could possibly need a hundred times over, but Claire knew nothing would ever be enough. Akela was shaken. She'd lost one of her friends, lost a man she'd worked alongside for a decade, and she wasn't allowed to grieve. She was there, interrogating us. Her questions hadn't been kind, but I didn't hold it against her.

"Commander. Please, listen. Rowan was not out of your sight for more than half an hour. The stablehands saw her enter, and they neither saw her leave nor re-enter, prior to your arrival. As for myself, I was with the Kings until shortly before you accompanied Rowan to the stables, and those working there can corroborate that I remained there the entire time," Claire said. "There is but one way out of the stables, and no shortage of guards, courtiers and servants in the surrounding area. We would've been seen. What's more, if one of us were responsible, we would've had to change our clothing."

Akela's fingers curled towards her palms, nails scraping across the tabletop.

"But..."

She didn't want it to be us. All she wanted was to know who had assassinated King Jonas, and I could sympathise with that.

Claire stood up. Akela moved for her axe, but Claire held her hands in front of her, reminding Akela that she was no threat. She was unarmed. We'd been searched for blades before Akela had sent the guards out of the room.

Akela didn't move her hand from her hip, but she didn't wrap her fingers around her axe, either. Claire placed a gentle hand on her shoulder and gripped it firmly.

"We will find who is responsible, Akela. Make no mistake about it. But you *are* wasting your time here," Claire said. "I have dealt with assassinations in the past. I may be a Knight, but I was ever tasked with more than slaying dragons. Tell Queen Kidira that we pose no threat, and that we will not rest until the matter is resolved."

Akela's gaze darted across the room, as unfocused as her scattered thoughts. She was on the verge of relenting when the door thundered open. It'd been locked from the outside and the latch scraped against metal as it was near-enough knocked off its hinges.

"I am saying we are *not* being disturbed," she snapped, ready to draw her axe, but Kouris ducked through the doorway. Her horns scraped against the ceiling, though her back was arched. "... Hm."

Akela bundled her hands into fists and tilted her chin upwards, meeting Kouris' gaze.

"Out," Kouris said. "It wasn't them."

"Queen Kidira, she is ordering me to—"

"*Out*. I'm ordering you as Queen Kouris to *get out*," Kouris roared, stomping towards Akela. She'd never come so close to flinching in her life. "If Kidira's having a problem with that, tell her to come speak with me herself."

Whether Akela recognised Kouris' authority or not was beyond the point. She didn't have a death wish. She stepped back and held Kouris' gaze for longer than anyone else would dare to, wanting to believe that she was right. We were innocent, and she'd done all she could to ensure that. She wasn't letting murderers walk free.

Akela left the room with a curt bow of her head. The door rattled in its frame behind her, left unlocked.

Nobody spoke, but something other than silence pooled between us. Kouris was trembling, breath ragged, and beyond the chamber with its steel plated door, I could feel the rush of death swarming through the castle, creating a trail from King Jonas' body, reaching out to me. How close did I need to be? My head pounded, dragging me out of the room, out of reality. I wanted to claw my fingers through the mist choking the corridors without moving an inch.

Kouris stopped me from drifting too far. Her voiceless ache became a growl and she threw her fists against the wall, horns scraping against stone as she tried to bring the whole castle down. Claire reacted faster than I could. Kouris' stature was never more evident than when she couldn't keep herself still, but Claire had no concern for her own safety.

She seized hold of Kouris' arm, fist on its way to the wall, and Kouris snarled, trying to throw her off. Claire gripped tight and pulled Kouris towards her, forcing her to bow. They stared at one another, and Claire kept her face close, in spite of all the fangs in front of her.

"Kouris," Claire said, placing her hands on her face. "Kouris, I am sorry."

"Weeks. I'm back here for *weeks*," came Kouris' mumble of a reply. "And look what's happening. Should've never come back."

"This has nothing to do with your return, Kouris. Do not blame yourself. If anything, it was a good thing that you were here, in the weeks leading up to his death. He was able to see you one last time."

"Leading up to his murder," Kouris said, but all the bite was gone. Claire's words had been of some small comfort to her. Her hands dropped to her sides and she leant forward, forehead touching Claire's. "Always got the feeling Jonas would be outliving all of us. Even me. He always had everything sorted. Back before Kastelir was founded, The Old West was the closest thing to a functioning territory in its own right, and now... Killed in his own castle. So much for any of that meaning a damn thing."

267

I didn't move towards Kouris. The way Claire and Kouris looked at one another as they spoke put me beyond their understanding of the situation. The finality of their every word was misplaced, and the permanence of which they spoke was lost on me.

King Jonas was dead, but he didn't have to stay that way. It'd take a thought, only a thought, and I could drive death out of him, as if striking a deal I'd never have to fulfil. I murmured, "I could—" under my breath, not meaning to be heard. Needing to remind myself of my power, more than anything.

Kouris and Claire towered over me. I stepped back, bumping into the table, and they stared at me as though it was too late. I began to wonder if there was light crackling between my fingers, if King Jonas had risen in the corridors beyond.

"No," Claire said bluntly. "Absolutely not."

"Why not?" I protested. "I could bring him back and it wouldn't even be hard. I could bring him back and Kouris wouldn't have to be upset. And neither would King Atthis or Queen Kidira or Akela, or the rest of the country! We'd be able to ask King Jonas who killed him, and there'd be no worrying about what would happen to Kastelir, or if anyone else was in danger, or..."

"*No*," Kouris said. "Your heart's in the right place, yrval, it really is, but you're only going to be causing more problems than you're fixing. I want to see Jonas on his feet, I honestly do, but it's not gonna be so easy as that. There'll be no use in it all if we're only trading his life for yours."

Trading my life for his. Did Kouris really believe that Queen Kidira would look upon what I'd done and demand I burn for it, even if King Jonas was returned to her?

"News of King Jonas' assassination won't remain contained to the castle. If half of Isin doesn't already know, they will by the morning," Claire said. They were both adamant, talking down to me as though I didn't understand the consequences of my own powers. "Dozens have seen the body and healers would've tried all they could to save him. There would be no doing this without anyone finding out, Rowan. Do you believe that Kastelir would accept a King raised from the dead? If Queen Kidira did not call for your capture, Kastelir would."

Kouris narrowed her gaze in agreement, but Claire's words didn't reach me. So what if they felt justified in King Jonas' continued death;

so what if they were only trying to protect me? There was an easy solution to the problem presented, yet they were convinced locking me away was the only thing for it.

I looked at Claire, and then at the ground.

"But you said..."

She sucked in a deep breath, mouth clamped shut in Kouris' presence. Kouris' gaze shot between me and Claire and bemusement gave way to understanding. She took a wide step back, giving Claire space to draw closer.

Claire tried to catch my eye, but my gaze slid back and forth like a pendulum whenever she moved.

"As a last resort, Rowan. There is no need to put yourself in that sort of danger, unless there is absolutely nothing more we can do," Claire said in a low voice. I couldn't look at her. "Please, Rowan. Don't throw away all you've earnt for yourself since leaving your village. Let the King remain dead."

I wrapped my fingers around her wrist when she placed a hand on my face. She pleaded with me as though my powers were beyond my control; King Jonas would leave death behind by virtue of me knowing he'd been murdered. My shoulders rose and I let go of her wrist, clasping my hands together to hold *something* back.

"Right. You're right. I won't do anything," I said, knowing I couldn't ask Claire to leave Kastelir after she'd sacrificed so much. "I'm sorry. It's just not *fair* and I wanted to be able to help, for once. I didn't speak to King Jonas much, but he was really nice to me when he had no reason to be. He didn't even have to look at me."

Claire gave me a smile that made me believe I'd be able to rein my powers in, and I took Kouris' hand as she returned to the conversation. She stood before me for one reason. Necromancy had saved her. Kouris understood why I wanted to bring King Jonas back. She didn't scorn necromancy in and of itself, but since returning to Asar, she'd told only me the truth, and for good reason.

They might think more of her in Canth, for having been brought back by a necromancer, but in Kastelir, they'd treat her like a shadow of herself.

"Supposed we'd better be getting to the bottom of this," Kouris said, heaving a sigh.

There weren't any chairs big enough to support her and her legs were no longer up to the task. She sat down with a thud that echoed throughout the castle.

I moved to her side and checked her horns for scuffs. There were scratches along the grooves of her horns, but they felt as though they'd been there for an age.

"It's alright, yrval. They might not be as tough as dragon-bone, but they ain't far off," Kouris said, wrapping an arm around my shoulders. "Reckon the wall's in a sorrier state."

I let her pull me against her chest and put my arms as far as they'd go around her waist. Kouris tilted her head against the wall, grey eyes closing. Urgency seeped out of her, making room for misery. I couldn't take her in my arms, couldn't let her hide from the word by burying her face in my neck, but I could curl up against her chest and let her know I was there.

"Do you think you might..." Claire began, trailing off. I heard her boots clip the stone floor and looked up to find her sitting against Kouris' side. "The faster we act, the better chance we have of getting justice for King Jonas. I know little beyond the fact that he was assassinated. Is there anything more you can tell me?"

Kouris took her time answering. Getting all the information we could from her was wise, but it didn't feel kind. With my ear to her chest, I heard her heart beating out of time with itself. I was confused, until I realised I was listening to two separate rhythms belonging to twin hearts.

"After meeting with you, Jonas went to deal with some agricultural matters, in the Old West. It's routine, as far as I can be telling. He meets with a couple of representatives, over on the second level. There were guards stationed at either end of the corridor, but it curves at a weird angle and there's some kind of blind-spot. Reckon he wouldn't have been out of sight for more than a few seconds. But aye. That was enough."

"And the murder weapon?"

"A blade. A dagger, most likely. Nothing left behind, though."

Claire took time digesting the information, more for Kouris' sake than her own, but mulling over facts in silence wouldn't help anyone. Once she was standing, she offered Kouris her hand. Kouris took it, but

270

did most of the work to get back to her feet.

"Shouldn't have been snapping at the Commander like that," Kouris said. "Come on. Let's be making ourselves useful, shall we?"

Kouris and Claire both hesitated, and I knew I was the reason why.

"I'll be fine," I said. "Promise."

I cut between them, opened the hefty door and ushered them out. I had no intention of bringing King Jonas back, but I wasn't going to let them shepherd me to my room, where I'd be no help to anyone. I was convinced I'd understand what I was seeing better than them; I'd be able to read the body in ways no one else could.

The castle beyond wasn't the one I'd become accustomed to. Nobody was going about their own business, anymore. Word had spread and there was only one thing on anyone's mind, guards, servants and nobles alike. They poured from their chambers, leaving their posts, filling every corridor and courtyard. The King was dead, that much they knew, but every group had their own ideas about how it happened.

An arrow had flown through an open window and struck him in the chest; someone had heard that there were Canthians in the city, a few days back, and anyone from across the Uncharted Sea was a grim omen in and of themselves; one of the King's guards had betrayed him; but no, no, it was an outsider, someone from Agados or Felheim.

The one thing they agreed on was that the assailant was still within the castle. Bells chimed from a far tower, either out of respect or as a warning, and with all the chaos sown throughout the castle, we had no trouble getting to the floor King Jonas had been murdered on. Nobody could agree where it took place, and the guards weren't stopping people from coming to their own conclusions and heading in the wrong direction.

We were stopped before we could get close.

Two guards crossed their spears, blocking the corridor, and one of them said, "I'm afraid you'll have to turn back."

"Move," Kouris ordered, but she was just another pane, to the guards.

Kouris would've snatched the spears from their hands and charged through, if she had to, but Akela overheard the commotion and poked her head around the corner.

"It is fine," she said, saving us from an altercation. "These ones, let them through."

The guards stepped to the side, relieved they didn't have to restrain a pane. King Jonas' body had been taken away, leaving only bloodstains smeared into the carpet and soaking the stone surrounding it. I breathed in and the scent of it stuck in the back of my throat. The trail of death had faded, but I could tell too much about my surroundings.

I knew where his body had fallen, how he had clutched at his chest; and it definitely was his chest, not his throat. I understood not only how long ago it had happened, but what had happened throughout each second that passed; I felt, to an unnerving extent, the last ounce of fear that had been bled from King Jonas' body.

Not using my necromancy in so long had created a drought within me, and I knew I owed death something.

"Commander, look," Kouris said while Claire knelt down low, eyes scanning the corridor. "I shouldn't have been so short with you earlier. You were only doing your job."

"No, no, you are correct, of course you are, Your Majesty," Akela insisted. "Ightham and Northwood, they are having nothing to do with it, and I am being too hard on them because I am angry. I am upset. You are understanding this, yes?"

"Aye," Kouris said, holding out a hand. Akela shook it firmly. "And just Kouris'll do. Been away for too long to be deserving any sort of rank."

Claire's search was fruitless. The corridor curved, leaving only a small stretch in the blind-spot of the guards stationed at either end. There was little in the way of hiding places, and she pulled the single cabinet from the wall, finding nothing within, behind or beneath it. There was nothing concealed behind any of the hefty painting frames, either.

"We are having the castle searched, but there are too many places to be hiding a blade," Akela said. She moved to the window spilling sunlight across the bloodstains. "The assassin, they are coming in this window and they are leaving by it."

I inched over, squeezing between Kouris and Claire. There was a drop, but not a considerable one. Had Kouris been outside, she would've been able to push herself onto tiptoes to look in.

"Don't reckon anyone could go unnoticed for long down there, meaning they knew Jonas' routine. This was well-planned, if nothing

272

else," Kouris said, staring into the walkway below.

"Akela. Should you require any assistance, I will do all I can to help," Claire said, when staring out of the window didn't instantly solve all our problems.

"Yes, yes, I am appreciating this, Ightham. I am interrogating you and Queen Kidira, she is being satisfied you are not guilty. First, I am speaking with the guards who are being stationed here when it is happening. King Atthis, he is locking them away, to be safe."

Promoted from suspect to interrogator, Claire followed Akela through the corridor and past the guards. I had to wrench myself off the spot. Kouris placed a hand on my back and led me on. I might have been the only one capable of fixing things, but I was the most useless one there.

Panic turned to sorrow throughout the castle, and those who weren't crying stood with their heads hung. Being dry-eyed would've left us conspicuous, had anyone been focused on us. They busied themselves consoling one another, assuring friends and strangers alike that rumours were just rumours, and that they must wait for an official announcement from the King or Queen before feeling anything too heavily.

I didn't want to stare at anyone, but sobbing so raw it twisted my stomach into knots clawed its way out of one of the chambers we passed. The door was slightly ajar, and I saw Katja at a table, face buried in her arms. I took another few steps before I stopped and tugged on Claire's sleeve.

"Katja, she's... Lady Kouris, she's upset and she's alone," I said. Claire furrowed her brow. So much had happened in the last few days that I hadn't had the chance to tell her we'd met. "I went into Isin with her. I think you'll be alright without me. I don't want to leave her like that."

Akela would've gone in my place, if she had the choice, and I pointedly didn't look at Kouris. Claire nodded and the three of them hurried on.

Katja had taken refuge in a drawing room. From the way she sobbed, I wouldn't have been surprised if she'd caused whoever had previously occupied the chamber to desert it. I knocked to no avail, and slipped into the room, quietly closing the door behind me. Katja didn't stop crying, not even to draw breath, and I ached more for her than I did for the entirety of the country that had just lost a King.

"Katja..." I said softly, wanting her to know I was there.

Her shoulders rose and she stopped shaking. She looked up, eyes red and face much the same. Her jaw trembled as she desperately wiped the tears from her cheeks, but they continued to spill, thick and heavy.

"Oh. Rowan," she mumbled, blinking through tears to see me. She sniffed loudly, doing what she could to compose herself. Trying to straighten out her dress, at the very least.

A stack of napkins had been left by a circle of silverware coated in biscuit crumbs, and I grabbed a handful, deciding they'd have to serve a new purpose. I handed one to Katja and slid into the chair next to hers.

"Rowan, I, uncle, he..." Katja tried, pausing to blow her nose.

"I know," I said, squeezing the side of her arm. She didn't need to explain herself, didn't need to say anything more, but she kept trying, in spite of all she'd been through.

"I was too late. Too late," she mumbled, and turned her palms upwards, fingers curling to form fists. I saw the blood streaked across her hands, staining the front of her dress. "I got there, but... Oh, he was already gone."

I gently wrapped my fingers around Katja's wrists, pulled her hands into my lap, and wiped them clean with a napkin. Her hands trembled along with the rest of her. None of this was new to me. I'd let the dead remain dead in the past, and I knew all I could do for her was to let her know I was willing to listen to whatever she needed to say.

"You couldn't have done anything," I said, but Katja's eyes flashed.

She tore her hands away from mine in a manner that would've been violent, had she not been lost to grief. She clasped one hand over the other, pulling them to her chest, and I sat there patient and silent, bloodied napkin held between my fingers.

Katja shook her head over and over, breath coming fast and heavy. Chair legs scraped against the floor as she backed away. Not from me, but from what had happened. I didn't say anything. I certainly didn't tell her to calm down, or that things were going to be alright; I remained as still as I could, not once looking away from her. Tears continued to fall, but there was clarity in her expression.

She needed me to know something.

"I—I *should've* been able to," Katja said, fists furling and unfurling in her lap. Her gaze bore into her palms, but I could only look at her eyes.

They darkened from the centre outwards, blue eyes turning black, the white of her eyes becoming like wet stone. "Why, Rowan? Why do I have this power if I cannot help when I'm truly needed?"

Katja swallowed the lump in her throat and all the energy flowing through her dissipated, along with the strain on her body. Her shoulders slumped and her hands fell limp in her lap. I knew that she felt as I had, when Claire had been carried off by Kouris, when I couldn't return life to the person who'd been placed on my table.

She wasn't the same, but she understood.

"You're a healer?" I heard myself ask.

"For all the good it's ever done," she said bitterly, and I wasn't afraid.

I'd imagined meeting a healer time and time again, imagined them *knowing*, but I didn't shrink away from Katja. My insides were in knots but nothing compelled me to run, to save myself. I put my hands on her shoulders and didn't care if she saw through me. I almost longed for it. The few seconds of respite from her tears were over, and she started to cry again.

I eased her towards me, letting her fall into my arms.

Katja buried her face in my shoulder and clung to the back of my shirt. I smoothed my hand across her long hair, letting her say what she needed.

"I-I never had a father," Katja said, words muffled by my shirt. "Never needed one, either, for I had two uncles. I have never been able to imagine how a person should do without them. But now, now I suppose I must learn, and quickly, without my Uncle Jonas..."

I squeezed her a little harder. I wanted to be kind, by my mind reeled with selfish thoughts. I wanted to know more about her powers, about the way it felt when she healed; if there was a wall she hit, something she couldn't tear down or scramble over.

"If only I were something *more*," Katja near-enough whispered. "Then I could... none of this would matter. None of it at all. Uncle Jonas, he'd, he'd come back to me."

She felt me tense and retreated from my arms. There I sat, something *more*, refusing to do anything. Refusing to help her.

"Katja," I said, desperate to force the words back inside of her. "You don't mean that."

I'd heard it plenty of times, from people in the same state as her. It tumbled from the lips of those who would do anything, *anything*, to have a loved one back, no matter how abhorrent. Necromancy was only ever desirable when it was out of reach, nothing more than a thought, a desperate wish.

The moment a person was brought back they were cursed, changed for the worse.

"I *do*, so very much," she insisted, and in spite of all I'd heard before, I believed her. "If only..."

She tilted her head forward and tears struck her knees. I took her into my arms again, knowing that she'd calm down and lose herself more than once in the ensuing days. As I held her, I knew that I was more powerful than all of this. I was stronger than her grief, stronger than the blade dug into King Jonas, again and again. Stronger than death itself, when I chose to be.

"Katja," I said softly. "I wish I could do something. I wish I could help you, but..."

Katja looked up at me. Her eyes were red and the tears were gone.

She didn't ask me to continue. Didn't dare to.

Taking my hands in her own, Katja squeezed them tightly and said, "Of course you do, Rowan. You're good. So very, very good."

CHAPTER NINETEEN

Claire wrote what I said word for word. The tip of the quill stopped when I paused to think, scratched across the paper when something came to me all at once, and she struck whole sentences out when I changed my mind.

There was much to tell my father, and just as much I couldn't say. I told him about Kyrindval and the pane, but I couldn't mention the castle; I spoke about my companions in general, sweeping ways, but could only mention *Rán* by name. Claire's paranoia hadn't ended with Luxon's life.

As I spoke, I came to appreciate how much had happened. I smiled at Claire, too focused on writing to notice me, and clasped my hands together under the desk as we waited for the parchment to dry.

The weather hadn't paid King Jonas' death any heed. A gentle breeze drifted in through the window, and the clear skies and rising warmth were only interrupted by the chirping of birds.

Claire placed the lid back on the inkwell and rinsed the quill's metal nib in a small glass of water.

"Have you ever tried to write? To read?" she asked, tapping the quill on the edge of the glass and drying the tip with a handkerchief.

"A few times. When I was younger," I said. "I just never really *got* it. The letters were always in the wrong order, even when Michael could make sense of them. He kept trying to teach me, but I guess I couldn't see what everyone else did."

I frowned. I didn't expect Claire to laugh, but felt as though she ought to.

"It happens," she said, quill back in its pot.

"Really?"

"Really. To varying degrees of severity, as well. Alexander had a similar problem, and a dozen tutors. It's called dyslexia. He now reads and writes well enough, albeit with no haste," Claire explained. I folded my arms across my chest and leant back in the chair. "You seem surprised to hear that."

"I always figured it was just me," I said. "Michael was always going on about how easy it'd be, if I just *tried*, but the more I tried, the harder it became. Even he gave up, in the end."

"It's a common enough affliction and not always dispelled by hard

277

work," Claire said, tilting the parchment to see if the ink was dry. "As I said, you most certainly aren't the only one."

I glanced over the letter, no longer able to remember which mark was supposed to make which sound.

"I just figured, you know, that I was good at... at what I could just *do*, without having to learn or really even try. Everything else was just kind of..." I shrugged. "Too much for me."

"Nonsense," Claire said. Satisfied the ink was dry, she stacked the parchment and lined up the edges with her palms. "You're more than capable, Rowan. Smarter than your brother in plenty of ways. Besides, did you not tell me that you had problems with your abilities early on? With scarring and the like? It sounds to me as though you have learnt a great deal about what you can and cannot do. It did not merely come to you."

I hadn't thought of it like that, but memories trickled back. Headaches came with the first few attempts at knitting lambs back together. They lasted for days, throbbing between my temples, pain distracting me from the rest of the world. Years on and I could rip out disease or bring back the dead with a thought, as naturally as breathing.

Claire was right. Having only myself to rely on didn't mean I hadn't learnt anything.

Seeing me smile, Claire rose to her feet and left the desk behind for one of the sofas.

Three days had passed, and despite the castle's best efforts, King Jonas' killer clung to freedom. I hadn't seen Claire in the interim, busy as she'd been, and Kouris too had been caught up in her own matters. I'd spent much of that time in my chamber, staring out at the city I wasn't bold enough to explore alone, and visiting Charley and Calais. I would've been glad of anyone's company, so long as they were able to talk back; I would've been beyond happy to see Claire, had she only been gone for three hours.

Which wasn't to say that being with her wasn't a little strange. It wasn't like the open road. There was nowhere for us to head, no beating of hooves to drown out our thoughts. I couldn't rush ahead to avoid looking at her, and it dawned on me that this was the first time we'd been alone together without any urgency rushing through us. She wasn't hurt. I wasn't furious for having discovered some new truth.

278

She'd simply sought me out that morning and asked if I should like to write to my father.

She'd helped me do just that. I should've thanked her and left. Instead, I tentatively moved to the sofa, sitting close to her, but not too close.

"So, um," I said, making a strong start. "Two days until the Phoenix Festival begins."

"Indeed. A day on the heels of the King's funeral," Claire said, leaning into the corner of the sofa. "But you needn't find an excuse to stay here, you know. It's fine that you're simply here."

I found it hard to believe that she wanted company for the sake of it being *my* company, and it was impossible to look at her when she fixed her gaze on me. I stared at my hands, far too rigid for the comfort the sofa offered, trying not to break out into nervous smiles.

Telling myself it was just Claire did nothing to help, because she was never *just* Claire.

I could lean against her, I told myself. I could lean against her and she wouldn't mind. She might even wrap her arms around me.

"Well," I said, continuing to find something wholly fascinating about the palms of my hands. "Can I kiss you?"

I hadn't meant to jump that far ahead, but Claire didn't bristle as I did.

"Of course you may," she said. "Why ever would it not be alright?"

I bit the inside of my mouth as Claire's fingers brushed my shoulder. It was all the convincing I needed to shuffle over. She put an arm around my shoulders and pulled me to her chest. Being so close to her hadn't made me any uncomfortable, only nervous in a way I didn't min..

"I don't know! I've just never really done this before," I said, hiding my face in the curve of her neck.

"*This?*" Claire inquired after a pause.

"This!" I repeated, gesturing vaguely at the two of us with the arm that wasn't caught between her back and the sofa. "All of... this."

Whatever *this* was.

Claire was silent for so long that I was forced to lean back and look up at her. When I did, she laughed dryly, but her expression was one of mild horror.

"What?" I demanded, hands clamping onto her shoulders.

279

One of her arms slipped down to the small of my back and she brought a fist to her mouth, trying to hold back her laughter. It didn't help.

"I apologise," she said, pursing her lips together and laughing breathily through her nose. "I am only laughing at my own expense, I assure you. I had assumed that you would have... well."

Claire pulled me close and kissed my forehead.

"Why would I have?"

"Why would you not?" she asked, placing a hand against my face so she could meet my gaze. She was beyond laughter now. She was looking at me in the same way I must've been looking at her, and there was a simple sincerity worked into her expression.

She coloured, just a little, across the bridge of her nose.

I was worried I was smiling too much to kiss her properly, until I did just that. Her arms tightened around my waist, pulling me flush against her, and as we kissed, I let myself be happy. I stopped worrying about the castle and all it contained, stopped worrying about all that had unfolded in the past few weeks and hoped that for a moment, Claire could stop worrying about the dragons.

Short minutes later, I found my face buried in Claire's neck. She ran her fingers through my hair, humming softly, and everything that had brought us there no longer seemed real. My village, Felheim. The country beyond the city and the castle beyond the chamber. It felt as though Claire and I had been there forever, on that very sofa, because surely acknowledging the past would be enough to send me tumbling back into it.

"There's been no one else, hm?" Claire couldn't help but ask.

"Not really," I said, but continued because Claire wasn't judgemental. She was only curious. "There were a few girls who came to the village when I was a healer, but that never really went anywhere. I've *liked* people, but I've never, um. Had the chance for... Look, everyone was always really focused on making sure I was always either working, or resting so I could work."

"I see. All work and no play," Claire said. "Well, you have Kouris and me now."

"What?" I spluttered. "No, I—"

"You're blushing," Claire said, kissing my nose. Before I could rally a more coherent defence, she said, "Will you be attending the Phoenix Festival?"

"Maybe," I said, happy to move the subject along. "I might as well see what it's like in a city this big, right?"

"It's a festival celebrating the fall of necromancers. Are you certain you wish to subject yourself to such things?"

I shrugged against her.

"I hear those things most days, and it's not like I haven't been to the Phoenix Festival every year since I was born."

I wanted the Kastelirians to sing songs that were familiar to me, with twisted lyrics; I wanted their versions of the tales of the Bloodless Lands to conflict with my village's, for Isin to accuse the necromancers of different crimes. If there was no consistency, there couldn't be any truth in it. The stories had been twisted like Kouris'.

"Why did you choose the phoenix for your sigil?" I asked, peeking up at her. "You said it didn't have anything to do with necromancers, but..."

"The phoenixes didn't turn against necromancers. No more so than anyone else was forced to turn against Kondo-Kana, and several of them were her allies. There are books written on the subject, hidden deep within the castle vaults," she said. "Were the phoenixes still alive, they would be deeply ashamed of how they have been remembered."

"But the Phoenix Fire... The phoenixes razed the necromancers in Myros, and Kondo-Kana killed the last of the phoenixes. Right?"

I'd wanted to attend the Phoenix Festival to dismiss the stories of the Necromancy War, yet I was using what I'd overheard to argue my point.

"The phoenixes fell in numbers a long time before any war began, and persisted after Kondo-Kana's death. History would like to paint phoenixes and necromancers as natural enemies, but in truth, the two worked side by side for as long as Myros stood. They were paired together as Priests of Isjin," Claire said. I wondered where this truth had been, all my life. "If anything, the extinction of phoenixes can be put down to the foolish notion that their meat would provide immortality, or at least longevity."

It wasn't right. The phoenixes died out because Kondo-Kana had found a way to stop them reviving themselves; they flocked to Myros in their thousands and sacrificed themselves to give our ancestors a chance to flee the Bloodless Lands. I wanted to believe her, but I couldn't shake off what I'd known all my life.

"So you chose the phoenix for your sigil because...?"

"Because I wanted somebody to represent them better than others were. I do not profess to know everything about phoenixes, but they caught my interest from a young age. Queen Aren would present me with gifts pertaining to them. Books, mostly. A dragon-bone knife with phoenixes carved into it," she said, voice becoming distant. "I took my name from one of the women who wrote on phoenixes, actually."

"Really? You picked your own name?"

"Indeed. Legally, the royal family's name is my name, but I did not wish to use it to grant me an unfair advantage. I wanted to be a Knight, and wanted people to see me as one; not as a royal playing dress-up," she said. "And so I picked an alias. I was young, at the time. Barely thirteen. But I believe it has come to suit me."

I'd always been a Northwood. My father had taken the name from my late mother, and once upon a time, the Northwoods had been spoken of warmly. I couldn't imagine not having that sense of stability to ground me all my life, something that marked my place in the world.

"I called you it for long enough, didn't I?" I said. "I think it suits you just fine, Sir."

Claire jabbed a finger against my side, scowling.

"Hearing you call me that sounds wrong," Claire said, pushing herself up with her palms and sitting against the arm of the sofa. "If you do wish to go to the Phoenix Festival, I shall endeavour to join you. I've little doubt King Atthis and Queen Kidira shall wish to keep me busy, especially considering the lack of results Akela and I have managed to procure, but perhaps Kouris will be able to convince King Atthis to allow me an hour or two to myself."

I pressed my nose to the line of her jaw. In that moment, the Phoenix Festival wasn't about necromancers, wasn't about what people thought my kin had done. It was about songs that meant nothing, words lost to the air, and only the high spirits of the festival-goers remained. It was about the colours and cheer, the food cooked out in the streets, and the long days of early summer, sun never setting, tavern doors never closing.

"I'd like that," I said.

If I started to doubt myself, started to believe that there was some truth in the songs they sang, I could look to Claire to ground myself.

"Come," Claire said, reluctantly prying herself from between me and the sofa. "I expect I shall be fetched within an hour or two. Let us find something to eat before then."

I didn't attend King Jonas' funeral. Bells tolled from sunrise till noon, within the castle and throughout Isin, and I saw crowds gather around the castle from my window. Most of the onlookers were more curious than grief-stricken, and only the distance between us made them quiet and respectful. The guards dealt with any who stepped out of line, and I saw as much of the procession as the Isiners at the gate did.

I'd been longing for the funeral, in a way. Once King Jonas was in his coffin, in the ground, that was it; it was done. My powers wouldn't spark beyond my control.

The castle's unusual silence left me restless. An assortment of clothing had been left in my room with a note atop it. I assumed it said I was free to rifle through the pile and wasted what time I could trying on different combinations. Several servants had fallen into the habit of knocking at my door and asking if I needed anything, anything at all.

That had to be Kouris' doing.

I had hot water and clean towels brought to my room. Sunlight struck the tiled area in front of the basin and I scrubbed myself down in earnest, catching my reflection in the mirror by chance. I'd been smiling to myself, but it didn't last long. My scars were still there, no matter how I tried to hide them. They were more grotesque than ever, bathed in light as I was. The colours clashed together as they spread from my stomach, across my ribs and up my back. There was no turning away from them.

I slapped my palm against the mirror, more frustration than force behind the movement. It shook in its frame as I scrambled to hide inside a shirt.

I distracted myself by pulling books off the shelves and flicking through them in search of pictures. It was to no avail. They were all full of the same: words and words, over and over, endlessly repeating themselves. I stared at the pages as though some meaning would work its way into my mind, but each one proved to be useless.

It was a relief when someone knocked at my chamber. I hurried to unlatch the door, supposing a servant wanted to know if I was ready for lunch, and found Katja stood on the other side.

She was dizzy, though not about to stumble, eyes misted red, cheeks blotched.

"Hey," I said, holding out a hand for her to take. I led her to the sofa, knowing she didn't want me to ask why she wasn't at King Jonas' funeral. "Do you need anything?"

"Water, if you wouldn't mind terribly," she murmured weakly, forehead rested against the heel of her palm. I moved to make her a drink, and Katja said, "I am sorry to bother you like this, dear. Oh, just look at me! I'm afraid this horrid thing makes me look far ghastlier than I feel, in spite of all today holds."

The *thing* in question was a beautifully simple funeral dress, but the fact that it was white was the only similarity it bore to anything I'd seen worn in my village.

"I simply had to get out of there, if only for a moment. The funeral is over and the guests are moving onto the wake, but the only people willing to engage in conversation with me are intent on feeling awful on my behalf. The guards do little more than nod and say *milady*. I had thought you might... well, I shouldn't like to presume, but..."

"It's fine, Katja," I assured her. I handed her a glass of water and took a seat next to her. "Is it over? Has King Jonas been buried?"

"Buried? Oh, goodness, no. There's a crypt beneath the castle, fit for royalty. His coffin will be placed there, forever on display, that we might make ourselves all the more miserable when guilt moves us to visit him," Katja said.

She placed the glass on a low table without taking a single sip.

Sighing, she slumped against the sofa. She closed her eyes and I didn't say a word, hoping the peace of my chamber was what she needed. I was considerably less relaxed than she was. I kept expecting a guard to burst through the door, ordered by Queen Kidira to find where her daughter had disappeared to.

"I really don't mean to keep you from your affairs, dear. What were you doing before I so rudely intruded?"

I gestured to the pile of books I'd flipped through. I was willing to answer any of Katja's questions, so long as it served as a distraction for her.

"Just looking through those for something to do. You're really not bothering me."

"Oh!" Katja straightened in her seat as though she'd been blind to the books, until I'd pointed them out. "Would you be so kind as to read something to me? Any of the books shall do. I hardly care for the material, at this very moment."

"I can't," I said. "Sorry."

"You can't what?"

"I can't read," I blurted out, finding something shameful in it for the way Katja stared at me, mouth agape. "I've never been able to."

"My word. Why ever not?" Katja asked, leaning towards me. "Did nobody think to teach you? How ever do you manage?"

I was glad to have taken her mind off her grief, but the questions rushed out of her, making me shuffle in my seat for the bewilderment I'd evoked. I knew she had no intention of being callous, but her shock served to make everything she said blunt.

"I never needed to read. I was a farmer, remember? My brother was always more than happy to read for me, if I ever needed help."

"Then why were you perusing these books?"

"I was looking for pictures," I admitted, feeling my face burn.

"Well! I should hardly believe it. An intelligent young woman like yourself, unable to read. That just goes to show, doesn't it, that you cannot judge a person by a single attribute alone," Katja said, pleased with herself for having concluded that I was worthy of consideration, despite my flaws. "Well, let's see here. *The Everlasting Kingdom*. One of the better histories of Myros, actually."

She flicked through a few pages and hummed to herself. I'd seen Michael do the same thing and expected to be there for hours, but Katja promptly snapped the book shut in her hand and placed it neatly atop the others.

"Did you know one of the scholars here actually speaks Myrosi? Remarkable, isn't it? He's one of the few people left on Bosma who can do so. Certainly the only person in Kastelir."

"What's the point in that?" I asked. "Who does he talk to?"

I thought it a perfectly reasonable question, but Katja chuckled to herself. The corner of my mouth tugged into a frown, but Katja wasn't looking at me. A ripple of anger crossed her features, as though she was silently scolding herself for daring to laugh on such a day.

"Goodness, I really must return to the wake, mustn't I? My mother shall be worried sick. I dare say she might even wonder where I am," Katja said wearily, gripping the arm of the sofa as she stood. "Someone has to console my cousins. That is, unless you might..."

I stared blankly at her. As much as I wanted to help, I couldn't go to the wake. Death and death alone would be on people's minds, and in lingering on it, surely they'd know what I was, what I'd wanted to do.

"I'm sorry, Katja. I can't," I said, not as firmly as I could've.

"Oh, Rowan. It'll be fine, I promise you. I know you spoke with my uncle. Why, I'd go as far as to say you knew him better than some of the lord and ladies and lieges who are supposedly grieving the loss of him," Katja said. She took my hand and pulled me to my feet before I could protest. "There are close to a hundred guests in attendance. Your presence shan't cause a problem, I assure you."

Katja squeezed my hand and smiled at me as best she could, eyes stinging with tears once more. A strange sensation crept up my throat, a sickness with no source, and it took all that I had within me to shake my head.

"I don't have anything to wear," I tried.

"That's what you were worried about? You ought to have said." Brightening, Katja took my other hand in her own. "We'll find you something suitable, dear."

"No." I shook my head, pulling my hands free. Katja reached for them again, fingers wrapping around my wrists as the sickness in my throat trickled down to the pit of my stomach. "I'd rather stay here."

Katja's jaw tensed and disappointment became her. It wasn't until that moment I appreciate how much taller she was than me. She stepped forward, grip tightening, tears threatening to spill over.

"It was such a great comfort when you came to me, Rowan. I had thought that, well, that there was some connection between us, and that you might..." Katja said in a whisper. My vision clouded and flashed with how unwell I felt. Her fingers were irons bound around my wrists, but I couldn't bring myself to move, to pull away. It was her nature as a healer making my stomach turn; something beyond her control, beyond her awareness. If I reacted, I'd give myself away. She'd know. "You were going to say something, the other day. I couldn't fathom what it was at the time, but now that I think about it, I—"

286

"Alright!" I yelped, prying my hands free. "I'll come with you, alright? Come on. Let's go."

I was at the door when Katja coughed to reclaim my attention.

"Your clothes, Rowan. You can't very well turn up in something so colourful," she said. "I suppose you couldn't read the note I left on these for you, could you? Not that it stopped you from putting them to use, I see."

Simultaneously revealing herself as my benefactor and digging through the clothes I'd left spread out across the armchairs, Katja managed to produce something that was suitable enough, she supposed. She handed me a white shirt and told me to change into it, back to me. I hesitated, clutching the shirt between unsteady fingers, but didn't ask her to leave the room.

I changed as quickly as I could, not about to demand anything of her. Not today.

She wasn't herself. She was as shaken as I was.

Katja insisted on brushing my hair. She was particularly ruthless, when it came to any tangles. Deeming me moderately presentable, she took my arm and I put any lingering discomfort down to my reluctance to leave my room.

The wake took place in one of the first parts of the castle I'd spent any real amount of time within, but I scarcely recognised the place. The banquet hall was awash in candlelight, revealing the room to be bigger than I'd imagined, and though the table resided within the middle, dozens of armchairs had been brought out for the dozens of guests. Some of them huddled together while others wished to mourn or eat in private, all of them draped in white finery.

Katja tilted her head at Queen Kidira, sat in the far corner. She scowled at Katja, but I imagined it was only because she had been worried. If an assassin could strike down a King, her daughter could hardly be considered safe, either.

The look she shot me was what it was.

Akela stood behind her, back straight, spear in hand, and I half expected Queen Kidira to send her my way and have me escorted out of the hall.

"Let's take a seat, shall we?" Katja said, tugging me towards a cluster of chairs. Some of them were placed back-to-back, and I took the lead, seating myself in the chair that Kouris' horns jutted over the top of. "There. Much better. Now I do not feel as though I ought to be seeking people out."

I was glad Katja didn't feel compelled to make rounds of the hall. No one looked at me as I came in, no one cared who I was. They certainly hadn't whispered *necromancer* behind my back. Still, I felt safer for sitting, hidden from most of the hall.

A portrait of King Jonas hung in the centre of the room. People gathered around it, gesturing to it as they sipped on their wine and nodded solemnly. A murmur of conversation filled the hall, and it was too little and too much. It didn't rise above the deep, sorrowful sounds the band drew out of stringed instruments on the balcony above, nor was it drowned out by the music.

"That's Sir Ightham, is it?" Katja asked, leaning towards me.

I'd failed to pick Claire out of the crowd, and for good reason. She was stood with her back to the wall, mirroring Akela in all ways, down to the spear in her hand and the Kastelirian armour she wore.

"That's her," I replied.

I shouldn't have seen Claire like that. Her reward for coming this far, for giving up all she had, was to be dressed in another nation's armour; she couldn't have felt any pride in the colours she wore.

"Not exactly what I was expecting," Katja remarked. "But I should like to speak to her regardless. After all, she is to be my sister-in-law."

A few feet away, a group of scholars too young to sit on the throne were discussing the effect choosing a new ruler would have on the economy. Others wondered out loud whether choosing a new Sovereign from what had once been the Old West was truly in the spirit of what Kastelir was supposed to stand for.

I listened to them until King Atthis' voice reached my ears. I hadn't realised he was there, without horns or antlers to give him away.

I didn't mean to eavesdrop, but it was hard not to overhear.

"You have been silent for half an hour or more," he said. "Something weighs upon your mind."

"We have just laid Jonas to rest in the crypt," Kouris replied gruffly. "Of course *something weighs upon my mind*."

People came and went, offering Katja their condolences, but I was invisible to them. Katja was subjected to tale after tale revolving around the most memorable parts of King Jonas' life and reign, while I had nothing to distract myself from the conversation unfolding behind me.

"And for twenty-seven years, you too rested in an empty crypt," King Atthis said.

"Then Jonas' life has been exchanged for my own. Is that it?"

"No, no. Do not give me *that* look, Kouris. This would've happened, whether you were here or across the Uncharted Sea."

Kouris grunted and a long pause followed. The lull in conversation was only interrupted by a third voice. It was nothing of interest. A servant scurried over to ask if more wine ought to be brought up from the cellars, and King Atthis dismissed him quickly, saying he wasn't to be bothered with such trivial matters for the rest of the day. The servant left, but minutes passed before either of them spoke another word.

"It's Kidira, isn't it?" Atthis asked. When Kouris gave no reply, he said, "You know you may speak freely to me."

"It's Kidira. Of course it's Kidira. It's always been her, yet she looks right through me. Won't speak a word to me. It's as though I'm not even here. Like I'm still back in Canth. If she doesn't look at me soon, doesn't speak to me, then I will know I *am* a ghost, dead these last twenty-seven years after all."

The woman who'd been speaking with Katja left her with the assurance that she was there for her, should she ever need someone to talk to, and without anyone vying for her attention, Katja caught the last of what Kouris said. She frowned, sympathetic, but gave the impression that she'd just as soon roll her eyes at her mother.

Kouris' words carried the ache she felt into my bones. If only she'd tell Queen Kidira what had truly happened. It'd never excuse what she'd done, the years she'd been absent, but it would start to make sense of what had happened. Surely that would mean *something* to Queen Kidira.

"What did you expect, Kouris? Did you expect to return and for everything to be as it once was? Kidira is not the woman you left widowed. For twenty-seven years she ensured that your memory was respected. She named her daughter after you. She felt nothing but pride when she spoke of you, believing you had faced your past and atoned for it. And then she discovers that you have merely run from Kastelir. Run from *her*. How is she supposed to begin absorbing any of that?"

"I had no choice. You know I didn't. I even asked her to go with me, but her duty was to Kastelir, and I understood that. I respected that. I had *no choice*," she hissed. "If I wasn't dead, Kastelir would've fallen apart in years. You think I haven't spent each and every day thinking of her? Praying at Canthian temples to those long gone gods of yours for a reason to come back here? I exiled myself from Kastelir, from Kidira. Thought it was better if I let her think me dead. Thought she might move on. Find a way to be happy."

"Come now. You know Kidira will never be happy until every violent thought in her Kingdom turns to ash and not a single Kastelirian goes hungry. Do not think she has been alone these twenty-seven years, either," Atthis said sternly. I dared to look across the room at Queen Kidira, certain she could feel my eyes on her. All the while, Akela stood behind her, back straight, chin raised. "You expected too much of her, Kouris, and not enough of yourself. You swore vows and broke them the moment the past came knocking at your door. Do not be surprised if it takes another twenty-seven years for her to set eyes on you again."

The words smarted. Over the back of the chair, I saw Kouris' horns bow forward.

"It's funny. I really thought I was doing her a favour. Or I convinced myself I did, to make leaving easier. Not that there was anything *easy* about it, trust me. But I always felt like there was some part of Kidira buried away that made her resent herself for loving me. Look at what I was, what the people believed I did. It was like this was always gonna be an inevitability."

The words came out thickly, difficult for Kouris to form, and no easier for me and Katja to overhear. We looked away from each other, hoping the conversation wouldn't pick back up, and from the corner of my eye I saw Katja stare at her hands with the same intensity that had turned her eyes dark days ago. She was stricken by a shade of guilt, having taken her mother's loss so lightly.

We were saved from wrapping ourselves up in the concept of twenty-seven years, in all that could be done and the way people changed, but didn't change, by a balding man in a long, loose thawb. He swooped over and bowed to take one of Katja's hands between both of his own.

"Lady Kouris! How it pains me to have to meet under such circumstances," he said, tone a tad dramatic, despite the sincerity lacing his voice. "If only I were able to congratulate you on the news of your recent engagement without such a tragedy overshadowing it."

"Lord Adiur," Katja said, smiling as much as seemed to be permitted at a wake. "I've had the pleasure of your friendship for long enough to feel the full effects of your well-wishes without you having to voice them. Please, don't trouble yourself. My spirits are eased to see you here. Is your good wife with you?"

"It would've pained her to miss His Majesty's sending off," Lord Adiur said, sweeping out an arm in the direction of a refined woman by the table, white-gold jewellery blending against the white of her suit. "She'll be over to see you in a moment, I'm sure. But I'm afraid I don't know your companion, Lady—?"

Lord Adiur fixed his eyes on me, graciously attempting to draw me into the conversation. I wondered how I was supposed to introduce myself without demoting his estimation of me. The presence of a farmer with no ties to the capital at the King's wake was likely as undesirable in Isin as it was in Thule, but Katja took it upon herself to say, "This is Rowan. She's as new a friend as she is dear."

"Well," he said, standing straight and clasping his hands in front of him. "I shan't say it's a pleasure to meet you. Not today, of all days. I'm certain you'll understand my wish to save such praise for the next time we meet, under thoroughly different circumstances. Although I would be remiss if I didn't tell you how glad I was to know Lady Kouris has a companion at such a time."

I smiled at Lord Adiur but didn't dare to speak. Thankfully, Katja reclaimed his attention and their conversation turned from pleasantries to that of a more personal nature. They spoke in the sort of hushed whispers that implied a pretence of privacy in such a crowded space, and Lord Adiur was convinced Katja must know something about who was to take King Jonas' place. I did my best to seem lost in my own thoughts, lest Lord Adiur entice me to reminisce about King Jonas with him.

He left after some minutes with a bow, claiming he'd taken up more than enough of Katja's time.

"I do wish I got to see him more often," Katja said. "He's a cousin of Uncle Atthis, actually. The resemblance isn't striking, I know, but they have always been on good terms. Ah, Rowan, dear. I do apologise for presuming to speak for you, but it's better that you don't say anything.

Your accent would give you away immediately, and there'd be no end to the questions we'd have to endure. It's for the best, wouldn't you agree?"

I sunk into my seat, doing as she wished. Keeping my lips pursed together. I listened for any more snippets of conversation between Kouris and King Atthis, but I made nothing out over the din, until the servant who'd interrupted them returned.

"King Atthis, Lady Rán," he said, short of breath. "I apologise for interrupting you, but—"

"For the last time, it's just *Rán*. Or *Representative Rán*, if you must give her some title," King Atthis snapped. "If you're here to update me on the wine situation, I strongly suggest you turn on your heels and avoid me for so long as you wish to remain employed."

"Go easy on him, Atthis," Kouris grumbled. "He's all out of sorts. What is it, lad?"

Curiosity got the better of me. I leant towards Katja's seat and looked between our chairs. King Atthis' elbow blocked much of my view, but I saw the servant clearly enough.

"I beg your forgiveness, Your Highness, but please," he mumbled, dabbing his forehead with a handkerchief. "Ianto Ires has come to seek an audience with you."

The name meant as much to King Atthis as it did to me.

"And you have brought this to me now because...?"

"Pardon, Majesty. He claims to speak for the rebels."

There was a decided pause. A cellist drew his bow across the strings, sending a low, resounding note through the hall.

"Why today, of all days? Does he believe me so weakened by grief that I would tear my country apart and condemn the scattered pieces back to war?"

"I-I'm afraid not, Your Majesty. He wishes to claim responsibility for King Jonas' death."

CHAPTER TWENTY

A dozen people overheard the servant and a murmur rippled through the room, catching Queen Kidira as it went. She rose to her feet, long white dress trailing behind her as she outpaced Akela across the hall. She didn't stop to question the servant and the guards didn't have the chance to open the doors for her. She threw them open herself and Katja grabbed my hand, pulling me along with her.

"Now, now, if everyone would remain where they are," Lord Adiur said to the rumbling crowd, convinced there was an assassin within their midst. "Their Majesties will have this attended to in no time, I assure you."

King Atthis let his cousin handle the sudden discord and slipped from the hall, doing his best to keep up with Queen Kidira. Kouris and Claire followed, and I had as little desire as I did choice to go with them. Katja's fingers dug into my wrist and she was too busy vying for her mother's attention to hear me say, "Katja, I don't think..."

We tore through a corridor and turned sharply, heading across a bridge connecting two parts of the castle. Katja's hand slipped from my wrist and she entwined her fingers with mine. I didn't pull away. I was caught up in it, now. I followed the others, glancing over my shoulder at Claire. She had less of an idea of what I was doing there than I did.

I thought Queen Kidira was storming blindly through the castle, but there was only one place visitors of the sort were taken to. It was the same room Akela had interrogated Claire and me in, door swarmed by a dozen guards. The servants who weren't in the kitchens, busy cooking up course after course for the wake, flooded the corridor, sharing descriptions of the man within for those who'd missed his entrance.

The few who caught sight of Queen Kidira scattered and the few who hadn't been so lucky held their breath in her presence. She wasn't concerned with them. Akela dismissed all but two of the guards and slowly, silently, the crowd sulked back into the castle's winding corridors, not yet daring to whisper amongst themselves.

"I am having this man brought before Your Majesties in the throne room, yes?" Akela asked.

"We'll speak with him here. He wants a spectacle and I will not give it to him," Queen Kidira said. King Atthis nodded in fierce agreement. Akela was about to unlock the door, but paused when Queen Kidira caught sight of Katja and said, "Why are you here? Return to the hall."

"I will not," Katja said defiantly, eyes brimming with tears. "This man is responsible for what happened to uncle, isn't he? I need to see him for myself."

"*Kouris*," Queen Kidira warned in a low voice.

"*Mother*," Katja returned, refusing to flinch.

Queen Kidira didn't waste another second. She turned her back to us and Katja took it to mean she'd won the right to follow her mother in.

Akela twisted the key in the lock, unfastening the bolts.

Ianto Ires had been left alone in the room, wrist shackled to the bar across the window. He sat at the table, arm held high, as though it was no discomfort to him.

He was a neat looking man, well-dressed, dark hair meticulously combed into place, but more than that, he was unspeakably calm. Ianto didn't panic at the sight of the King and Queen, nor did he cower when Akela walked up to him, spear still in hand.

Katja tugged me into the far corner, as out of the way as we could be in such a small, crowded room. Queen Kidira and King Atthis stood in front of Ianto, content to let Akela handle the interrogation. Queen Kidira refused to give Ianto the satisfaction of anger flaring within her, but the King had a harder time remaining calm. His hands clenched and unclenched into fists, teeth grinding together.

Claire was the last into the chamber. She pulled the door shut and Kouris charged across the room, hands slamming down on the table.

"You did it, did you? You put the knife in Jonas?"

Ianto flinched, more confused than alarmed.

"I made my terms clear to the servants," he said, speaking around Kouris. "I will only talk to the unlawful rulers of these lands."

Akela blocked his view of the King and Queen, mimicking Kouris' pose with a little less force.

"What? You are not understanding who you are seeing?" Akela asked. "Do not tell me you are thinking your northern Queen dead!"

Ianto stared at Kouris, lips parting, eyes narrowing. After a moment, he covered his mouth with his free hand and let out a sharp, breathy laugh.

"Dear me. I was but a boy of ten when you were *executed* for your crimes. That is, if you aren't simply another pane, propped up by these frauds. I would not be surprised either way! They have kept you hidden in some cellar, I expect," he said, laughing until it tangled in his throat and left him choking. His eyes watered and he pounded a fist against his chest, clearing the last of it from his throat. No one in the room stepped forward to help him. "I am a sick man, a very sick man indeed. I shall waste neither your time nor mine, whether or not you are who you claim to be."

Despite that, he looked between Akela and Kouris, waiting. He wanted to be questioned. He wanted them to grasp for answers. I stared at him, no longer wondering what sort of man would stab another to death in cold blood. I wondered what sort of man could sit there, brimming with pride and eager to brag about it.

Kouris raised her brow when Akela glanced at her, giving her the go-ahead to continue the interrogation.

"You are saying you sneaking into the castle and murdering the King, yes? You are coming here and you are claiming responsibility for it all?"

"*I am saying* that I am *claiming responsibility*, but I am not *killing your King* with my own two hands, yes?" Ianto said in a mockery of Akela's accent. Akela held his gaze and his lower jaw trembled, lungs on the verge of betraying him again. "Gracious. This one is entertaining. Where did you pick her up? Is this Kastelir of yours expanding its borders so? Well, as for the question: I set the plan into motion, but cannot claim to have a drop of Jonas' blood on my hands. I'm merely here as a formality."

No one but me was surprised.

King Atthis stepped forward and Queen Kidira gripped his arm, pulling him back.

"You are not doing it yourself, you are saying? You are not taking the knife because you are not having the guts to be using it? Well, I am certain you are wanting to tell me who is doing it! Nobody is wanting to be facing the gallows alone," Akela said.

"Indeed, indeed. The man you are looking for goes by the name of Tom," Ianto said.

"Tom," Kouris repeated. "How man Toms do you reckon you know, Commander?"

"Too many to be counting. Two of my cousins, they are being called

Tom. At family gatherings, this is being most confusing. And to be making matters worse, one of them is naming their son Tom. And there are many Toms who are soldiers, who are guards, and all of them, they are good, honest men. Well! One of them, I am thinking I am living without him quite easily, but he is not skinning a rabbit, much less stabbing a King."

Kouris put a hand on her chin and nodded for effect.

"Can't be saying it's a particularly common name amongst the pane and there's a shortage of Toms down in Canth, but I could probably draw up a list of ten or eleven knocking around Asar."

Ianto cleared his throat, irritated that Akela and Kouris were entertaining themselves at his expense. Queen Kidira took matters into her own hands while they were busy mulling things over. She stepped forward and parted Akela and Kouris with an outward sweep of her arms.

Queen Kidira didn't slam her hands on the table or lean towards Ianto, and still, the chain around his wrist rattled, chair legs scraping across the stone floor.

"Ires. You've had your fun," she said in a low voice, more exasperated than exhausted. "Tell me who Tom is, lest you're willing to find out whether the Commander's aim with a spear is as good as it is with an axe."

"A threat!" Ianto was nothing short of delighted. "But I needn't tell you who Tom is. He works – worked, I suppose – here. For no fewer than nine months, as it happens. But you never took the time to know him. The people who work for you are nothing but insects, are they?"

Queen Kidira didn't take the bait. She sighed and said, "We'll have to talk to Ocari," to King Atthis. "They'll know who he's talking about."

Ianto shuffled in his seat, eyes darting around the room. He caught my gaze for half a second, debating whether it was worth riling me up, and when Akela and Kouris began talking amongst themselves in hushed whispers, Ianto said, "Well? Too proud to ask me why I did it?"

King Atthis scoffed, more controlled than I'd expected him to be.

"The blanks are easily filled. You are part of the rebel group intent on tearing Kastelir apart, and you assassinated King Jonas to send a message. Your people are numerous and far-spread. You do realise you'll be executed for your part in this, don't you?"

"As I said, I'm a very sick man," Ianto grumbled. "My organisation wants you to know what we're capable of. You've sat on the throne for thirty years, Atthis. What claim did you have to our old territories, much less to this farce of a Kingdom? You made your own borders, ignored the treaties set up between other clans. You executed those with better claims to power than you and declared that your rule would be short-lived. That others would be voted onto the throne, that we'd all get a chance to shape this new land. And look what came of that! Three decades later and we have to carve the crowns off your heads."

Ianto's words were rehearsed and likely not his own. In the same way that Tom had been talked into doing as Ianto wished, Ianto too was being manipulated. He certainly wasn't a leader. His was being disposed of because his life was already forfeit. The disease he carried peeled off him in sheets and crawled through his veins, sticking to the inside of his lungs. It wasn't something a healer could wash away. He was far from brave in making a martyr of himself.

Facing the guillotine was a much kinder fate than coughing himself to death.

Katja let go of my hand and wrapped her arms around herself. The ebbing feeling of a disease she couldn't quell made her pale skin paler, face damp with sweat.

Queen Kidira put her hand on the edge of the table and drummed her fingers against it.

"Commander. I expect this *Tom* has been absent from work since the day of the incident, if not longer. Have Ocari give you his address, the name of a family member, anything, and take Ightham with you to bring him in. We shall keep Ires alive until we have the right person and you have retrieved all the information you can get from him. After that, throw him on the pyre," Queen Kidira said, and even Akela's eyes flashed as she nodded obediently.

"The... I am to be *burnt*?" Ianto asked, trying to tug the iron bar clean out of the window. For the first time, he understood the reality of facing his own death. A beheading was far easier to romanticise than having the flesh burnt from his bones. "But surely the standard method of execution ought to be employed here. The guillotine is, it's the—"

Queen Kidira wasn't listening.

"The necromancer held in Orinhal ought to arrive in time for the Phoenix Festival. Rather fitting. The people will enjoy the spectacle all the more if there are two executions that day."

"I—Commander, surely I am within my rights, surely it is lawful that..." Ianto tried, desperate to earn Akela's pity.

Only then did Queen Kidira lean towards him.

"You mock the Commander and then wish to seek her aid when it suits you?" she asked. Ianto froze in his seat, unable to reply. Stepping back, Queen Kidira fixed her eyes on Akela and said, "Burn him slowly," as she left the room.

The next few minutes were a jumble.

Akela had guards escort Ianto to a proper holding cell and the rest of us flooded out of the chamber. Katja ran after Queen Kidira, calling for her to wait, and the Queen stopped to place a hand on her daughter's shoulder. They headed off in one direction and King Atthis led Kouris in another.

I leant against the wall, heart doing what it could to crack my ribs apart.

The necromancer from Orinhal was still alive. He was being brought here, to Isin. I'd done all I could to push him from my mind, but he was coming to the capital to be burnt in the heart of the Kingdom. Orinhal was a large city, a wealthy one at that, but the death of a necromancer could never be wasted on it.

"Rowan," Claire said gently. "Are you alright?"

I shook my head. It was hard to look at her when all I could see was the Kastelirian uniform, when she'd stood by silently as Queen Kidira spoke of burning necromancers. But what *could* she do? Had anyone else bit their tongue in Queen Kidira's presence, I would've understood, but it was different with Claire. I expected too much of her and it wasn't fair.

"I'll—"

The doors slammed open and I leapt off the wall as though the stones were burning.

"Ightham, come," Akela said, tilting her head down the corridor. "We are finding Ocari at once."

I followed Claire and Akela. News of what happened had already spread through the castle, and every chamber and walkway were thrumming with rumour and exaggeration.

Ocari was too busy for gossip. They walked faster than we did, and I was on the verge of jogging to keep up with Akela and Claire. Three servants trailed behind Ocari, each carrying something that belonged in a different part of the castle. Ocari lectured a boy with a bundle of freshly cleaned sheets in his arms, telling him *exactly* how they were to be folded, and they didn't break their gait when Akela called out to them.

Akela caught up and squeezed between Ocari and the servant.

"Ocari, I am afraid I am not coming here for small talk," Akela said. "I am looking for a Tom, a Tom who is working here in the castle."

"Got a lot of Toms here, Commander. Three working down with the laundry, one who tends to the gardens, another two who—"

"Yes, yes, there are many, I am knowing this. But the Tom I am looking for, perhaps he is not coming to work since..." she paused, lowering her voice. "Since His Highness is murdered."

Ocari clapped their hands and the servants scattered. Ocari's work never ended but their expression became more serious than stern, understanding how important it was to put whatever they were in the middle of aside for the time being.

We were led to their office, close to the servants' quarters, and Ocari looked at me as though they recognised me as they opened the door. I would've waited in the corridor, but Claire ushered me inside. I stood in the corner, out of the way, while Ocari muttered to theirself, turning in a circle on the spot, trying to remember where *something* was.

The sheer number of books piled on the desk and lining the shelves made the small office smaller. A narrow ray of light spilt in through a high-up window, striking the floor by Ocari's chair.

"Ah," they said, pulling a ring of keys from their hip. They unlocked the top drawer of their desk and produced a stack of dog-eared documents. "Had a complaint yesterday morning. Well, I get plenty of complaints every morning, noon and night, but this one might be of interest to you. A cook in one of the eastern kitchens said one of their assistants hadn't shown since... you can imagine, I'm sure."

Ocari handed the note to Akela, who nodded gravely as she read it.

"You are having a way to find this Tom?" she asked.

Ocari gestured to Claire.

"Ightham. Top shelf, red book," they said as they took a seat.

Claire followed the orders without a moment's hesitation. I watched

299

as she pushed herself onto tiptoes and pried a hefty book from beneath two others; the uniform had become her. She wasn't Sir Ightham, wasn't a Knight. She certainly wasn't a Princess.

All of that was behind her.

The book thudded on the desk in front of Ocari and they closed their eyes for a split second, mouthing *eastern kitchens, eastern kitchens*, until they found whatever was locked away in the back of their memory. The spine cracked as they eased the book open and thumbed through a dozen pages.

"Let's see. The only address we have for this Tom is his mother's. Red Pine Street, down in the Gatholith District," Ocari said. "Listen, Commander. If you're saying that one of our own is responsible for this, one of the serving staff, then..."

"Ocari, my friend. I am not wanting you to worry," Akela said. "I am not accusing you of anything, and Their Majesties, they are knowing you are having nothing to do with this. You are keeping this place running for twenty years. There is no way you are throwing that all away."

Satisfied with Akela's promise, Ocari closed the book, dust flying as the pages slammed together.

We were gone by the time it was returned to the shelf.

It didn't take long to reach the Gatholith District. Michael would've lectured us on the history of the area, had he been with us, but in his absence, it was just another part of Isin. The streets were narrow, crowded with people running errands and children playing, and rows of washing ran between the windows, above our heads.

We reached the right street and Akela stopped to talk to a few men sat on their front steps, scrubbing dirty shirts against washing boards propped up in buckets. Akela drew an instant, honest answer out of the men, and they pointed us down the street, to the house at the very end of Red Pine.

There was a tavern halfway along the road. The doors were propped open with barstools and people spilt out onto the street.

"This truly marks it, then!" a woman shouted from within the tavern. "The end of King Jonas' reign."

"May he find rest in the Forest Within," someone called in reply.

The people in the street raised their glasses in agreement.

"May he rot in the crypt!" a voice boomed from the back of the tavern. "Imposters on the throne, the lot of them."

The people who'd raised their glasses jeered, but there was no force behind it. They did so in a tired, playful way, having had the argument time and time again. Still, a ripple of disagreement ran through the tavern, spurred on by barrels of ale and bottles of wine, and Akela slowed as she passed by, stopping a fight before it could break out.

"Watch it," the first person who spotted her called into the tavern. "Hey, watch it, I said! Look, the castle's sent out their finest."

Any disagreement went forgotten. The patrons sipped on their drinks, eyes fixed on us as we headed down the street, all of them suspicious, accusatory. They looked at Claire and Akela as though they were only there to abuse their power, district having been plagued by more trouble from guards than drunks.

"Ightham, cross the street. I am thinking, if this Tom is inside, perhaps he is running out of the window when I am knocking on the door. Go, go. You are watching for me, yes?" Akela said.

We did as she said. Claire stood to attention while I leant against a lamppost, both of us staring at the same window. It was propped open, curtains swaying in the breeze, and part of me wanted Tom to escape. He'd been manipulated by Ianto. There'd been so much self-righteous venom in that man's words that to me, coordinating the assassination was worse than sinking the blade in. I didn't want to feel that we were in the wrong, tracking Tom down like this, and I reminded myself that he'd waited for King Jonas.

He'd planned to catch him alone, and he'd stabbed him over and over, until not even a healer could save him.

"Did you know?" I asked Claire. "About the execution at the end of the Phoenix Festival?"

The only way I could ask without tensing was by not looking at Claire.

"I didn't. Had I any idea, Rowan, I would have told you immediately."

"It's fine." I cut her off before she could say anything else. "You have an entire Kingdom to look out for. It's important that you protect Felheim. Especially when you're not going to be able to do anything about an execution."

I wasn't comfortable with the words until I spoke them, but once I heard my voice drift into the warm air, I knew it was the only fair thing to say. Claire would do all that she could to protect me and I didn't have to test her. Pushing her to her limits for the sake of finding out what they were was the worst thing I could've done for Felheim, for her.

The necromancer would burn whether Claire spoke out against it or not. The only difference was that Queen Kidira might not keep her so close, should she dare to go against her laws.

"Is that your uniform now?" I asked, voice free of judgement. "No more dragon-bone armour?"

"It would appear so," Claire said, self-consciously adjusting the collar of her shirt.

Akela knocked on the door. Claire and I were far enough away for anything she said to be lost in the general buzz of the street, but we understood the situation when Akela knocked three times, louder and louder, demanding that someone answer the door.

A woman cautiously poked her head out of the door, unwilling to open it all the way. She let herself believe that Akela couldn't tear it off its hinges, if she wanted to. She couldn't be anyone other than Tom's mother and he couldn't be anywhere but cowering in the cellar, hoping he could hide away forever.

She was buying mere seconds for him, doing all she could to blind herself to the inevitability of her son paying for his crimes beneath a guillotine's blade.

Claire yawned.

I tore my eyes away from the woman futilely insisting that her son wasn't there and furrowed my brow at Claire.

"Kouris requested my company last night," she said, tightening her grip on her spear. "Insisted that we went drinking."

I turned away from her slowly, eyes back on the house Akela now had one foot inside.

"You tried to out-drink a pane?"

"*Tried* being the operative word," Claire said. "I could not refuse her. She needed someone to talk to."

"What do you and Kouris talk about?"

"The situation as a whole. Queen Kidira. Readjusting to the ways of Asar. You."

I opened my mouth but Claire took a step forward.

My eyes darted from the door to window and I saw what had caught her attention.

Akela had pushed her way into the house and fingers wrapped around the windowsill. Claire held out her spear and I gripped it with both hands as she set off at a sprint.

Tom's mother began to wail.

Tom flung himself through the window, landed heavily on his feet, and charged through the Gatholith District, desperately glancing over his shoulder at Claire. I lost sight of him in seconds. He knew the area, which streets were the busiest, and while no one purposely obstructed Claire's path, they didn't move out of her way, either.

The people of Red Pine took notice of me, now that Claire wasn't at my side. It was hard not to catch their attention with a guard's spear between my hands, and I drifted towards Akela, steel-tipped spear dragging along the stone of the street.

She wasn't restraining Tom's mother. She had her hands on her shoulders but she wasn't holding the woman back. There was no point: she couldn't do anything for him now. Akela was offering what comfort she could as the woman stuttered, "Y-you've got to believe me, C-Commander. Came r-right back here, he did, the moment it was d-done. They *tricked* him into it. Tom, he's, he's always been good, always h-helped me out," between sobs.

"Yes, yes. Your son, he is being used by these people. We are understanding the situation. The man who is making your son do this, he is already within the castle and soon, he is being executed," Akela said.

For a moment, the woman was able to lift her chin. There was justice in Ianto's death, but his execution was to be paired with her son's.

"Commander," Claire said gravely. She'd caught up with Tom and had dragged him back, one hand gripping his arm. He stood with his shoulders hunched, not looking at his mother, lest he burst into tears.

He was young. Much younger than I was. He couldn't have been older than seventeen and yet he'd spread so much hurt and turmoil through the Kingdom.

But more than that, more than he was scared, he was sorry for what he'd done.

It didn't make the blindest bit of difference. Akela put his wrists in shackles and Tom couldn't reach out as his mother tried to hold him one last time. He was going to be punished for what he'd done, no matter how regret churned within him, because there was no taking it back. No making it better.

Not for people like him.

"Listen, Ma. I'm sorry. I thought, thought..." Tom mumbled at the ground. "They told me it'd *help* Kastelir, that it was the only way for the people to be free, and..."

His mother wailed too loudly for his words to reach her. It was the only thing I ever heard him say, but his voice stuck with me as the people of the Gatholith District filled the streets, shoulder to shoulder. No one approached us, no one said anything, but the threat was implicit. They had the numbers to strike us down, if they so chose to live with the consequences.

I wondered whether they'd be more or less likely to come upon us like a tidal wave if they knew why we were marching one of their own back to the castle.

Claire and Akela took no pleasure in escorting Tom through Isin, but I found it hard to fall into step with them. The people of Isin narrowed their eyes at me and the spear in my hands became part of me. It was all they saw, only there to be brandished against them.

Kastelir may have been formed on the ruins of war and Isin may have sprung from the rubble left behind, but it hadn't thrived for long. The country wasn't crumbling apart, not in the way Felheim would have us believe it was, but there was something palpably stale in the atmosphere, something I was only just noticing. The Kingdom was held together by its own ideals, but it yearned for change.

I couldn't forgive the rebels for murdering King Jonas, but I understood the force that drove them. I understood wanting to be heard.

I handed the spear back to Claire the moment we were through the castle gates and walked with my head down, focusing on the white stone of the bridge beneath my feet.

"Rowan," Claire called, catching up to me. I stopped when she placed a hand against the back of my arm, though my gaze didn't break away from the edge of the bridge. "That was a necessity, I am afraid. Manipulated or otherwise, he had to answer for what he did."

"That's not..." *That's not it*, I wanted to say, but I couldn't put what *it*

304

was into words. Instead, I shook my head and said, "I understand. The King and Queen have to trust you, don't they? So if this is what you have to do for now, I guess we'll have to stay here for a bit longer, won't we?"

Claire hadn't expected that. Her surprise softened into something like gratitude.

"This won't be easy and it won't be over soon," she said. "I would not have caught up to him had I believed letting him escape would've been just."

I did my best to smile at her and said, "You'd better go."

The castle doors were pushed open and Akela led Tom inside, guards flanking him lest he dive into the moat.

"Indeed," Claire agreed. "If I have to remain in a foreign castle, I am glad I have you by my side."

She nodded firmly once she'd spoke, confirming that the words sat well with her, in whatever ways they'd altered between her thoughts and what had left her lips.

She headed into the castle before I could reply.

Before I could tell her that I was glad to be with her too, even if I felt no more comfortable in a castle where nobody knew who I was than a village where everyone's thoughts darkened against me.

CHAPTER TWENTY-ONE

The day before, funeral bells had rang out across Isin.

Isin was alive with a swell of cheer, music rising from every street corner. People had hung the last of the decorations days ago but it wasn't until the morning of the Phoenix Festival that the colours came to life. The oranges and golds of the banners contended with the beat of the sun and the clear blue sky ushered in the end of Etha.

"You sure you want to be heading down there, yrval?" Kouris asked as we crossed the bridge.

"I'm sure. There won't be anything like... *you know* until the last day, will there?" I said, taking her hand. "Besides, I haven't seen you properly in forever. I've missed you."

Kouris squeezed my hand, smiling around her tusks.

"Aye. There's been no shortage of things to do around the castle, I'll tell you that much," Kouris said, gesturing for the guards to open the doors. "Too bad about your dragon-slayer. Reckon Kidira's got her doing twice as much work as anyone else to prove herself."

I hadn't taken it too badly. The Phoenix Festival might've been over in an afternoon in my village, but it stretched for three days in Isin. There was always tomorrow for Claire and me, and it was just as important that I got to spend time with Kouris. I didn't want to pass up the opportunity to delve into the heart of Isin with her at my side.

People arrived from all over Kastelir to celebrate in the capital, and Isin's streets were awash with citizens and visitors alike. They all wore orange and gold, if only in the ribbons twisted in their hair. Tables longer and wider than the one in the castle's banquet hall were set up in open squares, interspersed with marquees and makeshift stages.

The festivals I'd attended had been made up of entertainment limited to song and dance, all of it revolving around the exodus from the Bloodless Lands.

In Isin, everyone put on performances of their own. Voices boomed from within tents and around fountains, filling the air with speech and song, and as we wandered towards Asos Square, the biggest open area in all of Isin, I heard people sing of the days of war, of lost loves and famed thieves. Asos housed a park littered with statues of people I didn't recognise and the biggest marquee of all stood in the centre. I saw dozens upon dozens of red lanterns within, ready to be sent up into the sky once night fell.

"Didn't exactly have the time to be getting you anything," Kouris said, gesturing to the stalls covered in trinkets all around us. "Anything you like the look of?"

The people sitting on benches or in the grass around us were handing each other neatly wrapped gifts, while those on their feet were being dragged between the stalls.

"You don't have to get me anything. I didn't know it was even a thing!"

"I know I don't have to," Kouris said, ducking down low. "I *want* to get you something, yrval."

I grabbed one of her horns and said, "I'm here with you. That's enough."

"Real cute," Kouris half-growled, standing up so quickly I was almost pulled from the ground. "Let's be getting the dragon-slayer something, aye?"

"You can stop calling her that," I said, reclaiming her hand. "You two are friends now, right?"

"If we weren't friends, I wouldn't tease her," Kouris said. "Gotta be having nicknames for everyone."

She tugged me towards a handful of merchants trying to raise their voices over the din, and had no trouble parting the crowd and securing us a place between the stalls.

"Wow. I guess they're really sticking to the theme," I said, staring down at the gifts on offer.

Wooden phoenixes from the size of my fist to the size of Kouris' were placed in rows around small metal goods; letter openers with engraved handles, pocket watches with feathers cast on the case, pendants encircling golden flames and talons; quills dyed orange and gold, and the bronzed beaks of eagles and hawks.

"Too much to choose from," Kouris said, crouching so that her chin was on my shoulder.

"Maybe this one?" I murmured, fingertips ghosting over the pendants.

Kouris' ear twitched against my face.

"That's the one alright. She's gonna love it," Kouris said. "Might even get a smile out of her."

I hurried to pick the necklace that had caught my eye, certain my face was burning. A small, silver feather hung from a thin chain, and when I held it out to the merchant who'd been watching me so eagerly he hadn't thought to be wary of Kouris, he said, "An *excellent* choice, young miss. We don't have another like it."

He wrapped it in a thin square of orange cloth and carefully took the coins Kouris held between her claws. I was confident in my choice until the necklace was tucked away in my pocket. I instantly knew it wasn't good enough, not when Claire already had her sigil for a pendant.

I endeavoured to forget about it and lost myself in the crowds as best I could, with a pane for company. Heat from the street vendors tasked with feeding hundreds mingled with all the people milling around us, and though there was already sweat on my brow, I couldn't have been happier.

I'd let myself believe in the worst of Isin, but the people had pulled together for the festival and were intent on doing nothing but smile and share gifts. It didn't matter who wore the crown, down in the city. It didn't matter how many empty seats there were in the throne room.

Nobody paid me any heed, now that I didn't have a spear in hand. Not when they could stare at Kouris instead. I became part of the buzz and flow of the city, so far removed from my old life that only then could I comprehend how truly grateful I was for Claire taking me away and Kouris staying by my side.

I took hold of her arm and used my free hand to eat the skewed chicken we'd brought.

"You know, the first Phoenix Festival – the first one in Kastelir, that is – wasn't this big. Definitely not as fancy," Kouris said, pausing to wrap her tongue around her skewer and pull the meat from it. "The castle wasn't finished then, not properly. Everyone was pulling together to get Isin built up and up. It was a way to be uniting the former territories through hard work. We all ended out in the city. Me, Kidira, Jonas, Atthis. We had our guards, don't be doubting that, but we hardly needed them. Everyone was so hopeful, back then. So glad to be done with the war that they were willing to put a lot behind 'em. We ended up having a picnic right here in Asos. The Kings and Queens, sitting in the grass and eating with bakers and butchers and builders."

Kouris smiled as she spoke. She was wistful in her own way but not

308

about to turn away from the present. We finished the food and she put an arm around my shoulders, winding through the thick of the crowd to a line of low benches in front of a stage. We sat and watched a man juggling knives, sunlight glinting off the edge of the blades to remind us how sharp they were. I couldn't say what it had to do with phoenixes, but I held my breath as I watched, certain the man would slip.

"We never had anything like this in my village. Never had much of anything, but I think the elders would've fainted if we'd had this much fun. Everyone got together in the village for a big meal – a *big* meal, it took most of the day – and then we'd go out into the streets and send up lanterns and sing whatever songs we weren't bored of," I said. It was hardly the stuff of Queens and Kingdoms but Kouris looked at me as I spoke, ears perking up. "I always liked the stories about the phoenixes rallying together to help the Myrosi people. Coming all the way from Canth, too! A lot of the songs made it sound like the phoenixes had been tamed like ravens, but Michael told a few stories where phoenixes had chosen their own names and decided to fight for themselves.

"I liked those stories. Not where they led, but... What *is* it like in Canth? Is there even a Phoenix Festival?"

The man on stage finished his act and Kouris and I clapped as he bowed. No one took his place. The seats around us emptied but Kouris and I remained sat there, leaving the rest of the entertainment for the hours ahead of us.

"There's something of the sort. Not celebrating the end of any war, though. It's there to remember the phoenixes. I'd say it was a solemn event but there ain't much solemn about Port Mahon," Kouris said, grinning. "Still, can't be claiming that anyone does *more* drinking than usual on that day. Last year, Reis sculpted a wooden phoenix half my height. Painted it and all. Took 'em months to work on, and what do they do with it? They wait until the middle of the night, when it's as dark as dark gets, and light the whole damn thing up outside the temple."

"Was, you know, everything you said about Reis true?" I asked, getting to my feet.

"Aye. Well, we didn't head to Canth together. They'd already been there for a good four years when I arrived. Their parents owned the ship Iseul and I travelled on, along with the port we pulled into. They were

309

the ones we had to pay our debt off to," Kouris explained as we meandered around Asos. "Now, Reis was only seven back then and they'd had to learn Canthian for theirself. I didn't speak a word of it and they helped me out. Stuck with 'em after that."

I was easy to think of Kouris as simply being absent for those twenty-seven years, yet she'd built up a life for herself. I hoped it would be the same for me. I hadn't gone so far as to leave Asar, but if I had to return to my village, I wanted to be different. Wanted to be someone new.

Children ran through the square dressed in feathered cloaks with oversized hoods. One smacked into Kouris' knee, pulled their hood back to see what they'd hit, and mouthed, "Whooooa," as their mother swooped in and snatched them out of harm's way. Kouris waved with a chuckle and we moved on to the performance drawing the largest crowd.

Kouris let me climb on her back without having to be asked. With my arms around her neck, I had the best view of the stage. Five people stood in the centre, draped in red cloaks, and spiralling towers and glassy-green buildings had been painted across the screen behind them. I didn't recognise any of the landmarks, but knew it was supposed to be Myros.

"And in the year seventeen eighty-six, the Necromancy War came to a halt after long, restless years," a man said. He spread his arms out wide while two actors either side of him stood with their heads bowed. "The King of the Everlasting Kingdom deigned to meet with the necromancers who had brought its golden age to an end."

A drum roll sounded from behind the screen and another of the actors looked up, throwing her hood back. The crowd jeered. Kondo-Kana, I assumed. I knew how the story went: the King met with half a dozen necromancers, offering peace, and one by one, they cut the throats of his generals. Michael said the story lacked originality and was handled far too brutishly.

It screamed that necromancers were to be loathed when a whisper would've sufficed.

"Alright up there, yrval?" Kouris asked.

I wrapped my fingers around her horns and hummed.

The play was one of few words and lacked the energy the pane around the fire pit had possessed. A man pulled back his cloak to reveal a wooden crown and one of the necromancers drew close, whispering in his ear. The King wasn't slaughtered, nor were his generals. He moved in jerky motions when the necromancer tugged on the invisible rope around his neck.

My stomach didn't churn. I didn't feel singled out by their portrayal of necromancers.

The most I felt was bored.

"The juggling was better than this," I said, propping my chin on Kouris' head.

We ventured away from the stage and left Asos to wander through the other squares. There was no shortage of songs to listen to or acts to watch and for an hour or more at a time, I was able to forget that any of this was about necromancers.

But I didn't delude myself. They were saving the most vicious of their songs for last, to make a real spectacle of the execution.

As we moved from one part of Isin to the next, I began to see cracks in the cheer. People scowled into their steins outside of taverns and I hurried by, not wanting to draw too much attention to Kouris. There were fewer pane wandering through Isin than I'd expected and I knew people were waiting for an excuse to pick a fight. Not every tavern was awash in orange and gold, and from within one that had forgone decorations, I heard them sing songs of King Jonas.

Died in his castle, died all alone,
The resistance drove a blade to his bone!

Kouris scowled. I didn't let her linger. We pulled away from narrow side roads and returned to the festivities. The scale of the festival changed, depending on what part of the city we were in, and they used empty crates as stages in the outer districts. I was determined to see as much of the city as I could and joined the locals in drinking homemade ale from dingy glasses.

Between a man telling jokes that went over my head and two women singing almost perfectly in time, Kouris caught the eye of a teenage boy helping an older woman carry a barrel of wine across the street.

"Oi, get this," he said, tearing his eyes off Kouris. "You know Ostin, right? Works as a gardener in the castle, yeah? He heard that Queen Kouris has only gone and come back."

I held my breath but there was no need to. Any pane would've jogged

311

his memory.

"Don't give me that nonsense. I have to put up with a new rumour about her every time someone spots a pane in the castle. Let the dead rest," the woman huffed, intent on getting back to work. "What's next? Suppose you're gonna tell me the necromancer they're burning is Kondo-Kana herself."

The boy frowned at the barrel and I laughed, once he was out of ear-shot. If only he knew how right he was. I smiled at Kouris, beyond glad to be with her. It was harder to believe there was any truth to the stories about necromancers when I was wandering through the streets of Isin with its long-dead Queen.

"I've been wondering," I said as we found ourselves back at Asos. "How'd you know to come back here?"

Kouris held her tongue, but only for as long as it took to find some-where to sit. We settled down under the shade of a young oak tree and nearby families enjoying picnics called their children back at the sight of a pane. It gave us all the privacy we needed.

"This'll probably disappoint you, yrval, but there's not much to it. Someone came and got me," Kouris said. "Now, there ain't many pane in Canth. Reckon I saw two in almost thirty years. So when a pane shows up on a ship one day, of course word's going to be getting back to me. Knew there was something wrong right away. They looked like they'd been used up. The last of their strength went into surviving the trip down and all they could talk about was the dragons and what Felheim was doing to 'em. They'd been sent to find me, but I didn't even get their name."

I folded my arms across her bent knee and propped my chin on the back of my hand.

"So you came back to help the pane, just like that?"

"Just like that. I marched down from the mountains to do the same a lifetime ago and I wasn't about to let an ocean stop me. To tell the truth, I'd been down in Canth for so long that it was almost as though Asar and Kastelir didn't exist. Almost as if I'd dreamt them up. It was a wake-up call, to be saying the least."

"Okay," I said, turning the information over in my mind. "But there's something else that I don't get. When Claire and I met you, you already knew who she was, right? How?"

Kouris' fangs showed when she grinned.

"Reckon I gave her a bit of a fright, showing up and knowing her secrets," she said, sounding too pleased with herself. "Truth is, I'd been watching her. Her and some of the other Knights. I didn't want to rush straight back to Kastelir and needed to see how the dragons were being used. So I went from one settlement to another, figuring out where to head next. That's how I found our dragon-slayer. I watched her put a sword through a dragon's head but she didn't stay and celebrate, like the others I'd tracked down. I'd never seen anyone so torn up about anything.

"She ran. Headed south. I lost track of her, for a time. But I knew she had to know something, so I took my chances and figured she'd head to Kastelir for help. If she hadn't left the continent already."

For all the time I'd spent convincing myself I was paranoid, there really *were* pane after us.

"I'm glad you came back," I said. "I mean, I'm not glad you had to leave Canth, or about the whole dragon thing. But I'm happy I got to meet you."

Kouris wrapped an arm around me and scooped me into her lap.

"I get your meaning, yrval. I'm glad I met you, too. Not glad you had to run away from your village, but glad you got out of there," she said, drawing close.

I thought she had something to add, but she remained exactly where she was, tusks inches from my lips.

"Um," I said, blinking. "... I kissed Claire."

"I know," she said. Her eyes flashed as she grinned. "No reason you can't be kissing me too, if you like."

My face burnt brighter than the festival banners and I put a hand on her shoulder, choking on a laugh as I pushed her back. Kouris went down easy, falling onto her elbows, smiling at me as I stared at her. She covered her chest with a great hand as though I'd wounded her and I huffed a sigh. Grabbing one of her horns, I pulled her close and kissed her forehead.

"There. That's only fair," she said.

We spent the rest of the afternoon doing much of nothing.

I laid my head on her lap, listening to music played in far off corners

313

and on nearby stages as sunlight filtered through the leaves above. People came and went, dragging instruments and children and partners along with them. Kouris and I drifted in and out of sleep until evening fell.

Asos Square emptied a little. The lanterns would be lit once the sun set and the marquee in the centre of the park promised a night of drinking and dancing. People went home to change into their finest clothing and I took the chance to stand up and stretch out, mind made pleasantly numb by the remnants of dreams. Kouris yawned widely, pushing out the full length of her tongue, convincing parents picnicking nearby that their children were going to be inhaled.

I was about to suggest finding something more appropriate to eat when someone called out, "Rowan!" from behind.

Akela and Katja had found their way into Asos. Katja hurried off the path and greeted me with a kiss on the cheek. They were both dressed better than anyone else in the city, better than anyone would be tonight. Katja wore yet another dress, this one light gold and rippling in the light breeze, and Akela had exchanged her armour for an embroidered silk shirt and neat black trousers.

"I'm glad to have stumbled upon you, dear," Katja said, clasping both of my hands in her own. How different she looked, now that the funeral was over; how much more comfortable I was around her, now that nothing flared up within me at the sight of her. "Have you been here long? I was only able to sneak out of the castle this last half hour. It isn't the celebration it ought to be, not with recent events."

"We've been here all day," I said, and didn't miss the way her gaze kept fluttering over my shoulder. "Oh. Right! This is, well. This is Kouris."

I stepped to the side, allowing Katja to approach her namesake. I didn't know how Kouris would react, and the memory of her marching away from the campfire burnt in my mind.

But when faced with Queen Kidira's daughter, she stepped forward and let herself grin.

"You must be Kouris," she said, holding out a hand.

Kouris shook it and said, "It's wonderful to finally meet you. I've heard so very much about you!"

"I hope one or two of 'em were good things."

314

"Almost exclusively," Katja said, clasping her hands behind her back. "Well, until a few weeks ago, that is."

Something went unspoken between them. They were nervous and excited, immediately aware of the role they played in each other's lives, but strangers nonetheless. They were willing to change that, despite how Queen Kidira felt about the matter, and I wandered over to Akela, giving them room to talk.

"I am afraid I am abandoning Ightham. Right now, she is enduring the endless ball," Akela said, not sounding sorry at all. "Still, it is not so bad. She is certainly looking the part."

I felt sorry for Claire, but when I looked at the castle in the distance, I was confident I could do nothing to rescue her.

Akela was in full support of finding something to eat and Katja and Kouris trailed behind us, tentatively getting to know one another. We found a vendor roasting a whole pig on a spit and Katja politely declined a serving at the sight of it. Akela ate enough for both of them and we strolled aimlessly, until Katja tugged on my arm.

"I saw a performance I thought would interest you, on the way here," she said brightly. "Would you like to see it?"

I nodded and Katja took wide strides down the street, pulling me along with her.

We didn't get far.

We reached a square Kouris and I had yet to explore, reminding me that there was more to Isin than could be seen in a single day, and a man in white robes did all he could to garner our attention.

"Ladies!" he called out. "Don't tell me two intelligent-looking women such as yourselves have been taken in by this disgrace of a festival!"

Katja raised her eyebrows and briskly walked over to the man. He was stunned into silence for a split second. Everyone else in the square was giving him as wide a berth as possible and we had to be the only people who hadn't run from him all day.

There were others dressed like him, brandishing rolls of parchment people swerved around as they might a sword.

"Religious sorts. Not what I had in mind. I must've taken a wrong turn..." Katja whispered to me. "Pardon me. Could you elaborate?"

The man looked as though he'd been rehearsing the words in his head for days. His enthusiasm caused him to falter.

315

"Indeed. Indeed I can! I represent the House of Light, the largest shrine to Isjin in all of Isin," he said. I doubted it was much to brag about. "My fellow devotees and I do not wish to cause trouble. Only to educate, to inform people of the ignorance that has been thrust upon them. If you are willing to listen, the Lightbearer Maethos is holding sermons all day in the shrine."

The man clasped his hands together and Akela let out a laugh deep enough to rattle every bone in his body.

"Lady Kouris, Northwood, we are moving on, yes? You are not being taken in by foolish sorts and their missing gods," she said. "If you are wanting to laugh at something, I am sure there are people on stages, and they are telling jokes even better than this one."

A passing woman nodded in agreement but I wished Akela hadn't said anything. I wanted to go to the shrine, if only for curiosity's sake, silently hoping Maethos' sermon matched what Claire had told me about phoenixes.

I'd promised myself to be more open with Katja but didn't say a word.

Thankfully, she took control and said, "Actually, Commander, I'm rather interested in this particular period of history. I've heard all there is on the subject from the Phoenix Festival itself over the years. I should like to gain another perspective on the matter."

Akela bowed without another word. We all turned to the worshipper but he remained on the spot for a handful of seconds. When he realised we were waiting for him to lead the way he almost tripped over his robes as he headed off.

The *House* of Light was an accurate description of the shrine. Unlike the one in Orinhal, the building hadn't been built with its current purpose in mind. It was the only house on the street that didn't have a hint of orange or gold marring it. The brickwork had been painted white, once upon a time, but the bright coating had long since faded, dulled by the elements and chipped around the edges.

A few people milled around, dressed for the Phoenix Festival. At least it wouldn't all be robed fanatics.

"Here you are, here you are," our guide said, holding the door open for us.

Katja and I stepped in, but when Kouris tried to duck through, the worshipper blocked her path.

"I'm afraid this is a house of *human* worship," he explained, no longer skittish now that his ilk were close.

"*Human* worship?" Kouris huffed. "And who are you thinking made the pane? Reckon we just crawled out from under a rock one day.?"

"I understand that Isin is responsible for all creation, but if one reads scripture, it is, um... quite clear that Bosma and all within it was designed to cradle human life, so..."

Kouris' horns knocked against the door frame as she leant close.

"A-and the ceilings are rather low," he added, bravery all but dried up.

I would've left with Kouris, not wanting to hear out anyone who would treat the pane in such a way, but Katja's arm was around mine. Akela put her hand on Kouris' shoulder and eased her back.

"Come, come. We are not wasting time on this nonsense. I am staying here and making sure that nothing is happening to Lady Kouris and Northwood, and you, you are going to the nearest tavern and you are bringing us drinks. It is a shame to be wasting the sunshine, yes?" Akela said.

Kouris' ears pressed flat against her head as she backed off.

The house had been converted into two large rooms, one of which was locked to us. A handful of people stood around the edges, and their faces screamed that they'd like nothing more than to bolt out of the front door. No one made eye contact with anyone else, not wanting to be recognised in such a place.

Murals covered the walls, some more crudely drawn than others, all following a similar theme. Suns and stars made up the background, shining brightly against the black, and in the very centre, a woman paler than the moon stood with her arms outstretched, flashing eyes almost closed.

Blazing comets surrounded her, but it was impossible to tell if they'd come from her hands or if she was reaching out to deflect them.

Katja stared in awe, silently mouthing something to herself, barely able to hold back a smile. Whether she was taken in by the House of Isjin was beyond the point. Katja was firm in her beliefs and standing there could only strengthen them. This was it. I'd let her know that I agreed with her. I'd find something in the sermon to cling to, something to justify saying what may well have been too much.

317

"To those who have torn themselves away from the temptations of the Phoenix Festival, I thank you," Maethos said, silently stepping out of the other room. Her robes were red, and she clasped a candle of the same colour between her hands. She carefully placed it on the floor, beneath the painting of Isjin. "I'm certain you have many, many questions and I've no doubt that there are plenty you haven't yet thought to ask."

"I've got to—" someone from the back of the room mumbled as they ran out.

Maethos arched her brow, looked around the shrine and fixed her eyes on mine. It shouldn't have made my heart clench as it did. It wasn't as though she'd picked me out by anything but chance: only a few of us remained.

"Tell me. What do you know of Isjin?"

"Um..."

What did I know of Isjin that wouldn't offend her was the real question. I could tell her all about Isjin's desertion of Bosma and the way she abandoned Myros to the will of the Bloodless Lands but I knew how ignorant I'd sound.

"I know about the Forest Within?" I ventured. Maethos nodded and gestured for me to continue. "When we die, we end up in the Forest Within a Forest. It's, um. A giant forest that you wander through, and anyone you want to see – if they're dead, that is – you just happen to come across them. The people who've seen it say it's peaceful. Relaxing. Except for the ones who go to hell. Which is the same as the Forest Within, except you keep walking without ever finding who you're looking for."

"Indeed. Although I should not separate the two concepts quite so radically. The Forest Within only becomes hell when the person you seek has no desire to meet with you. It may still be a paradise, in all other aspects. But what do you know of Isjin herself?"

I wanted to say something, if only *not much, honestly,* but Katja patted me on the arm and took it upon herself to answer.

"Not quite as much as I should like to. There is, of course, the creation story. I believe that most know of the way Isjin dreamt the world into existence, from within the void," Katja began. Maethos nodded, ready to take over, and Katja kept speaking. "When she awoke, Isjin discovered that a fearsome beast had fallen asleep on the edge of the void,

318

stopping her creation from flowing out into the emptiness that existed before all else.

"And so Isjin seized the beast, allowing her dreams to breathe life into the world, and tore the creature in two. Those two parts didn't wither, as she had thought they might. Instead, they became two distinct creatures: the dragons and the pane. They took their place on Bosma while humanity was still young."

"Quite. Very well spoken," Maethos said, bowing her head. Katja's face reddened a touch but she did what she could to remain modest. "The story is rather telling, today more so than ever. Think of what Isjin did with the beast, with the dragons and pane. She could have cast them back into the void, obliterated them wholly, yet she chose to let them live amongst her creation. In her infinite compassion, do you truly believe that Isjin would allow the phoenixes, beings of pure beauty, to raze themselves from Bosma?

"The phoenixes did not die fighting and we should not celebrate a sacrifice they never made. Simply put, the phoenixes were taken from us."

Most in the room remained unconvinced, but Maethos was engaging enough to hold their attention. She paced as she spoke, pointing to the murals, voice low and clear, promising some ancient wisdom.

"Taken from us?" I dared to ask.

"Taken by a time of war," she clarified. "Taken by politics, by greed. Not by necromancers."

I curled my fingers towards my palms, hands clammy. Claire had been right. I could only hope that my heart didn't beat so loudly it deafened me to what Maethos would say next.

The others flinched at the mention of necromancy and one person left, but Katja remained by my side, listening as intently as I was.

"Isjin shall not look kindly on us burning one of her Children," Maethos said, shaking her head.

"I... I heard the necromancers used to be Priests of Isjin, back in Myros. Is that true?" I asked, doing all I could to ignore the way Katja had turned to face me.

"It is, indeed it is," Maethos said, drawing closer. "The necromancers were held in the highest regard by Isjin, but without her guidance, they could only stray. They wandered down a path of darkness, though darkness was not in the hearts of all of them, and now live in the shadows of what they once were. We can but pray for them."

It'd been too good to be true. For a moment I'd believed that the House of Light might see me for what I truly was. But even the most devoted, those who drew scorn and mockery for daring to have faith, found ways to twist necromancy.

Maethos and the others aligned with the shrine didn't want to see me burn, but that didn't mean they were willing to see me as a whole person, either. They warped necromancers in their own way, to their own ends.

I'd come to the shrine to listen, to understand. I hadn't come to have pity forced upon me.

For once I took Katja's arm.

"Rowan, what are you..." she began, mortified by my lack of manners.

It didn't matter. I was leaving, and I wasn't leaving without her. I pushed the door open, charged out into the street, and once we were awash in sunlight, Katja said, "Goodness, Rowan. What's come over you? If you were uncomfortable, you ought to have told me. I'd hate to think I was responsible for subjecting you to things you didn't wish to hear."

"No, no. It's..." I began, running my fingers through my hair. I needed to get a grip on myself, on my surroundings. "Katja, I just wanted to..."

No sooner were the words out of my mouth than Katja's hands were on my shoulders. The familiar sickness swirled in the pit of my stomach and she met my gaze, eyes wide, pleading.

"Rowan, dear. Is there... what *is* it?" she asked softly.

I couldn't say whether I would've answered her or not. The words were on the tip of my tongue and the tightness in my chest would never ease until I spoke them, but all I could think was that I'd promised Claire to keep myself safe.

In the end, I didn't have to look out for myself. Kouris and Akela had taken a seat on somebody's doorstep across the road and were barely through their first stein of ale. The moment they saw us, they wandered over and Akela said, "Hah, I am winning! Kouris is thinking you are lasting half an hour, but I am saying, it is not even being ten minutes! You are owing me another drink and I am expecting it to be much better than this."

Katja pulled away but didn't take her eyes off me. I could see her thoughts churning behind them and I knew I'd given away more in how I'd acted than I ever could by voicing my thoughts and fears out loud.

"Alright, alright," Kouris said, slapping Akela on the back. "It's almost time for the lanterns. Reckon there'll be more than enough to drink over there."

Kouris and Akela led the way through the gathering bustle of the streets and as we headed back to Asos, Katja said nothing, did nothing. She didn't take my arm, didn't look at me. She only stared thoughtfully at nothing, two steps ahead of me the whole time.

CHAPTER TWENTY-TWO

No place on Bosma was ever so busy as Asos Square was, that night.

The first lanterns rose from the castle and once faint, orange lights hung above us like fleeting stars, the people of Isin sent the rest into the night sky. Street lamps and torches were doused for the ceremony and Kouris and I lit a lantern together, watching it float up and become lost amongst the lights.

Katja allowed Akela to send a lantern up for her and we moved into the marquee. A band played at one end, far more upbeat than anything I'd heard the day before, and barrels of ale and wine ran the length of the dance floor. People flocked to the centre, some already drunk, others working their way towards that point, and Kouris, Akela and I sat on the benches strewn around the edges, while Katja accepted a red-haired woman's invitation to dance.

Akela kept an eye on her. As I fetched us drinks, I was hardly surprised to learn that Katja possessed more grace than anyone under the marquee. I made my way across the dancefloor without spilling a drop from the steins and found Kouris and Akela chatting away like old friends.

Akela roared with laughter but I couldn't say why. The band and dancers and those sat drinking around the sides contributed such a cheerful clamour that we had to huddle close to hear one another.

"In the castle, we are only drinking wine that is older than I am, and we are being expected to appreciate how it is smelling of trees or grass," Akela said, holding up her second stein of ale, already half-empty. "But here, in the city, we are drinking properly! I am glad I am escaping the formalities."

"I guess babysitting isn't all that bad," I said, still on my first drink.

Katja took a break from dancing to sit by my side. She didn't treat me any differently than she had yesterday. It was all in my head, like always: I'd overreacted, assuming whatever I thought and felt was written all over me, for anyone to pick apart.

"Just a few months to the wedding!" she said. "I can scarcely believe it. It would've been sooner, if not for all that has happened of late... Oh, but you will come to the ceremony, won't you?"

"I... If you really want to me," I said. Katja knew nothing of what Felheim was truly doing or the moves Kastelir would eventually make against it. I gulped down a great mouthful of ale and said, "How did you meet the Prince? I didn't think Kastelir and Felheim had much contact."

"They don't, which is something I very much intend to change," Katja said, more excited by the prospect than her wedding itself. "Prince Alexander actually set things into motion. He's always been overshadowed by his siblings and felt it was about time he did something for his Kingdom. And so he reached out to us, writing to the Kings and Queen. The letter was not deemed of great importance and eventually came into my care. As for the rest... it is what it is!"

I wondered if we could use Katja's link to Prince Alexander. Their union would give the Kingdoms the opportunity to understand one another; perhaps one day Felheim could set aside fear of invasion and give up control of the dragons.

I quickly shrugged it off. It would've worked, someone else would've brought it up already.

"Heads up," Kouris said, tilting her horns towards the crowd gathered under the marquee.

I stared out at the masses, uncertain what I was searching for; not seeing Claire, though she was right in front of me. I was so used to seeing her in armour, leather and bone alike, that my gaze skimmed straight past the woman in the dress, still searching through the crowd for a handful of seconds.

Akela was right: Claire certainly looked the part. Queen Kidira must've demanded she looked presentable for the formalities and Claire was as comfortable in what she was wearing as I'd ever known her to be. Her white dress reached all the way down to her ankles, fading into greys and blacks at the bottom. Her hair was pinned up, simple and neat, neck and shoulders bare, save for the thin straps holding her dress up.

Claire lifted her brow and I realised I was staring. I hopped off the bench, caught my foot on the edge and almost tripped over.

She was more amused than alarmed and I managed a "Hi!", immediately regretting how little I'd had to drink. I held out my hands, not sure what I wanted to do with them, and brought them to my sides, well aware of how much I was smiling. I bit the inside of my cheek but it was no use. Out of the hundreds of people gathered and amidst all the attention she'd garnered, Claire was looking at me.

"Hi," I said. Again. "You look—your hair, it's, uh. You look nice."

Maybe I'd had too much to drink.

Claire was merciful and didn't laugh at me. Her face was red from the brisk walk into Asos and when she leant over to kiss my cheek, I managed to stop rocking on the balls of my feet.

"I wasn't certain you'd still be here," she said. "I came straight from the castle the moment my presence was no longer required."

Spending the day with Kouris had been perfect and I was grateful to have someone whose company I could enjoy while we were doing nothing but nap. I wouldn't have changed it for the world, but I lit up so much with Claire in front of me that I forgot I was supposed to speak. I was caught up in looking at her look at me, no longer aware of anyone around us.

Until one of the dancers bumped into my shoulder and spun off without realising they'd collided into me.

"Shall we?" Claire asked, gesturing towards the others.

"Right," I said, but didn't move. It was now or never. My fingers dipped into my pocket, brushing against the carefully folded clothing, and Claire remained patient as I sucked in a breath and said, "We got you something. Me and Kouris. It's for the Phoenix Festival. It's what they do here. What Kouris said they do here, anyway."

The corners of Claire's mouth flickered into a hint of a smile and my stomach sunk to my soles when I noticed the thin, silver chain she was already wearing around her neck. Of course she already had something of the sort, something that hadn't been bought from a merchant's cart.

Still, the words were out of my mouth and I didn't have much of a choice. I held out the handful of cloth to Claire and she peeled it back, taking hold of the chain between her thumb and first finger.

She held it up, silver feather twisting, and I looked at the floor, at my feet. Anywhere but at Claire.

"Rowan..."

"It was just, I saw it and thought you'd like it. It's fine if you don't want to wear it. I know you probably—"

"*Rowan.*" Claire tapped a finger beneath my chin. "It's beautiful. Thank you."

She took my hand, placed the necklace against my palm and unhooked the one she was already wearing. The end of the chain dipped into her dress and when she pulled it off, I saw the small silver key from

Praxis. Claire kept it in her hand as she turned around, crouching just enough for me to be able to put the necklace on for her.

With her hair up, there was nothing to hold out of the way, but loose strands brushed against my knuckles and my fingers weren't as steady as they could've been. My heart clenched like a fist with the fear that she wouldn't like the gift, and it was only then I began to understand that it wasn't *just* a gift.

I was trying to show her that I cared, and more than I could rightly say.

The chain was shorter than the one she'd been wearing and when she turned around, the feather rested beneath her collarbone. My heart released, pounding freely, and Claire hummed thoughtfully before putting the chain in her hand around my neck, key hanging from it.

"I'm afraid I wasn't aware of this particular Kastelirian tradition until the ball and had no time to get anything on the way here," she said. "Look after this for me. I don't have any pockets."

I laughed softly, knowing no amount of smiling was enough, and pressed my fingers to the metal as I tried to meet her gaze without my face burning.

"We should..." I said, spinning on my heels.

I meant to head over to the others but Claire caught hold of my wrist, turning me back around.

"What?" I asked when she didn't say anything.

Claire didn't move from the spot. A playful smile crossed her face and it was the most ominous thing I'd ever seen. She wrapped her fingers around my wrist, pulled me a step closer, and it dawned on me where we were and what everyone around us was doing.

"You want to..." I got half a sentence out and Claire nodded. "Um. I don't think I *can*."

Claire swept her arm out around the marquee, making her point without words. Knowing how to dance wasn't a requirement. Everyone was moving out of time with one another, some people entirely unaware of what the band was playing, and though shoulders were being bumped and feet were being stepped on, there wasn't a single person who wasn't enjoying themselves.

"I have spent the entire day watching nobles dance. Despite my current attire, I didn't once leave my station. Unlike Akela, I do not possess

325

the courage necessary to ask Queen Kidira for a dance," Claire explained. "Please?"

She held out a hand and I instinctively took it.

There was her answer.

"Did you used to dance a lot?" I asked, focusing so hard on where to put my hands that I forgot how to move. Claire took hold of my wrists, placed my hands on her shoulders, and put her hands on my hips.

"Indeed. There is always something to celebrate in the capital, if only to have an excuse to bring people together," she said, and then did the thing that'd been terrifying me. She stepped to the side, moving me along with her. "Balls and feasts are the battlegrounds of the high-born. Dance poorly and you lose the favour of three noble houses with a single step."

I made no reply, too busy thinking that I mustn't step on her foot, I mustn't step on her foot, and the music was hardly fitting. It was too fast, too upbeat, for the way we held each other close.

"And..." I dared to speak, since my feet had yet to betray me. "What's in those bags you locked away?"

"Things I couldn't bring myself to leave behind," Claire said, having enough faith in me to begin moving more quickly. "Belongings of sentimental value, for the most part. I thought them safer in Praxis than dragged all the way across Kastelir."

The song changed but we remained as we were. I knitted my fingers together against the nape of Claire's neck, content to lose myself amongst a sea of dancers and a cacophony of noises; people laughing, glasses clinking together, instruments coming to life. It wasn't the sort of celebration Claire had grown up attending, but the lack of tiled floors and ornate chandeliers didn't mean a thing to her.

Spending time around Kouris and Akela made it easy to forget that Claire was considerably taller than I was, but dancing served as reminder enough. She bowed her head to kiss me and though she'd done so before, this was different. Anyone could've seen us, anyone could've seen *her*, but she didn't care.

Claire kissed me and it didn't even occur to her to hide it from anyone.

Claire pulled back and I rested my face on her shoulder, not once stepping on her feet, not once caring how foolish I might've looked.

We danced for hours or minutes, until the band changed, and Kouris took the chance to swoop over and steal Claire from me. Claire rose to the challenge, thanking Kouris for her part in obtaining the necklace, and Akela spun me on the spot until I was dizzy from laughter. Katja watched from the benches and the four of us only stopped dancing to drink.

A drink turned into three and night gave up its dominion to morning. My entire body buzzed as we wandered back to the castle, and I almost believed that we'd travelled all that way for no reason other than to come together as we had. Claire and Kouris took my hands as the rising sun brought colour back to the city, and nothing could've convinced me that the Phoenix Festival would end in fire.

I slept through to midday, waking groggily, smiling so much that not even a yawn could stop my cheeks from aching. I stretched out, fell back against the pillow, and spent far too long telling myself I was going to get up in a few seconds. I eventually pulled myself out of bed to be rid of the slight headache ale and wine had left behind. A lunch that served as breakfast was brought to me, and I gulped down the better part of a pitcher, meandering over to the window.

The Phoenix Festival continued to consume the city and I knew of no reason why Queen Kidira wouldn't demand that Claire worked through today, as well. Half an hour of aimless wandering didn't bring me any closer to finding out where Kouris was, and I spent much of the day down in the stables with Charley and Calais.

One of them stablehands grudgingly let me walk them around the grassy castle grounds when she was certain there weren't any nobles taking lessons, and I guided them between trees, a rein in each hand.

They were both grateful for the rest, having carried us through Felheim and Kastelir alike, but being idle was starting to grate on them.

"Don't worry," I reassured them. "I'm sure we'll get out of here soon. Maybe we could ride out to meet Michael."

He'd written once, to tell Claire the pane were delaying their visit to Kastelir in light of recent events, but he'd be back within a fortnight.

The stablehand made frantic gestures to me as a group of children saddled up their horses and I guided Charley and Calais back towards the stables, only to have my path abruptly blocked.

"Rowan! Good afternoon," Katja said brightly. She fidgeted with her hands, pressing her palms together. Her duties around the castle must've stopped her from getting enough sleep. "Is this Sir Ightham's horse? He's absolutely gorgeous! And is this other one yours?"

"Calais and Charley," I said, introducing them.

Immediately losing interest in the horses, Katja lowered her voice, as though they were likely to eavesdrop.

"I hope this isn't too much of a bother, dear, but there's something I absolutely have to talk to you about."

I knew what it was.

The sun slipped from behind a cloud to glare down at me and coupled with the pounding between my temples, it was too bright to see, too foggy to think. I should've said that I didn't have time, that I was supposed to be meeting with Kouris or Claire, but Katja's suspicions would only be confirmed if I ran.

"Katja, I—"

"*Please*, Rowan," she said, gripping my hand.

Something in the way I looked at her betrayed me. She took Calais' reins and I followed on heavy feet, leading the horses back to their pens.

We headed through the castle without another word. There were hundreds of things Katja could want to talk to me about, I told myself. There was a problem with her upcoming wedding or Felheim had abruptly cut off all contact; her uncle's funeral had been two days ago and she needed someone to talk to; the castle was flooded with diplomats from the Old West, pleading their case for the crown, while others argued that anyone should be eligible for the throne, now that the territories were long-dead; she needed someone impartial to hear her out.

That was all.

Lulling myself into a false sense of security didn't work. I wanted her to ask me the things that made my insides lock up for the desperate relief it'd bring. I wanted her to know so that I'd no longer be terrified of her finding out; I trusted her, in spite of our conflicting natures.

"I'm afraid I don't have much time," Katja said, pushing a pair of chamber doors open. "I'm due back at the ball in a matter of minutes. My mother isn't particularly pleased that I left so early yesterday."

The room Katja led me to was undeniably hers. A portrait of her and Queen Kidira was framed above a desk and shelves upon shelves of books circled the sofas in the centre of the room.

Katja locked the door behind us.

"Oh, Rowan. You'll have to excuse me. I don't know how I'm to say this," she said, pacing the length of the room and backing me into a chair in the process. "I don't rightly know if I *should* say it. If I'm simply jumping to conclusions. Please, promise me that you won't hate me if I'm wrong."

She paused to look at me. I wrapped my fingers around the arms of the chair, unable to nod, to shake my head. I swallowed the lump in my throat and it was enough for her.

"Ever since we met, from the very *moment* I saw you, I've felt as though there's been an undeniable bond between us. I meant to let it pass, but... but it hasn't, has it? And I admit, I have said certain things to measure your reaction, hoping you might bring yourself to tell me the truth."

"Katja—"

"Yet I cannot keep this to myself any longer."

She stopped pacing altogether. She stood over me, face awash with a mix of pity and remorse, but not for me; for the way things were about to change. It was hard to breathe, harder still to speak, but I tried regardless, words coming out as a tangled whisper.

"Katja, please don't..."

My voice cracked and she knelt down, hands on my knees.

"Rowan, are you..." All strength slipped from her voice and I felt what she said more than I heard it. "Are you a necromancer?"

And then a strange thing happened.

The world didn't end.

Guards didn't rush into my chamber, dragging me away, and Katja didn't look at me any differently. My heart stopped pounding and I closed my eyes, thankful she knew, thankful the ground hadn't slipped out from under me. Frantic denial would've confirmed what she'd concluded and my silence worked in much the same way.

Katja pressed her forehead to my knees, shaking with relief in my place.

"Katja," I said, words coming out clearly. "You can't tell your mother. No matter what happens, you mustn't tell Queen Kidira.

"I won't! Oh, Rowan, I'd never do such a thing," Katja said, shooting back to her feet. She placed her hands on my shoulders and nothing inside of me recoiled or churned. Nothing could catch me off-guard, now we knew the truth about one another. "I swear to you, I shall never tell a soul."

She was the only person who'd ever worked it out for herself. I wanted to thank her for showing me it wasn't the end of all things, but when I stood, all I could say was, "I know, I know."

I trusted her. I had someone within the castle to help me, someone who could keep Queen Kidira from me, should the worst happen.

"I wasn't exaggerating when I said I had little time to spare," Katja said, dabbing the corners of her eyes with a handkerchief, having almost been reduced to tears. "There are guests from Agados here, come to see the... Well, I couldn't simply go another moment without asking. You'll forgive me, won't you?"

What was there to forgive? She'd been plagued by questions she'd forced herself to bottle up, subjecting herself to the same sort of strain I'd always been at the mercy of. She hadn't breathed a word of it to anyone else, hadn't told her mother as the law demanded she must. She'd come to me and she'd been nothing but understanding.

"There's nothing to forgive," I said, and the fear she was stricken with crumpled into nothing.

I felt Katja's absence more keenly than I'd felt her hands on my shoulders. There was so much I wanted to ask her, so much I could learn from her, but she was gone. With my bearings lost, I wandered the castle aimlessly, hearing a faint drone of music from within one of the larger halls.

Claire was inside, but had I slipped in, the dancefloor would've opened up and swallowed me whole, lest I mar the ball for a moment longer.

After suffering a few wrong turns, I found my way to Claire's chamber and let myself in. Not much had changed since I'd last been there and I found myself overwhelmed by how little there was to do. An empty wine bottle and glass had been left by one of the armchairs and I picked them up, leaving them on the edge of a table for a servant to collect.

I spent the rest of the day alternating between watching Isin from the window and napping on the sofa, and woke with a start when Claire slammed the door shut behind her.

"Oh," she said.

Just *oh*, neither irritated nor surprised.

It'd grown dark while I'd drifted in and out of sleep, and what little I could make out of Claire's expression made me realise I shouldn't have let myself in without asking. She was back in Kastelir's armour, hair obscuring much of her face as she fought to remove her gloves.

She threw them next to the empty wine bottle and dropped herself into a rigid, wooden chair.

"Are you alright?" I asked.

"Yes," she said, not missing a beat.

She wrapped her fingers around the bottleneck but it lifted too easily. She gritted her teeth and put it back down, glass thudding heavily against the table. I didn't move an inch or say a word, wanting to give Claire time to take deep breaths. She sat there with her chin propped on her fist, eyes turned away from me.

My first instinct was to ask if she wanted me to leave but I was afraid she'd force herself to say yes. When her shoulders showed no signs of relaxing on their own, I got to my feet, tiptoed over to the table and claimed a chair for myself. I didn't sit too close, didn't place my hand on her arm, but I didn't back away, either.

"What's wrong?"

Being more direct worked. Claire stewed in silence for a moment longer and drew in a sharp breath before it all came tumbling out.

"The Agadians have arrived, which ought to be no issue, but their long-standing ties with the Old West have deluded them into believing they have some say in who succeeds King Jonas. What's more, they are unsettlingly interested in the necromancer who is to be executed. King Atthis and Queen Kidira are of the opinion that Agados is a much more pressing issue than anything I have presented to them, and I am merely... I have been reduced to nothing but a guard, a footman, serving a foreign King and Queen," Claire said, elbows on the table, fingers tangled in her hair. "I have betrayed my Kingdom, and for what? That I might be kept under thumb, unable to help anyone? Why King Garland thought me worthy of his trust, I cannot say. I have—"

Her hands shook as her voice rose. I wrapped my fingers around her hand and squeezed it.

She turned to me, eyes dry.

"I apologise," she murmured. "I am merely tired."

"Didn't you get any sleep last night?" I asked, not yet sure where to start with the rest of what she'd said.

"I was not returned to my chamber for long when Queen Kidira had me sent for," she said, hands dropping onto the table. "I have always had some measure of difficulty falling asleep in a timely manner, but recent events have exacerbated that."

The dark marks under her eyes had told me that a long time ago.

My hands slipped from hers and I headed across the chamber to the rack of wine bottles arranged on a shelf, along with an assortment of glasses.

I picked a bottle at random and found it empty. I took another, supposing they were all good, and after wrestling with the cork, poured a glass for Claire and myself. I set the wine down on the table and she took it with some hesitation. Half a glass in and she relaxed as much as I could ask of her.

"I ought not to have said all that," Claire said, pressing a hand to her forehead and brushing her hair back. "It has been a long day. That's all."

I frowned over the rim of my wine glass.

"That's not all," I said as sternly as I knew how to. "If something's bothering you, you should tell me. I mean, *of course* something's bothering you, how could it not be, but you should be able to talk to me, right? I know what's happening, Claire. There's no reason to keep anything from me."

Claire looked as though she very much wanted to be convinced, but wasn't. She continued to stare at the tabletop, occasionally taking mouthfuls of wine, and I made myself be patient and still while she gathered together the means to say something in return.

"I do not feel good, Rowan. It is not very exciting, nor do I feel as though it creates anything of worth within or around me, but there it is. Depression," she said, placing the empty glass on the table. "Amidst all that is happening, I am endlessly *bored* by myself and my habits, and can only feel as though I am fated to make a mess of things. Again."

Claire had alluded to it before and Luxon had his own term for it. An *incident*. Talking about the past might take some pressure off the present, or at least give me some idea as to what I could do to help.

"What happened last time?"

Her lips parted but she gave no answer. Her eyes flickered over to the wine bottle but I took hold of her wrist before she could reach for it. I tugged her to her feet, pulled her onto the sofa and sat close, paying no heed to the way the tough leathers pressed against my sides.

"There were dragons. I wish I could start a story without saying *there were dragons*, but such is my life," she murmured softly, arm wrapped around my shoulder. I tucked my head under her chin, letting her say what she needed to. "I had been a Knight for a full year. A dragon attacked the town of Merion and when I arrived, the creature was curled up on the ashes, exhausted for the distance it'd travelled and the sheer amount of fire it had breathed.

"I fought it and I won. I managed to sink my sword into its side, between two scales, and stepped back to wait for our forces to rally and drag the creature back to Thule. But I had... I had not been thorough enough. The creature was only injured. Once there was space enough between us for it to spread its wings, it was in the air.

"It could not move fast or far, but it didn't need to. There was a village close by, not much smaller than yours, and the dragon pounced upon it. I charged after it, short a sword, and it did not have fire enough to raze the village in its entirety. I had become used to the stench of burning and what little remained of settlements, but in the village, the people were...

"They were still alive. The dragon lashed out, bringing down buildings, trapping them under the debris, and though I managed to retrieve my sword and finish the job, I could not, cannot, forget what I saw. What those people had to endure because I had not been careful enough.

"After that, I was not myself for a long time. Or rather, I feared I had become someone I did not recognise."

I wrapped my arms around her, not knowing what to say. Surely she had heard it all a hundred times before: that it wasn't her fault, that she had still saved those people. More than anything, I thought Claire needed the chance to keep speaking, so I said, "Is that why... you said you had a fiancée, and..."

"That was the start of it," Claire quickly interjected. "I became unruly. I did not wish to fight dragons; I did not wish to do anything. Luxon was right. No one else would've been afforded a second chance, as I was.

I was not kind to her. We are friends still, but much has changed."

In the minutes that followed, no sound filled the room but that of our breathing. It was enough for Claire that I'd listened to her but I didn't want that to be all the help I offered.

"Kouris and I would do anything to help you, you know. Anything for you. Even if that means running away from Kastelir and going to Thule ourselves," I said, making sure she was meeting my gaze. "But don't keep being so hard on yourself, alright? You were put in an impossible situation and you did what you thought was best. And you don't even know that it hasn't worked. King Jonas' death has just delayed things, alright? Don't give up now."

Claire closed her eyes, pressed her forehead against mine and said, "You're right. There are always other options."

"What about Agados? We could ask them for help," I said, tucking her hair behind her ears. "It seems like they're in better shape than Kastelir, anyway."

"Never," she said, wrapping her arms around my waist. "Agados has thrived in so far as it refuses to change. After the exodus from Myros, they refused to let in refugees, and even the pane have left the mountains Agados lays claim to. Kastelir, for all its faults, is the better option. The Agadians believe our roles are defined by body and birth and I should not accept their help were they to offer it."

I leant back against her and she stroked my hair, adding, "I shall wait a week. See what progress has been made, if any. If not, I shall return to Felheim and do what must be done.

"We'll figure something out," I promised.

I'd wanted to tell her about Katja, but what happened between us felt as though it'd been days or weeks in the past. Claire couldn't stand to take any more upon her shoulders and I resolved to handle the issue, or lack thereof, on my own. She pressed her nose to the top of my head, and had Claire been wearing anything else, had she been anyone else, we would've fallen asleep there and then.

"It's already dark," I pointed out.

I wormed my way from under her arm and held out my hands. She took them, frowning as she let me pull her to her feet. She was waiting for me to make my excuses and leave. In the past, I would've assumed that I'd overstayed my welcome, thinking it better to leave of my own volition than have her ask me to head back to my chambers.

Not this time. I placed my hands against her collarbone where one of the armour's buckles was pulled tight and Claire watched with a furrowed brow as I tried to work it loose.

"You need to—ugh," I said, frustrated when it didn't give. "You need to take off your armour. You can't sleep like this, Claire."

Amusement was a bizarre thing to see creep back into her features but it was there, no matter how faint. She undid the buckle on the first try and I watched as she pulled the strap tight before easing the prong out of the hole. I tried again with a strap at her side and she stood patiently as I removed the toughest and heaviest piece of armour from her chest.

She held out her arms and I removed her pauldrons and gloves, her leg plates and her belts, fingers not once faltering. I pulled the Kastelirian armour away piece by piece, slowly making my way to Claire beneath. She stepped out of her boots, left in nothing but a thin undershirt and leggings.

We left the armour in a pile on the floor and I led her to the bed, pushing the curtains to the side and tugging her in after me.

Claire found her way beneath the covers without putting up the fuss I expected. I burrowed in next to her, almost melting into her arms with the stiff armour gone. She held me close and I wrapped my arms tightly around her, not foolish enough to believe that my presence alone would lull her to sleep.

"It's alright if you can't fall asleep," I murmured into her neck. "But at least try to relax, okay?"

She kissed the top of my head and I did all I could to stay awake for as long as she was bound to. And though I knew that seeing nothing but dragons and flame behind my eyelids whenever I closed them wouldn't stop the same thoughts from plaguing Claire's mind, I couldn't banish the images.

I had my arms around her, yet I couldn't hold her close enough.

CHAPTER TWENTY-THREE

Claire awoke with the birds, but I remained at the mercy of exhaustion. The mattress rose as she pulled away from me and I made a few futile grasps at the empty space before rolling over. I heard the patter of feet against stone through the murk of my dreams, replaced minutes or years later by the clipping of boots. Claire appeared next to me for a brief second, back within her second skin, and kissed my forehead before leaving.

Hunger eventually lured me out of bed.

I could've forgotten what the last day of the Phoenix Festival meant, had I not run into Katja on the way back to my chamber.

She stopped mid-knock at the sight of me.

"Rowan! There you are, dear. Didn't you stay here last night?"

"No, I—"

She was in no mood for a reply. She took my arm and whisked me in the direction I'd come from, not giving me the chance to point out that I'd yet to have breakfast. A staircase I hadn't dared to venture up rose before us. It was wider than any other I'd rushed up or down in the castle, littered with as many guards as it was portraits.

They didn't attempt to stop me with Katja leading the way, but their eyes narrowed in scrutiny. The guards were more alert than ever and the arrival of diplomats from Agados had done nothing to relax them. I hurried up the stairs, wanting their eyes off my back, and reached a single room on the next level.

"I'm ever so glad I ran into you," Katja said, patting the back of my hand. "I'm afraid I need moral support. It's a dreary business, really, discussing official matters with my mother."

I came to an abrupt halt, hand slipping free of Katja's.

"Katja," I said, hating to disappoint her. "I can't."

"What ever do you mean?" she asked. "Oh. Oh, Rowan dear, do think it through clearly. You'll only ever draw suspicion to yourself if you actively hide from my mother. I honestly do apologise, though. I didn't think... No, no. You're right. You ought to leave."

Katja made a faint effort to smile, and turned towards the arching ivory doors at the end of the landing. Her shoulders rose and I doubted having Queen Kidira for a mother made it any easier to talk to her.

"I'm here now," I relented. "Might as well."

Katja brightened on cue and the door flicked open a fraction of a second before she had the chance to knock.

Akela stepped out, buttoning the collar of her shirt, and stopped with an, "Ah!"

She bowed her head and said, "Lady Kouris, Northwood," straightened her collar, and stepped between us, taking the stairs down two at a time.

Katja hummed flatly, watching Akela long after she was gone.

The door swung shut but Katja didn't waste time knocking. She stepped in and having heard Akela announce us, Queen Kidira didn't turn from her desk. She sat writing in a long, purple robe, not long out of bed, and Katja stood in the centre of the parlour, arms folded across her chest.

The chamber wasn't entirely unlike the others I'd visited throughout the castle, littered with bookcases and sofas and intricately woven rugs, though the fireplace against the far wall was large enough to cook a grown pig over. There were weapons in one corner, spears with carved shafts and engraved blades, lined up inside of a glass cabinet. There were few portraits within the room and the one that caught my eye was almost identical to the one in Katja's chamber. Nothing else in the parlour was particularly telling, though the boots discarded in one corner likely belonged to Akela.

"Good morning, mother," Katja finally said.

Without turning from her work, Queen Kidira said, "Good morning, Kouris. What is Ightham's squire doing with you?"

"We are *friends*," Katja said, offended on behalf of both of us.

"How nice for her," Queen Kidira said, inkwell ringing as she tapped the nib of her quill against the glass. "How may I help you? We both have a busy day ahead of us."

"I simply came to see whether you'd had a change of heart."

Queen Kidira reluctantly neglected her letters and stared right through her. Katja, to her credit, didn't flinch.

"The Agadians are biting at our heels over succession in the guise of *trade agreements*, and you wish to rescind the only entertainment in the Kingdom that might divert their attention for a few moments?" Queen Kidira asked.

"Entertainment? It isn't entertainment, and certainly not the sort

Agadians enjoy. You know as well as I do that they don't burn necromancers in Agados. The King would never squander something so
useful. Have you not asked yourself why they are so interested in this
particular execution?" Katja said. "Besides, it's archaic. It's *cruel*. We
ought to leave this sort of punishment in the past, where it belongs."

"Archaic?" The slight rise of Queen Kidira's brow was the closest I'd
come to seeing her laugh. "The Kingdom is scarcely older than you are."

Katja scoffed. I stared at the edge of Queen Kidira's desk, neither
daring to look at her or away from her, willing myself to get through it
without flinching. This was the real test. If I could endure Queen Kidira's
scathing beliefs about necromancy, then I could pass for something less
sinister around anyone.

"Yet you based these laws on mere *legends* that have been passed
down from Myros, as though—"

"As though necromancers were not responsible for the war?"

"In the same way that people are responsible for wars, perhaps. I hate
to be the one to tell you this, mother, but you are wasting a great opportunity," Katja said, waiting until Queen Kidira waved a hand in
something akin to interest. "We have a necromancer inside the castle
and uncle lies unmoving in a crypt."

Queen Kidira rose to her feet with a force that made Katja start. I
couldn't have backed away if I'd tried. She wrapped her fingers and
thumb around Katja's jaw, gaze burrowing into her, and Katja's fingers
curled towards her palm.

"I would never subject an enemy to that, much less a loved one,"
Queen Kidira said, letting go of her. "When you are Queen, you may
change whatever rules you see fit."

Katja's shoulders slumped and she looked to the side, letting out a
heavy breath.

"Ridiculous," she said, defeated. "Everyone knows you shall never
die."

A knock at the door concluded their short-lived debate and one of
Queen Kidira's maids brought in a freshly cleaned dress. Queen Kidira
nodded in approval and the maid bowed before taking it to one of the
adjoining rooms.

I thought that was to be the end of it. Queen Kidira would leave to
change, Katja would reluctantly attend the so-called festivities, and I

could slink back to my chamber and think about anything but fire.

"You," Queen Kidira said, tilting her head towards me. "What is your take on the situation? Has my daughter succeeded in brainwashing you yet?"

"I..." I had no choice but to betray Katja. My tongue was lead, only able to work itself loose when I dared to defend myself. "I'm from Felheim. It's not my place to question your laws. Your Majesty."

Queen Kidira's mouth slanted to the side and she left without another word, bored by my answer. I drew in a breath, blindly following Katja into the corridor.

"Well. I tried," she said, sighing drearily.

In a Kingdom of millions, she was the only one who had. I didn't get the chance to thank her, to apologise for not standing with her. She was swept away by a sea of scholars and servants, half of them insisting that she introduce them to the Agadian diplomats, the rest fussing over which dress she was to wear.

I wanted to spend the day with Charley and Calais but knew the open area would be full of nobles and guards with nothing to talk about but the executions. With everyone else occupied by the Agadian diplomats, the only entertainment available to me was in the form of books. I wasn't used to having so much time to waste. Back in the village, I worked from sun up to sundown and often longer, whether it was out in the fields or at the apothecary's.

I resolved to make myself useful and headed out in search of Ocari. It wasn't difficult to find them. The general rule seemed to be that if you didn't stop moving, you'd run into them, sooner or later. A flock of servants were hurrying down the bare-stone corridor between one of the larger kitchens and its respective pantry and I tailed them, keeping out of the way while they were issued their orders.

I darted after Ocari once the servants scattered, earning a raised eyebrow when I fell into step by their side.

"Yes?" they asked. Their tone was one of recognition, if nothing else.

"I was wondering if you needed help with anything," I said, well aware that my intentions were selfish. "I know you have everything running smoothly down here. But it'd be a favour to me, really."

Ocari took time out of their day to look me up and down as though I'd just asked to take on the role of Queen Kidira's personal handmaid.

"Enthusiasm goes a long way, but listen here. You're a Felheimer, brought here by a Knight we're pretending isn't a Princess and a pane we're pretending isn't Queen Kouris," Ocari said. "The less we know about you the better. And I mean that in the kindest possible way, I really do."

"Please," I tried, scurrying after them, before the woman with a mop in hand could get a word in edgeways. "Put me in a pantry and give me something to clean. No one has to know I'm there."

Ocari decided not to test how persistent I'd insist on being.

"Alright. But only because it's busy enough with the Phoenix Festival, never mind it coming on the tail of a funeral. Rest His Majesty's soul," Ocari said and nudged me towards a short, sturdy door. "In here. Sort out what's to be thrown, what needs to be eaten soon. Put whatever'll last in the bottom. Whoever was in there last made a fine mess of things. Didn't put a shred of bitterwillow in there."

I thanked Ocari and they dismissed my gratitude with a wave, drawing more servants and their questions with every step they took.

The room was bigger than the door led me to believe. Plain stone floors greeted me, along with walls scarred by thick shelves, packed from floor to ceiling with sacks of flour. There was a divide in the form of a severe looking cabinet halfway through the room, filled with jars of honey and preserves, and behind that, there were barrels of vegetables big enough to fall into.

It was hardly the most important job in the castle, or in that room, but there was a lot of work and it was all distracting. I tackled a barrel at a time, sifting through carrots and turnips and swedes, carefully pressing the pads of my thumbs against them to ensure they hadn't turned to mush beneath the skin. I was glad to be useful, even if it was in a way no one would ever notice.

I sat in the sunbeam speared through the small, square window so high up it touched the ceiling, and went long minutes at a time without thinking of fire. I didn't know when the executions would take place and it was better that way. They'd pass without my knowing and I wouldn't be tempted to make my way down to the crowd convinced they were witnessing vengeance fifteen hundred years too late.

The door swung open without warning and my thumb slipped through the skin of a potato that had seen better days.

340

I heard muttering from the other side of the cabinet, coarse words tumbling out in a language I didn't recognise, but the voice was instantly familiar to me.

I peered around the cabinet and caught sight of Akela mumbling hastily under her breath, hands held out in front of her as though the sacks of flour within reach presented her with an impossible choice. She'd left her armour behind for plainer clothes, hair slipping out of its ponytail.

"Akela?" I asked, wiping my thumb on the leg of my trousers. "Is everything okay?"

Akela's voice rose, undecipherable words coming out faster, abruptly leading onto, "*Northwood.* You are hiding away down here! Why are you doing this?"

"I'm not hiding. I'm helping," I insisted. "Aren't you on duty today? I thought you'd be needed, with all the Agadians."

Akela made a guttural sound and shook her head sharply, eyes back on the flour.

"They didn't need you to translate?"

I left the vegetables behind to help her stare at the shelves.

"Hah. No, no. The Agadians, they are understanding us well enough, and my Queen, she is speaking Agadian. They are understanding until they are disagreeing, that is, and this is being always. And then they are pretending that they are mishearing, waiting for us to be correcting ourselves," Akela said, scoffing. She pulled a sack of flour free from a shelf so high up even she had to push herself onto tiptoes to reach it. The bag hit her chest, covering her shirt with a thin film of flour. "I am not attending meetings with... with people such as they are. I am making a cake!"

"A cake?"

"Yes, yes. A cake! And if you are not keeping up, you are missing out," Akela announced, using the sole of her boot to kick the door open.

I glanced back at the vegetables, pretending I hadn't already made up my mind. The sight of them didn't compel me to stay. Ocari had tasked me with their care to be rid of me and I felt little guilt in delaying the process. Especially when the prospect of cake loomed in front of me.

More than that, there'd been a bitter note caught up in Akela's voice, the kind I hadn't thought to hear from her. She'd been muttering to herself in Agadian and I thought I might make better company than rows upon rows of flour.

Akela marched through the castle, destination fixed firmly in her mind, and burst into a small kitchen, tended to by a single cook.

"I'm afraid this kitchen is in use," the cook said when a sack of flour met the worktop.

"I am afraid I am making a cake for Queen Kidira, and if you are making me leave, then you are having to go to your Queen and explain why you are not letting Commander Ayad use your kitchen," Akela said, dusting off the front of her shirt and making matters worse. "How are you thinking she is responding to that, hm?"

The cook didn't argue. They held their hands in front of them and said, "Suppose I can be finding somewhere else to work, Commander," and headed out of the door I was propping open.

Akela pulled the cupboards open, well acquainted with their contents, and heaped bowls and whisks and sieves into her arms, raiding the larder for slabs of butter and baskets of eggs. I stepped to the side, keeping out of her way as she swung a kitchen knife like an axe, carving off a chunk of butter. I pulled the scales and a stack of weights away from the wall but Akela was already throwing handfuls of flour and sugar into a bowl, not wasting her time with precise measurements.

She slammed eggs open against the counter and the stove door creaked on its hinges as I pulled it open, getting the fire going. It was barely big enough for the cake Akela was whisking together under one arm.

"Do not be worrying," Akela said. "Queen Kidira, she is liking the more, hmm. Modest cakes! Sponge with lemon, this sort of thing, yes? Saying it is for her, it is only a ruse. We are making something having more substance, Northwood!"

Her idea of substance came in the form of cocoa powder, which she applied generously, turning the batter light brown. She placed the bowl on the counter, attacked it with a wooden spoon, hair coming loose, falling about her face.

With one arm holding the bowl in place and the other mixing, she tried to blow the strands out of her eyes. I pulled a chair across the room, legs scraping against stone, and hopped on it to pull Akela's hair free and tie it back up.

"Ah. Thank you," she said and I jumped down, holding the steel pans as she poured the mixture in.

"Everything okay?" I asked cautiously.

The spoon chiming against the glass bowl as the last of the cake batter dripped into the pans was all the answer I thought I was going to get, until she said, "Yes, yes. Or it is being fine, in some days."

I said nothing in reply, hoping she knew she could keep talking if she needed to, and opened the oven door. Akela stood back, waiting for the swell of heat to rise, and carefully slid the cake pans into the oven.

Sat on the counter, we ate the cake batter left on the spoon and whisk, cupboard doors rattling as Akela rocked her feet back and forth.

"... It is Agados. They are coming here and they are thinking they are having any say in who is taking King Jonas' throne. The Old West, they are trading with Agados for many, many decades, because Agados, it is having wealth and it is buying all the resources it is needing. There are veins of gold in the mountains," Akela eventually grumbled. "Agados, it is not being a good place. They are wanting to influence Kastelir and they are not listening to Queen Kidira, no matter what she is saying. They are not listening to my Queen and how are we knowing what is really happening in their country? Agados, it is being worse than you Felheimish and your wall."

"Claire said she'd never accept Agados' help, even if they offered it," I said, wanting to understand. "I hadn't really heard of them before this."

"Yes, that is how they are wanting it. They are keeping to themselves, they are only taking what they are wanting, and they are not letting outsiders and their ideas in. Their King, he is not leaving the Kingdom. Even now, even when they are burning a necromancer, they are only sending diplomats," Akela said. "In Agados, they are putting people into boxes and they are forcing them to play roles. I am not wanting this for Kastelir."

Perhaps Kastelirians didn't grow up on tales of Felheim's corruption, as we endured tales of Kastelir. Perhaps they grew up hearing about Agados' cruelty.

"Don't worry," I said, brushing flour off the bridge of her nose. "It doesn't matter what they have planned. Even if they don't listen to Queen Kidira, she'll probably just glare at them until they run back to their King."

Akela managed a laugh, boots thudding against the floor as she slipped from the counter. Not wanting to speak of Agados any further, she pushed herself onto tiptoes and retrieved a stack of chocolate hidden atop one of the cupboards. She dropped it onto the table, used her fist to smash it to bits, and threw the fragments she didn't melt down as a base for the icing into my lap.

Once the cake had cooled enough to bring it all together, it lived up to the smell that had preceded it. It was one of the best things I'd ever tasted, despite its haphazard creation. It was beyond indulgent, so rich a single bite was almost enough to make my eyes water, and Akela effortlessly made her way through a third of it.

"It's good. It's *really* good," I told her, wiping the crumbs from the corner of my mouth.

"Yes, I am knowing this," Akela said, licking icing from her thumb. "My talents, they are not all involving the swinging of the axe."

Akela was in better spirits but still wasn't herself. I jokingly suggested that she help me sort through the rest of the vegetables and she was in enough need of a distraction to agree. We sat on the floor together, picking at the cake, working until the light was so poor I could no longer discern between bruises and shadows.

"I am thinking, the festivities, they are done," Akela said, standing and stretching, holding out a hand to me. "Queen Kidira, she is expecting me, and I am needing to change."

Akela wrapped the remainder of the cake in napkins and left them in my care. We parted ways once we reached the carpeted part of the castle. I stuck to the edges of the castle, wanting to avoid the Agadians, in search of Claire and Kouris, hoping that either or both of them were free.

It didn't take long. Kouris rounded a corner, almost walked into me, and said, "There you are, yrval. Been looking all over."

She crinkled her nose, momentarily losing her chain of thought, tongue flicking out as though tasting the air.

"I, ah," Kouris started again, shaking it off. "We've got a few hours before Kidira's gonna be dragging the dragon-slayer back off for another round of politics. Thought we could all sit down for a talk."

Over the last few months, I'd been rudely awoken by an axe-wielding

344

assassin, confronted by a Knight who'd later ended up in a river, face split in two, been accused of killing a King and discovered that my Kingdom was founded on cruelty and lies. Had Kouris' words not been ominous, I would've known something was amiss.

"Cake?" I asked, holding out a slice.

Kouris' ears stuck straight up. She furrowed her brow and took a step back.

"No. No thanks, yrval," she said, waving her hands in front of her. "As I was saying, we don't have all the time in the world. Best be getting on with it."

I followed her with a shrug, supposing there was more cake for me and Claire. My stomach twisted at the thought of more chocolate but I knew that wouldn't stop me from taking another bite or two. Necromancy was of no help to me when it came to poor dietary choices.

Kouris was far from skittish but wasn't in the mood to run into anyone, either. I took three strides for every one of hers, congratulating myself on starting to recognise my surroundings, when Kouris turned into a corridor that made me wonder if there was ever an end to the labyrinth that engulfed the castle.

The staircase reminded me of the one leading to Queen Kidira's chambers, though no portraits hung on the walls and clumps of dust broke apart as I ran my hand up the bannister. Kouris pushed one of the doors open, not having to duck into the room, and for as displaced from time as the staircase had been, the chamber beyond was remarkably well-kept.

It was much like Queen Kidira's, spears notwithstanding, and though sheets were draped across much of the furniture, what was on display was big enough for any pane. Light ebbed lazily from the lantern on a low table, and I wondered if in twenty-seven years, the sheets protecting the furniture were the only change to the chamber.

"Good. She found you," Claire said, sat in an armchair at least three times as wide as it needed to be. Kouris took her place on the sofa opposite her and I joined Claire, leaning against the arm of the chair that came up to my shoulder.

"Cake?" I offered.

Claire's gloves were neatly folded on the table in front of her, and she took the cake eagerly, pulling away chunks with her fingers and eating without getting a single crumb on the side of her mouth or in her lap.

"This is good. Did you make it?" Claire asked, eating faster when she realised it wasn't only cake, but *good* cake.

Kouris drummed her fingers impatiently against her knee and I said, "I watched Akela make it."

I was eager to hear what they had to say. I knew it wouldn't be anything good, but the anticipation was making my skin itch.

"Here's the thing," Kouris said. "The dragon-slayer and me, we're thinking of leaving."

"Leaving? Leaving Kastelir, you mean?"

"Aye. Now, you know we had nothing but good intentions when we came here. The dragon-slayer thought she could get help for her Kingdom and I thought I could use my status to make that easier. Had Jonas been allowed to stick around, it just might've worked. But now Kidira and Atthis are too busy fighting with half the Kingdom over who gets to take the throne, and the other half wanna see 'em off their own. That's not even mentioning what's happening with Agados.

"It wasn't the best plan, but it was a plan. We saw it through and this one's stuck acting as Kidira's lackey, trying to prove her loyalties, and Atthis, he wants to act like nothing bad is gonna come of this. And if I'm to be honest, I reckon I'm hurting more than I'm helping. Can't be expecting to come back after so long and hope that nothing had changed. Doesn't leave us with many options, does it?"

Claire nodded as Kouris spoke, picking the last cake crumbs from the napkin. I handed her the other slice without looking away from Kouris. The thought of leaving Kastelir didn't frighten me. If anything, it made me realise how much I wanted to be out of the castle and back on the road, where Claire wasn't being made to dress as a foreign soldier, stripped of rank and honour.

"Where will we go? Back to Felheim? To Thule?" I asked, uncertain whether trading one castle for another would do us any good. "Are there people there who'd help us?"

Claire chewed thoughtfully.

"There *may* be, though I cannot say for certain. The King planned for this. Planned for me to follow in his footsteps. My entire life has been guided by him, and I have only become acquainted with those he approved of. He cannot be solely responsible for what is happening with the dragons. The web of those involved stretches further than I suspect," she said, sighing. "I did not expect Kastelir to help me, but I wished to warn them regardless. I have done just that."

"Okay. Okay," I said, rubbing my hands together. I knew one thing for certain, and that was that Claire wasn't going to *ask* to leave. We'd be running. She'd make an enemy of yet another King. "What about your mother? Queen Aren?"

The corner of Claire's mouth slanted downwards and she stared at the cake in her hand, picking at it without eating.

"The Queen has been ill for some time. Healers have purged the disease over and over, but only succeed in prolonging the decay. When I last saw her, I learnt that the healers were of little use to her. I should not like to trouble her, if such a thing is still possible," she said, jaw tightening.

I put a hand on the back of hers and squeezed it, letting go so she could finish off yet more cake.

Kouris' ears twitched as her gaze burrowed into the crumb-laden napkin.

I said, "Seriously, what is it?" to break the silence.

She didn't hear me.

"Pane don't like chocolate," Claire said and flicked a chunk directly at Kouris' nose. Kouris snarled, teeth snapping together, and Claire said, "Couldn't say why, though."

I laughed under my breath but felt it ripple jaggedly through my chest. Claire wrapped an arm around me as I leant against her, and I thought not only of the people we'd have to leave behind, of Akela and Katja, but those Claire would have to face. The King, the Queen. Her brothers. A slew of Knights who would surely stand against her, along with the entirety of a nation indebted to them for the dragons they kept at bay.

"Don't reckon we'll be going to Thule. Not straight away," Kouris said, having brushed off her nose half a dozen times. "Best to be heading to the source of it all, where they're raising and twisting their dragons."

"Oh?"

"The Bloodless Lands," Claire clarified. It all slid into place. Where else would they be able to manipulate beasts the size of barns without anyone else stumbling across them? "Or near enough."

"Isn't that dangerous?" I asked, questions spiking within me. "Do you think the Phoenix Fire is still burning?"

"It won't be safe, but none of this journey has been, thus far," Claire said. "And I doubt we shall get close enough to find out."

"They're not gonna see us coming," Kouris said, slamming a fist into her open hand. "They're not about to be wasting soldiers when no one ever crosses into the Bloodless Lands. That's just asking for their secrets to spill.

"Now, keep in mind that you don't have to be coming with us, yrval. We don't want to leave you behind but we're not forcing you into this. You've been kept in the dark for long enough and we wanted everything out in the open. We can take you back to Kyrindval, or—"

"No!" I said, bolting to the edge of my seat. "I followed you all the way through Felheim and Kastelir and up to Kyrindval, not knowing what was going on. And I'm not just going to go home or put up with Michael now that I'm finally starting to understand it. I want to help. Even if that just means carrying bags and washing the dinner things."

Kouris' lips curled into a smile, Claire pulled me back and neither of them said another word. They didn't have to. They hadn't expected me to stay behind and had only made the offer for me to refuse it. They wanted me with them. They'd set out on their own missions and I'd insisted on following along, but I was no longer a burden they were shepherding through Kingdoms.

I would've smiled but found it hard to greet the plan with any real enthusiasm. All three of us were already exhausted by what laid ahead: the weeks spent on the road, trying to remain inconspicuous with a pane in our midst, soft beds a distant memory. I closed my eyes, doing what I could to turn my thoughts away from the never-ending landscape that'd pass us by.

"I'll send a raven to your brother. Let him know to stay in Kyrindval," Claire said. "We leave at dawn."

CHAPTER TWENTY-FOUR

Claire returned to Queen Kidira's side and I headed to my chamber to gather my belongings and get an early night's sleep. The former didn't take long. I'd kept Claire's key around my neck since she'd placed it there and my only other belongings of worth were the clothes I pillaged from the room, hoping no one would miss them.

I slid the bag under a chair, aware it wouldn't go unnoticed if Katja turned up unannounced, and wrestled with the urge to find her and Akela. I confined myself to a chair and came to terms with the fact that I wouldn't be able to give them a proper goodbye, even if they inexplicably weren't busy. I'd say too much in holding back the goodbye I felt I owed them; there'd be a dull finality in everything I didn't say.

I wished I could write enough to leave a note. *Sorry* couldn't have taken more than a few strange swirls on the page. I knew this wasn't to be a momentary reprise from the castle. Fleeing Kastelir would make us their enemies and any friendships I'd nurtured were forfeit.

Sleep came in scattered bursts. I buried my face in a pillow and tried to convince myself I was already dreaming, but Isin was alive with the end of the festival, spirits raised at the expense of a necromancer's life.

I gave up on rest for minutes at a time, pulling the curtains back and wishing Claire would knock at my door; sitting with my feet dangling over the edge of the bed, wondering where the harm in heading out to find her was; inevitably falling back into the nest of blankets every time.

Birds sang to warn me of the encroaching dawn and I groaned groggily, mind finally willing to succumb to sleep. My joints ached, protesting every step I took. I would've felt better had I not slept at all.

I splashed water on my face, expecting it to work a miracle. The tips of my hair were barely wet when footsteps outside my chamber gave me reason to pause. I strained to listen but they passed straight by, lost in the winding corridors beyond.

Kouris would fetch our horses and I was to meet Claire by the servants' bridge we'd crossed upon leaving for Kyrindval. Another patter of footsteps passed and the moment the sun made its intent known to the night sky, I grabbed my bag and shot out of my room.

The corridor was clear but the rest of the castle was busier than I'd expected it to be. The Phoenix Festival had probably only wound to a close hours or minutes ago and if I ran into anyone, I could pretend to be drunk.

People fluttered by, dressed in nightwear, but none of them paid me any heed. I slipped past clusters of preoccupied people as easily as a shadow, and kept my destination in mind. I hoped another assassination hadn't caused the castle's residents to believe the walls were closing in on them.

"*Here?*" one man asked incredulously. "How many were lost?"

I moved too quickly to hear any reply. I darted down the staircase, found the ground floor, and happened upon a corridor that was unlikely to stay empty for more than a few seconds. I hoisted myself through the window, and landed on the narrow path between the castle and the moat. I jogged the rest of the way, and the shaky doubt that I wouldn't find the right bridge became something else when I turned the corner and found Claire, exactly I hadn't agreed to meet her.

She was at one of the upper bridges, and she wasn't alone.

Soldiers flanked her, but she hadn't been caught trying to escape. Her dragon-bone armour spoke volumes I wanted to deafen myself to.

"Claire!" I called out, sprinting the rest of the way.

Two soldiers caught my arms, holding me back.

"Afraid you can't come this way, miss," one of them said.

"Let her through," Kouris growled behind me, causing the soldiers to flinch as she stepped out of the castle.

Her eyes glinted and they let me go.

Akela was behind her, dressed in Luxon's ill-fitting dragon-bone armour, axe swapped out for a sword, but I couldn't spare more than a second to stare at her. I barged between the soldiers and Claire moved towards Calais.

"Claire!"

I gripped her arm and tensed at the smooth bone beneath my fingertips. She tensed, one foot already in the stirrup. She needed to leave and she needed to do it now.

"Rowan," she said. Her dragon-bone boots scraped the stone beneath as she put both feet back on the ground. "I have to leave. There is a dragon within Kastelir and I am the only one capable of slaying it."

"But..."

"This is my duty, Rowan. Please," she said, helm covering too much of her face. She was but a Knight once more, dragon-bone becoming her.

"Stay here. Wait."

The dragons she'd slain before were as nothing. The one that had found its way to Kastelir, that had been *sent* to Kastelir, was more vicious than any she'd faced before, all fire and fangs, intelligence burning brightly at its core. It wasn't that I didn't have faith in her, but the fear roiling inside of me had covered it in a thick haze.

"I..."

I'd spent so long focused on what Claire had lost, on all she'd left behind, and hadn't once dreamt she could slip into her old role so easily.

She didn't wait for me to say anything else. The gates swung open and the soldier shouted for her to move out. She climbed onto Calais, looked at me one last time, and mouthed *I'll be fine* as she gripped the reins.

"Northwood," Akela called from the back of her horse. Luxon's armour made her arms rest at awkward angles, but dragon-bone armour was not to be squandered. "Do not be fretting. In no time we are returning and then you are making me a cake to be celebrating, yes?"

Hooves beat against the bridge and armour clanged as the soldiers moved out. Kouris came to my side and she didn't have to say anything. I knew that she was leaving too.

"I'll take care of 'em," Kouris said.

All I could do was grip her fingers and squeeze them, arm falling limply by my side.

It wasn't until they were out of sight, gate locked behind them, that I could do anything but stare. The sun didn't waste any time in lighting up the sky and a faint smell of smoke drifted towards me from Isin, stirring me into action. I couldn't stay there. I had to get Charley, had to head after them.

Any of them could be hurt and it was up to me to help, to heal. It didn't matter if Akela saw me do it, if the soldiers knew what I was. We were leaving. Claire would slay the dragon and we'd be gone before anyone could think to march us back to the castle.

I charged towards the stables, colonnade in sight when a sharp, twisting sensation knotted my stomach so tightly I found myself doubled over, clawing at my skin through my shirt. I gripped the wall, took a deep breath, and saw Katja standing over me. She was so distraught by the news of a dragon that she had no idea what was flowing out of her.

"Rowan! My goodness, did you hear?" she asked.

She put a hand on my shoulder, steadying me, as though there wasn't an easier way to stop the sickness.

"Claire and Kouris," I said through grit teeth. "They've gone to fight the dragon."

"Sir Ightham and Kouris, they've...? Oh, Rowan, dear. I'm so, so sorry. But don't lose heart. They know what they're doing, don't they?" Katja asked. Comforting me helped her find her footing. Whatever had emanated from her faded, leaving a wave of nausea behind that had nothing to do with her. "Sir Ightham's a Knight, tried and tested. She'll slay the dragon before Kouris can think to help."

The word dragon sunk into me as though it was an accusation. I had known. All this time, I'd know what Felheim was capable of and I'd buried the truth so deep down that some days, I managed to convince myself I'd imagined it. Yet I'd known and done nothing to prevent this.

"How... how are they here?" I asked, desperate to believe it was nothing but a coincidence. A dragon had tumbled down from the mountains and mistaken a village for a meal; there was nothing more to it.

"No one can say. We haven't even known for the better part of an hour. We received word this morning, from the settlements overlooking the town of Hawlthan. It's *gone*, Rowan. An entire town, gone..." Katja said, teeth worrying her lower lip. "Come. I must speak with mother and uncle. Surely they'll have formed some manner of plan."

The faint din of Isin caught up to me, city awakening to grim news that bellowed through the streets, and I let Katja lead me away from the stables. I hadn't been thinking clearly. I never would've been able to catch up with Claire, Kouris and Akela, let alone help.

What would I be able to do with any ash the dragon created, other than watch it slip through my fingers?

Katja guided me to the throne room. Everyone in the castle had had the same idea: we only got to the front of the room by Katja being who she was. People recognised her and their faces lit up as though she had all the answers to all their problems.

"With all due respect, Your Majesties, we have long since said that the dragons may find their way to Kastelir," a man in long, green robes said.

"And you have long-since claimed that the pane would rebel and the phoenixes would rise once again," King Atthis snapped from atop the stairs. "*Next.*"

The King and Queen sat on their thrones, silence claiming the empty seats between them.

A soldier stepped forward, a young man with two yellow stripes on his shoulder, and said, "Your Highness, if I might take our forces along the perimeter, I could..."

"You could what?" Queen Kidira asked.

"I-I could buy Isin time, if nothing else," he said, trying to stare at Queen Kidira and King Atthis at the same time.

"You would not buy Isin seconds," King Atthis said, evoking a flutter of agreement from those gathered around him. "I will not send our soldiers out merely to die. Hawlthan had forces of its own and reports say it was but ash within minutes. I will not have you waste your time with heroics while the people of Isin work themselves into a panic. Half are still drunk from the conclusion of the Phoenix Festival and most haven't slept. Send your soldiers out into the streets to ensure the citizens do not tear Isin to the ground before the dragon has the chance to."

The soldier drew a breath, snapped a salute, and left with no words inside of him.

"No good," Katja mumbled under her breath.

She wasn't going to get an audience with her mother and uncle any time soon.

I slipped out of the chamber with Katja, head spinning, ringing. Claire was out there, Kouris and Akela too, and I didn't know how I was managing to put one foot in front of the other. People stopped Katja, eager for her advice, and as if underwater, I heard her tell them that she really was very sorry, but she didn't know more than anyone else. Their best bet was to hang onto the King and Queen's every word.

She stopped once, placed a hand on my shoulder and told me to wait where I was, able to tell how disorientating the world around me insisted on being. I leant against the wall, eyes closed, feeling as utterly powerless as every other person on Bosma. I couldn't reach out and rip the tendrils of death away from Claire or Kouris; I didn't even know whether Hawlthan was to the east or west, north or south.

Katja swung the door shut behind her and brought me back to my senses. I didn't know how long she'd been in the chamber, but it was long enough to find what she'd been looking for. She had a hefty black cloak draped over her arm and I couldn't bring myself to wonder why.

"This is it. This is our best chance," she said.

I opened my mouth to ask what she meant but she brought a finger to her lips, shushing me.

We worked our way lower into the castle, to parts I'd yet to explore. We weren't surrounded by servants and kitchens and dormitories. The ceilings were low, corridors narrow, and the walls were lined with torches that burnt away at the emptiness. If guards had been stationed there, they'd left at the threat of a dragon drawing closer.

Katja took a torch to brandish against the darkness and glanced around skittishly, taking slow steps to her destination. She turned each time she mistook one of my footsteps for someone following us, and the fire reflecting in her eyes made it all too easy to mistake her nerves for excitement.

"Where are we going?" I asked, but she silenced me again. The distraction of the dragon was the only thing stopping me from digging my heels into the bare stone and never moving again, but even with my thoughts twisting through the corridors and escaping the castle, rising up, up, like smoke, my surroundings worked their way under my skin.

I was on the verge of shuddering. Something was waiting for us at the end of the corridor, something that reached out to me, slipping between the light from the torches and the darkness, beckoning, almost—

"No," I breathed more than I said. I stopped and Katja had no choice but to do the same. "The crypt. You're taking me to the crypt."

Feigning ignorance wouldn't help. The inexplicable pull of the door made me want to press my palms flat against the dark stone walls and hook my fingers around the steel rings that held the torches in place.

I wanted to make myself immoveable, deaf to what Katja would ask of me.

"We need to turn back," I said slowly, lest I startle the flames around us. "This isn't a good idea."

"Rowan," she protested, kneeling to place her torch on the floor. I swallowed the lump in my throat and she cupped my face with both hands, smiling weakly. "Rowan, dear. I know it's a lot of ask of you. I know it's more than I should ever ask of any one person, but please. I am begging you. Think of the good you'll do. Sir Ightham, Kouris and

354

the Commander are riding across the country at this very moment, for the good of Kastelir. I'm not saying we ought to have gone with them. Perish the thought! They are soldiers and we are not; we only ought to do what we can. This is your duty to Kastelir, Rowan."

Her eyes were wide and pleading and I was already defenceless. I'd wanted this. I'd wanted to bring King Jonas back. I'd begged Kouris and Claire to let me try, yet I was desperate to turn my back on the one person who'd been fighting for necromancers, for people like me.

"I can't. Your mother, King Atthis, they'd..."

"They *need* him back, Rowan. Surely you've seen the mess Kastelir has already made of itself, the disaster we're on the cusp of. Should the Agadians get their way..." She drew in a slow breath, jaw tightening. "You won't simply be bringing back one man. Nor will you merely be returning my uncle, or indeed a King. You'll be bringing together a country intent on tearing itself to shreds."

My heart raced faster than my thoughts, powers swirling inside of me like a torch in the dark. After all I'd witnessed, after all Akela had told me of Agados, I was finally in a position to fix things. Katja wasn't merely pleading her case to *me*, begging because I was her friend; I was the only one who could bring Jonas back, who could stop Kastelir becoming what Akela feared it would.

And I was leaving.

Once the dragon was slain and Claire and Kouris were back, we were leaving.

"Okay," I said in a voice stronger than my own. "But not here. Not in the castle."

"The entire castle is busy, it's our best chance to..." Katja blurted out, belatedly realising I'd agreed. Her hands trembled as she stepped back, heel knocking the handle of the torch and sending it rolling in a semi-circle across the floor. The shadows shifted, making her eyes darker. "Thank you. Oh, Rowan. Thank you."

She crouched and felt for the torch handle without taking her eyes off me. Something heavy lodged itself within us and between us and I didn't question her. I didn't ask her why she was pushing the crypt's tombstone of a door open despite what I'd just said.

No torches blazed within. Katja held hers up high, making the cave of a room deeper for all the flickering shadows that painted it. It was a crypt meant for Kings and Queens alone and only so much room had been sent aside for it. Being there with Katja, next to King Jonas' temporary resting place, made the prospect of death seem very small indeed.

"We'll take uncle back to my apartment in the city," Katja said, staring at the sarcophagus' stone lid. *Take him*, she said. Not *steal his corpse*. "We can – you can – do what needs to be done there."

I said nothing, unwilling to give myself the chance to change my mind. Katja hooked her fingers around the sarcophagus' lid and I did the same. On the count of three we put all of our strength into lifting it. I focused not on helping the daughter of a Queen steal the body of a King while a dragon plagued the country, but on the stone biting into my fingertips, catching and tearing skin that healed straight over. I almost offered to heal Katja's fingertips, until I realised that her hands were doing the same.

Sweat clung to my forehead but we moved the lid enough to see the body within and hoist it out. The corpse didn't unsettle me. Bitterwillow had been packed around it, stopping it from going too far to rot, and no stench rushed out at us. I didn't fixate on his sunken face, on how still and empty he was. I saw ways to fix him, to drive out the force that would see him reduced to bones, then dust.

I reached for his shoulder but jumped back when Katja yelped, "Rowan! What are you doing?"

"I'm moving him," I said slowly, wanting to make sure I understood the question. "We need to get him to your apartment, Katja."

"Not like that!"

"How are we going to get him out of here, then?"

"Your powers! Goodness, Rowan, use your powers, wouldn't you?"

I stared at her as blankly as King Jonas stared at the backs of his eyelids. Katja held her arms out in an expectant half-shrug, lips slowly parting when she realised I had no idea what she was asking of me.

"You don't know? You *don't* know, do you?" Katja said. She would've laughed, had we been anywhere else. "I don't have time for this. I don't have time to teach you, I... It's a corpse, Rowan. It's a corpse and you're a necromancer. Think of yourself as a puppeteer. It's on strings, invisible strings, that only you can pull."

She ran her fingers through her hair, twisting a handful of it atop her head. Katja might not have time to teach me but I didn't have time to let her down, either. I ignored how absurd it sounded, moved back to the King's body and told myself that moving a corpse without touching it was no more ridiculous than raising the dead with a thought.

I stared at him, picturing what would happen if I lured death towards myself without giving it the chance to be torn from the frame it had chosen. I focused so hard that my temples ached and my eyes burnt, willing King Jonas to rise, to clamber out of the sarcophagus.

The corpse's fingers twitched and I almost send myself ricocheting into an early grave.

Katja pressed her fingers to her lips and I did it again, mind screaming *move, move, come to me, come to me.* The sight of King Jonas' limbs moving independently of one another was worse than the sight of his corpse, worse than he must've looked with his face paling, blood rushing from the wounds. He moved like a spider with too many legs, too many joints, and I backed away as I lured him towards me.

Each movement he made tore my nerves, sending jolts through my spine and wrists. I'd never make it out of the crypt, much less to Katja's apartment. I thrust out an arm, wanting it to stop, and the corpse did the same.

My vision cleared. The movement hadn't cost me anything at all.

I didn't need to control it. It only had to copy me.

"It worked! Rowan, we really did it," Katja said, jittery. "I was afraid it was all nonsense. The only proof of it was hidden inside a dusty old tome and it made no end of foolish claims, stating that necromancers were wont to burn more easily than parchment and... It isn't the time to be rambling, is it? Come, come."

I held out my arms and King Jonas' corpse did the same thing, allowing Katja to put the cloak on it, hood up.

There was a heat in my veins, a connection I hadn't felt in an age. Not since I'd brought Peter back. Katja stopped me from leaving, gripping the back of my shirt and causing the corpse to grind to a halt.

"Rowan, your eyes. They're... rather unsettlingly bright," she said. "No matter. The sun isn't holding anything back today. Just keep your head down and it'll be of no concern."

We kept to the less travelled passages within the castle, shortcuts Katja had learnt as a child, and no one stopped us from walking straight

357

out of the castle and into Isin.

The morning was beautiful, and the clear, wide sky soaked up the panic roaring within every house, street and open square. King Atthis had been right about the people. Those who were still drunk swayed on the spot and gave the soldiers and guards few problems to deal with, but the rest of the citizens were convinced the King and Queen knew something they refused to share with the rest of the city.

Rumours moved quicker than we did and people declared that a dragon would be upon Isin within mere minutes. Some were gathering what they could, delusional enough to believe they could run beyond a dragon's reach. No one paid us any heed as we moved quickly and quietly towards what had once been Autíra.

I forced myself to think of dragons, to dwell on Claire fighting one at that very moment, but couldn't believe any of it. How could it be true? How could anything else of note be happening in the world while I was making a corpse march through the streets?

Katja's fingers shook as she unlocked the door. She missed twice, key scraping against iron and wood, but she did her part and got us out of the city, out of the frightened eye of the masses.

The boots King Jonas had been laid to rest in thumped up the stairs, and the corpse stood in the centre of the living room, coming to stop with a sense of finality I couldn't account for. For a wretched moment, I didn't know how I was supposed to separate the two of us. I couldn't imagine giving up such complete control, but I forced myself to picture dry bark being torn from a tree and King Jonas crumpled to the ground for the second time.

Katja knelt and laid his body on the floor more slowly than she needed to. Hesitant, almost.

"This is the easy part," I said for my benefit more than hers, wanting to test my voice.

Katja nodded, lips pursed together as she batted away a stray tear that dared to show itself.

I knelt opposite her, hands hovering over King Jonas' chest. I hadn't been lying. It *was* the easy part. So easy that I barely knew how it happened, how it worked. There was nothing mechanical about it, no procedure I had to follow. I didn't focus on one part of the King in particular, didn't force my mind to linger on the wounds that had let death rush into him.

All I did was imagine him as he ought to be, sitting up of his own volition, muscles versed in fluid movements, and so it was.

King Jonas' eyes opened and it was the only the harrowing gasp for breath that tore Katja's gaze from me. She'd watched me the whole time, more eager to see what I did than witness the results for herself, but I was instantly forgotten. King Jonas lashed out to protect himself from a blade that was no longer there and Katja threw herself against him, clutching him tight.

"Uncle! Uncle, you're safe!" Katja's voice was thick with tears and I scrambled back, placing myself out of sight. "It's alright. Please, you're safe."

"Kouris?" King Jonas asked. The man who'd been stabbed to death in his own castle, the man whose wake I'd attended, placed his hands on Katja's shoulders and eased her back. "You have to be careful, there was a—a boy with a knife, a..."

"I know, Uncle. I know. It's alright, I promise you. You were hurt, but I brought you here. I barely managed to heal you in time, but it's alright. Mother caught the man who did this to you," Katja said softly, and it was only when I heard her take credit for my work that I comprehended what I'd done.

All my power spluttered inside my chest, washing out of my body and taking more than it ought to. I gripped the wall, sure that I'd never be able to support my bones, much less my thoughts. I'd let Claire down. I'd brought back a King, a good man, and though I could see how much it meant to Katja and knew it would mean even more to Kastelir, I'd broken my promise.

I'd put Claire at risk in putting myself at risk, practising necromancy to its fullest when I knew that Queen Kidira would never hesitate to have a pyre stoked.

Katja didn't need me anymore. I slipped from the apartment as quietly as I could, depending on her sobbing to distract from the door closing behind me. I charged straight back to the castle, despite what I'd done. The panic outside was infectious and in my haste, I began to mistake the shadows of birds and banners for those of dragons.

Claire's key rested heavily against my chest, sending news of what

I'd done across the Kingdom. It wasn't until I reached the bridge I realised I had no way of getting into the castle on my own. I had no proof I'd ever set foot inside, and the guards were doing all they could to keep walls of Isiners back. I ducked through seas of bodies and thudded against the guards' crossed spears, but Ocari was stood halfway across the bridge, directing servants this way and that, escorting out the ones who insisted on being with their families.

"Ocari! Tell them to let me through. Please!" I called out. A nod from them was all it took. The guards grabbed my collar and pulled me through the gap beneath their spears. "Thank you!"

I charged around the castle, to the bridge I'd last seen Claire on. It was all for nothing. No one awaited me. I grabbed the arm of a passing servant and asked if the Commander and the others were back. He shook his head and the next two guards gave me the same answer.

Once I stopped, I didn't know what to do with myself. I crouched by the wall of the castle and as the hours slipped away, I convinced myself that the worst had happened. I bit the inside of my mouth, willing to pay any price for what I'd done, so long as Claire, Kouris and Akela were returned safely to me.

Fear and disgust twisted in my gut, but some part of me wanted to smile. It was fear doing it, it had to be. The power I'd wielded thrummed through me, urging me to try something else. Something more. I hadn't known I could control the dead until a few hours ago, hadn't believed the tales of necromancers raising armies of pane and dragons alike, and couldn't imagine what else had been kept from me. There was too much raging inside of me.

I wanted to tear the power out, like poison from a wound.

"Northwood!"

The word echoed in my head, weighing nothing, meaning nothing. I had become a thing, a creature defined by its powers, by death, and... Northwood. Northwood. That was me.

That was Akela's voice.

The glare of the sun made my vision flash. Akela stumbled as she stepped towards me but didn't fall. She blocked out the sun and I saw burns lining her jaw, dipping down towards her neck. Blood gushed from her split lip and her face was bruised, but her armour had done all she'd asked of it.

"Akela..." I said weakly, nails scraping across the ground. "Claire and Kouris. Where are they?"

Akela took a step forward, tried to kneel, but the armour wouldn't let her.

"I am telling you not to worry, Northwood. Kouris, she is behind us. She is bringing Ightham," Akela said, blood staining her empty smile. "Perhaps you are wanting to look away. It is not looking nice, this is true, but we are having healers. And your Phoenix, she is rising again, yes?"

A swarm of guards dragged Akela inside, two of them helping her stand, and I shook with such force as I waited for Kouris to appear that I didn't know how the castle still stood.

My powers became me. It no longer mattered if that's all I was, because it meant I could help Claire and Kouris. I could save them from whatever wounds they'd suffered, whatever agony they were in.

The gates swung open and there was no missing Kouris. She didn't run across the bridge. Couldn't. At a distance, I could feel the pain peeling off Claire. Kouris held her in her arms and that clear, dark mist hovered all around them. It was different from the time Claire had been cut open. The buzz wasn't louder, wasn't angrier. It was settled, as though there was no turning back from this.

The stone cracked white beneath my hands, spreading from my palms.

No shadows covered it and slowly, I pushed myself to my feet.

Kouris didn't stop as she passed but I saw enough. Claire was unconscious and long since, too. Her helm was on, but only because it couldn't be removed; every inch of her face was burnt, charred flesh bound to the dragon-bone. Every ounce of the agony Claire had been in echoed through me.

"Yrval, don't be looking," Kouris said, shifting Claire in her arms so her shoulder blocked my view. "There are healers. We've got healers for this kind of thing."

I stood there, useless, watching Kouris head into the castle with Claire in her arms, knowing Kastelir would never let me help those I cared for the most.

CHAPTER TWENTY-FIVE

I found Kouris, or Kouris found me.

I wandered the corridors, head full of what I'd seen, and Kouris placed her hands on my shoulders to stop me from drifting forever. I barely registered the touch. She turned me on the spot and crouched down low, eyes meeting mine. The fear of what could've happened rushed into me. It was hard to believe that reality wasn't going to shatter.

"I was worried," I mumbled, crashing into her chest. She put her arms around me, rising to a fraction of her full height, and I clung on as though it would stop her from ever leaving again. "I was so worried about you, Kouris."

"Aye, yrval. I'm sorry we had to be running off like that," she said. I buried my face in the orange cloth draped across her chest, inhaling the stench of smoke clinging to it. She hadn't been to the healers yet. An ache rattled within her bones and I drew it out, gulping it down like a drowning person clawing their way towards land. Kouris tensed, then pressed her lips to the top of my head. "No need to be worrying yourself. I'm a tad more fireproof than you lot."

I gripped the front of her armour and looked up at her, wanting nothing more than to tell her the truth. I'd made a mistake. I was scared and it'd made me foolish and we needed to leave because of it. Katja wouldn't be able to convince King Jonas to remain confined to his apartment, if she'd intended to leave him there at all. She hadn't known I'd planned to leave, didn't know I'd been delayed; King Jonas could walk through the gates at any moment, completely beyond my control.

But I couldn't say that to Kouris. I couldn't lie to her, either. My tongue stuck to the roof of my mouth, immovable until I found another truth.

"... I love you, you know," I mumbled and Kouris' ears drooped, pressed flat to the sides of her neck.

Bowing down, she kissed my forehead, nose and mouth, tusks brushing against my skin.

"Same to you, yrval," she said softly. I clung to her again. "It's okay, it's okay. We all made it back in one piece, didn't we?"

I shook my head, teeth grinding together. They'd barely been gone a day, yet I'd undone all the work I'd put into escaping my old life.

"I want to go. We *need* to go. We need to leave Kastelir, so we can really fix this," I wheezed pathetically.

"What you need is to go see our dragon-slayer," Kouris said, easing me back. "Come on. Let's get you to her chamber."

I let myself be led when I never should've come back to the castle. I should've headed out of Isin and made camp, waiting for them to join me in the morning. Yet there I was in front of Claire's door, arms stuck to my sides. Kouris hesitated, pushed the door open and steered me inside.

"She'll be back in a bit. They had to, ah..." Kouris said, rubbing her jaw. "You'll be seeing her soon enough."

There was a bag on the sofa, fully packed. We'd been hours short of freedom and I wondered when I'd started thinking of the castle as a cage. I could've left at any moment and no one would've noticed. For Kouris, being there trapped her in the past, and Claire was bound to it by her own guilt. She never would've forgiven herself if she hadn't been there to face the dragon, but that was nothing compared to what she'd been put through today.

"Kouris. The dragon, it's...?" I said, gripping her wrist as she made ready to leave.

"It's all taken care of. They're dragging it back to Isin. They'll be picking at its bones like vultures, no doubt," Kouris said. "Get yourself something to drink, alright? Looks like you're in need of it."

I sunk into an armchair once I was alone, but couldn't bring myself to touch what little remained of the wine. I stared at the door, expecting guards to burst in and drag me away. King Jonas was risen and *I'd* done it; they'd know. How could they not?

I wanted to scream or sob, to pull at my hair, but my mind wouldn't let me move. And so I stared at the door until it creaked open.

It wasn't the guards. Of course it wasn't. Katja had a plan and she'd never let them find me.

Claire had caught death's attention twice. I'd seen her teeth stained red and her skin splayed open, flesh branded by a dragon; twice she had come back to me without a scratch on her. She took slow, heavy steps across the room, walking as though her body was still riddled with wounds.

She fell into an armchair and stared, as I had, at the door, making a statue of herself. I didn't know what to do for her, didn't know whether I ought to get her a drink or say something. I rose to my feet, took a step and she shattered. She covered her face with her hand and began to cry.

She wasn't loud, but tears streamed between her fingers. Her shoulders shook as I wrapped my arms around her. She let herself be pulled close, clung to the back of my shirt, and I murmured, "Claire, Claire," running my fingers through her hair. I didn't tell her it was alright. I didn't tell her not to cry.

"We'll get away from this," I whispered. "We'll leave tomorrow morning, just like we planned."

It was enough for her to catch her breath and look up at me with tear-streaked cheeks. I brushed my thumbs across her face, jaw trembling beneath my fingertips.

"Leave? We cannot leave, Rowan. Not now," she said, falling back against me, energy spent in a handful of words.

If I tensed, Claire thought nothing of it.

"Why?"

"Felheim will not stop now. There will be more dragons and Kastelir is not prepared," she said, strength returning to her voice when she spoke of dragons. "Akela is passable but unrefined. It is up to me to teach them how to deal with dragons."

It didn't matter. Whether King Jonas returned to the castle within a minute or a week, it didn't matter. The last sliver of hope I'd clung to in a desperate attempt to keep myself calm was gone; but Claire was in my arms and this wasn't about me. I could face the consequences, so long as I knew Claire was safe.

I could leave on my own. It didn't have to be the end of the world. I could head to Kyrindval and send word from there, doing all I could to help from afar.

"Is it always like this?" I asked, moving beyond fear.

"Always," Claire said, tears no longer flowing so freely. "In Thule, a Knight's return is celebrated days later for this very reason. It is said that there are only a handful of Knights, but that is not true. Knights come and go. There are dozens, hundreds, eager to be trained; dozens ready to take our place, when we fall. We are expendable: healers are not.

"We are sent to face dragons. If we survive, we are brought back to

364

the capital and…"

She drew in a heavy breath, shoulders rising. I remained silent, giving her the time she needed to find the words, and ran my fingers through her hair, uneven along the edges, singed ends cut away.

"They cut me out of my armour," she eventually said, looking away from me. "There were healers and so it did not hurt, naturally, and yet…"

"It doesn't matter if it didn't hurt," I said, not daring to blink. "You still had to go through all of that. You still saw it, felt it. I'm so sorry, Claire."

Grimacing, she bit her lower lip. While her gaze was fixed on the wall, I quickly wiped my eyes with the back of my hand, desperate to be strong when she couldn't. What she said next came out so quietly that I knew the words weren't meant for me, not entirely. They slipped out like a confession, all the dark things she had ever thought about herself hidden amongst something far grimmer.

"Every time I seek out a dragon, I do so as though I am to die. I do not *want* to face them, Rowan, but I must. I must. I consider fleeing, saving myself, but once I am at its jaws, once I am *burning*, I want nothing more than for it to be over," she said, huffing a dry, bitter laugh. "Bitterwillow only diminishes reaction times. I feel how I am changed so deeply that I cannot believe I can ever be rid of it. And yet I am, every time. Until I look in a mirror and my eyes do not quite focus."

Claire had taken me away from a world that sought to turn me against myself, once they'd got all the use out of me they could, and I wanted nothing more than to take her away from *this*. The dragons, the politics. All of it. I wanted to take her as far away as I could, down to Canth, where she could fish in the ocean and no one would ever ask her to offer her life in exchange for theirs.

But I knew she'd never leave. Not even if I asked her to.

"I understand," was all I said, in the end.

"Do you?" she asked, not unkindly, but without missing a beat.

I hadn't meant to make any of this about myself, but while she'd sounded sceptical, there was a dull sense of hope grating against her words.

"I'm a necromancer. I should be able to wash away any wound, and yet… I have scars, Claire. Scars that don't look like scars should look, or feel like they should feel. Because of mistakes I made, they'll never go away. And every time I need to use my powers, every time I'm almost hurt, I'm *terrified* that I'll do something wrong again. That there'll only be *these*."

I didn't give her the chance to reply or myself the chance to falter. I took hold of her wrist and pulled her hand towards my stomach, under my shirt. Claire's fingertips were warm but I sucked in a breath, muscles pulling taut beneath her palm.

Claire kept her eyes on mine as her fingers grazed the web of scars laid out across my stomach, brow furrowing, lips parting. I stared back, trying not to shake, but she didn't see me. She was trying to picture the hard, raised ridges that rose and fell beneath her fingertips and I found myself nodding shallowly before she'd asked anything of me.

She tentatively took hold of the hem of my shirt and hitched it up enough to see my stomach. I didn't breathe, didn't tremble. For years I'd hidden away, and now Claire's eyes were flickering across every inch of me. It would've been too much, had she not pulled me into her lap, bowing her head to kiss my scars.

The fear was gone, anger and resentment along with it. Claire saw the mess I'd made of my body and drew me closer.

Her hands ghosted across my sides, nose nudging the hem of my shirt up. I held up my arms, fabric soon forgotten. Claire kissed across my ribs, tracing the shapes of scars, and all the heat in the world pooled in the pit of my stomach.

"Rowan," she said, bringing herself to look up. "You're beautiful."

My knees sunk into the seat of the armchair, between its arms and Claire's hips, and I cupped her face with both hands, leaning down to kiss her. Her parted lips pressed against mine, hands resting on my hips, and I kissed her as though I never intended to stop; as though there was no other way for her to know what she meant to me.

She returned the kiss in kind, lifting her hips to meet mine, hands smoothing across my back. Her nails ran lightly between my shoulder blades, drifting down to the scars spread across my spine. I rolled my hips as she kissed my neck, the line of my jaw and the shell of my ear, and when I grasped at her shirt, she only stopped me to lift me clean into the air.

I wrapped my legs around her waist and she kissed me still, taking the few steps we could've made easier and fell gracefully against the bed.

The curtains dimmed our surroundings, but not so much that I couldn't see her face when she knelt over me, her body when she let me tug her shirt off.

Her hair fell about my face and she kissed me slowly, pressing herself closer with every breath. She tried to move but I caught her by the shoulders, nails digging in, and she murmured, "Rowan...?" as my head sunk back into the pillow. I gave her the slightest nod, body tensing and relaxing until I couldn't keep still, and she kissed her way across my chest, back down across the scars she was already familiar with, until she reached my hipbones.

I wasn't leaving, come the morning. Dragons weren't outside the castle, weren't crossing over from Felheim, clinging to the wall and clawing their way over. The room beyond the bed didn't exist, much less the castle enveloping it. There was nothing but Claire, nothing but her warmth; her fingers, her mouth; her name leaving my lips in a whisper, a murmur, a gasp.

It was dark when I opened my eyes. I hadn't drifted off for more than a few minutes, hadn't succumbed to sleep completely, and Claire pressed herself against my back, knees tucked against mine. I nestled against her, arms around my waist and nose pressed to my nape, and told myself I wouldn't sleep. I wouldn't be able to take in the feel of her skin against my own, her breath skidding across my neck, body aching pleasantly.

I only closed my eyes to blink, but they grew heavy, resistant to the idea of opening. The next thing I knew, I was blinking them open, faint yellow light spilling in through the gaps in the curtains. Claire had turned during the night and I pushed myself up with my palms, fingers gently brushing between her shoulder blades. The last few hours had been stolen from me, and as light cut across my fingers, highlighting her freckles, I knew I couldn't leave. Not without saying anything.

What I could do was go to Katja. Morning found me clear-headed and I knew King Jonas hadn't returned to the castle. Being an outsider was enough to cast suspicion on me when he'd died. They would've broken down the door and pulled me from under the bedsheets, had he wandered home. If Katja were still with her uncle, she'd be able to tell me what to do. She might be able to convince him to overlook what I'd done, in exchange for his life.

Nobody would take kindly to tales of a grave-robbing necromancer, but Kyrindval was still a last resort. I had to try. I kissed Claire on the shoulder, quietly slipped out of bed, and tracked down my clothing with no small amount of difficulty. Plans almost ruined by a stray shirt, I stepped into my clothes as quietly as I could, but kept hoping to hear Claire stir.

Hoping she wouldn't let me leave until she got the truth out of me.

"I'll be back soon," I whispered, legs unsteady.

I closed the door silently behind me and waited on the other side, ear pressed against it, but no sound made its way through.

I slipped out with the servants attending errands. The castle wasn't anywhere close to running normally, but the wheels were still turning. It was another gorgeous day outside, clear skies signalling the arrival of a summer that was bound to be hotter than any in years, but the city itself was a mess. Remnants of the Phoenix Festival lingered. Makeshift stages and stalls hadn't been cleared away, thanks to the commotion, and banners and flags hung from windows, ripped when they were lucky enough not to have been trampled in the street.

The Kastelirians had expected to deal with a hangover, not a dragon. People wandered the streets, hands on the back of their heads, unable to settle down in their homes, barely feeling any safer within the walls of the city. More damage had been dealt to people's spirits than the buildings, though I had to wind around a few upturned carts and what remained of broken windows. Some were still intent on leaving Isin, thinking themselves safe if they moved, while others had turned fear to giddy adrenaline and were running through the streets and gathering what they could from battered shop fronts.

Guards and soldiers patrolled the city, shepherding citizens away from the areas that had taken the brunt of the damage, Asos Square in particular. For all the trouble there was to be found, no one looked my way twice.

How apathetic they made the Felheimish look, when it came to dragons.

The former Autíra hadn't gone unscathed, but any shattered glass was being swept up as the residents went about their day. It wasn't until I was stood at the end of the street, Katja's apartment in sight, that I knew I was going to have to leave. No matter how good her intentions were, Katja couldn't be expected to protect me over a King. Especially not when that King was family.

I'd go to Kyrindval. Kyrindval was hardly a bad place, but Claire and Kouris wouldn't be there.

But it wouldn't be forever. It would take weeks, months. Years, perhaps. No longer, now that King Jonas was back. I could do that. Kravt or one of the other pane could help me send letters, and I'd accept responsibility for how rashly I'd acted.

The sun rose above Isin's wall. I lifted a hand to block out the glare but something beat me to it.

My vision flashed in the sudden absence of light, colours blotting out the darkness, and a thud like a mountain falling sent the wall shaking to its foundations. Throughout Isin, the buildings and trees and streets themselves trembled, but the people remained still, failing to comprehend what they saw, desperate for some way to react.

The bright-dark haze cleared, and purple scales gleamed, but I couldn't believe what was in front of me. A dragon swallowed the sun whole, claws sinking into stone, causing the wall to crumble. With a roar that made my head ring, the fhord leant forward, fire flooding the edges of Isin. A wave of heat struck me and all at once, everyone was screaming, "Dragon! *Dragon!*"

The spell was broken.

I turned on my heels and ran as the Isiners did, as if there was any escaping it. The people charged every which way, streets becoming rivers raging into one another, and I had to fight the urge to wrap my arms around my head and duck every time debris made craters of the street. The guards atop the shattered wall served as the first invitation death was extended, that morning.

I charged towards the castle but shadows beat me there.

Dark shapes swarmed the street and the sky was full of orange and red. Six kraau flew in from the east and barrelled towards Isin's highest point. They crashed into the castle, claws hooked against window ledges, winged arms wrapped around high towers, and used their tails to beat the buildings, before resorting to fire.

I ground to a halt as everyone darted around me. Thick plumes of black smoke rose from the wreckage the fhord left behind. I saw everything we'd come so far to protect in ashes. I wanted to fall to my knees and give up there and then.

Another dozen dragons swooped across the city, leaving torrents of fire in their wake, each finding their own district to lay claim to. The sound of towers shattering, buildings being uprooted and thrown across the city, was the only thing louder than the screams rising above the smoke. There was such a cacophony of fear rattling through the trembling bones of Isin that the clear blue sky drew in all the clamour.

I couldn't think clearly. Claire and Kouris would be able to get out of the castle and if I kept charging towards it, I'd be greeted by walls of rubble and smoke, guards struggling to evacuate people. I'd be one more person in the way, and there were those around me who needed help.

I ran towards the streets already in ruin and knelt by those who'd been forced to stop.

"It's fine. I'm a healer," I told them, no longer content to hold my powers back. I fixed legs crushed by falling rafters, burns sustained from smouldering rubble, and ran off to the next person before anyone could react to what I was doing.

The flames rose and the dragons roared. I kept moving towards the fire. It was the end of the world, as far as I could see: there was no escaping it, only giving others a chance to make it out of Isin. Some chose to stay back and help. Not many, but enough to help me pull people from under crumbled walls and misplaced chunks of roofs. I was numb to everything unfurling around me, even as wounds wore away and ran up the lengths of my arms, into my chest.

"Thank you, thank you, thank you," people said, tears streaming down their faces as they made ready to run. "I owe you my life!"

I wondered how many of them had crowded around to watch the necromancer burn, two short days ago.

There was no shortage of dead and dying. I felt myself tugged in every direction and ran where the pull was the strongest and the smoke thickest. It faded to nothing the moment it flooded my lungs, but I choked on it regardless, covering my mouth and holding my breath for as long as I could.

A dragon's tail swung overhead and I pressed my back to a building, as though they were tracking down targets, rather than destroying all that laid in their path, living or otherwise. An orange wing spread out and the creature took off, leaving being the sound of wood cracking with heat, buildings falling in on themselves. Those who could had already make it out of that part of the city but bodies lined the street, slumped against walls.

I grabbed a corpse under the arms, dragged it away from the smoke and knocked the death out of it. The corpse became a woman once more. She didn't want to believe she'd been dead and ran away from me as though she'd tripped, hit her head, and relied on me to bring her back to her senses.

I wanted to make bodies rise and march themselves to safety, but if anyone saw me, that would be the end of it. People feared necromancers at the best of times. There wasn't a thing that would stop them from going for my throat and throwing me into the fires.

I pulled two more bodies down the street, wiped away the burns and brought them back, and ran after the last one I could see, through the smoke. The old woman didn't have a single burn or broken bone, but the smoke had got into her lungs and still coiled within. I wrapped my arm around hers, trying to pull her away from the collapsing building behind, but it was coming down too quickly and my arms were already aching.

I risked bringing her back there. I forced the smoke out of her and her eyes opened as she let out a splutter, choking on nothing.

"I... I'm alive?" she asked as I urged her onto her feet, pointing towards the end of the street with less smoke spiralling down it.

She stared at me, slowly piecing together what had happened, but the deafening thud of part of the castle falling from the open sky spurred her into action. She started running without taking her eyes off me, without thanking me, and was gone within seconds. I remained where I was, crouched amidst the smoke, uncertain whether I was doing these people a kindness. I was giving them another chance, but who was to say that chance wouldn't end in fire?

I needed a moment. The heat was stifling, making my head spin, and I didn't notice the man standing over me until he called out, "Hey! I saw what you just did."

My gaze shot up and my hand inched across the ground, fingers wrapping around the edges of a dislodged brick.

I recognised him. He was the soldier who'd implored King Atthis to let him take their forces outside of the city, only now his armour was torn to shreds and his face was burnt, fingers bloody.

"You're a necromancer..." he said, dirt and soot mixing with blood and sweat.

The brick scraped across the ground as I pulled it closer, eyes fixed fast on his, but the sound was lost to the turmoil overtaking the city.

I waited for him to draw his weapon, to call for help, but his eyes welled up.

"You have to help me," he said. "Please. My husband, he's, he's..."

I rose to my feet and the brick clattered against the ground. I grabbed his arm, followed him through the smoke and drew out all he breathed in, all that stained his lungs. The soldier shook but didn't stop for a second. We came to the ruins of a bakery at the end of the street. An arm stretched out from beneath a crumpled wall. The body was fine from the chest down, but I couldn't bring him back until the huge chunk of stone had been dragged off his skull and shoulders.

"Come on. We need to move this," I said, wrapping my fingers around the edge of the fallen wall.

I grit my teeth, eyes stinging with tears from the heat and smoke, and the soldier and I put all our strength into lifting.

"We were only trying to help people," he mumbled as we got absolutely nowhere. It was too heavy for us, would've been too heavy for half a dozen of us, but no one was venturing this far into the smoke. "We got everyone out, but, but..."

My fingers split open on the wall and healed over with grit caught under them. I heaved again, arms about to give. I coughed into my shoulder and with one last futile effort, the wall lifted easily.

"What?" I wondered out loud, opening my eyes to find Kouris next to me, straining to hold up the wall. "Kouris! You're..."

But what was there to say? There was no room left for words. The soldier hadn't flinched in the presence of a necromancer and didn't at the sight of a pane, either. He pulled the crushed corpse of his husband from beneath the wreckage and Kouris dropped the wall, dirt and dust flying into the air.

I knelt by the dead man, hands ghosting over his skull, and drew the broken bits of bone back into place.

"Both of you, thank you so much," the soldier said, clinging to his husband as he stirred in his arms. "Come with us, please. We'll get out of here together."

I was determined to help, but it'd been clear from the start that we were fighting a losing battle. I looked to Kouris, felt the smoke coiling within her, and knew that I couldn't ask the two men to help us find Claire. They had to get out of Isin without any detours.

"There's someone we have to find. Go, go!" I told them. The soldier nodded his head over and over, understanding but not liking it one bit. His husband, still disorientated, hadn't breathed a word, and ran when he was told to.

"Where's Claire?" I asked Kouris.

I gripped the front of her leathers and took all the smoke she was plagued with upon myself, no longer having to think about it. All the death and decay in the surrounding area was sifting into me. My veins pounded with it, limbs heavy, eyes burning bright.

"We can't afford to be looking for her, yrval," Kouris said. "The whole city's gonna be a sea of fire within minutes. We've gotta help who we can and get ourselves out of here. She's gonna be doing the same thing."

I couldn't argue with her. I wasn't going to leave without Claire, but I wasn't going to waste what little time Isin had left. Kouris let me climb on her back and I clung to her horns, desperately searching through the smoke and flames, surroundings already unrecognisable. It'd been minutes since the sum total of damage within Isin was smashed glass and torn banners, but now the city was beyond salvation.

"Claire got out of the castle, didn't she? And the others? Akela's out too, right?" I asked as Kouris leapt over a toppled statue. "Everyone's going to get out, aren't they?"

Kouris growled and darted into a narrow side-street as a kraau circled overhead, looking for its next perch.

"We got as many as we could out. Everyone wanted to be the first out, though. Can't tell you how many were knocked into that damn moat."

There were fewer and fewer people to help as we charged through Isin, searching for a way out of a maze made of makeshift dead-ends. I sensed bodies in the flattened buildings around me, trapped under more layers of stone and wood than Kouris and I could claw our way through.

My heart ached for Kouris every time we happened upon a dragon.

They were her kin, forced to commit atrocities beyond their under-standing, and the only way to put a stop to this all was to kill them. We stumbled across a kraau's back legs and Kouris bowed down low, dodg-ing its swinging tail.

A glint of white caught my eye through the grey and I called out, "Claire!" before I could be certain it was her.

Kouris ground to a halt and my forehead cracked against one of her horns, but I hadn't been hoping against hope. Claire changed course, ran towards us, and relief turned bitter in my throat when I realised why she was wearing her armour.

"There you are," she said, voice on the verge of cracking.

She didn't let herself reach out to me.

I crashed into her, clutched her arms and said, "Claire, Claire. You have to come with us! You *have* to."

There'd be time to explain where I'd been later.

She shook her head, eyes flickering away from me beneath her visor.

"You know I must stay and fight. I've no choice, Rowan," she said, taking a step back.

"*Please*," I begged. "You might be able to stand against one dragon but not against all of these."

"Listen to her," Kouris said. "You don't owe Isin your life."

"If I am even able to save two lives, it is a fair exchange," Claire said. "I came to protect the Kastelirian people against this, Kouris."

"Fuck 'em," Kouris growled. "You're not throwing yourself away. Not for a thousand of 'em. You need to survive Isin if you want to help the whole damn country."

Claire hesitated, but I knew she'd never turn away from her duty.

"This part of the city was lost first. There is still much that can be saved, west of the castle. I have to go," she said. I opened my mouth to snap that I was going to go with her, but she backed out of my grasp. "You have to go, Rowan. Kouris, take her to Kyrindval. Take care of each other. Promise me that."

Kouris wouldn't look at me and I knew it was because she was going to do all she could to tear me away. She stepped forward, bowed down and pressed her forehead to the front of Claire's helm as she gripped her shoulders.

"You meet us there, Claire," she said. "Swear that you will."

374

"No!" I said, reaching out to grab Claire. Kouris wrapped her arms around me and lifted me clean off the ground. "Don't!" I called out after Claire, reaching for her as she drew her sword and took slow steps backwards. "Don't, Claire. Don't leave me, please! I can help! I can protect you!"

She disappeared into the smoke and I screamed after her, calling for her to come back, howling her name. I beat my fists against Kouris' shoulders, fighting to be free, but none of it amounted to anything. Kouris didn't flinch. She headed further and further from Claire, turning as sharply as one of the castle's spires planted itself into the centre of the street ahead.

"It's alright, yrval, it's alright," Kouris murmured. "She wants you safe. You can do that much for her, can't you?"

"Kouris, she's going to get hurt. I... I need to, I..."

Kouris murmured something under her breath in Svargan, but I knew a curse when I heard one.

Darkness descended upon the shattered streets ahead of us. The fhord that'd clawed its way through the wall crushed what remained of the buildings to make space for itself, purple wings fanned out, obscuring the sky as it roared at the sun, making ready to breathe.

There was no absorbing the size of it, not even when it stood before us. I was smaller than its largest fang and as I slipped from Kouris' arms to stand motionless by her side, I knew that no matter how quickly we fled, we wouldn't escape its reach.

"Yrval," Kouris said softly. Too softly.

She reached out, taking my hand in hers and I entwined our fingers as I stared up at the dragon. There wasn't a scratch on it, despite all the damage it'd done, and my other hand trailed through the air, wanting to find Claire's.

The dragon lowered its head, plumes of smoke rising from its nostrils, and I did all I could to brace myself, to fight the flames they moment they raged against Kouris and me. Its jagged fangs parted, long tongue tasting the air, and as its shoulder blades pushed back, I held out a hand, desperate for it to stop.

Heat spiked in the air and Kouris tugged me to the side, meaning to leap into one of the barely-standing buildings, but my mind was still screaming for the dragon to stop, stop: and it did.

The fhord gave one final sharp, short roar and came crashing to the ground like a stone.

My fingers twitched and all the exhaustion in my body was replaced by fire in my veins, my bones. The death I'd drawn from the Isiners rushed out of me and filled the dragon, bringing it down, down like the castle no longer rising against the horizon.

I wanted to laugh, overwhelmed by the force locked inside of me, but the sound caught in my throat, sending a bolt of pain between my temples. I doubled over, gripped the sides of my head, and my palms grew slick with the blood that trickled out of my ears. My head throbbed, but I was still standing. The taste of copper rushed from the back of my throat and Kouris caught me as the ground rushed up to meet my knees.

"I can do it," I said, shaking with certainty. For all the blood streaming from my nose, it was my eyes Kouris was staring at. "Come on! We can find Claire and get rid of the other dragons, Kouris, please..."

"Yrval, shh. Shh," she said, as though she hadn't heard me.

Kouris rocked me in her arms, holding me close to her chest and as I saw her mouth words that had been replaced by a high-pitched whine, my body began to tremble in her arms.

A grim, harrowing force rushed through me. It wasn't the smoke flooding the city or even the mist of death that rose with the heat. A darkness came over me that I couldn't run from, couldn't banish, and Kouris faded as the ringing in my ears turned to a screech, then stopped.

I awoke to another sort of darkness, prickled with bright lights.

I stared blankly, barely able to blink at the night sky draped over us. Miles away, Isin burnt brightly under midnight's shroud. I felt myself sway to and fro, to and fro, accompanied by the rhythmic thrum of heavy footsteps.

I was in Kouris' arms, nothing left inside of me. Beside us, figures moved away from Isin, away from the smoke that blotted out stars, and I saw Akela at my side. Blood spilt from a gash on her cheek, eye bruised, dark and angry. She did nothing to tend to her wounds and stared straight ahead as we marched on and on.

I bundled my fingers in front of Kouris' shirt. She looked down at me, eyes silver-white, like the moon. I mouthed Claire's name, unable to find my voice. Kouris' ears twitched before they drooped. She could only shake her head. I didn't dare to part my lips, after that.

I didn't dare to breathe too deeply.

In the aftermath of the attack, there was nothing left for us but the hollowed-out night. I watched with wide, dry eyes as the fires of Isin fell beneath the horizon, flames flickering and fading without a sound.

In the disquiet that followed the devastation, I thought no voice would ever be raised again; no word could ever be uttered to make sense of this, and the thought of speech in its entirety became senseless and cruel.

In the end, it was silence that took the last of Kastelir.

The Complete History of Kastelir

The Sky Beneath the Sun

Gall and Wormwood

UPCOMING TITLES

Bitfrost

The Shattering of the Spirit-Sword Brackish

Sam Farren started writing the way many young authors do: they really, *really* wanted to post some fanfiction. After dabbling in both transformative and original works for many years, they developed a passion for representing lesbian, bisexual, trans women, and woman-aligned non-binary people of all sorts in fantasy worlds. *Dragonoak: The Complete History of Kastelir* is their debut novel and the first instalment in a trilogy.

Born and raised in the south-east of England, Sam still resides there, along with a pile of snakes and lizards. They currently work fulltime with animals, write in lieu of sleeping, and deeply appreciate any and all support via their published works.

If you've enjoyed this novel, please consider sharing a review or recommendation on social media. Please remember that *Dragonoak* is a small, independent publication, and has been created with relatively few resources. *Dragonoak* has been worked on day in, day out, for over five years, and any errors are not for lack of hard work!

They can be found on twitter at SFarrenBooks, or contacted directly at farren.books@gmail.com

Made in the USA
Middletown, DE
17 July 2017